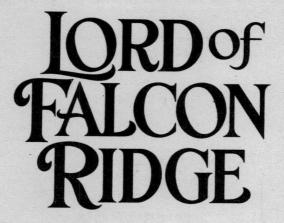

LORD of FALCON RIDGE

CATHERINE COULTER

D0311629

JOVE BOOKS, NEW YORK

LORD OF FALCON RIDGE

A Jove Book / published by arrangement with
the author

PRINTING HISTORY
Jove edition / April 1995

ISBN: 0-515-11584-3

A JOVE BOOK®
Jove Books are published by The Berkley Publishing Group,
200 Madison Avenue, New York, New York 10016.
JOVE and the "J" design are trademarks
belonging to Jove Publications, Inc.

PRINTED IN THE UNITED STATES OF AMERICA

10 9 8 7 6 5 4 3 2 1

Gunleik said, frowning at Cleve, "You don't look like a man who's enjoyed himself all through a long dark night with a new wife who worships you."

"Gunleik's right," Hafter said, adding his frowning to Gunleik's. "You look like you've got a cramp in your bowels. That, hmmm, or you've done something incredibly stupid with your new bride."

It was too much, damn their interfering eyes. He shouted, "Damn all of you. My bowels are just fine. You want the truth, you damned meddlesome sods? Very well, I failed her. I fell asleep like a stuporous goat."

Rorik groaned and struck his fist against Cleve's arm. "You didn't. Truly, you fell asleep? Quickly? Aye, I see by the guilt in your eyes you did. By all the gods, Cleve, you give us all a bad name."

"I'm going to the bathing hut," Cleve said and left them to stare after him. He didn't look at his new wife.

To my brother-in-law, John Blaise Pogany,
a smart and sexy guy who can sell you a house,
account your books and mix you a drink.

You're neat, Blaise.

CC

LORD of
FALCON
RIDGE

1

Malverne farmstead
Vestfold, Norway
A.D. 922

CLEVE DREAMED THE dream the first time on the night
of his daughter's third natal day. It was in the middle of
the night in the deepest summer, and thus it never darkened
to black until it was nearly dawn again. He was sleeping
deeply in that soft gray dark of the midnight summer when
the dream came. He stood on a high, narrow cliff listening,
sniffing the warm, wet air. Below him was a raging waterfall roiling through slick boulders only to narrow with the
tightening of the banks before it shot out over a lower cliff,
crashing far below beyond where he could see. A light mist
fell about him. It was suddenly so cold that he shivered.
He pulled his warm woolen cloak closer.

All around him were thick stands of trees and bright
purple and yellow flowering plants that seemed to grow out
of the rocks themselves. Boulders and large stones were
scattered among the low, scrubby brush. He followed the
snaking path, making his way down through the narrow cut
in the foliage. A pony awaited him at the bottom: black as
night with a white star on its forehead. It was blowing gently. Cleve knew the pony. Although it was small, it seemed

right to him. He realized that just as he knew the pony, he knew this land of crags and misting rain and air so soft and sweet it made him want to weep.

There was a single wolfskin on his pony's back which he knocked askew when he jumped onto its back. A moment later, he was racing across a meadow that was filled with bright flowers, their sweet scent filling the air. The misting rain stopped and the sun came out. It was high overhead, hot and bright. Soon he felt sweat bead on his forehead. The pony turned at the end of the meadow toward another trail that led eastward. He pulled the pony to a stop, turning it away to the opposite direction. He felt sweat stinging his eyes, wet his armpits. No, he didn't want to go that way, just thinking of it made his belly cramp with fear. No, he wanted to ride away, far away, never to have to see . . . see what? He sat atop the pony's back shaking his head back and forth. No, never would he go back. But then he knew he would, knew he had no choice, and suddenly, he was there, staring blankly at the huge wooden house with its sod and shingled roof. This was no simple home really, but a fortress. He realized then that he heard nothing, absolutely nothing. There was so much silence, yet men and women were working in the fields, carrying firewood, directing children. A man with huge arms was lifting a sword above his head, testing its weight and balance. There was no laughter, no arguments, just a deathly silence that filled the air itself and he knew that was the way it always was. Then he heard low voices coming from within the huge fortress. He didn't want to go in there. The voices became louder as the immense wooden door opened. Through air that was thick with smoke from the fire pit he could see men sharpening their axes, polishing their helmets. He could see women weaving, sewing, and cooking. It all looked so normal, yet he wanted to run from this place, but he couldn't. Then he saw *her* standing there, her golden head bowed, so small she was, so defenseless, and he backed away, shaking his head, feeling a keening wail build up inside him. She'd spun, dyed, and woven his woolen cloak for him and he clutched it to him as if by doing so he could clutch her and save her. A part of him seemed to know the danger she was in; he also knew he was helpless to prevent what would happen. He was outside the fortress now, but he could still hear the calm, low voice that was speaking from somewhere within. It was deadly, that voice, just as deadly as the man who possessed it. Soon he would be silent. Soon, all would be silent, except for her. The low, deep voice murmured on until it was pierced by the woman's scream. That was all it took; Cleve knew what had happened.

He ran as fast as he could, looking frantically for the pony, but the pony was no longer there. He heard a cry of pain, then another and another. The cries grew louder and louder, filling him with such unutterable emptiness that he saw nothing, became nothing.

He gasped, jerking upright in his box bed.

"Papa."

He heard her soft voice before he could react, before he could pull himself away from the terror he couldn't see, a terror that gnawed at him just the same. He knew, he knew . . .

"Papa. I heard you cry out. Are you all right?"

"Aye," he said finally, focusing on his daughter. Her hair, as golden as his own, fell in tangles around her small face. " 'Twas a vicious dream, naught more, just a dream. Come here, sweeting, and let me hug you."

He tried to believe it was just a dream, nothing more than a simple dream concocted out of the barley soup he'd eaten for the evening meal.

He lifted his daughter onto the box bed and pulled her into his arms. He held her close to his heart, this small perfect being whom he'd magically created. He tried not to think of her mother, Sarla, the woman he'd loved who had tried to kill him, particularly not so soon after that dream that still made his heart thud against his chest and made the sweat itch in his armpits.

Kiri kissed his chin, curling her thin arms around his neck. She squeezed hard, then giggled, and that brought him fully back into himself. It had been nothing but a strange dream, nothing more.

She said, "I kicked Harald today. He said I couldn't use his sword. He said I was a girl and had enough to do without learning to kill men. I told him he wasn't a man, he was just a little boy. He got all red in the face and called me a name I know is bad, so I kicked him hard."

"Do you remember what Harald called you?"

She shook her head against his chest. He smiled down at her though he felt more heartache than he wished to let on. He couldn't protect her forever from the truth. Children heard the adults talking. Sometimes they spoke of that time so long ago and spoke of Sarla, then looked sideways at Kiri, who looked nothing like her mother. No, Kiri was the image of him. Were they trying to see Sarla in her? Aye, of course they were.

He hugged Kiri to him. He loved her so much he ached with it. This tiny scrap of his, so perfectly formed, a face so beautiful he knew someday men would lose their heads at the mere sight of her. Yet from her earliest months Kiri had clutched at her father's knife, not at the soft linen-stuffed doll her Aunt Laren had made for her. It was he who arranged the stuffed doll where Kiri slept so Laren's feelings wouldn't be hurt.

To his now sleeping daughter he whispered, "I dreamed of a place that seems not so different from Norway, but deep down I know it is. There was mist so soft you could believe it woven into cloth, all gray and light, and yellow and purple flowers that were everywhere and I knew they were everywhere, not just that place in my dream. It was very different from any place I have ever been in my life. It was familiar to me. I recognized it. I knew more fear than I have in my life."

He stopped. He didn't want to speak aloud of it. It scared him, he freely admitted it to himself. He hadn't been himself in that dream, but he had, and that, he couldn't explain. He kissed his daughter's hair, then settled her against him. He fell asleep near dawn, the lush scent of those strange flowers hovering nearby, teasing the air in his small chamber.

Malverne farmstead
Vestfold, Norway
Nearly two years later

"Damnation, Cleve, I could have killed you. You're just standing there like a goat without a single thought in his head, ready to take an arrow through his heart and be the evening meal. What is wrong with you? Where the hell is your knife? It should be aimed at my chest, you damned madman."

Cleve shook his head at Merrik Haraldsson, the man who had rescued him along with Laren and her small brother, Taby, five years before in Kiev. Merrik was his best friend, the man who'd taught him to fight, to be a Viking warrior, the man who was now striding toward him, his bow at his side, anger radiating from him because he feared Cleve had not learned his lessons well enough. It was an uncertain world. Danger could appear at any moment, even here at Malverne, Merrik's farmstead, a magnificent home surrounded with mighty mountains and a fjord below that was so blue it hurt the eyes when the sun shone directly upon it.

Cleve waited. When Merrik was just an arm's length from him, Cleve turned smoothly to his side, gracefully kicked out his foot, connecting with Merrik's belly, no lower, for he didn't want to send his friend into agony, then he leapt at him, his knee in his chest, knocking him backward. He landed on top of Merrik, straddling him, his knife poised at his throat.

Merrik looked surprised. He said nothing. He brought his knees against Cleve's back, hard, knocking the breath from him, even as he jerked sideways, hitting upward with his mighty arm, trying to throw Cleve to the ground beyond him. Cleve dug his knees into Merrik's lean sides, closed his eyes against the pain in his back, and held on. Were Merrik an enemy, he would be dead, the knife sliding clean and quickly through his neck, but this was naught but sport and there was more pain to be borne, more grunts and curses to turn the air a richer blue than it now was in late spring, more breaths to explode into the warm afternoon light, before Merrik would allow him to declare victory, if that would indeed be the outcome. Merrik was a cunning bastard and Cleve still hadn't learned all his tricks, even after five long years.

Oleg shouted from behind them, "Enough, both of you. You'll kill each other and then what will Laren do? I'll tell you what. She'd take Merrik's big sword and hit both your butts with the broad side. Then she'd kiss Merrik until he wanted to rut more than he wanted to fight." He was laughing, standing over them now, hands on his hips. Oleg was a big man, golden as most of the Vikings were, his eyes as blue as the summer sky.

Finally, when Cleve lightened the pressure from Merrik's throat, Merrik splayed his hands upward in the dirt. "I am defeated. Actually, I'm dead, truth be told. You and that bloody knife, Cleve. You've gotten much too adroit with it. Then you've got the gall to toss it away and use your elbows on me, a trick I taught you."

"You were angry, Merrik. You've told me often enough that a man is a fool if he allows himself to be angered during a fight." Cleve grinned down at him. "Actually, I don't think you had a chance, angry or not."

Merrik cursed him, loud and long, until all three of them were laughing and others had come to them and were telling some of their own tales of cunning and guile.

Cleve climbed off Merrik, then offered his hand to his friend. Merrik could have broken Cleve's arm, could have thrown him six feet with a simple twist of his body, could have brought him eye to eye and crushed the life from him, but he'd claimed defeat, and thus the sport was done, at least for now. There was always another day to test each other's strength.

Suddenly, Merrik was as serious as he'd been when fever had come to Malverne the past spring and killed ten of their people. "Listen to me, Cleve. You can never relax vigilance, you know that. There is always trouble somewhere, and if you blink, the trouble can be right in front of you. Remember just weeks ago my cousin Lotti nearly died when a wild boar came into the barley fields? She was lucky that Egill was nearby. You can never nap, my friend, never."

Cleve remembered well enough and the memory still made his blood run cold. Cleve adored Lotti, a woman who couldn't speak but who could communicate just as clearly as those who did by moving her fingers. It was a language of her own creation but all the Malek people, her children, and her husband, Egill, understood, and spoke thus to her as well. Cleve himself had learned some words over the past five years but he doubted his fingers could ever be so adroit as Lotti's or Egill's.

"I was thinking of a dream I had," Cleve said. No sooner had he said this than he wished he'd kept his mouth shut. Dreams were always important to Vikings, each one remembered was spoken about, argued over endlessly, until all were satisfied that it posed no danger to any of them.

"What dream?" Oleg said, handing each man a cup of pure fjord water, so cold in late spring that it constricted the throat.

"A dream that has come to me five times now."

"Five nights in a row?"

"Nay, Oleg, five times over the past two years, it has come unexpected. It has become fuller, richer, I suppose, like one of Ileria's tapestries, yet I still can't grasp what it means. But it means something, I know that it does. It's very frustrating."

"Tell us," Merrik said. "A dream that returns in fuller detail could mean something very important, Cleve. It could portend things to come, mayhap dangers of which we know naught as of yet."

"I cannot, Merrik. Not yet. Please, my friend, not yet. It's not about here or about you. It's about the past, the very distant past."

Merrik let it go. Cleve was as stubborn as Laren, Merrik's red-haired wife, particularly once he'd made up his mind. As they walked down to the fjord to swim with a half dozen of the men and boys, he changed the subject. "You leave tomorrow for Normandy and Rollo's court. You will tell Duke Rollo we will come to Rouen to visit after harvest." He paused a moment, his face lighting with such affection that Cleve was glad Merrik's sons weren't there to see it. "Tell Taby I will teach him a new wrestling trick. By all the gods, I miss him. He's ten years old now, a handsome lad, honest and loyal."

"You couldn't have kept him with you, Merrik. As Rollo's nephew, he belongs in Normandy." Aye, he thought, Rollo had subjugated northern France so that the French king had been forced to grant him the title of the first duke of Normandy and cede him all the land he already held. It was important that Rollo's hold never be weakened else the country would again be ravaged by marauding Viking raiders.

"I know, but it doesn't make me miss him less."

"I will tell him his brother-in-law misses him so much that he failed to thrash a former slave." Cleve thought about that time five years before. Merrik had been trading in Kiev. He'd wanted to buy a slave for his mother, but had seen a small boy in the slave ring and been drawn to him. He'd bought Taby and then rescued both Cleve and Laren, Taby's sister, from the merchant who'd brought her. Merrik had loved Taby more than any other human being, save his wife, Laren, even more than his own sons.

Cleve waited until Merrik smiled at that, then continued. "I think Rollo wants to send me to Ireland to see King Sitric, at least that's what his messenger hinted at. Sitric was once a very old man near to death. Yet when we visited Rouen last year, Rollo told me that Sitric is again a man in his prime. Magic was wrought by a foreign magician called Hormuze, who disappeared after he'd wrought this change in the king. I can't believe it, but most do. Odd, all of it. Do you know anything about this King Sitric, Merrik?''

"I? Know about Sitric? Nay, Cleve, not a thing. Not a single thing.''

Cleve knew Merrik was lying. He also knew he wouldn't ever find out why or what precisely he was lying about. Not unless he could find out from this King Sitric himself or if he could manage to find more guile than Merrik possessed. He doubted that would happen.

"Laren and I are pleased that you've become Rollo's emissary. You have a wily tongue and a quick mind, Cleve. Rollo is lucky and he knows it.''

"I could be an utter fool and Rollo would still reward me since he believes I saved his beloved Laren and Taby.''

"Rollo is fortunate,'' Merrik said, and clapped Cleve on the back. "Since you aren't a fool, he can make good use of you as well as reward you.''

2

Dublin, Ireland
Court of King Sitric
A.D. 924

THE FIRST TIME Cleve saw her she was arguing with another woman, a woman older than she, a woman endowed with the most glorious silver blond hair he'd ever seen. It wasn't her mother, but perhaps an older sister. He couldn't make out their words, but there was enmity in the air—bitterness and resentment of longstanding.

The young one said, anger thick in her voice, "You evil witch, I won't let you hurt her again, do you hear me?"

"Just what will you do, you interfering little bitch? Go whining to your father? Mind your manners, show me the respect I'm due, or I'll make you regret it."

"Just living with you is the biggest punishment anyone could endure."

Suddenly, without warning, the older woman, so exquisitely beautiful in her pale blue robe, that incredible hair long and loose to her hips, swung her arm as hard as any man and struck the girl's cheek. The girl staggered back, lost her balance and hit her hip against a stone bench.

He was poised to run to her, to do something, he didn't know what, when the girl bounced back, ran straight at the older woman and grabbed a good amount of that beautiful hair in her fists. She tugged hard and the woman began to yell, hitting her, struggling madly, but the girl didn't let go. She was as determined as that scrappy little dog Kiri had begged him to keep when they'd been in Rouen just three weeks before.

It couldn't go on and it didn't. The older woman finally pulled free. She stepped back, panting, her face pale with rage and undoubtedly pain. Her beautiful hair was disheveled and tangled. "You'll be sorry for that, Chessa. By all the gods, I'll make you sorry. You think you're so important here, so above me and my sons. Well, you're not. Your father's important, not you. His sons are important, not you. And I'm more important than all of them. Aye, you'll regret this." She turned and strode from the garden through a small door Cleve hadn't noticed before.

"Are you all right?"

The girl turned at the sound of his voice.

"Who are you?"

Her breasts were heaving. They were nice breasts, full, straining against the soft linen of her gown. She was smaller than he'd first thought, seeing her leap at the older woman without a shadow of fear. Her eyes were as green as the wet moss beside the river Liffey. She looked ready to leap at him and pull out his hair, too. He said mildly, in his soothing diplomat's voice, "My name is Cleve of Malverne, messenger from Duke Rollo of Normandy."

She looked him up and down, all disdain and unveiled dislike. He waited for her to recoil, to say something that would hurt. He knew she would. After all, she'd certainly spoken her mind to that other woman with the incredible hair. But she said instead, more than a hint of sarcasm in her voice, "Not just a messenger from what I hear. You represent the duke, don't you? You're his emissary. You're here to negotiate some sort of agreement with the king."

"I suppose you could say that."

The sarcasm thickened. "All of you emissaries, you talk like limpets, don't you, so low and quiet, your words slicker than wet skin. You come here from your kings or from your dukes and you want something. A fat minister from King Charles's court in Paris was here just last month. He was oily and kept looking at me as if my robe was lying at my feet. He made me want to bathe. None of you say anything, but you say it nicely and hope the other person is stupid. Well, I'm not stupid. At least you're not oily and I feel like I still have my robe on. Now, why were you spying on us? What do you want?''

"That was quite a lot you just said.'' He smiled at her, and still waited for her to flinch, to step back from him, but she didn't. He continued, more than curious now because she hadn't flinched, hadn't looked at him and recoiled. ''Actually I was merely learning my way about. I heard voices and came into this beautiful garden. I'm rather glad you didn't succeed in pulling out that other woman's hair. It's far too beautiful to be left in knots on the ground.''

"It is her pride, that hair of hers.'' She sighed. ''Her hair is strong, curse her. I did try, I yanked as hard as I could but it did no good. It's the first time I've managed to get so close, and I failed. The gods know what she'll do to me now. She always manages something that hurts.''

He took a step closer. He could see the red hand print on her left cheek. He reached out his hand, then realized what he was doing, and withdrew it. ''Are you all right?''

"Oh, yes. She's struck me so many times that now I hardly even notice. This time was different though, but still, we fight whenever we're within the same chamber.''

"How was it different?''

She was thoughtful for a long moment. Finally she said, her brows knit, ''There was deep hatred this time, not just annoyance or irritation. I'm full-grown now and she can't bear that, although I don't understand why.''

"Who is she?''

"My father's second wife.''

"Ah, the stepmother. There are many tales about their vanity and evil. A skald I know well tells of a stepmother who turned her stepdaughter into a pumpkin and left her in a field to rot. Luckily for the pumpkin, a child came along, kicked it, and when it moaned with pain, the child touched it just right and the stepdaughter reappeared. The child ran away.''

''That didn't sound like a diplomat. Perhaps you are human after all.''

''Perhaps one day you will hear the full tale. Now, about your stepmother.''

''Yes, that's what she is, and my father loves her, despite her vanity, her temper, her meanness. She's given him four sons, you see.''

''I see.''

''You needn't repeat any of this,'' she said, her eyes narrowing in warning.

''Why should I? Surely it isn't all that interesting. Who would I tell who would be amused or hold me in higher esteem?''

She snorted, actually snorted, and he was, for just an instant, enchanted. ''There you go again, not saying anything, just asking a stupid question that doesn't carry as much weight as a bee's wings. I don't think I'd be a good diplomat.''

''No, probably not,'' he said in that same mild voice. ''You haven't answered my question. Why should I tell anyone about you trying to pull out your stepmother's hair?''

That jaw of hers was stubborn as a stoat's but nicely rounded, quite soft looking, really. ''Oh, very well. You'll find out anyway, the way you sneak around and speak so softly like you're licking honey. She's Queen Sira, the king's wife. He used to call her Naphta, after my mother, but she hated it so he let her have her own name back again. That was after the birth of her first son.''

''It all sounds very complicated. I take it then that you're the king's daughter.''

''Yes, I'm Chessa.''

''That's an unusual name.''

''Not as unusual as the one I was given at birth. Everything changed when my father married Sira. Your name is unusual as well.''

"Perhaps," he said, "but I have grown to like it."

"You have one gold eye and one blue eye, as if the gods couldn't decide which would suit you best. They're really quite nice.''

"The gods or my eyes?"

She grinned up at him and shook her head.

He waited, but she said nothing more. He smiled down at her as she silently braided her hair, and thought, *She never once flinched at the sight of my face.*

King Sitric's chamber was large and airy, the walls white as a dove's back, clean and free of spider webs. There were woven mats covering the packed earth floor. The furnishings were simple: a large box bed with several white wolfskins of great value spread over the top, a large carved mahogany chest at the foot of the bed for clothing. Highback chairs were arranged in small groupings, the king's fashioned with finely etched chair posts as befitted his rank. He was eyeing his daughter, wondering why she'd come to his chamber unexpectedly, why she was pacing about like a young tigress. What on earth had set her off? She turned then and said, "I'm not at all certain I like him but he's very handsome. It's strange, but he doesn't appear to realize it and thus puff himself up with his own conceit. Every handsome man I've ever met has believed himself fascinating to females. He has the look of a Viking with that golden hair of his, but I heard that he isn't one of them. And his eyes. One is golden and the other is a deep deep blue. They're beautiful, just as he is.''

King Sitric raised a very black brow at his daughter's words. "Mayhap you could tell me who this handsome man is that you're not certain you like? Someone new here at the palace? Do I know him, this man with one golden eye and one blue eye?" But now he realized who she was talking about and he waited, so surprised he couldn't find words to say in any case.

"Of course you do, Father. He said he was Cleve of Malverne, come from Duke Rollo of Normandy. Surely he isn't one of those Frenchmen. Why, they are all short and oily, like that minister who was here. He is tall and well made and—"

King Sitric said very carefully, "You said Cleve of Malverne? From Duke Rollo?"

"Yes, he chanced to come into the garden behind my chamber. I demanded to know who he was and he had to tell me."

"Handsome, you think?"

"Oh, yes, but he's like all the rest of those mealy-mouthed diplomats who come here wanting you to do things for their masters. He's smooth as an adder in his speech but he doesn't really say anything."

"Perhaps you are just a bit prejudiced, Chessa. I had hoped that by now you would have forgotten that unfortunate incident with Ragnor of York."

Her chin went up and her father smiled. She was so very different from her mother, soft-spoken, submissive Naphta, whom he'd loved more than wisdom and nearly more than his own life as well, but not more than his small daughter's life.

He hadn't sought to temper his daughter's forthrightness or her blunt candor. No, he'd had to leave her weapons so she could stand toe to toe with his witch of a second wife, who needed more discipline than he ever managed to mete out to her. She always distracted him with that lithe body of hers and her passion. By all the gods, her passion made him mad with lust even now after eight years. But he had to control her, for she was a witch, and he knew that she detested Chessa, seeing her as a threat, which was ridiculous.

"I have forgotten Ragnor, Father. He was naught but a foolish boy. Indeed, I gained my revenge on him, then spit his name into the dust. He has been gone from my mind for a long time now."

"Don't lie, Eze. You still smart from the wounds. He

hurt you with his talk of everlasting adoration.''

"You haven't called me Eze in a very long time."

"It's true, you're really more Chessa to me now than Eze. It just slipped off my tongue. You still don't mind your name, do you? You know I had to change it. As you became older Eze sounded more and more strange in the court. People remarked on it so I changed it to Chessa, a long-ago Irish heroine.''

"Just as Naphta sounded strange?"

He stiffened. "Aye, if you will. But we are not speaking of your stepmother.''

"Thank Freya for that," she said, then fell silent. She rarely digressed. Once focused, she usually never wavered. He was content to wait. She said at last, "It's true, Father. I don't think often of Ragnor. I can't believe I was so gullible that I actually believed his lies. But I did gain revenge on him, that is—oh—''

This was interesting. This closemouthed daughter of his rarely let anything slip. He saw that she was chagrined. "What did you do, Chessa?"

"You don't really wish to know, do you?"

"What did you do, Chessa?"

"I ground up malle leaves with some fist root and added just a touch of ginger to make it tasty. Ragnor loves ginger. I heard that he puked up his guts for a good three days.''

He laughed, he couldn't help himself. Thank the gods she hadn't killed the officious bastard. He wouldn't put it past her. But no, she'd exercised restraint, a quality her stepmother couldn't seem to master. She'd grown up well, he'd seen to it. He was proud of her. She learned from mistakes and never, to his knowledge, repeated them. It was a pity she was only a woman.

Chessa smiled in relief. She loved her father dearly. She hated to distress him. She said now, without thought, "Will you invite this Cleve of Malverne to dine with us?"

"Why?"

"To see if he will speak like a man and not continue like a smooth-pebbled rock skipping over the water."

"You aren't simply content to stare at his handsome face? At his golden eye and blue eye? At his well-made man's body?"

"For a while, perhaps. Nay, for more than just awhile. But you know, Father, his voice is very nice and pleases me."

"Very well. Oh, I hear you and your stepmother were fighting today. What about this time?"

"Did Cleve of Malverne tell you?"

"No, sweeting, he did not. Why would he? How would he know of it? What did you fight about?"

"I would prefer not to speak of it."

"You will do as I tell you. What, Chessa?"

"She struck little Ingrid again."

"What did the girl do this time?"

"She wasn't fast enough with Sira's hair comb. Sira bruised her ribs she struck her so hard with her fist."

"I will speak to her," he said. "Try not to fight with her, Chessa, all right?"

"Certainly. Do you want yet more sons off her? Is that why you allow her to be so damnably wicked?"

He sighed, smoothed his hands over the soft linen of his purple robe, and said, "You are still young—"

"I am eighteen. Most girls are married and have babes by my age."

"Nonetheless, you are innocent in the ways of men and women. Sira gives me much, Chessa, much that you can't begin to understand."

"She gives you her body whenever you ask? You needn't deny it, I know that's important to men. But I've seen her naked, Father. She's borne four children. Her breasts are lined and so is her belly. All right, so she doesn't have extra flesh, but still—"

"The childbirthing lines make no difference. It's the way of life. It doesn't lessen a woman's beauty. No, it's other things, things you can't understand as yet."

"Things Ragnor wanted to teach me but I wouldn't let him."

"He touched you?"

Chessa had to smile at the sudden grimness in her father's voice. Debauching his wife was one thing. A man touching his daughter was quite another.

"Yes, but I put a stop to it. That's when he began spouting all his lies about loving me beyond the time of doom. I swear to you, he actually said beyond the time of doom. I could but stare at him. He was a fool."

"I will make you a bargain, Chessa. You keep away from Sira and I will endeavor to teach her a bit of humility, a bit of kindness toward others."

"I wish you good luck," Chessa said, and left her father's chamber.

What Sira would probably do, he thought, knowing himself quite well, was to seduce him. He'd forget his own name in the process.

Cleve knew the man was after his blood. He waved the stranger toward him, taunting him. "Come, little man, come to me. We will see who can kill. Come, you sniveling little coward."

Little was hardly the word for the man. He towered over Cleve, broad as a strapping bull, his fists huge. He was filthy, his stench nearly overpowering.

He lunged, his hands outstretched. He would try to crush Cleve against his chest, squeezing the life from him.

Cleve let him think he would get his way easily. He took a step back, as if suddenly afraid.

The man in his filthy bearskin laughed. "No more smart words for me, lying scum? Now, I'm coming to you just as you asked me to, and I'm going to make you feel more pain than you imagined a man could feel."

"Tell me, who sent you?"

"Ah, I'll tell you that just as your tongue is bulging from your lying mouth."

"Will you, or are you too stupid to even realize the man's name?"

The man yelled.

Cleve judged the distance, calmed himself in the very deepest part of himself, the way Merrik, Oleg, and others had taught him to. He raised his hand in a fluttering gesture, then dropped his arm. The movement made the man laugh. He strode toward Cleve, blocking his escape, moving him ever backward, toward the dark fetid alley.

"Are you afraid I'll still escape you? Who wants me dead? Who paid you to kill me?"

Cleve saw the shadow against the moonlit side of the building.

"Don't you dare hurt him!"

"Damnation," Cleve said, recognizing that voice. He called out, "Get out of here, Chessa. Go away."

"Nay, I'll take care of this miserable bastard. Coward, leave him alone."

Cleve sighed, positioned the hidden blade between his fingers and raised his arm. "You want me dead?" he shouted at the man who had half turned at the sound of a female voice.

"Aye, and now," the man shouted, whirling back toward Cleve again with renewed fury.

Cleve calmly released the knife. It gleamed in the dim light. It embedded itself in the man's throat, the tip of the knife coming out the back of his dirty neck.

At the very same moment, he heard Chessa call out, "There, you miserable creature, how does that feel? Go away and leave us alone."

The man stared at Cleve, disbelieving, then he opened his mouth to speak, but only blood gushed out. He fell forward heavily onto his face. It was then that Cleve saw the knife sticking out of the man's back.

She'd stabbed him. She'd actually stuck a knife in the man's back.

"Are you all right, Cleve?" She was running to him, her hands out to touch him.

He stopped her in her tracks. "Why in the name of the gods are you here in this dark place?"

"How odd. You sound angry. I saved your life and

you're angry about it. Men—all of you are conceited oafs, none of you is worth a blade of grass.'' She bent over and pulled the knife from the man's shoulder. It was then she saw the point of another knife protruding from his neck. She straightened slowly, eyeing him. ''You killed him.''

''Yes, damn you, and I didn't want to, at least not yet. He hadn't yet told me who'd hired him to murder me. And you had to come along and play the dragon slayer. Next time, keep to your own affairs.''

''I'm sorry. I just thought I was helping you. I was afraid he would hurt you and I couldn't let that happen.''

''Why not? I'm only a diplomat who never says anything in a straightforward manner. You loathe who and what I am. The dinner with your father was so strained I'm surprised that anyone ate anything at all. Even the servants felt it, one of them nearly dumping some stewed cabbage on my lap. Then you brought it to a dramatic end. What are you doing here?''

''I wanted to speak to you. I saw my stepmother eyeing you like a succulent piece of honeyed almond bread during our dinner, and I knew she'd get you into her bed and so that's why I said what I did. It wasn't all that dramatic.''

''You wanted the dinner to be over with quickly so your stepmother wouldn't seduce me?''

She nodded. ''You needn't act so surprised. I truly didn't mean to insult you so terribly. It was expedient.''

''You called all diplomats mangy curs whose fleas jumped on all those who came too close. A man could find himself dead for saying such a thing.''

''Actually, I said they were your master's fleas, and they defiled anyone they touched.''

''Forgive me for not rendering your insult perfectly. Your stepmother had no intention of seducing me. No, she was looking at me for another reason, one that's right in front of your damned nose. She felt nothing for me save distaste. By all the gods, you're blind.''

''No, you're the blind one. Of course she was eyeing you with lust. You're beautiful. No matter what else Sira is, she enjoys a handsome man when she sees one. You're very unlike my father. He's black haired and dark skinned, just like me, and you're golden and beautiful. Aye, she enjoys looking at handsome men, she—''

''Be quiet and go away. You're wrong and your dislike of her is making you sightless and stubborn. I'm left with a mystery I don't much like. Didn't your father tell you to keep to your sewing? What the devil are you doing wielding a knife with such enthusiasm and talent?'' He thought of Kiri, the most skilled five-year-old girl child with a knife that he knew of. By all the gods, he didn't want her to follow in this damned girl's footsteps.

''I thought he would crush you to death. Would you prefer that I shriek and faint?''

''In this case, aye. Go away now, Chessa, I must think about this.''

''I saw someone hiding near the edge of those trees, watching and waiting to see what happened.''

Not only had she rushed to save him, she'd perhaps even seen the man who'd hired the assassin to kill him ''Who?''

''It wasn't a man. I don't know who she was. She wore a cloak and hood pulled up tightly around her head. But I know it wasn't a man.''

Cleve could but stare at her. He wasn't at all certain he believed her.

3

"**M**Y DAUGHTER TELLS me you were very nearly killed last night. An assassin, she said."

Cleve said in his low, smooth voice, "Just a thief, sire, or perhaps the man believed me to be someone else."

"But what were you doing there, Cleve? Thieves and outlaws abound in that area."

Cleve merely shrugged, saying nothing. He had no intention of telling the king that he'd received a message, telling him to come to that dank, filthy alley. Nor did he tell the king that his daughter had followed him there. He didn't imagine that she had told her father anything, just that he, Cleve, had spoken to her about what had happened. So she trusted him not to betray her. He probably should have told the truth then. Her father should have more control over her. Still, he kept his mouth shut, his lie stark and bare for the king to chew on. The king knew it was a lie, Cleve saw it in his dark, clever eyes.

"I don't think it was just a common thief," King Sitric said, stroking his jaw, a strong jaw, not an old man's jaw. Cleve thought again of the stories he'd heard of the magician Hormuze who'd renewed the old king, making him a vigorous man in his prime.

"I will assign one of my men to accompany you whenever you leave my palace. I don't want Duke Rollo's emissary to die whilst he is dealing with me.''

"As you will, though I hardly believe it necessary. A one-time attack, nothing more.'' Actually, Cleve wanted another attack. He wanted to know who was behind it. And he didn't want the king's daughter in the way the next time.

"Now, back to our negotiations. Duke Rollo wants my daughter, Chessa, to marry his son, the future heir to the dukedom of Normandy.''

"Yes, his wife died in childbed some two years ago. William is in need not only of a wife but of a strong father-in-law, to use as leverage when the French king bares his fangs, which his nobles force him to do with great regularity. In return, you will dower your daughter only modestly, for your wisdom and the magic of your reign are held in deep respect by Rollo. It is the blood of your blood that he wishes to have.''

King Sitric drummed his fingertips on the chair posts of his throne. The king looked particularly fine this morning, in his white robe, belted with stout linen embroidered with diamonds and emeralds. His lustrous black hair was clubbed back and tied with a black woven strip of linen. Cleve said nothing, merely waited for the king to speak. He'd had nearly this same conversation with the king for the two previous days. They'd discussed the state of the Norman duchy, the power gains made by the French king, Charles III, the fact that Charles wanted Chessa to marry his nephew, Louis. But Sitric didn't trust King Charles, something he hadn't said exactly, though Cleve was practiced at observing.

They'd come to agreement on all details surrounding the marriage. Many things they'd spoken of, yet the king had for the third time asked Cleve to repeat Duke Rollo's request. He said at last, "It is an offer that interests me. How old is William?''

"He is nearing his thirtieth year.''

"It's good he isn't older.''

"Aye, to your daughter perhaps it is preferable. But what matter? A man can father children until he greets death at his doorstep. That is all that is important. With your daughter and all your sons, I'd believed you to be an ancient, but here you are in your prime. It surprised me, sire.''

Cleve waited in vain but King Sitric didn't take the bait. He said only, ''We will speak this evening, Cleve of Malverne. Would you care to dine with my family again? Perhaps my daughter will mind her tongue tonight. Perhaps my queen will show restraint, though it is not in her character, truth be told.''

''For your daughter, sire, a possibility,'' Cleve said. ''For your queen, I know not.''

Sitric sighed. ''I do know,'' he said, and sighed again.

That evening Cleve was again ushered into the king's presence by Cullic, the king's personal bodyguard. Cullic was beautiful and dark and as cold as the moon at the winter solstice. It was said he came from Spain. He said nothing now, just pointed Cleve toward his chair at the long, narrow linen-covered table. There were platters of broiled mutton and roasted geese, the birds' heads and necks propped up with slender golden sticks, making them look quite alive, thoughtful even. There were dishes filled with peas, stewed onions, and cabbage. Fresh loaves of rye bread piled high in baskets sat beside each plate. These were no simple wooden plates for the king of Ireland. They were of the finest glass from the Rhineland, pale blue all over with gold threads shot throughout. The drinking glasses were the same precious blue and filled with sweet wine that the king's subjects would likely never taste unless they stole it. The knives and spoons were of polished reindeer bone with handles of carved obsidian. The previous evening, there had been pale green glasses and dishes from beyond the mountains to the south of France. This king was wealthy and he looked young. Cleve would give a good deal to know the truth of his reign. King Sitric was dark skinned, his eyes black as the night at the winter solstice, his hair the same pure black as his daughter's. He looked oddly foreign this evening, but perhaps it was just the light of the soft oil-wick bowls that sat on the table and rush torches on the walls of the chamber that gave his face an exotic cast.

"Ah, I see you don't readily identify that dish, Cleve," Chessa said, rising. " 'Tis a mixture of *glailey* fish and eggs. Quite tasty, really."

As before, she was looking straight at him, her head cocked slightly to one side. She wore her hair differently this evening: green ribbons twisted through her braids which were in turn wrapped around her head. Her hair was the deepest black imaginable, with no hint of red. He looked away. In the beginning Sarla had looked at him the way Chessa looked at him now, with no revulsion in her face, no repugnance in her eyes. No, he wouldn't let that happen to him again. Ever. He had Kiri. She was all he wanted.

He was here to negotiate the princess's wedding to William Longsword, son of Duke Rollo of Normandy. William was a good man, a powerful man, a man Cleve respected and admired, a man not too old for Chessa to be content with him. "I have never heard of *glailey* fish before," he said, trying to make polite conversation with this strange girl who failed to wince when she looked at his face.

"They swim in long, narrow ribbons near the shore in the river Liffey," she said, leaning toward him. Her eyes were a deeper green than they'd been the day before, a deeper green than the ribbon in her hair. He expected her eyes to hold mystery—the hint of secrets to tempt men beyond endurance. But her eyes were as clear as the pools of water after a gentle afternoon rain. Cleve reminded himself that no woman was guileless, not a single one of them, save Laren. But if this princess was so frank, why didn't she see him clearly? Why didn't she at least flinch when she looked at his face? "I take my brothers there. Brodan caught the *glailey* we're eating."

"Chessa, I told you that I don't want you taking the boys anywhere outside the palace grounds. You can't protect them. They're all-important, not for your silly pleasure.

You're a princess, a lady, not a slut of a fishwife. Stay away from the princes.''

"I will do just as I please, Sira."

The queen with the exquisite silver hair half rose from her seat. "I won't have you speaking back to me, Chessa."

"Now, Sira," the king said, "the boys love their sister. The babe is making you tired, I know. Cleve, would you like some plover eggs? Chessa tells me they're baked inside a barley mixture."

"What? You're going to bear yet another child? Isn't four enough?"

"It will be another male child," Sira said, her hands lightly rubbing over her still-flat belly. "A man can't have too many male children. They are worth something, unlike girls, who have little value."

"I wouldn't say that," the king said as he slid a spoon full of peas into his mouth. "I told you, Sira, that Duke Rollo of Normandy wants Chessa to wed his son and heir. I would say it makes her of infinite value."

"What are you talking about, Papa? You want me to marry someone who lives in Normandy? That's a world away. Those people are Vikings, they're—"

"She isn't worthy," Sira said. "It's ridiculous, as I told you. Nay, you must wed one of our boys to the French princess. The power is there, not in the Norman duchy with that old man, Rollo. He is an old man, nearly dead. His son won't withstand the French. He will be defeated and killed and what will you have? A daughter without any help at all to you. Nay, my lord, 'tis Brodan who must marry into the French house. Let Chessa marry Ragnor of York. Truly, my lord, she isn't worthy of this."

"And you are worthy?" Chessa's face had become markedly red. "As for the Danelaw, the Saxons will soon defeat the Vikings and there will be no more Danish rule. Ah, but that's what you want, isn't it, Sira? You want me to be in York and perhaps left in a ditch after the Saxons take the capital. Aye, you'd like that. But just look at you.

You're not a princess yourself, you're just an accident, you're naught but a—''

"That's quite enough," Sitric said easily. "Sira, would you care for some wine? The merchant Daleeah arrived from Spain just this afternoon. It's a heady brew and as sweet as your mouth."

Cleve saw that the queen was furious, but wise enough to hold her tongue in front of her husband, and even, perhaps, in front of him, though he couldn't imagine why she would care about what he thought of her. As for Chessa, she was staring blankly down at her serving of *glailey* fish and eggs. All knew that the Danelaw was growing weaker by the year, the inroads made by the Saxons drawing closer and closer. It was a matter of time and the Vikings would lose their hold and their rule. He wondered if this prince of the Danelaw, this Ragnor, would ever even rule.

Warfare was more open tonight. The queen and Chessa scrapped back and forth, but there wasn't much heat in Chessa's insults. Cleve wondered what Chessa thought about her probable marriage to William Longsword. It would doubtless be to her liking. What woman wouldn't prefer wealth? He didn't care. By Freya's grace, he wanted only to lead his life, raise his daughter, and find a willing female once in a while to ease his body. Surely it wasn't too much for a man to wish.

The next morning the king summoned Cleve to his throne room. No one else was there. Nothing new in that. Whenever he'd spoken to Cleve, he'd dismissed his ministers, even the servants, all save his bodyguard, Cullic. When Cleve had remarked upon it the first day of his arrival he'd said that servants could serve two masters and he had no intention of granting them that opportunity.

"I give my consent," he said as soon as Cleve entered. "You may leave today and inform Duke Rollo of my decision. I will send Chessa to Rouen when he so desires the marriage to take place."

Cleve bowed low. "As you will, sire."

"Cleve."

"Aye?"

"You did well. You're an intelligent man. I believe you are a man to trust. If you tire of Rollo, I would offer you service here."

Cleve thanked Sitric and turned to leave.

"You were wise to keep away from my daughter. She seems to regard you differently. It is unexpected. I want this marriage. I foresee that Duke Rollo has begun a dynasty that will only grow in power and in conquered land."

"Perhaps you are right about Rollo. His will is strong." Cleve paused but a moment, flicked a speck of dirt from his sleeve and added, "I have no reason to wish your daughter's company." He left the king's presence, neither saying more.

Malverne farmstead
One month later

"Papa."

"Aye, sweeting," he said, lifting Kiri up above his head, then lowering her and holding her close."

"You were gone far too long. I don't like it."

"I don't either. I had to travel from Dublin back to Rouen before I could come home to Malverne. But I told you how many days it would be. I am home three days early."

"That's true," she said, and frowned. "Sometimes I think you add days just to try to fool me. Did all go well?"

He was silent for a very long time, his long fingers lightly stroking down his daughter's back. She wiggled and he scratched her left shoulder. "Everything went as Duke Rollo wished," he said finally. "Now, go to bed, Kiri. I'll tell you all about Taby on the morrow. Your uncle Merrik is right. Taby is a golden child, strong and kind. Ah, here is Irek, come to sleep with you." Irek was fat now, nearly full grown, black and white save for a gray spot on his nose. What sort of dog he was, no one could begin to guess. He was ferociously protective of Kiri, barking wildly if he believed anyone wanted to harm her. Harald, Merrik's eldest son, kept his distance when Irek began to growl.

In the full darkness of the night, he dreamed again the vivid dream that hadn't come to him in nearly three months. He was tossed into the dream just as a man could be tossed overboard into a storm-maddened sea, with no warning, no portent. It was real and he was there and the scent of those purple and yellow flowers filled him, just as he seemed to feel the lightly falling mist against his face. This time he didn't begin on the cliff edge looking down into that ravine that was filled with boulders and crashing cold water. No, this time, he was there, at the door of that house with its sod and shingle roof, with the thin trail of smoke that came from the single hole in the roof. He was shaking. He didn't want to go into that fortress. He heard that deep, compelling voice. He knew she would scream soon. He tried to run. Where was the pony? He reached out his hand and lifted the single iron latch. The huge wooden door swung open. Suddenly the voice was quiet. She wasn't screaming. There was dead silence. The room was long and wide, and at the end of it there was a high dais, behind it huge square-cut shutters. The floor was hard-packed earth. One end of the huge hall was curtained off. He knew there were small sleeping chambers behind that curtain, four of them. There were benches all along the walls. Hanging from thick chains over the fire pit was a huge iron pot, steam rising out of it, thickening the air with white mist. Silence still reigned even though the hall held many men, women, and children. Even the three dogs sitting there on their haunches were as silent as the people. He hated it. He feared it. He took another step into the hall. He saw a woman standing over the fire pit stirring something in a huge iron pot. There was a man drinking from an ornately carved wooden cup. He sat in the only chair in the room, its back high, its arms exquisitely carved to display a scene showing Thor defeat-

ing his enemies, his sword raised, the look of triumph ferocious on his thick wooden face. The chair looked to be
very old, but the man was young, his hair black and thick,
his face lean, his hands long and white and narrow. He was
garbed all in black. His sleeves were so loose they would
billow out in a wind. Other men were sitting along the
bench where several women served them wooden plates of
food.

The man in the chair looked to be brooding, his chin
resting on his white slender hand. But he wasn't really
brooding, Cleve somehow knew. He was watching a young
girl who was working at a loom in the corner. Then he
glanced at the woman attending the iron pot over the fire
pit. The woman looked from the girl toward the man. There
was both rage and fear in her eyes. She said something, but
the man ignored her. He kept his eyes on the girl. Softly,
he told her to come to him. Cleve shrieked at her not to do
it, not to go to him, and for the first time in the dreams,
she actually seemed to hear him. She turned, as if searching
out where he was. Then, as if she saw him, she spoke to
him, but he couldn't hear her words, couldn't understand
what she wanted to tell him. He watched her walk slowly
toward the man, and he was afraid and he was angry, as
angry as the woman who still stood at the fire pit, her eyes
never wavering from the elegant man who sat in that royal
chair.

He knew he was dreaming, but again he couldn't make
himself awaken. He could feel the man looking at him now,
and he saw the man frown. Then the man rose and waved
the girl away from him. He was walking toward Cleve. He
would kill him, Cleve knew it, yet he couldn't seem to
make his feet move, he couldn't speak. The man came
down on his haunches in front of him. Oddly, he merely
stretched out his hand and smoothed the golden hair back
from his brow. He said, ''You look as shaggy as your sheep
dog.'' He drew a slender knife from its scabbard at his
waist. Cleve was so afraid he thought he'd vomit, but the
man merely sliced off the long shank of hair that fell over

his forehead. Then he patted Cleve's cheek and rose. He said, "This is a man's business. Go outside and play with your pony." But Cleve looked toward the woman at the fire pit. She avoided his eyes. He looked toward the girl and she nodded, saying nothing, just nodded at him until he turned and nearly ran from that huge hall.

It was then he heard a scream. He didn't turn. He couldn't bear to turn, he just ran and ran and ran. . . .

He jerked awake, his breath hitched in his throat, and he knew then that his mind was stitching together long-forgotten memories and making him relive them, making him face who he was and what he'd been a long time ago. He slept again as the dawn came and the air was still and deep as his sleep was now.

And once he was wide awake, he remembered.

Laren and Merrik, the lord and lady of Malverne farmstead, walked with him up to Raven's Peak. They were silent, waiting, for they knew that something important had happened to him and they were content to be patient, to let him tell them in his own good time.

Cleve said nothing until they reached the top of the peak. He stared out over the fjord and the barren cliffs opposite before turning to his good friends with a smile. "My name isn't Cleve. It's Ronin. My mother's ancestors are Scottish Dalriada and were originally from northern Ireland, many generations ago. They journeyed to the west, first to the outer islands, then to the mainland both north and south of the Romans' two walls, where they fought the Picts, the Britons, and the Vikings. They finally gained their own land and settled. They're now called the Scots. They were united with the Picts by Kenneth in the middle of the last century."

"By Thor's might," Merrik said. "You're a Scot, truly? From where does your family hail?"

"In the northwest, on the western shore of a river called Loch Ness. It's a savage land, Merrik, more untamed than Norway, but it doesn't have the months of frigid cold.

There are outlaws aplenty. There is much trading. There is beautiful land that goes on and on, and it changes from flatland to deep valleys to mountains that are so vicious, so barren and rugged, that you pray to survive them. There are glens and small secluded places where waterfalls crash downward onto boulders older than the hills themselves. You would enjoy yourself there.

"Merrik, you remember the dream I told you about? Well, I've had it on and off now for over two years. It's grown bolder, fuller in the past two years. Last night I dreamed it again and this time when I awoke in the morning, I knew. I remembered." He paused a moment, pain filling his eyes. "I am half Viking. My father was Olrik the Ram, and he was a powerful Viking chieftain, as was his father and his father's father before him. He was known as the lord of Falcon Ridge, his fortress was called Kinloch. I look like him, with my golden hair. As for my strange eyes, I have no idea if they are from him or from my mother. I was too young to know when I was taken. I wasn't born a slave, but like Laren, I was made into one. As I said, my mother was Dalriadan, small and fair skinned, hair as red as an angry sky before sunset. She was very beautiful. My father captured her on a raid and married her. They settled northward near the coast. I have a brother and two sisters, all older than I. My brother was Ethar, my two sisters, Argana and Cayman."

"The lord of Falcon Ridge," Merrik repeated slowly. "I have heard of him. Perhaps it was from my father. What happened? Why were you sold into slavery?"

"Yes," Laren said, touching her fingertips to his linen sleeve. "How came you to be a slave if your father was so powerful?"

"My father died when I was very young. My mother married another Viking warrior who was powerful in a neighboring area. I remember he was cold and hard and he wore only black. He brought silence to Kinloch, and fear. Aye, I remember even as small as I was that he terrified everyone. I remember that I was out one day riding my pony. I stopped when I saw someone I knew, and whilst I was talking to him I was struck on the head and left for dead. I didn't die, but I was very ill. A man found me, brought me back to health and sold me in Hedeby to a man who liked . . . well, it's not important. My stepfather—I can't remember his name—he was a bully, but he was so cold, how well I remember that, the unnatural coldness of him and everything he touched. He took my father's place and everything changed. Surely it was he who wanted me killed, but I didn't die, though the result was surely the same since I was a slave for fifteen years. It was never his plan to raise me to take my rightful place, though I wonder why he killed me before he killed my older brother, who was the rightful heir. That's a mystery. Doubtless after I was gone, he spawned more children off my mother. As to what became of my brother and sisters, I don't know. I remembered in this last dream that he wanted my sister, Argana. She was only a girl, no more than twelve. But I knew he wanted her and my mother knew it as well. He beat my mother, I remember that. I remember hearing her screams, his low, deep voice, so calm, so very black, and her screams.''

Cleve looked from Merrik to Laren. There was regret and deep, deep anger in his eyes. "I want to go home," he said. "I pray my mother and my brother and sisters are still alive. It has been nearly twenty years. I want to know if what I suspect is true: if this man, my stepfather, tried to kill me, if he killed my brother, so he could take what is ours. I want vengeance.''

"I will go with you," Merrik said, and rubbed his hands together. "I grow bored with all this damned peace, not a single squabble in over six months now. At the last meeting of the *thing* in Kaupang, there were only silly complaints— a man who'd stolen a pig from his neighbor—matters that didn't deserve the time it took us to travel there. Even the raid into the Rhineland whilst you were away being a diplomat wasn't much of a challenge. I will go gray before I test my sword again. You say your land is savage? You swear my sword won't hang lifeless by my side?''

"More savage than you can imagine. But don't forget, I was but five years old.''

"I will go with you as well,'' Laren said. "Merrik is right. It's time for an adventure.''

Merrik opened his mouth, then wisely closed it.

Cleve said slowly, "I was born Ronin but I've been Cleve for twenty years. Cleve I will remain.''

4

DUKE ROLLO OF Normandy, a man of many more years than were allotted to most men, sharp of eye and strong of will, and ready for any adventure, leaned forward, and said, "Cleve, Laren has told me of your beginnings. I, too, wish to see that you regain what is yours, that you find your family, though it has been nearly twenty years, a long time. People die. Few are like me and my brother, Hallad. Ha, that Hallad. I am convinced that he will sire another child even as he is being laid out for burial."

"This is true, sire," Cleve said. Laren's father, Hallad, had sired another three sons off his young wife he'd wedded five years before. He was still as hail and hardy as Rollo. It sometimes terrified Cleve. It reminded him of King Sitric of Ireland, a young man who was older than death, if judged by years. Had Rollo and Hallad been touched by the same magic?

"But surely you would rather speak of the marriage between William and Chessa, daughter of King Sitric."

"Oh, aye. It is time and William knows it. He doesn't

really want this marriage, but he will do it. He misses his wife, you know.''

"He must breed more sons," Cleve said.

"He understands what he must do. You told him that the princess was comely.''

"Aye, she's comely.''

"Is she submissive?''

"There is a brightness about her.''

"Does that mean submissive?''

"Not exactly, sire, but surely William won't know disappointment in her. But you didn't ask me these questions before. The marriage is arranged. Merrik, Laren, and I will remain here until the princess arrives for her marriage. William has asked that we wait.''

"Aye, I know it. Merrik will spend all his time with Taby, Laren will tell me skald's tales, and you, Cleve? What will you do?''

"I will bask in the brightness of your court, sire.''

"Ah, well, don't tell me then, what you will really do. Ha, I'll wager she's a comely young girl. That's it, isn't it?''

It was the truth, but Cleve merely smiled, a sated smile. Her name was Marda, she was buxom and merry, and she pleased him mightily.

"Then you, Merrik, and Laren will travel up the eastern coast of the Danelaw to Scotland. Will you take Kiri with you and that damned cur of hers? Do you need more warriors?''

Cleve nodded. "Kiri and Irek, aye, they'll come. It will be our home. We don't have need of more warriors. We will have two warships and forty men. It seems that all Merrik's men grew bored and testy. All want to trade, mayhap fight and plunder and enjoy new women if they can.''

"Aye, it is a man's way. Merrik's warriors are amongst the best. Still, I should like to send some of my own warriors with you. Just a few, Cleve. My captain is Bjarni, a man who is loyal to me and stronger than the oak tree from which I hang scoundrels.'' Rollo sat back in his huge throne and rubbed his shaven chin. "I do not like Laren going. She is a woman. She could be harmed. Taby would not like it.''

"She survived for two years as a slave, sire. She is able to see to herself.''

"She is a woman. Women haven't the strength of men.''

"She is nearly as skilled as I with a knife. 'Tis true Merrik's sword drags her arm to the ground, but a knife will kill as true as the mightiest blade.''

Rollo grunted, still displeased. "Ah, there was another matter, Cleve.'' Rollo paused. "It's about Ragnor of York.''

"What about him? I was told by Sitric, after I'd offered him a goodly amount of mead, that Ragnor had tried to seduce Chessa, but failed. She was hurt by his lies and Sitric told me that she gave him a purge that had him puking up his innards for several days.''

"She doesn't sound at all submissive, Cleve.''

"I would say rather, sire, that she was wronged and took her revenge.''

"She should have allowed another to avenge her.''

"Just as Laren should have waited for a warrior to rescue her and Taby?''

"Oh, aye, Cleve, you have your smooth, clever tongue. Your wit tires me.''

"Forgive me, sire. What is it you wished to tell me about Ragnor of York?''

"He has decided he wants the princess. His father has told him that he was a fool to try to deceive her, to seduce her without marrying her first. Ragnor, from the tale you just told me, would probably rather flay the flesh off her back than wed her now. Purged him, did she? Puked up his guts? What did she use?''

"Malle leaves mixed with ginger, something Ragnor likes, she told her father.''

"Did he have his ass bare as well?''

"I don't know if the malle leaves have that result.''

Rollo laughed, a low rumble, then louder and louder until he threw his head back, striking it against the back of the huge throne. He grunted and leaned forward, allowing one of his bodyguards to rub the back of his head.

"More to the left, near my right ear," Rollo said as the man massaged his head as gently as he would a babe's.

"Did I tell you, Cleve, that William just laughed when I told him I was getting old and I should step down for him? Aye, he laughed and laughed, but he didn't hit his head. He's young and thinks ahead."

"William knows that wisdom and leadership remain constant in a man of your abilities, sire."

"That sounds like a diplomat's hollow praise, Cleve."

"That is what the princess told me. Do I speak with false praise? Say meaningless words? Very well, if it pleases you to hear the truth, I would agree with William. Keep to your place, Duke Rollo, until you can no longer rise from your bed. You have fought hard to gain your place, you have brought prosperity to a land that had been nearly torn asunder by avarice and battle and rapacity. Enjoy your power now, for all men must die. Valhalla might be what one would desire for eternity, but I think I should prefer the joys of the mortal world for as long as I could. Aye, sire, keep your throne and power for a while longer. William doesn't mind. Your people don't mind."

"I raised him well," Rollo said. "Did you say that the princess insulted you?"

"Aye, she did, said I had a tongue like an adder, a tongue that lolled about spewing honeyed words but said nothing."

"She sounds difficult, Cleve."

Cleve just smiled. The princess wasn't all that difficult. However, William had no heavy hand with a woman, so Cleve imagined that her marriage to him would be pleasant. He wondered what Chessa would think of her father-in-law.

"In any case, I hear that Ragnor wants her. Wants to wed with her. He's a man, not a boy, all of twenty-one, but he's a selfish creature, spoiled. I can't imagine that he would have any kindness for a girl who purged him." The duke laughed again, this time throwing his head forward. Still, his bodyguard stepped up, ready. "Until she is here in Rouen, we must take care that Ragnor doesn't take her."

"I will fetch her myself, sire," Cleve said, then wondered why he'd said it. He didn't want to see Chessa again until she was standing beside William before a Christian priest. Then she would be William's wife and nothing more would matter.

Duke Rollo shook his head. "Actually, I have already sent two warships to Dublin. They should return shortly. Now, where is Laren? I wish to hear a story. She keeps me guessing, what with the queen who was captured by a lord of Bulgar and how she kept him at bay by telling him stories. Aye, Laren is wily. She is sly. She is a good skald."

"I believe she and Merrik are with Taby. Merrik misses the boy sorely."

"Aye, I know it, but now he has his own sons. What are their names? I forget such things now."

"Kendrid and Harald, both the image of their father. They will be men of valor. But it makes no difference. Taby is the son of Merrik's heart. I hope his own sons will never realize it."

Duke Rollo rubbed his chin, felt the sagging skin, and frowned. "Nay," he said, "this princess doesn't sound at all submissive. Think you that William will have to beat her?"

"If he did I fear he would receive an unwanted and unexpected purge."

"A woman is submissive when her belly is filled with a babe. William will see to it immediately. Think you she's a good breeder, Cleve?"

He pictured her in his mind's eye. Not all that tall, slender waist, full breasts, the size of her hips unclear because of the draped, full-cut gowns she wore. "She seemed of adequate size, sire." He pictured his hands splayed, nearly meeting around her waist. Then going lower to spread over her belly, letting his fingers span outward. Aye, she was large enough to bear children.

But not William's children. Not Ragnor's children.

As he left the duke's presence Cleve wondered from whence that errant thought had come.

Dublin, Ireland
Court of King Sitric

She'd caught a netful of *glailey* fish and was laughing as she scooped it out of the river Liffey only to have one of them wriggle through the net and fall back into the water. "You escaped me and 'twas well done," she called to the wildly escaping fish, only a small blur now.

Chessa was alone, Brodan having been escorted back to the palace by two of Sira's bodyguards. He'd complained, but the bodyguards had their orders. Chessa had told him to go. They'd catch *glailey* fish another morning. She loved Brodan. Nearly eight years old, he was bright and loving, like their father, thank Freya's beneficence, and not at all like that witch, Sira. He was usually a very serious boy, studying with the Christian scholars, dreaming silent dreams whilst he was awake.

But her father wasn't all that loving.

He'd told her that morning that William had sent two warships to take her to Rouen. She would leave on the morrow.

She'd said, her chin up, for she'd thought and thought about it, "No, Father, I don't wish to wed with William. I don't wish to leave Dublin. I don't wish to marry a man I've never met. I won't do it. Besides, he is nearly your age. I don't wish to wed my father."

He'd held to his patience, she recognized the slight stiffening of his shoulders, the pursing of his lips. "Men come in all ages, Chessa. They are still men. As for William, Cleve told me he was only thirty, not old at all."

"Women come in all ages as well. Let this William marry one who is closer to his age than I am. There are still eleven years between us."

"He needs a young woman, one to bear him children."

"I refuse to become like Sira, who breeds one child after another. It is all she does. It is all she is. No, she is also a witch and mean-spirited and—"

"We are not speaking of Sira," the king said, and she saw now that he was losing patience and sought another path to convince him.

She placed her hand in his, as she'd done when she was a small child, and he, her protector, her father, the only being in the world, as far as she was concerned. "Papa, please don't send me away. I will try to be kinder to Sira. I won't take the boys to the river to throw the nets for the *glailey* fish. I will try to soften my words."

Sitric laughed, he couldn't help himself. "You make vows you cannot keep, my sweeting. Nay, now listen to me, Chessa. You are a woman grown, 'tis time for you to wed, time for you to leave me. William is a fine man, Cleve assured me of that. I questioned him closely. William will treat you honorably."

And that, Chessa thought now, shoving her hair out of her eyes, was that. This was very probably her last day of freedom. Even now her servant was packing her huge wooden trunk with soft linen undershifts, wool gowns dyed soft reddish brown from the madder plant. Ah, and the linen gown of brilliant gold, dyed from a lichen that grew close to the Affern Swamp. Her father had given her a special wool gown of pure scarlet, dyed with the rare orchid lichen from many miles to the south, stitched with intricate embroidered designs. She had a woolen gown to match each of the gowns. She had elaborate brooches to wear on the shoulder, dainty earrings of the purest silver, gold, and ivory. She had gold neck chains and a chain of colored beads presented to her by one of her father's ministers. She was a princess and she would go to this William looking like a princess.

That made her smile. Her feet were bare and dirty, her hair hanging down over her forehead, smudges of muddy water on her cheeks. Her hands were as dirty as her feet and her back hurt from bending over to net the fish. Her brown gown was tucked up, leaving her legs bare to her knees.

If this William could but see her now perhaps he would turn on his royal heels and run the other way.

She thought of Cleve and wondered if he would be in Rouen. She'd thought about him a lot, truth be told, for the past month. She still hadn't found out who had tried to have him killed. That was odd, for what could he have done to earn such enmity?

She rubbed the small of her back and looked back toward the town. It was all wooden buildings, many of them connected by wooden walkways since it rained so often here and the paths became muddy holes very quickly. The fortifications were also of wooden poles, thick and sturdy, strongly bound together, with walkways along the ramparts. Dublin was a trading center that was gaining fame by the year, and that meant more enemies wanted to seize it and rule in her father's place. There were always Irish raids by local chieftains, unwilling to accept Viking rule.

She sighed, knowing she must return to the palace, knowing that her father was having a special banquet for her, this last evening of her life in Dublin. She imagined how delighted Sira would be to see the back of her, though she knew that Sira had argued and shrieked at King Sitric not to go through with the marriage. All Chessa could think was that Sira didn't want Chessa to be above her in rank. But she wouldn't be, would she?

She picked up her skirts and made her way through the thick water reeds. The wind picked up. The thick willow trees that overhung the river Liffey swayed and whispered in the still air. It would rain soon. Even now the clouds were rolling in from the Irish Sea. Aye, it would be a grand storm, and it would be upon them soon now.

She picked up her skirts higher and began to run. She dropped her sandals, leaned down to grab them up, and heard something behind her. She whirled about to see a man standing there, tall and muscled and smiling.

She calmed herself. "Who are you?"

"My name is Kerek. You are Princess Chessa?"

"Why do you wish to know?" She stared at the huge man, his thick red hair threaded with white.

"Aye, you are she." He took a step toward her, still smiling, and she tried to duck around him. He grabbed her arm, whirled her about, pulled her against him.

She'd left her knife in her chamber.

She forced herself to ease against him. His hold on her loosened. She raised her foot and kicked him hard in the shin. He yelped and she threw the knotted net of *glailey* fish in his face. He released her and she was running faster than she ever had in her life. He was on her in an instant, nearly pulling her arm from its socket as he yanked her about.

She raised her leg to strike him in the groin, but he was faster. He cursed her, then, calmly, he raised his fist and sent it squarely into her jaw, grabbing her arms even as she went flying backwards.

Chessa fell against him.

Kerek picked her up and threw her over his massive shoulder. When she awoke some minutes later and reared up, he merely brought her down in front of him and said, "Will you lie quietly or shall I knock you out again?"

She felt dizzy and sick. She didn't want him to hit her again. She merely nodded.

He slung her over his shoulder again. She closed her eyes, wondering who this man was and what he wanted. Her father had told her so very many times that she wasn't to wander outside the palace fortifications alone. It was dangerous. She'd never paid him any attention.

He'd been right and she was a fool. She looked at the ground, knowing that the man was carrying her toward the harbor where all the trading ships docked. The market was near. There were always people there. Someone would help her.

He wove through a good dozen traders hawking fish, shoes, soapstone bowls. She reared up and screamed at the top of her lungs, "I am Chessa, daughter of King Sitric. Help me!"

The man hit her hips hard, laughing as he did so. "Aye, my sweeting, you're a princess, a beautiful princess. Everyone is looking at you, admiring your Royal Highness's beauty. Ah, your gown is beyond fine, isn't it? The dirt on your face ennobles you right enough."

"Help me! I'm Princess Chessa, help me!"

But the people were just staring at her, some of them pointing, some of them laughing now.

"Aye, she's a muddy little lark," said a woman who was examining a jeweler's silver armlet.

"Those dirty little bare feet of hers are as royal as the hairs in my husband's nose," another woman shouted, this one rubbing her large hands on a trout that was still wriggling.

The man's hand hit her bottom again, this time much harder and she sucked in her breath.

"Quiet now, sweeting," he said aloud, all jovial and loving. "Don't give laughter to these good people at your own expense. Or do you do it because you like the feel of my hand on your sweet buttocks?"

He was through the market then, and he walked faster. "I will make you pay for that," she said quietly.

"You think so, do you? Well, we will see, won't we?" She tried to jerk away from him, and he laughed. "I don't know if my poor master will enjoy you," he said. He broke into a trot, bouncing her up and down until her stomach knotted with cramps and nausea.

Then he was carrying her across a wooden ramp onto a large trading ship. He lowered her to her feet and she would have fallen had he not held her arm.

"Come along," he said, and dragged her along solid pine planks between the rowing spaces. At the stern of the ship was a large covered area for sleeping and cargo. He shoved her into the area. There was a man there, seated on a chair, which was so silly she would have laughed if she wasn't still trying to swallow the wretched nausea, for his head brushed the top of the leather canvas.

Aye, he was seated there in the shadows as if he were in a throne room and not aboard a trading ship beneath a sheltering canvas.

"She looks like a slut," the man said. "She looks like a slave." Chessa froze. Surely life couldn't be this unfair. By all the gods, she'd rather be off to Normandy and marry this William Longsword.

"Aye," Kerek said, "but at least she was alone and I had not a bit of trouble with her."

"I don't believe you. She would fight the forces of the Christian's devil before she would meekly give in to any man, despite his size."

"Very well," Kerek said, and there was admiration in his voice. "I did have to think quickly, but I won, for she is here."

"Aye, and in my power at last. Hello, Chessa. Didn't you think you would see me again?"

5

CHESSA STARED AT Ragnor of York.

"Aye, I've got you now, you little bitch, and you'll not escape me."

"What do you want, you miserable piece of swamp weed?"

Ragnor stood slowly, took two steps toward her, and slapped her hard. She fell to the rug-covered wooden planks. Pain seared through her hip. He stood over her, his hands on his narrow hips, looking down at her. He was quite pleased with himself. He was smiling down at her.

"I like you at my feet, your face down. It becomes you. You will never again speak to me with any words save modest ones. Do you understand, Chessa?"

She looked up at him, standing there over her. She swallowed words she knew would only lead to more pain, though she wanted to shriek at him, tell him what she thought of him, throw herself on him, and pound that smirk off his silly face.

"I asked you a question, Chessa. Answer me."

Still, she couldn't get her throat to work, couldn't seem to make meek words come out of her mouth.

He kicked her in the ribs. She jerked at the pain and pulled in on herself, hugging her arms around her.

"Answer me," he said, his voice shrill now.

Kerek said, "You don't want to risk killing her, my lord. Perhaps she has no breath to answer you, perhaps—"

"Keep your opinion in your throat, Kerek. She's willful, stubborn, and has more pride than any hundred women. I will enjoy breaking that pride of hers. Aye, and I will. She fed me poison. She would have killed me if I hadn't been so strong."

She got herself to her knees, her palms on the floor, the pain in her ribs pulling and prodding at her, but she managed to draw her breath. She looked up at him then and said, "Why did you bring me here?"

He raised his foot, but Kerek grasped his arm, saying urgently, "It is a modest question. She doesn't realize why you have taken her. If you tell her, the knowledge will make her even more modest, even more sweetly meek."

Kerek was blind. She would never be meek and Ragnor knew it, but he did slowly lower his foot. When he'd raised it, she'd flinched, and that had pleased him. Perhaps Kerek was right. Perhaps he'd shown her that she would come to accept him as her master. "Attend me, then," he said, and sat himself again in his chair. She was on her hands and knees in front of him, her hair loose from its thick braid, all that sinful black hair, as black as the hair of the heathen Picts who lived northward in that savage land of Scotland, the damned feral beasts who stole sheep and cattle and women from the outer farmsteads. At least her hair was shiny and clean, unlike the greasy matted hair of the Picts. He supposed she was comely enough. Her eyes were an odd green, near moss green, and that made her more acceptable to him as a wife. He'd wanted to bed her, but that hadn't happened, and in instances of rare honesty, he knew it had been foolish of him to try to seduce her. She was a princess and even the future ruler of the Danelaw didn't bed a princess and walk away.

But he didn't want to marry her. He wanted Inelda, the daughter of a Norwegian jewelry merchant in York, her hair so blond it was nearly white, her eyes the palest blue. By Freya, he wanted her, but his father demanded that he wed

Chessa, that damned bitch who'd turned him down, who'd poisoned him, who'd made him puke up his guts. Inelda only turned him down because she was so very innocent, so shy. And she really hadn't said nay to him, only whispered that she was afraid, not of him, oh, never of him, but of what would happen if he got her with child. What would she do? Ah, she was so very afraid. He adored her for her fear, knew that once he'd wedded Chessa, he would return to Inelda and make her his wife in everything but name. He would take care of her. She could breed a dozen children, he didn't care. He just wanted her.

"Attend me," he said again when Chessa raised her head to look at him. To look *up* at him. "You asked why I had you brought to me. I'm taking you back to York. You will wed with me. You will be the future queen of the Danelaw."

"So," she said slowly, the pain in her ribs less now, "your father still orders you about, does he?"

He leaned forward, grabbed her braid and yanked it upward until her face was at the level of his knees. "You will keep silent or I will make you regret it." He was shaking with rage. "By all the gods, I would like to beat you senseless. But I won't. Instead I'll do what I did in Dublin. I'll bend you to my will with my words again, and you, you silly girl, will listen to me and believe me. Admit it, Chessa, you wanted me, you loved me, you wanted to marry me then. You wanted me to bed you."

To his surprise, she nodded. "Aye, I believed you loved me and thus I was open to you. I believed that you were honest and sincere. I believed you were a good man. But then I saw the truth in you and it sickened me. You sickened me. I sickened myself because I'd believed you. Would that I had more malle leaves and fist root. You liked that drink, didn't you, since I added ginger? You puked and puked, I heard, and it pleased me no end. It wasn't poison, but I'm pleased you were so ill you believed it was."

He was utterly still. "I wanted to kill you for that."

"You deserved it. You were a liar. You deceived me. You were dishonorable."

"I merely wanted to bed you without having to see your damned face every day. You poisoned me."

"I told you that I didn't. If I'd wanted to kill you, I could have. I just wanted you to be so sick you'd want to die but you wouldn't."

He dropped her braid. He remembered too well the awful pain in his belly, the unending cramps, the bile, the smell of himself after days of sickness. He would pay her back for that. But let her guess now what was in his mind though he wanted to strangle the life from her. "No more honeyed words for you, Chessa. I wanted to bed you and I will, and I don't care if you like it or not. You try to harm me again and you will have an accident and I will make a good show of grief when I tell of it to my father."

"You won't touch me, Ragnor, or I'll kill you, I swear it. Ah, how I wish I could have seen you puking up your guts. Aye, I heard about it and I laughed and laughed because you got what you deserved. You wronged me, Ragnor. I merely took my revenge. Is that not what a man would do? Why not a woman, then?" She stopped then, knowing that more pain would come because his face was pinched, his eyes red with rage. But she couldn't keep the words unspoken. It was the truth and she had to say it. Now she would pay for the truth.

The air around her thickened with his anger. He dropped to his knees in front of her. He took her throat between his hands and tightened his fingers. She grasped his wrists, trying to pull loose, but he only tightened his grip. She struggled, jerking sideways, pulling him down with her. Suddenly, he released her throat, shoved her onto her back and came down over her. "This is all I ever wanted from you," he said, pressing his palm into her belly. "This is what I will have from you."

He ground himself against her and she froze. She felt the weight of him, the shape of him, the hardness and force of his body, and she hated it.

"My lord, the captain wishes to leave now. He wishes to speak to you. Please, my lord."

Ragnor had forgotten that Kerek was there, standing only a few feet away, watching. His father believed the damned Danish bastard to be such an excellent bodyguard for him. He called Kerek a man of good sense and reason. Now here he was trying to intercede on the princess's behalf. What did he know of anything? He was an old man, lust in him long dead.

Ragnor reared off Chessa and rolled to his feet. He looked down at her, lying there, her arms over her chest, her face pale. She lacked the lovely pallor of Inelda; Chessa could only pale to a dull golden color. He looked at her eyes, that odd green that looked so mysterious with her black hair, mysterious and veiled, hiding knowledge from him. Her eyes weren't warm and inviting as Inelda's eyes were.

He shook himself. "I will return to you. If you are good to me, I will give you no reason to complain to my father. If you hide your arrogance well from me, I will wait to take you until we are wed. If you displease me at all, if you speak to me with insolence, I will strip you and take you in front of any of the men who wish to look. Do you understand me, Chessa?"

"I understand you," she said, her only thought of how she would escape him.

"You look like the filthiest of my father's sluts. Kerek will bring you water to bathe yourself. I don't know if it will be enough, but you will make do. I have brought clothing for you. Array yourself so that I can bear to look upon you."

"If I hadn't been fishing at the river, I would have been safe from you. That I look like a slut from my exercise was to your advantage, otherwise this man couldn't have taken me."

"Oh, I'd have gotten you, Chessa," Ragnor said with a laugh. And with that, he left her.

Rouen,
Duke Rollo's Palace

"She's been taken," Bjarni said, still out of breath, for he'd run from the dock to the palace. "Stolen away without a trace. The king is frantic."

Rollo turned to Cleve. "Could she have run away? Did she not wish to wed William?"

"What she wanted didn't matter. It wasn't her decision to make. It was her father's." Cleve sighed. "Someone took her. Who would benefit the most?"

Bjarni said, "King Sitric believes it to be Ragnor of York. He said that the Danelaw king, Olric, wanted her to marry his son."

Cleve laughed, unable to help himself. He told Rollo what Chessa had done to Ragnor of York. "Thus, sire, I cannot imagine that Olric ever planned to negotiate with Sitric, for he knew it wouldn't work. Nay, he simply took her. He will wed her to Ragnor and it will be done."

William, who should have been profoundly distressed by the news, said in an almost cheerful voice, "Aye, it is most probably Ragnor of York. Lothaire the Bald, one of King Charles's ministers, also told me that Olric of the Danelaw wanted her for his son. Even King Charles wants her, though his eldest son is only eleven years old."

"You never said a word of this to me," Rollo said, bending those compelling dark eyes of his on his only son.

William merely shrugged. "The French want one of Sitric's sons to wed into their family. They don't want the Irish alliance with Normandy that Chessa would bring. Thus it wouldn't surprise me that Charles assisted Olric and Ragnor to kidnap the girl."

"This *girl* is to be your wife, William."

"Does it really matter, Father? She will not be dishonored. She will one day be a queen. I will continue as I have. I have my son dear Margaret gave me. Eilder will follow me. He will survive. I need no more sons.''

Duke Rollo looked at his son, who was thirty years old, and said, ''You are a fool. To love a dead woman so much that you put a dynasty into danger makes me want to search inside your head for reason.''

Cleve, scenting an old squabble, cleared his throat, and said, ''I will go after her.''

''Aye,'' Rollo said. ''You will fetch her back here, Cleve. William will do his duty by her and wed her and he will have a dozen more sons. It is necessary. Our line won't die out, not because of your love of this damned dead woman.''

Cleve cocked his head toward William.

William said slowly, knowing there was no hope for it, ''Aye, Cleve, bring her back. The matter was agreed to and I will honor it.''

''Merrik will enjoy the adventure,'' Cleve said.

''As will I,'' Laren said quietly from behind him. ''As will I.''

''Papa,'' Kiri said, and held out her arms to him. Laren released her and Cleve knew that he would have to be very careful in his rescue.

It was very dark. Chessa heard the men talking outside as they bent over their oars. They complained that the wind had died and now all of them would have to exhaust themselves with the rowing. They complained that Ragnor was pushing them too hard. He wanted to be in York in another four days. They were sailing in the Channel between Normandy and England, she thought, so very close. Soon they would turn northward and sail past East Anglia into the North Sea until they reached York. Then she would escape.

She wondered if Cleve knew yet she'd been taken. She wondered what he thought, if he worried about her, if he wished to see her again, safe and unharmed. She wondered if he ever thought about her the way she did about him. She saw his beautiful face clearly, the clean gold of his hair, the fascination of his one golden eye and his one blue eye. She didn't wonder at all what William or Duke Rollo thought.

She sighed, settling herself on the mat, pulling the woolen blanket more closely about her. As she had for the past three nights, she worried that Ragnor wouldn't keep his word. She worried that he would come and rape her. She knew Kerek couldn't stop him if he decided to force her, but she believed now that he would try to aid her. Kerek's thick red hair was whipped by the wind, his face deeply seamed from years in the sun. He was as strong as a much younger warrior, but there was softness in him, kindness that made her think frantically of how to get him to help her. He couldn't bear Ragnor, that was clear.

He had spent much of his time with her during the past three days. To protect her in the only way he knew how. He brought her food, water, and stiff conversation, for he was but a man of modest means and place, and she was, after all, a princess.

She was a princess only because her father was brilliant, she thought, smiling to herself. All these kings wanted her for her pure northern bloodlines and her father's strength. If only they knew the truth.

"Princess."

"Aye, Kerek. It is very dark tonight. There is no moon at all. How does the man at the tiller know where the men should set their oars?"

"There is the faint glitter of the North Star. The navigator is a man who's eyes know every speck in the heavens. Were it raining, I vow he would still be able to see the right path."

"What do you want, Kerek?"

He didn't answer immediately, and she said again, "Why are you here?"

"To keep him away," he said at last. "He has drunk too much mead. He talks to the men. He laughs and he boasts. He claims he will break you in before he takes you to wife. He claims if you aren't to his liking, he will give you to the men, then throw you overboard and claim an accident to his father, Olric. He doesn't like you overmuch. He won't ever forget how it was you who made him sicker than an asp biting the Christian devil.''

"But he needs me," she said, wondering exactly how true that really was.

"Aye, but he doesn't know it. He wants his father's throne. He is tired of the restraints his father places on him. Ragnor is a man with a boy's passions and a boy's selfishness and greed. The Danelaw grows weaker. Soon the Saxons will conquer York, take all our lands, and there will be no more Viking kings, all will come under the kingdom of the Saxons. It is but a matter of time. When Olric dies, Ragnor won't have the ability or the skill to keep the Saxons at bay.'' He was silent for a good number of minutes, sitting cross-legged beside her now beneath the thick leather tarp. "I believe you could keep the Saxons from defeating the Danelaw.''

"I? I am naught but a woman.''

"That is true. But there have been other women who were strong, warrior women who led men into battle and overcame the enemy.''

"Aye," she said quietly. "I've been told stories about Boadicea, the queen of the Iceni. She fought bravely against the Romans, but she lost eventually, Kerek. She died, and thousands of warriors with her.''

"Men followed her into battle. It is said her warriors killed seventy thousand Romans before they themselves were defeated and put to the sword.''

"You believe me another Boadicea?''

She could feel his eyes on her in the darkness. He said, "You are still very young. It is too soon to tell. But I saw the cold disdain in your eyes for Ragnor. You spoke fiercely to him even knowing that he would hurt you. You didn't cry or whimper. You showed no fear.''

"That doesn't mean I am a warrior woman. That simply means that I am stupid.''

"You avenged yourself. You didn't seek out a man to use for your revenge."

"It was naught to grind up the malle leaves and the fist root."

"How did you convince him to drink it?"

She laughed. "He believed I would still let him bed me, though I had told him earlier he was goat offal and a river snake. He simply didn't believe that a woman could ever mean what she said. Thus, when I smiled at him and offered him a ginger drink, he leered at me and drank it down. He didn't become ill until late the following day. He didn't realize what I had done."

"He was sicker than a river snake tied into knots. The men laughed behind their hands."

"I am still a woman, Kerek," she said. "I believed him, you see, truly believed that he loved me. No, I am no brave female to save anyone. I was nothing but a fool."

"Had you ever known another man before?"

"Nay, but still—"

Kerek rose to stand in the opening. "I have come to know you in the past days. You will grow and learn. Ah, it begins to rain. The wind has suddenly risen. We will see if the navigator can truly sniff out the stars to keep us in the right direction."

"I would just as soon he ran us aground."

Kerek said quietly over his shoulder, "I would take you again for Ragnor. Know that I do it for the Viking Danelaw, not for that puffed-up little prince."

Chessa eased back down onto the mat, pulling the blanket to her chin. He believed her a warrior woman? Kerek was mad.

They left Rouen to sail up the Seine into the Channel with two warships and two trading vessels. Merrik had said, "We have soapstone bowls of fine quality and reindeer combs and beautiful armlets fashioned by Gyre the Dane. York is a fine trading center. We will gain much silver." He grinned down at his wife. "Besides, I wish to find you a gown of scarlet, a color you have never managed to get right with all your dyes.''

Naturally, the trading vessels also carried household goods—clothing, chests, fishing nets, seeds for planting—for none of them knew what they would find when they reached Scotland and sailed into the trading town of Inverness that sat at the end of the Moray Firth. Cleve had willingly given Kiri over to Laren, who grudgingly accepted being in charge of one of the trading vessels and his daughter.

"I want to stay with you and Merrik," Laren had said, eyes narrowed on his face.

Merrik said easily, "The men would welcome your presence and your skald's tales, but Oleg has begged me to allow you to oversee the second trading vessel. We haven't enough leaders, he told me."

"You lie with the ease of a dying man who swears he will sin no more."

"It is why you adore me."

She laughed, she couldn't help it, swooped down, and swung Kiri up into her arms. "Come, love, you will see your papa tonight."

Later, as the men rowed into the Channel, Merrik said, "It worries me that Kiri is with us. You should have left her at Malverne with the boys, or even here with Rollo."

"Nay," Cleve said. "We are going home, Merrik. I will protect her. Besides, you know that she doesn't like to be apart from me."

"That's not the half of it and you know it. She doesn't eat, she won't play with the other children. She does the chores Laren gives to her but there is no joy in her. She looks like a pinched little ghost. It scares everyone to see this little girl waste away when her papa isn't there."

Cleve said, "You see, I am right to bring her with me, despite any risks. Choosing the correct number of days I'll be gone is beyond difficult. I'd rather worry having her with me than worry having her waste away if I didn't return in the time I promised her."

"I doubt not we will manage to get Chessa back, but there will be problems, Cleve. We will have to take her to Rouen before we can voyage up to Scotland."

"Aye, I know it, and I dislike the delay, but this girl Chessa is a good sort, as women go. She is bright. She is really quite beautiful. Her eyes are greener than the hills behind Oslo after a heavy rain."

Merrik eyed his friend thoughtfully. "You like her?"

"Aye, I like her. She was open and friendly."

"But you didn't trust her."

"I would have to be an ass to give my trust to another woman."

"Cleve, you must forget Sarla."

"It isn't to the point, Merrik. It makes no difference if I believed her a crone or a Christian's angel. She's a princess. She is to wed William. It is good for William that she is open and friendly, or at least pretends to it."

"If Ragnor of York has raped her, no man of high rank will wed her and you know it."

Cleve just looked at his friend, his hand unconsciously going to the beautifully worked knife at his belt.

This was interesting, Merrik thought. He made his way to where Eller sat, tapped him on the shoulder, and took over his oar. Soon he was stripped to his loincloth, his back glistening with sweat.

6

THE SKY WAS darker than the bottom of a witch's cal-
dron. The storm was close now. There was no wind, no
movement of any kind. The huge wadmal square sail was
hanging loosely as the flesh on an old man's neck. It was
hard to breathe, the air was so thick and still. It seemed
that the earth had simply stopped.

The storm was closer now. It had to be because surely
they couldn't continue like this, the warship like a ghost,
eerie and silent in the water, no sound, no squawking of
gulls overhead, no lapping of waves against the overlapping
oak plank sides of the ship. Even the sea serpent's head
that stretched up above the prow looked strangely ghostly,
as unearthly and terrifying as it must to the natives when
they saw a Viking warship coming out of the fog, a demon
come to take them to hell. But now it was different.

They waited, unwilling to move, silent as the still water
around them that would become their tomb.

She stood in the opening of the covered cargo space
looking out at the men who sat on their sea chests, bent
motionless over their oars. Even they had stopped rowing,
becoming as still as everything around them. They were
silently praying to Thor, to Odin.

Ragnor's ship lay off the coast of East Anglia. Kerek
had told her that Ragnor was drunk. He was sprawled be-

side the rudder, too frightened to do anything but drink the last of the warm mead. Kerek told her in a low voice that the captain, Torric, wondered if they would see morning. Torric had seen the beginning of a storm like this only one other time in his life, off the western coast of Norway, but that time the air wasn't warm and dead the way it was now. It had been frigid, so cold that the men accepted death when the storm blew in on them because if they were hurled into the sea, they would be frozen in an instant.

Torric was then a lad of ten years old when he and one other warrior had managed to ride the storm out, landing on the rugged rocky shores near Bergen.

Now Torric walked to where Kerek and Chessa stood. "It will be here very soon now," he said, his voice a whisper.

She said nothing. What was there to say?

Then Kerek was pointing, nearly panting in his excitement. "Look, yon, 'tis an island. See how the blackness has parted over there? It is an island, I'm sure of it. Surely Torric, if the men row with all their might we can reach it. There must be a safe harbor there."

"Aye," Torric said, hope in his voice. "Aye, I see it. The gods have shown it to you. It wasn't there before, I would swear to it."

She waited silently, listening to Torric yell at the men, urging them to row with all their might, telling them they would survive if they made it to that island.

"It's the storm that makes for the strange lighting," Kerek said. "I think it's raining hard over the island. The splurges of lightning make it visible. Go inside now, Princess."

"Oh, no, Kerek, I will watch. Isn't there anything I can do to help?"

"You can stay alive," he said, and left her.

It seemed but moments later that a sheet of rain cascaded down upon them. She watched one man plucked up by a mountainous wave and tossed into the sea. No one could do anything. Torric yelled louder for them to row, row, harder and harder still.

Hawkfell Island

"My lord, all the boats are pulled ashore, lashed down, and covered. We're ready for the storm."

Rorik Haraldsson, Lord of Hawkfell Island, nodded, raising his face as rain swept in. He sucked in his breath at the force of it. It had been years since he'd felt anything this violent. Everything had been done that could be done. Now they would simply wait.

He turned back into the longhouse. The long rectangular structure was already filled with a faint blue tint from the smoke held inside the huge closed house. He walked to his wife, Mirana, who was sewing calmly, probably a blue shirt for him, since she'd long ago declared that it made him look even more magnificent than he actually was.

He rather liked the way she always complimented him and smacked him at the same time. There wasn't a sweetly compliant bone in her entire body and he loved her dearly. He knew she would kill anyone who tried to harm him, kill anyone who threatened their island, their people, their children. He trusted her implicitly, something he didn't believe many men could say about their wives or their friends. She looked up as he approached, but she didn't smile. Her face was pale, and he noticed with a frown that her fingers were none too steady with her needle.

He cocked an eyebrow at her. "Is it blue, wife?"

"What? The air? Of course it's blue. The smoke can't escape, you know that, what with the doors closed against the storm and—oh, your shirt. Of course it's blue. It's just the color of your eyes. I must make you many of them before your eyes fade to some dull color and I forget what they were once like. By all the gods, Rorik, it sounds as if Thor has unleashed all his anger on us."

"Aye, but what do you expect? I told you not to do those

woman things to my body. The gods don't like mere women to seek to dominate their menfolk, they know that men are weak of flesh and always eager to take whatever is offered to them." He grinned shamelessly at her.

She was out of her chair, the beautiful blue shirt tossed on the chair arm, and at him. She was hitting his chest with her fists, laughing, biting his shoulder.

"Mama, don't hurt Papa. Surely what he did wasn't that bad, was it?"

Mirana turned to look down at her little girl, Aglida, so beautifully golden that it closed her throat to look at the child. "Your papa," she said, sweeping the little girl into her arms, "is a great jester. He thinks himself amusing when he is only outrageous. He believes he can crush me down with his humor, when in fact he falls short and—"

"Papa is perfect," Aglida said, reaching for Rorik.

"She will get over this," Mirana said and handed their daughter to Rorik.

"Nay, she will be just like her mother and worship me forever."

She gave him a shove, then kissed him. "I will surely make you pay for your humor, my lord."

"Aye, you will. You always do. It pleases me. Now I see that you tossed my shirt aside like a bone you chewed on. I only have one chest filled with blue shirts. I cannot afford to have you toss one aside."

"Aye, it's just like a bone Mama's chewed on," Aglida said. "I'll sew you another shirt, Papa. It will be as beautiful as Mama's, mayhap better."

"Mama's what, sweeting?"

"Rorik, be quiet. Come, Aglida, 'tis time you slept."

All had watched the play between the master and mistress. All heard the laughter, saw the smiles. All knew they were doing it apurpose, to ease everyone. It worked. A woman giggled when her husband patted her buttocks. A child yelled at another to throw her the leather ball. Conversation became louder. The children began playing again. Their parents began speaking of sleep.

Rain crashed against the sod and wood-shingled roof, making the big wooden beams creak and moan, sounding, Old Firren said, like a battle between the gods, and it would be men who would lose.

It went on and on, lessening for long periods of time, then beginning again. It was near midnight, all the Hawkfell people still awake, the children at last asleep, waiting and listening.

The door burst open and Hafter ran in. "A ship," he shouted. "There's a ship in the harbor and it's breaking up against the shore."

The men were out of the longhouse in moments, running through the wide palisade doors and down the narrow path that led to the beach.

Rorik ran out onto the dock, the rain slashing against his face, so much of it, he felt he would drown if he opened his mouth. Great slashes of lightning rent the sky. The warship was heaving to its side, the great sea serpent's head dipping beneath the huge waves.

He heard men shouting, saw them desperately trying to row the ship to shore, but it sent them spinning. Then it seemed as if the sea, in a furious spurt, shoved the ship onto the shore so hard that several men were flung overboard. Rorik shouted to his men. They were at the ship in moments, pulling the men from the water, watching others gathering their chests before they realized that they were ashore and would remain there. For a moment, several of the men simply stood on the swaying ship, just staring at Rorik and his people, disbelieving that they had survived. Very soon they would fear they'd only survived the storm to be killed here. He strode forward, shouting above the noise of the rain and thunder, "I am Rorik and this is Hawkfell Island. We won't harm you. Come, you're safe now."

Still the men hung back. They could be easily butchered. They had knives at their belts, swords, helmets, and shields in their sea chests.

"Come," Rorik said again, knowing well their thoughts,

knowing he would distrust any unknown man who didn't try to kill him on a strange island in the middle of a storm.

The men were looking at each other and he knew they realized they were helpless. Suddenly, a woman jumped from the ship onto the beach. A *woman*! Rorik dashed the rain from his face only to hear her call out, "Lord Rorik, it is you, isn't it? Thank you for your welcome. We believed ourselves lost but the gods brought us to you."

Then another man jumped after her, shouting, "Don't listen to her, she lies, she's my prisoner. I am marrying her, don't listen to her."

This was surely strange, Rorik thought, wondering what the gods had vomited onto his island's shore. He reached the woman, realized she was very young, and said, "I have no idea what is happening here, but don't be afraid."

"Don't touch her!"

Rorik looked at the man, who would have looked ready to kill him if he hadn't been so pathetic and frightened. "Who are you?"

The man drew himself up as if suddenly remembering that he wasn't a drowned rat. "I am Ragnor of York, son of Olric." He even tried for a swagger. "I will take over now."

Rorik could have taken the man's neck between his hands and choked the life out of him in moments. "You are in no condition to make demands or give orders. Get your people together and we will go to the longhouse."

"Aye, my lord," another man said to Ragnor. "We are safe now and we owe this man our thanks."

"I'll cut out your damned tongue, Kerek," Ragnor said. "As for you," he yelled after Chessa, who'd walked to stand beside this Rorik, "you will do nothing that angers me, do you understand? You will tell this man no lies. You will remain silent and meek."

Chessa said nothing at all. She pulled sodden strands of hair from her face and looked up at the rain-soaked man who towered above her. She stood close enough so that he blocked some of the rain from her face. "The captain, Torric, is injured. I believe his leg is broken from the mast falling on him. He is a good man. Please help him.''

Rorik turned and said, ''Hafter, take two men and get Captain Torric. Mirana will see to him. Now, you appear to know me. What is your name?''

''I am Chessa, and you're Lord Rorik of Hawkfell Island?''

''Aye.''

She gave him a brilliant wet smile. ''Do you remember a young girl named Eze, daughter of Hormuze, the greatest sorcerer of all time?''

Rorik stared down at her, looking closely at her, studying her. The last time he'd seen Eze she'd been only ten years old, a serious child who'd shown no fear of him or of his men. He'd used her to free his wife, Mirana, from Hormuze. Now she was grown and by some miracle she'd been thrown onto Hawkfell Island. He said slowly, ''By all the gods, this storm will go down in memory.''

''You are a beautiful man, my lord, but still you are not as beautiful as my papa.''

Rorik threw back his head and laughed deeply and nearly choked on the water that swept into his mouth. ''And just how is your beautiful papa?'' Hormuze had disguised himself as an old graybeard, looking every bit as old as the king of Ireland. He'd killed Sitric and taken his place. He'd wanted Mirana simply because she'd looked so much like his long-dead wife, Naphta. But he'd had to settle for Sira, Rorik's cousin. He'd made his own prophecy come true— that Hormuze the magician had wrought magic to make the old king young again. It was now a favorite tale in many countries. All believed it, for the young Sitric was proof.

''He has four sons and he still loves Sira, more's the pity.''

''Four sons? By Thor's toes, he doesn't rest, does he?''

''She's pregnant again.''

''Ah, so she's still a witch?''

''She's more than a witch, she's—''

But Ragnor refused to go quietly. ''Don't listen to her,

damn you! She's lying. She's naught but my wife, naught but a slut, naught—''

"What is going on here?" Rorik said, looking down at the lovely woman before him.

"I will tell you," Ragnor said, shoving Chessa behind him. "And then you will obey my orders. I am Ragnor of York and you are nothing but the peasant who clings to this pile of rocks and mud."

Rorik said to the man Kerek, "Who is this fool to say that my island is a pile of rocks?"

"His mind is disordered," Kerek said. "Come," he said to Ragnor, "I will assist you to Lord Rorik's longhouse. Your wits are disordered from the storm and the mead."

"I won't leave her alone with him. He just might try to steal her, he might try to rape her. He's a Viking and a warrior. He's up to no good, he's—"

Rorik shoved his fist into Ragnor's jaw. The man collapsed where he stood. He said to Kerek, "I wonder why no one's murdered him yet. Take him to the longhouse. Follow my line of men up the path. When he awakens, mayhap he'll come to understand the way of things."

Chessa said, shaking her head, "I doubt he's capable."

Mirana rose and wiped her hands on a linen cloth. "He will be all right. Utta and I straightened Torric's leg and bound it between two thin slabs of timber. Entti gave him very strong mead to drink. Old Alna cackled over him, said he was a lovely lad, and that made him smile even though she drooled on him a bit. He will sleep for many hours now."

"Thank you," Chessa said. "Where is this Old Alna?"

"Over there by the fire pit, picking her two remaining teeth," Mirana said. "Just look at you, Eze, all grown up, and so beautiful. I hadn't thought to ever see you again, truth be told. Aye, and you've grown up very well."

"I would say she's more than beautiful."

Chessa laughed up at Lord Rorik, who'd come to stand beside his wife. "You say that, my lord, because I look so

very much like her. My papa was right about that. I am
sorry he took you, Mirana, and all because you looked like
my mother. I vow I would have rather had you for a stepmother than that miserable Sira. Come, Lord Rorik, tell the
truth. It is because I look like Mirana that you think me
comely.''

"You think me so lacking in clear sight? You're very
little like Mirana. Her hair is a rather dull black, not all
shiny like yours, and her eyes are the color of the mainland salt marsh grass, all sort of a wet green, while yours,
Eze—''

"Why do you call her that name?" It was Ragnor and
he wasn't drunk now. He was stroking his hand over his
jaw as he strode up to Rorik as if he were lord, his chin
thrust out, looking like naught but a sullen boy in a man's
body. "It's an ugly name. It sounds foreign. Why did you
call her that name?"

Chessa said quickly, "It's a nickname from my child-
hood. You see, Ragnor, Lord Rorik met me when I was
very young. He will soon come to call me Chessa, a name
very popular amongst the Irish Dalriada.''

"Chessa," Rorik said. "It's a lovely name. Lovelier than
that ugly name of my wife's—Mirana. It sounds like some
sort of fish in the North Sea. Perhaps she isn't too aged for
me to give her another name.''

Mirana poked her elbow in her husband's ribs. "He
plays dangerous games, does my lord,'' she said. "But so
long as he wears the blue shirts I sew for him that perfectly
match the blue of his eyes and he doesn't gain flesh, I will
not fling him into the sea, at least I won't fling him in
during this storm. He isn't a strong swimmer and I would
doubtless have to leap in after him to save him.''

"I don't understand what any of you are talking about.
This woman is insulting this man and he insults her back
and you're all laughing and it's stupid. Listen to me,
Chessa, none of this matters, not that they knew you when
you had this foolish Eze name, nothing. You're going to
marry me and you won't tell this man any of your lies.''

"I thought you said she was your wife and a slut and—"

"Hold your tongue," Ragnor said, and immediately shut his mouth when he felt a large calloused hand close over his shoulder.

"What did you say, little worm?" Hafter said close to Ragnor's ear, and then he squeezed, feeling the bones crunching together.

Ragnor yelped.

"He will learn manners quickly with such instruction," Rorik said. "Release him, Hafter. You would think that he would remember my fist in his jaw for at least an hour. He is too young to have such flaws in his memory. It will lead to his death if he isn't careful."

"His brain was drowned in the storm," Hafter said, squeezed one last time, and shoved Ragnor forward. "If he ever had one of any size at all." Ragnor managed to keep his balance, just barely.

"You mangy little bastard," Hafter said after him. "No wonder the Danelaw will soon fall to the Saxons, what with the likes of you holding the reins of power. Is it true you're the son of Olric?"

"Aye, and soon that old man will be well dead. Then I will return and kill all of you."

Kerek said, "Now, my lord, you lose your temper for naught. These good people have saved us. Our warship is destroyed. We are cast upon their kindness. I beg you to moderate your speech, to accept their generous bounty with smiles and gratitude."

Ragnor cursed and strode away. Chessa heard Old Alna cackle.

"My lord."

"Gunleik, how many did we save?"

"Seventeen, Rorik. This man Kerek told me that nine men have been lost. Still, it's not bad, given the fury of this storm."

"I remember you," Chessa said, looking up at the grizzled man, not that old, but the years he'd spent as a warrior were etched deep in his face. "You were already at Clon-

tarf when Lord Rorik brought me there to exchange me for
Mirana. You helped Lord Rorik.''

"Aye, I did. Who are you?"

"I'm that little girl, Eze. All of you saved my papa."

Gunleik stared at his friend and lord. "This is passing
strange, Rorik."

"Aye, but you'll get used to it. Her name is Chessa now.
Ah, Kerek, go see Entti. Mayhap Entti will give Ragnor
something warm and tasty, something that will make his
bowels rampage. Then he can enjoy the storm on many
trips to the privy."

Chessa laughed aloud. "Oh, goodness, that would be
splendid, Hafter. Who is Entti? Does she know all about
the malle root?"

"Entti is my wife," Hafter said, and there was such pride
in his voice that Chessa wanted to meet the woman who'd
inspired such feeling in a man. "Ah, here she is. Sweeting,
have you a potion that would improve the manners of one
of our guests? Chessa here says the malle root is passing
good."

The woman had magnificent dark brown hair that swayed
down her back as she walked, thick lustrous hair with ribbons threaded through it. She was carrying a small babe
who was asleep, his head against her shoulder, his thumb
in his mouth. "You mean our magnificent lord from York?
He is a paltry creature. He yells to all who will listen that
she is his wife. Are you?"

"No. Actually, he kidnapped me. Were it not for the
storm, were it not for Kerek just chancing to see the island,
were it not for you, all of us would be dead now. Or, if we
had survived, then I would have to find a way to escape
him once we reached York. It's all complicated, because
there's William and I don't want to marry him either, but
my father negotiated the wedding treaty."

"William?" Rorik said. "Duke Rollo's son?"

Chessa nodded.

"William is a very nice man," Mirana said, frowning at
Chessa. "It's true that he's still very much in love with his

wife, who died, but he would keep faith with you—"

"Ha," Entti said, handing Hafter the sleeping babe. "That means nothing, Mirana. William's too morose not to keep faith. A girl shouldn't have to wed a man in love with another woman even if she is dead."

"At least he isn't too old," Rorik said.

"He hasn't lost his teeth or grown a fat belly," Mirana said.

Chessa watched Hafter grab his wife's hand and drag her away. Entti leaned down, bit his hand, then, to Chessa's astonishment, she kissed that same hand where she'd bitten it. Mirana was laughing, Rorik was just shaking his head. "You are to marry William," he said, "yet Ragnor kidnapped you. Gunleik is right. All of this is strange. What do you wish me to do, Chessa?"

She looked toward Ragnor, who was seated between two of his men, the three of them speaking in low voices. "He's a snake," she said. "Treacherous. But he's also a bully and a coward. Do you think perhaps I could kill him?"

"You *what*?"

"She said, my lord," Mirana said calmly, "that she would like to kill him."

"Well, that's different. I thought she wanted to mill him like flour for bread. Now, wife, I believe everyone is dry and has found a place to sleep. I see Old Alna is licking her chops over that man Kerek who's speaking to her. He is Ragnor's protector?"

"I suppose so. I wish he wasn't, since he is a good man."

"I thought you liked him. He seems a steady man."

"Aye, he's the man who kidnapped me. He did hit me, but he had to, else I would have brought him low. He was only doing his duty."

"Naturally then you would be overcome with goodwill toward him," Rorik said, and a golden eyebrow shot up. "You will sleep with my wife and I will remain out here with all the men. I want to ensure that this Ragnor doesn't try to kill us in our sleep."

"He's such a worm," Chessa said. "I wonder how I could have ever believed otherwise."

"This," Mirana said, taking Chessa's arm, "is a story I look forward to hearing in all its splendid detail."

"Aye," Rorik said, patting Chessa's shoulder, "And I want to know all about King Sitric, that old man magically made young again by Hormuze. Mirana, take Aglida and the boys and put them to bed."

"Aye, my dear lord," Mirana said, and gave him a smile that was identical to Chessa's. Rorik just stared at the two women, standing there side by side, their black hair thick and curling slightly, no red streaks, just the midnight black of the sky outside in the storm. So many memories overtook him in that moment. Life remained ever interesting, he thought, as he took a woolen blanket and joined Hafter near the fire pit.

7

THE MORNING WAS warm and balmy, the sky a bright blue, scattered with white clouds. The water was utterly calm; the waves washed gently onto the shore. Kerzog, a huge mongrel whose tongue was as long as a longboat plank, Rorik was used to saying, raced after the receding waves, then barked loudly as the sea rushed back in, many times curling around his hind paws. Rorik breathed in deeply. "Were it not for all the broken branches and refuse tossed onto the shore, I wouldn't know that just two days ago a storm tried to tear us apart."

"Aye, you're right," Gunleik said as he leaned down to pick up a piece of oddly shaped driftwood, thinking he could carve something nice for his wife, Erna. A dolphin, perhaps. "What think you of the warship, Rorik?"

Rorik straightened from his examination of the ship. "We can repair the ship well enough for the men to row it to York. The mast sheared off completely. We can do nothing about that. The rudder needs repair, but it can be done."

"We will take one of your warships," Ragnor said, striding across the beach. "I have looked at both of them and the trading vessels too. I believe I will have one of each. You will consider it your tribute to me."

Rorik merely looked at Ragnor of York, who was more

ragged than most of his men. None, evidently, had offered him clothing, else he simply hadn't thought of it.

"Aye," Ragnor said more loudly, for now Kerek and six of his warriors were behind him. "We'll take that warship over there. It looked sound enough for us."

"I see," Rorik said mildly. "And will you return it to us once you've done with it?"

"Naturally not. It is your tribute, as I told you. We will leave after the morning meal. I told your wife and that toothless old hag to prepare extra food for us for our journey. She looked at me so strangely that I think she must be simple. I told Chessa to ready herself. Also there is a young girl who much pleases me. Her name is Utta. I will take her with me. She would be honored to be my concubine."

Kerzog growled, showing vicious yellow teeth.

Rorik grinned and said in that same mild voice, "I doubt her husband would be honored at the notion. My dog doesn't like it either. The dog's name is Kerzog. Her husband's name is Haakon. Perhaps you could speak to him about taking Utta. He's the tall man over yon, helping lift away the broken mast. I will call him for you."

"Nay, my lord, that isn't necessary," Kerek said quickly. "Lord Ragnor merely jests. He wouldn't want a girl who was wed to another man."

"Mayhap not," Ragnor said, eyeing the flexing muscles of Haakon's arms and back. "However, I will have that warship and one of the trading vessels."

Kerek said, "My lord Rorik, this is difficult. I must get my lord Ragnor back to York, the princess with him."

"Nay, it's not at all difficult," Hafter said. "You will keep your mouths shut, else I and my men will kill each of you slowly and with a good deal of pleasure. You will keep quiet until Lord Rorik decides what is to be done with you. Is that clear enough, even for you, lackbrain?"

Ragnor shrieked, "Nay, I am Ragnor of York, you cannot speak to me like that. *Lackbrain?* Not even my mother ever called me that. I'll have you flogged." He paused a moment, eyes frightening in their anger, then he calmed, as suddenly as the sky had after it had nearly killed them in the storm. "Listen, Rorik. You must help me. You must give me what I demand."

Kerzog looked ready to leap. "No, down," Rorik said, pulling on Kerzog's ears. "Kerek, do remove him. He grows wearisome. Not my dog, your master. As Hafter says, I will inform you what you will do and when you will do it."

"My lord, come with me. The island isn't at all a pile of rocks. There is no mud now. It's quite beautiful with a lot of arable land. We can explore, perhaps—"

Ragnor turned and struck Kerek hard in his mouth with the flat of his palm. "You stupid old graybeard, how dare you treat me like a witless child? How dare you take their side? I'll flay the flesh from your coward's back, I'll—"

Rorik heard a furious yell. He saw Chessa scrambling down the path, running straight at Ragnor. She was red in the face, from exertion, and from anger, he realized. She didn't stop, but ran right into Ragnor, shoving him hard in his chest with her fists, pushing him backward, kicking his shins with first one foot then the other, yelling into his face all the while, "You filthy bully! Kerek tries to keep you alive but you are too stupid to realize it. Leave him alone. I will hurt you badly if you strike him again."

Ragnor tried to grab her, but she was like leaping fire, her hands flying out to hit him hard in his belly, in his chest, in his face. He yelled when she brought up her knee and kicked him in the groin. Then she snorted as he doubled over, and coolly shoved him off the dock into the water. She turned and said in a voice as sweetly calm as the beautiful morning, "Are you all right, Kerek?"

He looked at her from his great height and said, "I must take you to York, Princess. Surely you realize it is the Danelaw's only hope. You must marry the worm."

"You're being ridiculous, Kerek. I would kill him or he would kill me. I'm not this Boadicea or any other warrior woman you can come up with. I am nothing but an ordinary woman. Ah, Ragnor cut your cheek with that silver ring of his. Let me bathe it for you.''

But Kerek stepped back. "You are a princess. It isn't right.''

"Let me tell you just how much a real princess I am," she said, but was interrupted by one of Ragnor's men who came forward and said to Rorik, "Ragnor cannot swim, my lord. Should one of us save him?''

Rorik could only stare at the man. Then he threw back his head and laughed deeply, turning only when they heard yells from Ragnor, who was clutching one of the slimy wooden supports beneath the dock.

Hafter said, "It took only two days for our people to show Ragnor's warriors that any life is better than the one they live under that little bastard's thumb.''

"Aye, Arek," Rorik said on a sigh. "Save him, though it pains me to tell you to do so. He is the future king of the Danelaw and thus we have no choice but to keep him alive. Even Ragnor is preferable to rule by the Saxons.''

"The Saxons aren't beginning to seem so bad, Rorik," Hafter said.

Old Alna cackled by way of an answer, for she hadn't heard the question, her hearing now wandering away from her as much as her mind. The lovely captain Torric was drinking one of her potions that she'd sweetened with honey and ground-up almonds. Actually it was one of Utta's potions, for Old Alna's eyes were too blurred to tell most ingredients apart. "You'll be seeing Valkyries soon," she said, and the captain sighed, "but not real ones, just Valkyries I'll conjure up for you with my potion.''

"I see several now. Who is that beautiful Valkyrie giving her breast to the babe?''

"Eh? Ah, that's Entti. Look not too interested, Captain, else her husband Hafter just might gullet you and my sweet lady's nursing of you would all be for naught. Hafter is possessive of Entti.''

"She has a beautiful breast," Torric said, and drank

down some more of Old Alna's potion.

"The other one is just the same."

"Aye, 'tis probably true. Will I see it?"

"She's not showing it to you, Torric. She's feeding Verad, greedy little stoat, and being modest about it. It's just that Mirana has moved to stir the huge pot of stew and thus you can see clearly. You'd best keep your eyes on my face. That will give you incredible dreams of beauty."

Captain Torric groaned at that. Old Alna cackled. "I was once that beautiful, my breasts that full and round."

Captain Torric groaned again and closed his eyes for Mirana had moved again to stand in front of Entti. "What is happening with Lord Ragnor?"

"My master hasn't killed the ass yet, if that's what you're asking me, Captain. Aye, my lad, finish the potion. Before you sleep, you'll believe me beautiful. You'll want to wed with me. You'll want to bed me."

Torric moaned again, stared at the potion as if it had become poison. But he drank it down nonetheless for his leg pained him a great deal. "I'm glad Rorik hasn't killed him. King Olric placed both Kerek and me in charge of his safety, but it is difficult, for Ragnor is difficult, nay, more than difficult. He swaggers and boasts and all want to kick his teeth down his throat. But it's odd, you know. When he decides to play a man with wit and charm, even a man who's brave, a man who feels compassion for others, he can actually do it. Kerek told me that was how he first won the princess's heart. I can't imagine any man fooling her, but he did it. He dished himself up to her as a generous, kind man who adored her. Ah, but then he showed his true colors. They're not pleasant colors, at least never around me and the other men." He sighed, wishing he had more potion. He was feeling sweet and soft in his belly. He no longer felt his broken leg. He didn't even feel his tongue.

"I don't know what to do. Kerek wants the Princess Chessa to marry him. He's convinced that she will make a better man of him."

"It would be a wager I wouldn't take," Old Alna said.

"The gods know she has little enough to start with. A man can't be molded as can a loaf of bread."

"Less than little enough to start with," Torric said, and tried to shift his weight. He felt as if he were floating, his head light, his body thrumming with the pleasure of no pain. He could sell casks of the potion. He could become a wealthy man. "What was in that drink?"

Old Alna cackled.

Mirana said over Old Alna's shoulder, "How do you feel, Captain?"

"Another Valkyrie," he said. "Are your breasts as beautiful as Entti's?" He smiled vaguely, then sighed himself into a stupor.

"He just saw one of Entti's breasts, for little Verad was suckling hard. He's a lovely man, this captain. I remember once when I was even younger than you, Mirana, when I became lost and this fierce man found me and—"

Mirana smiled as Old Alna continued to tell her of a long-ago adventure with a man she'd never seen before but who was, she claimed, the best lover she'd ever had.

Soon Old Alna was sleeping too, huddled next to the captain. Mirana covered both of them, wondering as she did so if Alna had also drunk of the potion.

Kerzog bounded up to her just as she was turning back to the fire pit. "No, don't do it, you brute," she yelled at him, but it did no good. He was happy to see her, full of energy after being penned up during the long storm. His run on the beach hadn't been enough for him. He knocked her down and held her there, licking her face. She tried to cover herself with her hands, but Kerzog was used to that ploy and was butting his head beneath her hands, licking her all the harder. "Rorik," she yelled. "Help me."

Rorik was laughing, as was Chessa behind him. "Good dog," Chessa said, and leaned down to hug Kerzog.

"You'll be sorry you did that," Rorik said, but it was too late. Kerzog, a lover of women, released Mirana, eyed Chessa, who looked remarkably like his mistress, even smelled a bit like his mistress, and leapt against her, his two front paws on her shoulders. She stumbled but managed to keep upright. She was laughing, hugging the huge dog, then pulling on his ears.

"She's grown up well," Mirana said to her husband as he pulled her to her feet. He dipped the corner of her tunic in the barrel of water and wiped her face.

"Aye. But what will we do with her? Ragnor wants her. William is supposed to marry her. By all the gods, I dislike problems of this sort. Do you suppose we could send her back to Dublin? Surely this must be Sitric's decision."

Chessa said, her voice sharp as the knife in Rorik's belt, "I don't want to go back. My father would force me to go to Rouen, to William. I don't want this William. I don't know him. He could be as offensive as Ragnor. I could think of him like a brother. Would you want to marry Ragnor, Mirana? Would you want to marry a man you felt was your brother, Mirana?"

"Or you could come to love him as a wife should a husband," Rorik said. He cuffed Kerzog, then picked up the dog's favorite stick and threw it out the open doors of the longhouse.

"I repeat, Rorik, I don't want to go back. Would you want to go back to Dublin and live with my stepmother, Sira?"

Rorik blinked, then laughed. "By the gods, that isn't a fate I should seek out."

"That wretched bitch," Mirana said. "She would have killed me if she could. She wanted Rorik, you see. She was cruel to you, Chessa?"

"When I got to be old enough I was cruel back. It's just that my father is blind to her wickedness. He enjoys her body, you see. She is with child again. She has already given him four boys. *Four*. I like my brothers. Indeed, the eldest, Brodan, is a dear boy, albeit very thoughtful and mayhap too solemn. He is a Christian and takes his studies very seriously. Sira forbids me to play with them. I don't think I can go back now. I would perhaps stick my knife through her wicked heart."

"Oh, dear," Mirana said. She turned to look up at her husband. "What are we going to do?"

"I had thought," Rorik said, "that Sitric was going to discipline Sira, teach her submissiveness to him. That was what he claimed he would do when he took her that night."

"She doesn't behave horribly in front of my father, at least not so horribly that even he is taken aback. She's wicked, not stupid. Never stupid. Besides, he is quite used to the carping between us. He pays it little attention, just blames her foul moods on her pregnancies."

Kerek came into the longhouse then, carrying a shivering Ragnor in his arms as if he were a small child. Ragnor's face was blue, his teeth were chattering.

"I'd rather hoped he would drown," Rorik said. "I suppose now that one of your men must give him some dry clothes."

"I rather hoped so too," Mirana said. "He was eyeing Utta as a goat would a succulent boot."

"Does Sira still have her beautiful hair?" Rorik said.

"Oh, aye. My father let her rid herself of the dye on the day she presented him with his first son. I attacked her once and tried to pull out that hair of hers. Cleve saw me do it. I think he was stricken like every other man by her beautiful hair." She sighed. "Papa told me I didn't understand about men and women. I think Sira pleases him immensely in the marriage bed."

"Cleve," Rorik said, staring at her blankly, "by all the gods, what is this? You know Cleve?"

She cocked her head to one side, a movement identical to Mirana's when she had questions about to bubble over. "Certainly. It was he who negotiated the wedding contract for Duke Rollo, curse him to the Christian's devil. What's the matter? Isn't that his name? He said he was Cleve of Malverne. Do you know him as well?"

"Oh, aye, that's his name," Mirana said. "We have known Cleve for five years, ever since Rorik's brother, Merrik, brought him out of Kiev."

"What was Cleve doing in Kiev?"

"He was a slave."

"A slave! But surely that's not possible. Why, Cleve is a beautiful man, utterly splendid, and he is very smart and he speaks well, perhaps too well because he's a diplomat, and he has to say nice smooth things so he doesn't offend anyone, but—" She stopped speaking, aware that Rorik and Mirana were staring at her. She gulped, then said more slowly, "Perhaps I am wrong about him. Isn't he a good man? A very handsome man who isn't vain about his comely face and magnificent body? Isn't he a warrior of some skill? He threw a knife and struck this assassin right in his throat. I didn't actually see him do it since I threw my knife as well and struck him in the back, but I did see his knife sticking out of the man's neck." She stopped talking again, aware that Rorik and Mirana were still staring at her, their mouths open. Kerzog barked, sat on his haunches, and let his tongue loll free of his mouth.

"Very well," Chessa said. "I can accept whatever you tell me. Was I just as wrong about him as I was about Ragnor of York? You will tell me the truth about Cleve."

Rorik cleared his throat. "Everything you've said is true. Cleve is a very fine young man. He has known cruelty, too much cruelty, and he is smart and speaks well, and Merrik has taught him warrior skills during the past five years, but—" Rorik stopped talking, looking down at his wife, who simply smiled and shook her head.

"I must see to our midday meal. Shall we feed Lord Ragnor, do you think, Chessa?"

"He has dry clothing. Surely that is enough."

Two days later the men had nearly finished repairing Ragnor's warship. "It's a fine ship," Hafter said to Rorik as they watched the men paint the sides with thick black pine tar. "Sixty feet long, not as long as the *Raven's Wing* of yours, but still, adequate. The keel needed some work, but it's sufficient to get them to York. Six oars were lost, but it doesn't matter. The others are sturdy enough, as are the oar holes."

"Has Ragnor bothered you?"

"Aye, but every time he comes near me, I simply call out to Haakon or to Aslak. I think Lord Ragnor is afraid Haakon will pound him into the surf."

"Both of them would. Then they'd kick him and stick a knife in his soft belly."

Aslak yelled, "By the gods, Rorik, here comes a fleet of ships. Who can it be? Outlaws? Viking raiders?" Rorik wasted no time. He yelled out to his men to arm themselves. In but a moment the men had dashed up the path to the longhouse to get their swords, shields, arrows, and axes. They were ready for battle within minutes.

"At least we have seventeen more men to fight with us," Rorik said, looking at Ragnor's men, standing close with his own men.

"No need," said Hafter. "Look, Aslak is waving to the lead warship. Its stem is the Malverne dragon. It's Lord Merrik come to visit us."

"I wonder," Rorik said slowly, "if Cleve is with him. By the gods, does he have a surprise awaiting him if he is with him."

Cleve saw her immediately. He stood in the entrance of the palisade gates and just stared at her. He shook his head. He'd heard the incredible tale the men had told him as they'd climbed the path to the palisade atop Hawkfell Island. But still he hadn't believed it. There was no escape to plan, no rescue to save an innocent young girl from the miserable likes of Ragnor of York. He supposed he was both relieved and disappointed. He supposed he'd wanted to prove himself. He frowned. Prove himself to whom? Certainly not to her. Damnation. He didn't believe this. She was here and she was staring at him as hard as he was staring at her.

She was here and she was safe. Now she was shaking her head, as if she couldn't believe he was really there. He saw her shake her head once, then again, then look at him once more. He saw the recognition in her eyes. Then she was running toward him, her lustrous black hair long down her back, flying out behind her intertwined with scarlet ribbons, glistening beneath the bright morning sunlight. She was calling out his name and laughing. Her arms were stretched toward him. He didn't move, couldn't seem to bring himself to move out of her way. He felt the shock of her when she threw herself against him, hugging him tightly. She clasped her arms around her neck and rose on her tiptoes. "Ah, Master Cleve, you've come. This isn't what I expected. The gods aren't usually so kind to mortals. You're here. Ah, but I've missed you and thought of you endlessly, wondering what you were doing, if you were thinking of me and what you were thinking. I've wanted to see you so very much." She kissed his chin, his cheek, because he quickly turned his face aside so she wouldn't kiss his mouth, so she wouldn't kiss the scar by accident. He didn't think he could bear to see the revulsion on her happy face.

In the next moment, Chessa realized his arms were at his sides. He was standing there like a pillar, not saying a word, not doing anything. Except suffering her. Her arms fell away. She quickly stepped back from him. Her eyes dropped to her sandals. She felt humiliated. And everyone had seen what she'd done. Everyone had seen him reject her. Everyone. The shame of it ate to her soul. Just seeing him like that, so very unexpected, had sent her right at him, joy suffusing her. She was a fool. She didn't know men, had no idea what they were like, what was in their minds. Aye, she'd been wrong again.

She knew she had to do something. She couldn't just stand here in front of him like a child scuffing her toes into the dirt. She raised her face. He was pale.

"I'm sorry," she said, and her chin went up. "You surprised me. I wasn't expecting you. You were a friendly face, nothing more, just someone here for me, someone I knew. No, not that, it's just that I've thought of you so very much, no, I don't mean that exactly, and—"

"I know," he said. "Are you all right, Chessa?"

"Aye, I'm fine. I suppose the men told you everything that has happened?"

Cleve nodded. "Not all of it, but enough for now. You can tell me the rest before we leave."

"What do you mean, leave?"

"To return to Rouen for your wedding to William. We were at Rouen awaiting your arrival for the wedding when we heard that you'd been kidnapped. It seemed the likely man to have done it was Ragnor of York. Thus we were coming after you, to rescue you."

Chessa nodded, feeling blessedly numb.

Cleve said, his voice deliberate, "Then we were returning you to William."

She nodded again, feeling nothing at all, thank the gods. "But why did you stop here at Hawkfell Island?"

"Lord Merrik of Malverne and Lord Rorik are brothers. We had planned to stop here. That the storm brought you here as well is something I hadn't even considered." He took a step toward her, his voice low. "Chessa, try to understand. I have no choice in this, in little of anything really. I only have choice in my own life and even now my own future hangs in the balance."

She said nothing, but she wondered what he meant. He had no choice in anything? Did that mean that he would want her if she weren't a princess, if she weren't promised to marry William? She had no idea what was in his mind. He was very smooth. Very closed. "I see," she said, turned, and walked away.

Rorik, who was standing next to his brother, Merrik, said, "She spoke of Cleve with such enthusiasm before you arrived that I wondered if there was something between them. There is, but it's all on her side."

Merrik said, looking at Cleve, who was standing in the same spot, watching Chessa disappear into the longhouse, "You know that Sarla and her treachery made him very suspicious of any woman. By Thor's hammer, Rorik, Sarla even tried to murder him. She tried to steal away Kiri and hold her for ransom. How would you feel about women were you Cleve?"

"I don't know," Rorik said. "As for Cleve I believe he could love her but since he negotiated the marriage contract for Duke Rollo, his honor would make him withdraw from her. It's odd. She doesn't seem to see the scar on his face. She called him beautiful, both of face and body. She went on about him endlessly."

"If Sarla ever saw that hideous scar she didn't say anything either," Merrik said.

"Oh, she saw it. It repelled her. She told Ileria that if his body weren't so well-formed, if he didn't give her such pleasure, she wouldn't let him close to her. She said she could forgive his face since he worshipped her so completely, since he made her forget Erik. When Ileria told me that, I wanted to kill Sarla. But Chessa is honest in her feelings, in what she said, in what she believes."

Merrik cursed quietly.

"You're right," his brother said. "Nothing is easy in life."

"It's all a damnable mess," Merrik said.

8

RAGNOR OF YORK eyed Cleve with growing rage. The man was hideous with that white slashing scar from the edge of his eyebrow to nearly his chin, a curved scar that looked like a half moon. He hadn't heard about that scar. It made him look mean, even vicious. It made him look dangerous. He was built strong and tall as a Viking, his chin was smooth, his hair golden and long, clubbed back in a queue. He was calm and he spoke in a smooth, reasoned way. His eyes were fascinating, it was that simple. They held him, even though he didn't want them to. One golden eye and one blue eye. Surely the gods had cursed him, surely he was unclean. Ragnor hated him. He wondered if women admired him even more with those strange eyes. Ragnor hated him even more from that moment to the next. He wanted to kill this Cleve, who shouldn't have come, who shouldn't have been friends with this peasant, Rorik, who himself crowed like a cock on this stupid pile of rocks he called his island.

Cleve was also the emissary for Duke Rollo, the bastard who wanted Chessa for his son, William. It was Kerek who had told him this, all pleased with himself, and Ragnor had let him talk even though he already knew all of it, but it was Kerek's duty to ask all the questions of these lowly creatures and then give an accurate report to him, Ragnor of York, his master. It mattered not what Ragnor already knew.

Aye, surely this Cleve was lowly. What was a slave even if he did become an emissary? By Odin-All-Father's beard, he remained a lowly man with a smooth tongue. Ragnor didn't even know if this Cleve's tongue was that smooth, for he'd said little, merely sat quietly on the bench against the wall of the longhouse, watching and listening. Ragnor hated him for his control, so effortlessly exerted.

Ragnor said finally to Kerek, "We won't allow him to take her anywhere." He still stared at Cleve, unable to look away from him. Those damned eyes of his. "The man's a slave, naught more than a miserable slave."

"He's a free man," Kerek said. "Lord Merrik freed him some five years ago. He's Duke Rollo's emissary. I have already told you this."

"Aye, but you didn't draw the right judgment. None of that matters. He's offal even though he does perhaps speak well. He could die easily. He should have in Dublin if— but that isn't important now. He's here and he's alive. I will have Chessa."

"Aye, you must have the princess, but we must move very carefully, I don't want Cleve slitting your throat."

Ragnor looked up at Kerek in some surprise. "You sound passionate. Do you want her for yourself? Aye, you lust after her, don't you, Kerek? She's a proud little bitch, surely you've seen that. She'd never part her legs for you."

"She won't for you either, my lord."

Ragnor hissed, rising from the table, so angry he wanted to kill anyone, and Kerek was the closest.

"Sit down," Kerek said, his voice suddenly so cold that Ragnor would have shivered if he'd been a small boy. He started to tell Kerek that he would hit him again, when Kerek said easily, "I know how we will keep the princess."

"You do?"

"Aye, sit down again and listen to me. *My lord.*"

Ragnor sat down and tossed down a cup of mead. "I want that girl, Utta. She made the mead. She's excellent."

"You can't have her. Now listen to me. *My lord.*"

"I don't like you now, Kerek. I don't like what you've become from a moment ago to now. Now you're mocking me and I won't stomach it. I allowed it before because you recognized that you were nothing compared to me. You knew that I was your master and you knew to obey me. You knew that you were to protect me with your life. But now, you seem to be insolent. Stop it or I will kill you."

"If you kill me, you bloody fool, the princess will shove a knife into your meager heart. Is your mind so small you don't remember how all you did was strike my face and she attacked you and knocked you off the dock?"

"She took me off guard. Also, I didn't want to hurt her. It doesn't look well for a strong man to harm a small girl. I allowed it, even allowed her to kick me and shove me, but she will pay for that. I will kick her in the ribs again. I liked having her on the floor in front of me. I liked having her pant. That was nice."

Kerek wondered how he'd let Ragnor get him off his course so easily. "Listen to me. *My lord.* William of Normandy will only marry a virgin."

"Aye, no man of power would marry a girl other men had taken. So what?"

Kerek wanted to tell him that he was the stupidest cretin he'd ever known, but he merely smiled, thinking about Chessa, knowing she would come to deal well with Ragnor and with Olric, that she would some day save the Danelaw. He knew it. She wasn't just an ordinary woman as she claimed. She was young, untried, but he knew what was in her, aye, he knew. He would make this marriage happen. Then he would advise her, teach her, let her discover herself the strength within her. And Turella would be there to teach her as well. Both of them would be there for her, always. He said patiently to Ragnor, "If you had raped the princess then William would have to relinquish her to you, for he couldn't trust any issue from her body if perhaps she were pregnant."

Ragnor stared at Kerek. "By Thor's hammer, you're stupid, Kerek. I wanted to take her but you stopped me. I could have planted my seed in her belly, but you stopped me.''

Kerek pictured his hands around Ragnor's neck. He could practically feel the soft flesh sinking into the bones. He forced himself to control. ''It doesn't matter that you didn't rape her. You need simply say that you did.''

''But she will deny it. I could beat her, then perhaps she would stay silent, perhaps even nod her head when I said it. But I would have to beat her senseless to gain that result.''

''You can't beat her senseless, else Lord Rorik or Cleve would surely kill you despite your high position. That is the only thing that stills their hands against you. You must simply say that you forced her, that she is no longer a virgin, that indeed you forced her several times.''

''She will deny it and try to kill me for saying it.''

Kerek shrugged. ''No woman wants to admit to being raped. Even the princess wouldn't want to admit to it.'' Ah, but the princess wasn't like other women. She had the soul and spirit of a warrior. She would grow stronger under his tutelage, his and Turella's. He said thoughtfully, ''If she does deny it, why, who ever believes a woman? However, to be certain, I will say it is true also.'' He said as an afterthought, ''I won't let her kill you.''

''You're wrong about all of it, Kerek. She will scream and yell and probably attack me. She will do the same to you. She will never be submissive. She will never willingly obey me. I don't want her. Let my father do away with my mother, she does naught save pull weeds in that garden of hers, then he can marry Chessa. I want that girl Utta. The mead is delicious, sweet and strong, and it makes me want her more each time I look at her. I think she wants me too and that's why she makes the mead so well. It is for me that she brews it, not for Haakon, her brute of a husband.''

And Kerek thought, *Let the gods give me grit.*

She was avoiding him. Strangely, it bothered him. He didn't like it. She seemed pale to him, withdrawn, which was difficult, for Hawkfell Island was crammed with people. The longhouse bulged at mealtimes. At least a good dozen men slept in the outer room of the bathing hut, and on the nights it was warm enough, most slept outside, close together for warmth, all the blankets on the island in use. Some men even slept in the byre.

What was she thinking?

He remembered her joy when she saw him, when she realized he wasn't a ghost or some sort of chimera, but he was himself, Cleve of Malverne, and he was here on Hawkfell Island. She'd run to him, her arms open and she'd kissed him and spoken so freely to him. He'd wanted to feel her mouth on his, but he'd known he couldn't and had turned his face away.

He turned slightly, careful not to put his weight on Kiri, who was sleeping as deeply as only a child could sleep. Cleve wondered if she was dreaming, and if so, what her five years could conjure up for a night tale. She sighed and he hugged her, bending his head slightly to kiss the top of her golden head.

He saw Chessa's face clearly the moment she realized this small girl was his daughter. She'd looked from one to the other, for Cleve was holding his daughter and she was staring candidly back at Chessa. Chessa said at last, smiling at Kiri, "You look just like your father. You will be more beautiful than any woman on the earth."

"Really?" Kiri had said. "I'm as beautiful as my papa?"

"Aye, you are, I swear it."

Kiri said then, "You aren't nearly as beautiful as my papa, but you are honest and your eyes see well."

Cleve laughed, tossed his daughter into the air, then caught her in his arms again. She was shrieking, and he tossed her up again. "You're shameless, Kiri. The princess will believe you conceited and thus your beauty will be lessened, just as a cupped hand over a lit candle dims the light." But he kissed her eyebrows and hugged her hard against him until she squeaked.

"But she said I looked just like you, Papa."

"Aye, Cleve," Rorik said. "Don't argue with your babe."

Kiri held out her arms to Rorik, who took her, hugged her, then kissed her. He breathed in the scent of her flesh. "You smell just like Aglida. Now, Chessa, do you think my little daughter is also beautiful? Will she be the second most beautiful woman on earth when she grows up?"

Ragnor walked up to them, trying to swagger, but he only managed to look a bit drunk, his walk crooked. "What is all this stupidity? This is a little girl child. She is of no account at all. Why do you speak of her becoming beautiful someday? Someday, we will be old or dead and her future beauty doesn't matter. Come along, Chessa, I would speak to you. You are to be my wife and you must begin to be submissive to me now. Come."

Chessa sighed as she turned to Ragnor. "Go away," she said only.

He looked shocked. "You would tell me to leave you? You don't wish to hear my words in private? You want all to hear what must be said?"

"Go away, Ragnor. I don't care what you say. You have been drinking Utta's mead, haven't you?"

"Nay, not yet. Kerek said my head must be clear and thus it would follow that I would reason well and my tongue would speak fluently. Come along or all will know what I must say."

Kerek nodded slightly to Ragnor. He was surprised. The man had managed to gain everyone's attention. All were closing about them now. All were listening.

"It matters not," Chessa said. "Nothing about you matters. Your warship is ready. Leave Hawkfell Island. No one wants you here. I do wonder how many of your men will return with you."

"That is another matter entirely and doesn't concern you. You're naught but a woman and know nothing of importance." Ragnor stopped, hearing Kerek gently clear his throat. He cleared his own then and waited a moment before he said again, "You must come with me. This is important and it is private. Very private."

"Out with it, Ragnor," Rorik said. "Chessa doesn't care, so say what you will say."

"She can't marry William of Normandy."

Cleve said easily, "Naturally she can. She will marry William. She must marry William. It is done. The only reason you still live is because you will become the King of the Danelaw. Don't push the limits of our patience."

Chessa just looked at Cleve and he knew in that moment that she would fight it, that she would refuse to wed William, and then what in the name of the gods would he do? He would lose faith with Rollo, he would lose faith with Sitric. And what would happen to Chessa?

Ragnor said with all the pride of a Viking raider who'd just plundered an abbey, "The princess can't marry William of Normandy because I've already bedded her. I've taken her many times. She isn't a virgin. She could be carrying my babe, the future ruler of the Danelaw. Aye, the future ruler but only after I've been king for a very long time."

There was pandemonium.

Kerek lowered his head to hide his grudging smile. Ragnor had done well. It never ceased to amaze him how Ragnor could play the dignified man, logical and fluent. He waited to see how the princess would react. He looked up to see her staring blankly at Ragnor, her mouth opening. He prepared himself for her yells, her passionate denials. He prepared himself to lie. It was for the best. He had no choice.

Suddenly, she closed her mouth and said, innocence radiating from her as soft light from a rush lamp, "But what difference does that make, my lord? So you raped me many times? I hated it as I hate you, for you were nothing but a clod and cruel and selfish, but who would care about that?"

Ragnor looked like a fish tossed onto shore, his mouth gaping open, then closing. He looked as if he were suffocating. He just stared at her. Kerek said quickly, "Princess, it matters not. There is no shame for you, none at all. You simply must realize that Lord William of Normandy can no longer accept you as his wife. A man of power must have a virgin bride.''

''I see,'' Chessa said slowly. ''But not really. Ragnor raped me. I didn't welcome him to my bed. He gave me no choice in the matter. Am I not to have William because this little worm forced me so many times?''

It was Merrik who blurted out, ''Have you had your monthly flow since he raped you the last time?''

Mirana and Laren each grabbed one of Merrik's arms and shook him. ''Hush,'' Laren said. ''You're embarrassing Chessa. This should be done in private.''

''Oh, I will answer him,'' Chessa said, squaring her shoulders, looking directly at Cleve. ''I haven't had my monthly flow.''

Without warning, Cleve threw himself on Ragnor. He lifted him off his feet, pounded his fists into his mouth, then into his belly, and threw him a good six feet across the longhouse. ''You damnable bastard, raping a lady, a princess. By all the gods, I don't care who you are, I'll kill you.'' And he was on him again, leaping to land on him, straddling him, pounding his fist in his face, slamming his head against the packed earthen floor, then jerking him to his feet, easily avoiding any blows Ragnor attempted.

''I cannot allow this,'' Kerek said, and ran to the two men.

''Wait,'' Rorik yelled, seeing Kerek draw a knife. Four men dragged Cleve off Ragnor, whose lip was bleeding in two places and would have both eyes black within hours. He was sweating and shaking, obviously in pain. Rorik prayed Cleve hadn't hurt any of his innards. What was he to do?

Rorik was smart enough not to release Cleve, who was panting, staring at Ragnor, who was being tended by Kerek. Ragnor's other men were staying back.

Merrik said very quietly, ''Cleve, stop it. Gain control of yourself. We will solve this problem. You cannot kill the little bastard. You cannot. None of us can, despite the provocation.''

"Aye, I can and I will. Didn't you hear? He raped her, he forced her, and hurt her. By all the gods, she hasn't had her monthly flow."

All the men's hands tightened on him.

Chessa didn't want Ragnor's blood on Cleve's hands. "I thank you for defending my honor, Cleve. But it isn't necessary."

Cleve turned on her. His face was still flushed from rage and exertion. He was still panting. His knuckles were bleeding from the blows he'd landed on Ragnor's face. He actually shook his fist at her. "Listen to me, Chessa. You will begin your monthly flow and you will begin it now. You will marry William. Do you understand me?"

"Since you're yelling at me, it's difficult not to understand you."

"Don't you twist my nose, Chessa. You will marry William. You must marry William."

"But Ragnor said that I can't since I'm no longer a virgin. Is it true that a man with pride and honor and power wouldn't want me just because I was raped? Aren't I still the same, still Chessa? Do I speak differently, act differently just because Ragnor raped me so many times?"

Cleve lurched away, taking the men by surprise. In the next instant he'd reached Ragnor and his hands were about his throat. He was pulled off again, cursing, wild as a berserker. Merrik had never seen Cleve so lost to control. He pulled back his fist and slammed it into his friend's jaw.

"He must sleep on this," he said, rubbing his hand. "His rage was too great for him to see reason. When he awakes, we will speak to him."

"Thank you, my lord," Kerek said. "I didn't want to kill him to protect Ragnor."

"What did you say, Kerek? That you would kill to protect me? It's wise for you to become respectful to me again. Many of these men are vicious. I just might need you to protect me."

Kerek closed his eyes for an instant. Chessa said quietly, "You see him as he really is, Kerek. I won't wed him and you can't force me to. No one can."

"I must try, Princess," Kerek said, sighed, and turned back to Ragnor, who was drinking a wooden mug of mead and looking toward Utta like a slavering goat.

Cleve woke up on a groan. He felt fire in his jaw. He opened his eyes to see Chessa over him, holding his head in her lap, lightly touching a wet cloth to his chin. He felt the warmth of her, her softness. He immediately pulled away from her and sat up, swinging his legs over the side of the box bed. "Where are we?"

"In Rorik's and Mirana's bedchamber. I bandaged your hands. You scored your knuckles."

Cleve remembered what he'd done. He closed his eyes and cursed.

"Merrik said he had to strike you. He said he'd never seen you so angry. He said—"

"Be quiet. I must think."

She folded her hands in her lap and leaned back against the thick wooden planks that separated this bedchamber from the next one. She was content to wait. He'd tried to kill Ragnor. His rage had been magnificent. She began to fidget. "Have you finished thinking, Cleve?"

"Be quiet," he said again, turning even more away from her. "My jaw hurts."

"It took four men to pull you off Ragnor and you still fought them. Do you remember now if you come from a race of warriors?"

"Aye, I do, and don't sound so damned proud of me," he said, turning now to look at her. "As if I'm your child and you're pleased I went mad as a berserker. I don't know what happened to me. It won't happen again. I won't let it. Damn you, you made me do it."

"I know," she said, a tiny smile curving up the corners of her mouth. "I'm very powerful, mayhap even a witch. Every man who comes near me does exactly what I wish him to do. You were no exception, though I thought you might be and—''

''Be quiet. You can taunt and mock Ragnor. You won't do it to me. Be quiet.''

''All right. Ah, here's Kiri. Come here, little sweeting. You can see that your papa's just fine.''

Kirk looked frightened and it smote Cleve. He quickly drew her up onto his lap and pulled her against his chest. ''I'm sorry that I was so unlike myself, Kiri.''

''I thought you were splendid, Papa.''

Women, he thought, rubbing his bruised hands together. Were they never too young to be perverse?

''I'm just sorry that Uncle Merrik had to hit you. He's very sorry. He told me so. Laren said she wished Oleg had been here, that he'd have been so pleased to see you boil over like one of her stews in the cooking pot.''

''I don't believe any of this,'' Cleve said, setting Kiri on the floor. ''Go play with your cousins. I'm all right. Go, Kiri.''

''They're not really my cousins.''

''It's close enough. Go.''

She skipped away from the box bed, but at the door, she turned and said, ''Why did you get so angry, Papa? Why do you care who she marries? She's not even beautiful like you are, like she says I am.''

''Go,'' Cleve said, and watched her dash out of the bedchamber. He said, turning to Chessa, ''I mean it. You must start your monthly flow.''

She laughed. ''But I'm still not a virgin.''

''William is thirty, more seasoned, more mature. He will understand. After all, a girl is only a virgin once. A man who demands a virgin is a fool. William isn't a fool.''

She said, ''If he, a future ruler, doesn't demand that his wife be a virgin, then he must really be seasoned.''

''Damnation, he isn't old. He is but five years older than I am. He is wise because he was married to the same woman for ten years before she died. He adored her. He was faithful to her. He isn't a fool because he's never been a fool. You will be able to trust him.''

"Perhaps this William isn't a fool, but you are, Cleve. Do tell me, why did you attack Ragnor?''

He looked at her as if he wanted to strangle her.

9

"I DEMAND THAT you kill this man, this former slave, Cleve who isn't anybody, he just pretends to be important. He must die. He dared to strike Ragnor of York, son of Olric."

Rorik looked at Ragnor's black right eye, the swollen bruised jaw, the reddened flesh of his throat. "Why do you speak of yourself as if you were another?"

"I am of royal blood. Royalty speak like that when they wish others to obey them immediately, just as I'm ordering you, Rorik. Kill him."

"If everyone was dead that you ordered to be killed, the earth would have no more people on it. You may forget your demands. However, I would think it wise were I to give Cleve your share of mead. It is rotting what little brain you have left."

"I am *Lord* Ragnor."

"Your ship is ready to leave for York," Rorik said, knowing he didn't have too much longer to keep himself from attacking Ragnor just as Cleve had done. "I hope you have sufficient men left to row you back."

"I have more men than I need."

"That's good, because I think some of the men won't go back with you."

Ragnor just stared at him, then yelled, "Utta, bring me

some mead. Kerek, come here and tell me that Rorik lies.''

Rorik just shook his head and quickly took himself out of the longhouse. He patted Entti's shoulder as he passed by the bread trough. He'd rarely in his life seen so much dough. She was singing softly while she kneaded the dough. It was a relief that Ragnor was leaving on the morrow. Rorik feared that the island's stores of barley, rye, and wheat would be severely depleted. They were eating more and more fish. Rorik wanted to go hunting on the mainland, beyond the salt marsh, for pheasant and grouse, perhaps even a wild boar, but he didn't dare leave the island for fear of what Ragnor would do. Nor did he want to make Ragnor Merrik's responsibility. Both his men and Merrik's men were staying close, keeping a tight watch on Ragnor and his men. But his belly was growing tired of fish, even Utta's roasted herring and baked sea bass, even wrapped in oiled and spiced tartar leaves.

He greeted his brother by the palisade gates. ''Where are you going, Merrik?''

''Hunting. Aslak and Hafter are going with me as well as another dozen or so men. I knew you wouldn't wish to leave what with that fool Ragnor about causing trouble. Also I'm leaving a goodly number of men here. We're going in relays. I should have begun this yesterday. By Thor's toes, my belly is tired of fish, even though it is wondrously prepared.''

Rorik had to smile at how much alike he and his brother were. He said, ''It's a good idea, one I was just mulling over. I will allow my men to do the same. By the gods, my muscles are turning soft. Where is Cleve?''

''If Chessa has her way then he's probably with her.''

Rorik grunted. ''Has she obeyed him yet? Has she begun her monthly flow?''

''I don't know. She's a stubborn woman.''

In the stand of pine trees at the top of Hawkfell Island, Cleve said, ''Does your belly cramp?''

''Why should my belly cramp? Utta makes the best porridge I've ever eaten. Even the fish is excellent but I'm getting very tired of it.''

"Your monthly flow, Chessa. Don't you have belly cramping when you begin your monthly flow?''

"Cleve, perhaps you'd best send a message back to Duke Rollo and this William. Tell them that I'm not at all a nice fresh young princess. Tell them that I am still nice and young but I'm no longer fresh. Tell William that if he weds me I will be able to compare him to another man. I understand men don't like that and so that is why they demand that their wives come to them untouched by other manly hands and other manly parts.''

"Men are not so paltry.''

"It is not my experience. Ragnor seemed wonderful to me at first, then he proved his falseness. You may well ask how I could have been so blind, seeing what an ass he is now. Well, I was.

"Then my father decides I'm to marry a man I've never seen, a man already long married, a man you say is seasoned and mature, and then the first man kidnaps me and rapes me, many times. And now you want to send me to the mature man. Mature makes him sound dreadfully tiring, Cleve. Haven't I suffered enough?'' She held her face in her hands and sobbed.

"I'm sorry, Chessa,'' he said, pulling her into his arms. "By the gods I feel like a miserable sot.'' His arms came around her back, squeezing her against him. He felt her arms go around his back as well. He felt her breasts against his chest. He felt the warmth of her breath against his throat. He leaned over and kissed the top of her head. "I'm so sorry. It wasn't your fault. I wish I'd killed Ragnor, the rotten little bastard, despite who he is. Did he hurt you badly?''

She just nodded against his shoulder, saying nothing, the sobs still coming.

"Do you think he hurt you internally?''

"I don't know. He kicked me hard in the ribs. He told me he liked to see lying me at his feet. He liked to see my pain. Then he fell down on top of me.''

He kissed her again, this incredible girl who believed him more beautiful than the gods, this adorable girl who was a princess and thus far above him. She'd been dreadfully hurt and now all he could do was see that she was hurt even more.

''You must marry William.'' He kissed her ear. ''Oh, damn, Chessa, you're a princess. You must marry William, there's no choice, for either of us.''

''I will consider it if you will send a message to him telling him what has happened.''

''It would take days for the message to reach him and days more for a messenger to return here to Hawkfell.''

''You would prefer then to take me there to face him, for me to tell him what happened, then perhaps see the disdain on his face that said clearly what he thought of me? You aren't a very kind man, Cleve.''

''Nay, I didn't mean that,'' he said, and squeezed her harder. He kissed her temple, her flesh soft and warm from the sun overhead. ''Chessa, you're promised to him. Your father and Duke Rollo agreed.''

''Everything has changed,'' she said, and that, at least, was the truth. She kissed his throat. She raised her hand and lightly touched her fingertips to his mouth. ''Cleve, everything has changed,'' she said again. ''Do you disdain me? Do you hate me now because I've been used by Ragnor?''

''By all the gods, no, you stupid woman. You're you and that would never change.''

''Then why can we not simply—''

''You said you were blind at first with Ragnor. Look at my face, damn you. Look!''

She looked up, staring at him straightly. She cocked her head to one side in question. ''I don't understand you. You're beautiful. I would never tire of looking at you in my life.''

He couldn't believe her. She was lying. ''Damn you, don't you see the scar? Are you playing me for a fool? Do you enjoy mocking me? I'm hideous, ugly as a monster, uglier than the dragon stem on Merrik's warship. Look, Chessa.''

She smiled at him, drew his head down between both her palms and kissed the scar, her mouth soft, too soft, and it touched him so deeply he didn't know whether to shove her away or kiss her until neither of them could breathe. Then she said, ''You attacked Ragnor for what he did to me. If you would show me the man who did this to you I would attack him and kill him.''

He stared down at her, stunned and disbelieving. He said slowly, ''It wasn't a man.''

''A woman struck you?''

''Aye.''

''At least that was all she did. You're alive and you're here with me.''

''Not for very long. Once you begin your monthly flow, we must return to Rouen.''

She was silent then, still held in his arms. The sun was bright and warm overhead. Oystercatchers flew over the fallow barley field. Just behind them flew a glittering trio of dunlin. Sea gulls squawked loudly. Curlews spun wildly through the pine and fir trees behind them.

''You sound as if perhaps you don't want me to wed with William. You are holding me. Perhaps you want to wed me yourself.''

''No,'' he said, ''I don't.'' He leaned down and this time she raised her face and he kissed her mouth. By the gods, she was soft, giving. He wanted to devour her, but he held himself back. He shouldn't be touching her, much less kissing her as if she belonged to him. ''No,'' he said, and broke away from her. ''No, I don't want you. I will never want another woman for the rest of my life, that is, I would want a woman to ease me, but not a wife, not a mate. I have Kiri and I will see that she grows strong. I will see that she has no guile, no cunning, to bring a man low.''

She stood there panting slightly, her breasts heaving, and his eyes were drawn there, and he could but stare at her breasts, and he wanted desperately to feel her breasts in his hands, to taste her with his mouth. "Go away, Chessa. No, you won't, will you? Very well, I'll go. I don't know what game you're playing. All women play games to make men flounder about like the sea bass I caught yesterday. It doesn't matter. You will begin your monthly flow and I will be safe from you. You will be safe from yourself. You will see me as I really am. You will recognize my ugliness. You will wed William."

Without another word, he turned on his heel and nearly ran back toward the longhouse.

"He does want me," she said to a pinwheel performing intricate turns above her head. "Aye, he does want me."

Mirana said to Chessa, "Kiri has asked me how you can be a princess since you don't have beautiful golden hair and bright blue eyes like she does. She doesn't think you look like a real princess at all. Nor," Mirana added, "does she like you looking at her papa the way you do."

"Did you tell her I can't seem to help myself? Cleve is a stubborn man. He cares for me, I know it, he knows it, but he won't let me close. Some of his reasons are murky, others quite stupid, even others utterly false. Why can't you simply tell him that I'm as little a real princess as Sira is a queen, bred for the position?"

"I cannot do that. Surely you see why, Chessa. As for Cleve's reasons, murky or not, stupid or not, nothing will sway him. As for Kiri, I only told her that you admired her father. I told her that if a princess looked at her father in an admiring way, why then, her father was of unquestioned nobility."

"Is that true?"

"I don't yet know the full truth, at least those truths from Cleve's dreams. He remembers that his father was the Lord of Kinloch, on the western side of Loch Ness, in Scotland, near the trading town of Inverness. He remembers his stepfather, the man's coldness and cruelty toward his mother. Does he remember correctly? Are they truly as things were?

When you are, well, settled, Merrik and Laren are going with him to Scotland, back to Cleve's home, to set things aright if there is anyone left to set things aright with.''

''Hasn't it been a very long time?''

''Aye, twenty years. I truly don't know what Cleve expects, but he must go home, he must see what there is left. He had a mother, an older brother, and two sisters. Life is very uncertain. They could be dead. It is likely.''

''When I am settled,'' Chessa repeated slowly. Then she smiled at Mirana, this woman who looked so much like her. She knew how she wanted to be settled. And she knew now how she would gain it. It would not be well done of her. She didn't care. She was fighting for her future.

Chessa took another bite of Utta's porridge, swallowed, drank a bit of goat's milk, and said, ''What did Kiri's mother look like?''

''Sarla? Ah, that is a tale. Sarla always seemed so gentle, so very sensitive and kind, her voice always low and soft. Even her hair was a soft brown, as soft as she was, her eyes a lighter brown. She was quite pretty, really. It's just that one usually didn't notice because she was so very quiet. After her husband, Erik, died, she and Cleve became lovers. She became pregnant with Kiri. But then Laren's father, Hallad, came to Malverne and wanted her. Hallad is Duke Rollo's brother. He was very rich and could offer her more than she'd ever had in her life. She decided to marry him. Cleve told her she could do as she wished, but he wanted his child from her first. She tried to kill him and thankfully all was discovered. Sarla stayed at Malverne until Kiri was born, then she, well, she died.''

''Did Cleve love her?''

''Perhaps at first. If someone tried to kill you would you still love him?''

Chessa smiled, took another bite of porridge and said, ''I don't blame Ragnor for wanting to take Utta. She is a wonderful cook.''

''Aye, when I first came to Hawkfell Island, she was but eleven years old. Her cooking kept me alive.''

"Alive? What do you mean?"

But Mirana only patted her hand. "Ah, there's a tale for a long winter's evening. I have much to do since we have so many hungry men here. You must decide what you wish to do, Chessa. Oh, have you begun your monthly flow yet?"

Chessa rolled her eyes and said nothing.

That evening, Chessa moved closer to Cleve when Laren, not only the mistress of Malverne but also its skald, stood before all the people to tell them a story.

"She's a female," Ragnor said, wiping the mead from his mouth. "How can she be a skald? That is ridiculous. Where is a real skald? Where is a man?"

"Be quiet. *My lord,*" Kerek said. "They have been kind enough to allow you to remain in the longhouse, hold your tongue." He poured him another goblet of mead. Ragnor, who recognized that insolent tone, knew that he didn't want to hear it again, thus said nothing, merely accepted the mead and drank deep.

Laren said slowly, "Let me tell you about the great king Tarokamin, who was born in a land far to the south. A land called Egypt where there is a long river called the Nile that divides the country into two parts and gives it life. You see, all else in this country is naught but desert, mile after mile of sand, empty and barren.

"For thousands of years, the kings in this country built mighty stone monuments in which they were buried with untold riches. The more powerful the king, the greater the wealth buried with him. The monuments were called pyramids. They were very large at the base then, with each level, fewer stones were used until there was but a point at the top of the monument."

"There isn't a country like that," Ragnor said. "A country with the name Egypt. As for these pyramids, who would want such a stupid sort of burial monument? A point at the top, you say? That is ridiculous. I am learned and I know there's nothing like anything you've described."

"This is a story, my lord, naught more," Laren said, smiling at him through gritted teeth. "Listen now and learn of Tarokamin. He wanted a monument greater than any king who had come before him, greater than his father's, greater than his grandfather's, whose was the greatest to be seen in the land. He ordered a Babylonian master craftsman to oversee the work. He hired hundreds of overseers. One hundred thousand slaves quarried the stone and hauled it to the site where the huge monument was to be erected.

"King Tarokamin married and had a son who was more precious to him than his wife, than his army, than all his jewels, but not more precious to him than his burial monument. He would go to the afterlife when he died, but he would still be immortal, for all who came after him would see his monument and know that he had been a great and wealthy king.

"The years passed. His son grew to manhood, a handsome, strong young man. Every day of his life he looked upon his father's monument. Tall now, taller than anything he had ever seen in his life. Two thousand men standing side by side couldn't come together around the base of the great stone pyramid so massive a structure it was. It would soon be completed, this stone mausoleum that would house his father's bones in magnificently decorated chambers, hidden in the bowels of the monument.

"The day came when his father told him he was to marry his sister. Don't be shocked. This was the custom of the land, one we find very strange, but it is what the kings did. King Tarokamin hadn't married his sister because he didn't have one. He had married a princess from a neighboring kingdom. But he knew how things were to be done.

"However, the son hated his sister, hated her with a soul-deep hatred. He told his father he wouldn't marry her. He told his father that he could never produce children by her because he hated her so much. He said she was wicked, that she had many lovers, that she was vain and grasping. No, he wouldn't marry her, not ever.

"His father told him that if he refused, he would give

her to his younger brother and he, the beloved, favored son, would be banished from the land. The son bowed his head. He knew how proud and stubborn his father was. He also knew the custom and he knew he couldn't flout it. He felt sorry for his brother, who was gentle and uncertain, not good material for a king.

"The next day he was gone, his two servants and six of the king's soldiers with him. Tarokamin was distraught. They could find no trace of his favorite son. Never was he seen again until three days after the old king had died." Laren had lowered her voice until her final words were barely above a whisper.

There was utter silence, all the people leaning forward, all their attention on Laren, and now she smiled at them and said again, "Tell me if you can what became of the son?"

Merrik laughed. "She has done it again. I keep thinking I will come to understand her mind, but it has been five years and I still have not succeeded."

"Wait," Cleve said. "Laren, you said the son wasn't seen again until after the father died?"

"Aye, that's right. He wasn't seen again until three days after the old king had died."

"Ah, then he came back with an army and overthrew his younger brother," Chessa said. "He then took his rightful place as ruler." Cleve nodded as did most of the people.

Laren shook her head.

Rorik said, "Perhaps the younger brother went out and found him, waiting outside the kingdom."

Laren shook her head again. She looked at Hafter, at Entti, whose babe was sleeping on her lap, at Mirana, at all the people, one by one.

"Come, tell us, Laren," Aslak shouted. "What did happen to the son? How was he seen three days after his father died?"

Suddenly Ragnor laughed. He rose from the bench, belched and laughed more. "You are all fools. Anyone who is of royal blood would know the answer to her foolish puzzle.''

Everyone looked at Ragnor, many fists raised in his direction. He drank down more mead. Laren wondered how he still sat straight on the bench or managed to stand. She saw rage on Merrik's face and said quickly, ''Aye, my lord? You know the answer?''

''Certainly,'' Ragnor said. ''Shall I tell you?''

''If you can,'' Rorik said, wishing he could forget that Olric, king of the Danelaw would exact retribution were his son killed.

Merrik nodded. He rather hoped Ragnor would make an ass of himself. After all, the rest of them had.

Ragnor said to Laren, ''You said he hated his sister and refused to wed with her and for this reason he was forced to leave his country and his younger brother would succeed the father when he died?''

''Aye, that's correct.''

Ragnor belched again and laughed. ''You're fools, all of you. Listen to the answer. His sister hated him as much as he hated her. How could it be otherwise? Thus, he left and none ever heard of him again. When he was seen three days after his father's death, it was in the massive mausoleum that you call pyramid. Aye, he was found and all recognized his clothes and the jewels he wore, but he was naught but sand and bones. You see, the sister killed him, she avenged herself for his humiliation of her, and placed his body in the old king's hidden burial chamber. She was probably aided by this Babylonian craftsman who would know where the burial chambers were hidden. He was her lover, wasn't he?''

''By all the gods,'' Laren said, staring at Ragnor of York. ''You are perfectly right, my lord.''

Ragnor preened like a jackdaw. ''Let me also tell you that the sister wasn't blamed for the murder. All believed the king had killed his son and placed him in the burial chamber. Since he loved him, they would be together for eternity.''

"That's right, Lord Ragnor."

"I can't stand this," Rorik said, got up, and left the longhouse.

Ragnor laughed and drank more mead. "I am a prince. Of course I would know the answer. Don't raise your fists at me, remember who I am, remember who my father is."

Ragnor said, looking as if he would soon be patting Laren on her head like a puppy that has just performed well, "Perhaps I am wrong. She told a fine tale. I liked the question at the end. It holds interest for a smart man. Aye, you did well, Laren. Perhaps a female isn't such a bad skald after all." And he pulled off his silver armlet and handed it to her.

"Thank you, my lord," she said, stunned.

Cleve said to Chessa, "I will go join Rorik. This is too much to bear. By all the gods, I want to kill him."

Kerek left Ragnor bragging and braying to any of his men who would listen and came to Chessa, who was watching Kiri playing with a leather ball. "You see, he isn't always stupid, though he did brag a bit too much about his superiority."

"You're right, that was well done of him," she said, not looking up at him.

"Don't you believe that if a man is clever, as Ragnor just proved to be, that he can be taught other things?"

"You mean like kindness, good judgment, generosity, common sense? Ah, and humility? That quality surely crowns all others. Shall I continue, Kerek?"

Kerek ground his teeth. "A man can't be everything that is to your liking. You cannot demand a god. A man must have some flaws."

"Leave it be, Kerek," she said, patting his arm. "Leave it be. I won't wed him and there's the end to it."

He said nothing. Chessa sighed and took herself to the fire pit to help Mirana and Entti clear away the remaining food from the evening meal.

10

CHESSA WAS SLEEPING deeply, dreaming of Egypt, that
land very far to the south, that land of endless sand and
heat that seared the flesh off the bones. She remembered
the feel of the heat. She remembered the trees and the delicious dates as she picked them and stuffed them into her
mouth. She remembered the soft white linen she wore, the
open sandals. But above all she remembered the heat.

She also remembered a woman, her voice, her softness,
and she knew in her dream that it was her mother, Naphta.
She moaned softly, and the sound from deep in her own
throat brought her awake.

She stared up into a man's face. In the next instant, his
fist landed on her jaw and she fell into blackness where
there was no more sand, no more heat, just emptiness and
peace.

When she awoke, she wasn't in Mirana's box bed. She
was alone and her hands were bound. She shook her head.
A pain seared through her jaw where the man had struck
her.

She was sitting up against a bale of hay in a small hut.
Light came through the cracks in the wood plank walls.
Her ankles were also bound. She was still in her white linen
nightshift that came to her knees.

When the small door creaked open some minutes later,

she immediately stopped trying to pull her hands loose of the rope. Kerek bent over and came into the hut. He was carrying a bowl and a hunk of bread.

"Good morning, Princess," he said. "I hope you feel all right. By the gods, your jaw is bruised. I told that fool to go easy with you, not to hit you. He's large, he could have merely held his hand over your mouth."

"Who was that man?"

"One of Ragnor's men. I couldn't come for you because I'm being watched too closely. I will make Ottar pay for this, the clumsy bastard. Does your jaw hurt?"

"Of course it hurts. Why did you have me taken?"

"Come, you know why."

She sighed. "Untie me, Kerek, and take me back to the longhouse."

"Nay, after you've eaten I will take you to the warship. Even now Ragnor is gathering the men together."

"Oh? Are there enough men who want to return to York with him? It isn't just you?"

"He is promising them more silver if they return with him."

"Do they realize he's lying to them?"

"You won't speak like that of your future husband, Princess, and he will very shortly be your husband. I will ensure it. I promised the queen."

"You, Kerek, you will ensure that Ragnor keeps his word and gives them more silver?"

"No, I will ensure that you marry him."

"Listen to me, Kerek. Your loyalty to him is—I don't know what it is. Let me go, else I swear to you that your wretched master will be very unhappy if you force me back to York."

"We will see about that. Why did you tell everyone that Ragnor raped you? I have wondered and wondered and come up with no answer. Ragnor believes it is simply a sign that you want him, thus your compliance. He is wrong, of course. Why did you do it?"

She said nothing, merely looked at the bowl of porridge

in Kerek's large hand. He untied the ropes around her wrists, then rubbed the feeling back into them. She began to eat Utta's wonderful porridge, laced through with honey.

She said at last, "It was Ragnor who said he'd raped me. I merely agreed with him."

"Why?"

"I don't wish to marry William of Normandy either. It seemed an excellent way to make him break the marriage contract."

"There's more to it than that," Kerek said. "I didn't want to believe it, but I've seen you looking at Cleve. His face is ugly as a monster's. He isn't handsome like Ragnor. Why do you look upon him the way you do?"

"He isn't ugly. He's beautiful. I've finished the porridge. Let me go now, Kerek."

"I can't, Princess." He leaned over her and stuffed a cloth in her mouth. Before she could spit it out, he tied another cloth over her mouth, knotting it at the back of her head. He quickly tied her hands. He said to her as he wrapped her completely in a thick wool blanket and lifted her over his shoulder, "I'm sorry about your discomfort, Princess, but I couldn't take you to the warship earlier. The palisade gates are well guarded. They wouldn't have let me pass, not carrying something over my shoulder. Now all Ragnor's men are carrying their belongings to the warship. No one will question me."

He opened the small door, looked both ways, then strode with her over his shoulder, well hidden in the blanket, toward the palisade gates. The gates were wide open, men, women, children, goats, chickens, and cows all milling about. Men were climbing back up from the dock, others carrying foodstuff or clothing down to store on the warship.

Kerek whistled as he walked down the long path to the beach below. There was a lot of activity. It appeared that many of Ragnor's men did believe he would pay them more silver. He wondered if Ragnor really would. Probably not. He didn't care.

"You've got her?" Ragnor said staring at the fat woolen

blanket over Kerek's shoulder.

"Aye, I only had to stuff a cloth in her mouth and tie her hands. I will speak to Ottar. He had no right to strike her. He hurt her. I didn't even like tying her up but I knew she wouldn't come with me willingly."

"I told him to strike her if he needed to, so speak not to him, Kerek," Ragnor said, then he turned away, saying over his shoulder, "I must return to the longhouse. I will be back shortly. Have everyone ready on the warship and at their oars."

Kerek stared after Ragnor, wondering what he'd left at the longhouse, wanting to strike him for ordering Ottar to hit Chessa if he wished to, which he had. He carried Chessa on board and beneath a new leather tarp that covered the few goods that had survived the storm. He laid her gently on the wooden planks and unwrapped her. She looked up at him, her eyes deadly with anger. He quickly tied her wrists a bit tighter and rose. "I am sorry, Princess, but it must be." She made a furious gurgling sound. He just shook his head and sighed. He stayed with her a few more minutes, saw that she was breathing more easily and then went out to the men. There were only thirteen men there to row them to York. He would row as well, and he hoped that even Ragnor would take his turn at the oars. They would have to row as quickly as they could for Kerek had no idea how long it would be before Chessa was missed and a hunt was mounted.

They had to hurry. He said to Torric, who was propped up against the rudder, his leg stuck out in front of him, "Why did Lord Ragnor return to the longhouse?"

Torric rolled his eyes. "You'll not believe it, Kerek."

"Believe what?"

Then he heard a yell, looked up to see Ragnor running as fast as he could down the path, the girl Utta slung over his shoulder, unconscious. Kerek could only stare. Torric was right, he couldn't believe it. That stupid bastard. He'd told Ottar to mould a blanket in Chessa's shape in the box bed so anyone looking in would think she still slept. It would have bought them time. But now that ass Ragnor had ruined everything. He'd simply grabbed Utta and carried her off.

There was nothing he could do. He yelled, "Everyone prepare to row until your hearts burst, else you'll be food for the fish."

When Ragnor reached the warship, Kerek yelled, "Drop her, Ragnor, leave her, else they'll come after us and kill us all."

"Nay, she will make me mead and let me bed her. You've seen how she looks at me. She wants me. She won't mind that I can't wed her. You'll see. When I bed her, she'll scream my name. Think you I should demand that when she screams, she screams Prince Ragnor or Lord Ragnor?"

"Damn you, you idiot, drop her on the beach!"

Ragnor raised her off his shoulder and tossed her to one of his men, his mightiest warrior, Olya, who caught her against him as if she were naught but a small child. He looked at Kerek and just shrugged. Ragnor yelled even as he jumped onto the warship, "Row, damn you all, row!"

But it was too late. Kerek watched helplessly as men swept down the path yelling at the top of their lungs, carrying swords, axes, knives. Some had even picked up rocks beside the path. At their head was Haakon, Utta's husband. Had Ragnor grabbed her right out of her bed? Had her husband still been beside her?

Behind him were Rorik, Merrik, and Cleve. Kerek would die for this fool of a man, all of them would die.

He said to Torric, "Tell Olya to throw the girl Utta back onto the beach. Do it or we'll be butchered."

Ragnor screamed, "Row!"

They obeyed Ragnor, muscles straining, they rowed, but still it wasn't enough. Haakon and two dozen warriors splashed through the waves and climbed over the side of the warship. The fighting began.

Torric tried to rise, but Rorik merely frowned at him and brought the flat of his sword down on his head. Torric collapsed and fell beneath the rudder. As for Olya, he dropped Utta on the center wooden plank, drew his sword and fought with all his strength and skill. He got a sword through his belly, another through his chest. Because they were Vikings, because they were trained warriors who would never surrender, most died. Three were groaning, helpless, when it was over.

Kerek, as had been his vow to the queen, had protected his prince. He now stood at the stem of the warship, waiting to be slashed apart. The men had stayed away from him until the others were either dead or helpless. Now it was his turn. He expected no less. Ragnor was behind him, the bloody coward. Suddenly Ragnor raced around Kerek, grabbed up Utta and pulled her upright in front of him. He pulled the knife from his belt. He screamed at Rorik, "Keep them back or the girl dies. I care not though she makes the best mead I've ever drunk."

There was instant silence. The boat swayed and rocked in the waves, for they were still close to shore. Slowly, all the Malverne men and the Hawkfell men fell in behind Rorik, staring at Ragnor, and the still-unconscious Utta held in front of him like a shield.

Though his hand shook, Cleve said in his calm diplomat's voice, "My lord Ragnor, it is over for you. If you wish to live, you will at once release Utta. You will lay her down very gently. You will not so much as make a shadow on her throat with that knife. Do you understand me?"

Ragnor didn't know what to do. It was all Kerek's fault. If only he'd captured Utta instead of that arrogant Chessa, who looked at him as if he were naught but a worm, even after he'd solved the skald's riddle. He called out, "Haakon, I will buy her from you."

Kerek saw Cleve gently touch Haakon's arm. "No, don't move." To Ragnor, he said in that same calm voice, "Release Utta now. You, Kerek, and Captain Torric will survive if you do as I tell you. Mirana will tend those men's wounds."

"You're nothing but a slave, Cleve, you're ugly with

that scar sliced up your face. I don't know why Chessa thinks you so manly and beautiful. She must have a squint. You've no right to even speak to me. Go away, all of you.''

Suddenly there was a moan, a woman's moan. All the men looked toward the small covered cargo space to see Chessa on her hands and knees, her mouth tied with a rag, trying to crawl through the opening.

"You damned bastard," Cleve yelled, all his diplomat's calm vanished, and ran right at Ragnor. "I don't care who you are or what your damned father may do. You'll die now, you gutless worm!" The ship rocked wildly, throwing Ragnor to the side. At that moment, Utta awoke, shook her head to clear it, saw her husband's white face in front of her, and sent her elbow back into a soft stomach.

Ragnor yowled. She was free. She rolled aside just as Cleve leapt upon Ragnor. He dragged him down else they'd both have gone flying over the side of the warship. He pounded Ragnor's head against the center plank, the thud sounding loud and painful.

"Kill the damned bastard," Haakon yelled out, grabbing Utta and holding her steady.

"Wring his fool's neck," Hafter said. "Slice off his mangy parts."

"Please, Cleve," Kerek begged. But this time Rorik held him back and said, "If Cleve wishes to kill him, let him. He is responsible for the death of all of these good men."

Cleve was red-faced with rage. He sent his fist into Ragnor's throat, then quickly drew the knife from its sheath at his waist.

"No, Cleve."

He stopped cold. She'd but whispered the two words, but it stopped him. He looked at Chessa, who was still on her hands and knees, but she'd managed to work the gag from her mouth even with her wrists bound. "No," she said again, trying to crawl to him. "Don't kill him. I don't want you declared an outlaw and it is what King Olric would do, at the very least. He would even send men here to Hawkfell Island. He's not worth it. Don't kill him, Cleve.''

He slowly withdrew the knife. Ragnor was looking up at him, so terrified that he couldn't even groan at the pain in his ribs and his head.

"Has he hurt you, Chessa?"

"No, I'm fine. Could you please release me?"

Cleve rose slowly, looked down at Ragnor, then kicked him in the ribs. Ragnor yelled, then screamed, "Kerek, I'll kill you for this. It's all your fault. You took her and look what happened."

Kerek turned to Utta, who was still standing close to her husband. "I'm sorry he did this. He is sometimes ungoverned. Will you kill him, Haakon?"

Rorik said nothing, just looked at his man.

Utta said, her arms around her husband's back, "Nay, Haakon, leave him be. It is as Chessa said. You would be made an outlaw and I won't want our children to know their father had to flee to survive."

"Our children?" Haakon said blankly.

"Aye," she said, smiling up at him. "At least we will have the first one in seven months or so."

Merrik shouted at Chessa, "Have you begun your monthly flow yet?"

They would return Lord Ragnor, Kerek, and Torric to York once they'd taken Chessa to Rouen for her marriage to William. The men made the decision, then informed the women.

"I see," Mirana said after Rorik had finished. "You mighty men thought this all through, did you? You doubtless sat about swilling ale and weighing this complicated decision. How pleased I am that you deign to inform us of your plans. How tired you must be after all your mental discussions. Would you like some more ale, my lord? Are my lord's feet weary? I could go onto my hands and knees and you could rest your feet upon my back."

Rorik looked harassed. "Stop your sweet attacks, Mirana. Nay, they're vicious, you just speak sweetly. Damnation, someone had to make the decision. You women—'' He paused, taking in Laren and Chessa, and beyond them, Entti, Amma, Erna, Old Alna, all the women of Hawkfell Island, falling in behind their mistress, ready to kill for her if need be, their loyalty always to her, not to him. He wasn't happy. He turned to his brother. ''Merrik, you will speak to Laren before she makes a skald's tale of this and casts us all in the role of the Christian devil. Make her see reason. As for you, Cleve, take Chessa away from here and tell her to begin her monthly flow. She has no say in anything. Her father has made the decision for her.''

''Laren,'' Merrik said in his softest voice, which was just beneath a roar, ''surely you don't agree with Mirana. Surely you won't mock me as she does Rorik. Surely you won't make this pitiful little happening into a skald's tale, will you?''

''A Christian devil is too good for you, Merrik,'' his wife said, standing toe to toe with him, even though she reached only to his chin.

Suddenly Old Alna cackled. ''I think we shouldn't cook for them anymore. No more porridge from Utta. No more ale. No more roasted boar steaks. What say you, Amma?''

Amma, a strong woman, a large woman, grinned up at her huge husband, Sculla. ''What say you, husband? Do you want your belly to shrink just because you've been an ass?''

Cleve interrupted in his best diplomat's low, calm, smooth voice, ''We are getting far afield. I will ask the women just one question. Choose from amongst you who will give me your answer.''

''What is the question?'' Utta asked.

''Who should Princess Chessa wed?''

The women withdrew, drawing together into a tight circle, speaking, all talking at once, until Mirana held up her hand. ''Let us go outside. I do not wish the men to hear this. Doubtless they argued and insulted each other and yelled and carried on, but they will deny it and make us feel like fools when we do the same."

When all the women had left the longhouse, Rorik clapped Cleve on the back. "That was well done of you."

"Aye," Merrik said, grinning like a Viking who's just plundered a rich town, "what else can they decide? They must decide exactly what we decided. There is no other way to settle things."

"They are women," Cleve said. "Women aren't like men. They don't think like we do." He shook his head, sat on the bench, his hands between his legs, and just stared down between his shoes.

The other men drank ale, sharpened their axes, their swords, played with the children, pulled Kerzog's ears. The three wounded men lay in the corner, watching, but saying nothing. They wondered what would become of Lord Ragnor. All three hoped he would magically drop dead in his tracks before the fool managed to get all of them killed.

"Papa, what's happening?"

Aglida climbed onto her father's lap. "Mama isn't pleased with you, is she? What did you do?"

"Nothing, sweeting. It's just a thing that happens between men and women. Where is Kiri?"

"She followed Aunt Laren outside with the women."

"It won't be good," Cleve said, shaking his head back and forth. "I was stupid to suggest it."

"There is nothing else they can decide," Merrik said.

"What if she doesn't begin her monthly flow?" Rorik said.

"She could begin it and not tell us," Hafter said. "I will order Entti to tell me the truth."

The men stared at Hafter as if he'd grown another head. "You will *order* Entti to spy for you?" Rorik said, then he laughed, low, deep laughter, and soon all the men were jesting and laughing and drinking more ale.

The women came back into the longhouse, Mirana at their head. "We have decided what will happen." Slowly the men rose. They didn't say anything.

Mirana smiled at her husband. "My lord, we agree that

Ragnor, Kerek, and Torric must be returned to York. It's unfortunate that we can't kill them since they richly deserve it, but there it is. We'll return the other three men as well."

"You see," Rorik said to Cleve, "I told you there was no other way for them to decide."

"As to Chessa marrying William. She doesn't wish to and we agree with her. She wishes to marry Cleve."

Cleve stared at Mirana, just stared, knowing he was turning pale, knowing that he'd been a fool to ever give the women the chance to add their agreement to the men's.

He said finally, breaking the thick silence, "I won't marry the princess. For that reason. She's a princess. I am nothing, less than nothing."

"You are the son of the Lord of Kinloch," Laren said. "That's what you told us."

"I don't even know what this Kinloch is. It could be a bloody rock in the middle of Loch Ness. It could have been overthrown and the Scots could now control it, or the Picts, or the Britons. I could have dreamed it all in my dream. I could have made myself another boy who was captured. It isn't possible."

Laren cleared her throat. "Cleve, we know that two times now you have attacked Lord Ragnor when he was hurting Chessa. It is obvious to all of us that you want her."

"Aye, I want her, she's a woman and she's beautiful and I haven't had a woman in far too many weeks. By Thor's axe, what does that have to do with anything? I am a man. All men need to have a woman to see to them."

"I think perhaps we'd best steer clear of that," Merrik said, eyeing the women uneasily. "Laren, you women are thinking with your hearts, not with your heads. Cleve has negotiated the wedding contract. He must bring the princess to William. He has given his word. His honor is at stake."

For the first time, Chessa made her way to stand in front of the women. "You say it is Cleve's honor at stake. It is my life at stake. I have listened to all of you. Now it is time for the truth, the truth that four of you already know, perhaps all of you know."

"Chessa, no—" Mirana said, grabbing her sleeve.

"Leave be, Mirana. It's my future, not yours. Leave be. I beg that all of you in the longhouse swear to keep silent about this for I wouldn't have my father harmed. Don't forget to take away Ragnor and Kerek and the three wounded men. Do it now. Leave Captain Torric. He's so drunk with Alna's potions he doesn't know where he is."

There were murmurs of assent.

"Don't, Chessa," Rorik said.

Hafter, Aslak, and Sculla carried the three wounded men from the longhouse, all of them swearing on pain of death by Thor, by Odin, that they wouldn't say anything if only they could remain. Ragnor looked bored and Kerek started to open his mouth, saw the look on Rorik's face, and closed it. Hafter raised an eyebrow at Rorik, who just shook his head. Ragnor and Kerek were herded out after the other men.

Chessa just looked at Cleve for a long moment. He looked both utterly bewildered and furious. He said, "What do you have to say, Princess? Be quick about it for I would leave to return you to Rouen—to your bridegroom, to the man you must marry, for there is no choice for anyone, least of all you. I trust you will begin your monthly flow on our journey."

She said slowly, looking straightly at him, "Cleve, listen to me, for I tell you the truth. I am not a princess."

11

THERE WASN'T A sound in the longhouse. Even the children were silent. Kerzog was sprawled on his belly, his head on his paws, not moving except for his tongue lolling out.

"Did you hear what I said?" Chessa said, staring at all the men and women around the huge chamber. "I said I wasn't a princess. Before my father killed King Sitric of Ireland, he was Hormuze the magician. I'm his daughter." She couldn't understand why people weren't shocked, weren't yelling that such a thing couldn't be true.

Of course, she thought. Everyone knows. They've known since the beginning. Their only surprise was that she would admit it.

Mirana said, "Chessa, everyone knows the truth. Just after your father Hormuze married Sira and became the king of Ireland—renewed and young again—he sent a skald here the following winter solstice and he told the incredible tale of how the mystic Hormuze had wrought the change in the king and made him young again and given him a wife who would give him sons. All believed it. Those who didn't realized that your father would be an excellent king and thus kept their mouths shut. You see, your father wanted us to know that everything had come about just as he'd predicted. If I remember aright, Sira was pregnant with the first son.''

Cleve looked at Merrik. "When I asked you about that tale, you denied any knowledge.''

"Naturally. It was never to have been spoken of and hasn't, until now. Thank the gods we got Kerek and Ragnor out of here. Chessa was right, I wouldn't trust Ragnor any more than I'd wager Mirana could outrun Kerzog.''

"It's true?'' Cleve asked, now looking at her. "Chessa isn't a princess?''

"Actually,'' she said, clearing her throat loudly. "I'm from that far-away land to the south called Egypt, the land Laren spoke about last night. My father wanted Mirana for his wife because she looked so much like my mother, but she had already married Lord Rorik.'' She sighed. "So he took Sira. Papa was so certain he could improve her. She was wild and vicious and ruthless, excellent qualities, I believe, in a king, but not in a queen. I don't think he dwells on it much now.'' She looked at Cleve now. "I'm not a princess. I'm just me, no royal blood, nothing to interest William of Normandy, nothing to interest Ragnor of York. My father even changed my name because he didn't want anyone to remember Hormuze or that I was his daughter or to take the chance that someone might think that King Sitric had the look of Hormuze.''

Cleve said, "Now I know the full story. It's an excellent story. Nay, I believe it. I have but to look at Rorik's face to know it's true. As for your not having royal blood, why then, neither does William. His father, Duke Rollo, wasn't royal until he negotiated the treaty with King Charles III. But now he is royal simply because of that treaty, just as you are a princess simply because your father is now a king. None of it makes any difference. I gave my word to Duke Rollo that I would bring you to him. I will keep my word. You will begin your monthly flow.''

She looked at him straightly, holding herself very still. "I will marry no man but you.''

Cleve strode to the door of the longhouse.

"Where are you going?"

He turned to look at her, standing there, her hands clasped in front of her, her black hair loose down her back, braided strands threaded with strips of yellow linen, her linen gown of soft saffron making her skin look golden, making her eyes look greener, which surely wasn't possible. She'd just said it in front of everyone. She would marry no man but he. She was beyond foolish. She was beyond blind. Just looking at his face should have turned her against such a notion. It was an infatuation. Surely she would wake up one morning soon and realize that she didn't want him, and perhaps wonder how she could have ever believed that she had.

"I must think," he said, and fled the longhouse. No one said anything until they no longer heard his retreating footsteps.

Chessa just stood there after he was gone, just stood there seeing nothing really, hearing the voices around her becoming thick now, louder, for now everything must be discussed and argued about. Everyone had an opinion. Everyone would be heard.

She heard Rorik say to Mirana, "You should have told her it wouldn't work. To claim a man like that with no warning, especially a man like Cleve, who doesn't really know who or what he is, a man who doesn't want a wife, and that's understandable given what was done to him."

"Why doesn't Papa want a wife?"

"Oh, dear," Laren said as she scooped Kiri up in her arms. "Your papa, sweeting—well, it isn't that he doesn't want a wife, he just—"

She stalled and Merrik said, patting Kiri's golden hair, "Your papa has much to do, Kiri. You know that. We are going to Scotland to return to where he was born. All this is uncertain, thus he can't have a wife right now."

"Why not? She could help him just like Aunt Laren helps you. She could tell him the right of things when he gets confused, just like Aunt Lar—"

''I know, Kiri,'' Merrik said quickly, trying not to laugh. ''It's just that things are, well, very difficult right now.''

Chessa said, ''Kiri's right. Why can't he marry me?''

''Chessa,'' Rorik said, ''be quiet.''

''No, I won't. Kiri, your papa can have me for a wife right now, this afternoon if he wishes it. This evening if Mirana must have time to prepare for a celebration. I would help your papa learn about where he came from and why he was left to die as a small boy, then sold as a slave like your Aunt Laren.''

''I don't know if you should marry Papa,'' Kiri said, looking at Chessa. ''You look just like my Aunt Mirana.''

''That just makes her very lucky, Kiri,'' Mirana said and grinned.

''Maybe my papa doesn't want a wife because he loved my mama so much. Maybe my papa just doesn't like you. I don't know.''

She wiggled out of Merrik's hold and ran to the doorway.

''Sweeting,'' Laren called after her, ''just play outside with your cousins. Don't go beyond the palisade.''

Cleve returned in early evening, a sleeping Kiri in his arms. ''We spent the afternoon on the eastern cliff, watching the dunlin and oystercatchers.'' He said nothing more, paid no attention at all to Chessa until late that night when everyone was preparing to sleep. He walked to her, just stared down at her, but said nothing for a very long time. There was a food stain on her bosom, her hair was loose, her face flushed from the heat of the fire pit.

''Look at my face,'' he said.

She looked at his face.

''What do you see?''

She smiled up at him. Slowly, she raised her hand and traced her finger over his mouth, his nose, his eyebrows, smoothing them, then at last, she lightly traced her fingertip down the curved scar. ''I see you,'' she said. ''I see the man I want, the only man I will ever want. I see you and I want to smile and laugh and perhaps do a little dance. I want to kiss you and touch you. What I see is the man the gods fashioned just for me. Now, Cleve, look at my face.''

He looked at her face.

''What do you see?''

He didn't touch her as she had him. He said, ''I have never seen eyes the color of yours. I had thought your eyes like Mirana's, but it isn't true. The green of your eyes is different, darker, nearly black in this dim light, and there is a slight tilt to the corners of your eyes that makes you look like you're keeping secrets, that you know things that other people don't know. Is that true, Chessa?''

''Nay.''

She wanted very much to kiss him. She'd kissed Ragnor several times and thought it strange, this touching of mouths.

''Cleve,'' she said, standing on her tiptoes. Her heart was pounding so loudly she was certain he must hear it. She spread her palms on his chest, feeling the heat of his body, feeling the steady pounding of his own heart.

''Do you see anything else, Cleve?''

''I see a woman who will not do as she's bid.''

''That's all you see? Strange eyes and a woman who won't be led about by the nose? I feel your heart, Cleve. It's beating very fast now.''

''If you were closer you'd feel how hard my sex is. It means nothing, Princess. I'm a man and a man is always ready to bed a comely woman. It's no more than that.'' Then his hands were on her wrists and he was gently pushing her away from him.

He stepped back from her. ''Merrik, his men, and I are taking Ragnor, Kerek, and Torric back to York. It should only take five days, no longer than eight days, depending on the weather, depending on things I can't begin to think of. When we return then we'll go to Rouen. In the meantime you will begin your monthly flow. I don't think you're pregnant. After all, you don't want to bear Ragnor's child. No, I feel that you are just being stubborn. You refuse to obey your father's wishes and thus this is how you go about gaining your own way. If you refuse to wed William, I will return you to Sitric.''

"But didn't you hear me? I'm not a princess.''

He shrugged. ''I said it before and it's true. Since you are the King of Ireland's daughter you are thus a princess. You could have left Ragnor in here and told him that. He could have told the world. It makes no difference. Now, we're leaving in the morning. I bid you good night, Princess.''

She stared after him. He felt he had to keep his word, both to her father and to Duke Rollo. She had to come up with a good reason why it was no longer so important. But it was much more than that. The woman he'd loved had tried to murder him. Surely that would make a man wary of women. She realized that she had to prove herself to him, prove to him that he could trust her, prove that he was safe with her, that he would have her loyalty forever.

But what if he really didn't want her? But she didn't believe that was true. She wouldn't allow it to be true. All had seen him become as ferocious as a berserker those times she was attacked. She supposed she had to tell him the truth. Not only wasn't she a princess, she was also still a virgin. By Thor's hammer, she could just see his face when she told him that. She realized that she'd dug a very large hole at her feet and she was fast slipping into it. It had seemed such an excellent idea at the time. After all, if she wasn't a virgin then William wouldn't want her, thus she was free, she could have Cleve and surely, when at last he came to her, her virginity would have pleased him.

Now she knew it wouldn't. He would know she'd lied. He would believe she was no better than Sarla, that wretched bitch Chessa wished were here right now, right this instant. Surely she'd kill Sarla for what she'd done to Cleve. She wondered how much more there was to the story than the bare bones she'd been told. Probably a lot more.

Merrik, Cleve, and all twenty of the Malverne men left the following dawn. All the Hawkfell Island men and women were there to see them off. Chessa, Laren, and Mirana stood close together on the dock as the men loaded the warship with provisions. Entti handed Merrik a large skin filled with ale, saying, "This isn't intended for Ragnor's gullet. It's for the first night you're sailing from York, having rid yourself of these three."

Old Alna was there to say good-bye to her Captain Torric. She patted his bound wrists and cackled. "Aye, my pretty boy, you would have fought to have me. I was more beautiful than those young twittering crows who stand here with me."

Captain Torric said, "But Alna, if you were ever that beautiful, then it would have been my grandfather to have fought to have you and perhaps then I would have been your grandson."

She cuffed his ear, then cackled. "You keep that leg straight, Captain, it will heal faster, and take this potion." She handed him a small vial. "If you weren't leaving, my pretty boy, I'd give you another vial and it would be a love potion and you would fall in love with your grandmother." She laughed and laughed, and Captain Torric looked desperately toward Merrik, who just grinned and said, "Consider Old Alna a gift from the gods, Torric."

Laren smiled at her husband, but didn't say anything. She'd already told him ten times to keep a keen eye, for she didn't trust Ragnor at all. As for Kerek, he was even a greater danger, for he was obsessed with having Chessa for Ragnor, for the Danelaw.

Cleve said nothing to Chessa, but stood off to the side, speaking to his daughter. He kissed her, set her down, and told her to go to her aunt Laren.

He waved at her, and the men shoved off. Within minutes, the bright blue-and-white striped wadmal sail was but a dot in the distance. The Hawkfell men gathered up their weapons, their tools, and took themselves off to hunt.

"Look at the pinwheels," Mirana said. "They're fighting with the gulls. I find them fascinating. They soar and dive and drive the other birds wild."

Chessa looked at her as if she'd lost her mind.

"Forgive me, Chessa, but I've always had a fondness for birds, but it doesn't mean I don't know what you're feeling." She sighed.

"You're not a damned princess like I am," Chessa said. "How could you begin to know what I feel?"

Mirana laughed. "That's better. Cleve will return and then we'll see."

Chessa looked at all the women's faces surrounding her. "Oh, dear," she said. "There's something else I'm not."

Mirana stared fixedly at two curlews who were racing away from a spraying wave. "I don't think I want to know."

"I'm not pregnant."

"You began your monthly flow?"

"Yes, but that doesn't matter. It's worse than that."

"What is this?" Laren asked as she came upon the two of them.

"She started her monthly flow," Mirana said. "She isn't pregnant with Ragnor's child."

"It doesn't matter."

"Of course it matters," Laren said. "When at last you have Cleve for your husband, you won't have to worry that you carry Ragnor's child."

Chessa looked from Mirana to Laren and to the other women who were clustered close. She said on a miserable sigh, "I'm a virgin. I lied. I hoped no one would expect me to go to William if I wasn't pure. I was wrong."

"But that's wonderful," Utta said, then her eyes widened. "Oh, dear," she said.

"Aye, this is a new twist to the problem," Entti said. "If Cleve knows you're a virgin, he'll carry you off to Rouen and you'll be wed to William before you know it. Oh, dear. What do you think, Amma?"

That tall strong woman with the strength of many of the Hawkfell Island men looked ready to swim after the departed warship. "What I think," she said slowly, "is that you must bed Cleve the moment he returns from York."

All the women gathered around on the dock, arguing for a good long time. There were no jests.

Laren said at last, "Listen, all of you. It's not Chessa, it's Cleve. I told Chessa about Sarla, but not all the wretched details of it. It will help her and the rest of you understand why he is running as fast as he can away from her."

"Sarla tried to kill him," Old Alna said, spitting off the dock, interrupting Laren because she was, after all, older than anyone on Hawkfell Island, and thus she could do as she pleased, and Laren bowed to her to continue. "You know that, Chessa. What you don't know, sweeting, is that she lured him with love words up to the top of Raven's Peak, made passionate love with him, then when he was lying there blissfully happy, believing her happy as well, she struck him on the head with a rock, and shoved him over. The gods saved him. He landed on a ledge. Laren's little brother, Taby, saw it all, but Sarla threatened him, told him that she would kill Laren and Merrik if he told anyone what he'd seen. But in the end, he told Merrik, and thus Cleve was saved, but barely in time. That's enough to make a man's innards cramp when he thinks about a new woman. Aye, I hear that when he beds any of the women at Malverne, there is always an oil lamp burning. When he is through, he sleeps alone. He has less trust for a woman than the men had for that Ragnor."

"Tell me how you know all that, Alna," Laren said. "You were here on Hawkfell Island when it all happened, far away from Norway."

"I gave your beautiful husband a potion that loosened his tongue. He told me everything, smiling the whole time. He even told me how lovely I looked."

"I believe it," Laren said to Mirana. "Except for the last part."

"I knew all that, save the details of it, just as Alna said," Chessa said impatiently. "But Sarla was just one woman. Surely he's far too smart a man to think that all women are like her."

"Aye," Laren said. "That's true. But understand, Chessa. She was the first woman Cleve knew as a free man. He trusted her. He gave himself to her. He loved her. Then she tried to kill him."

"But Chessa is different," Mirana said. "I can't believe Cleve so blind as not to see it."

"Men," Amma said, drawing herself up even taller, "even my precious Sculla, sometimes becomes over-wrought and ceases to reason. It is what has happened to Cleve. He does think that all women are like Sarla. What's more, he believes himself hideous with that scar. He has made himself believe this and thus it is how he sees him-self. Since he is a man, it will be difficult for him to see clearly. Also he believes he must deliver up Chessa to Duke Rollo else he will have broken his sacred word."

"Men and their sacred word," Mirana said. "More wars have been fought because of their wretched sacred word."

Chessa said slowly, "Surely my father wishes for my happiness more than anything. He wants the alliance with Normandy, no doubt about that, but can't he make a sep-arate treaty with Duke Rollo, without sacrificing me in the bargain? How can I make Cleve understand that my father won't curse him if he weds me himself? His father is, after all, the Lord of Kinloch."

Laren turned then to look at the top of the path. Every child who lived on Hawkfell Island was up there, all of them huddled together, the older ones holding the younger ones, all of them staring down at their mothers.

Kerzog came bursting through the knot of children and tore down the path, barking and panting. He saw Mirana and Chessa standing close together, and skidded to a stop on the dock. He eyed one, then the other. In a burst of joy, he leapt on both of them. Chessa cried out as she felt herself flying backward off the dock to splash into the water, Mir-ana landing on top of her.

Old Alna cackled madly.

*   *   *

By the end of a week, the women began to fidget. The Hawkfell Island men spoke of the weather with galling confidence. Aye, a storm had slowed them, had even blown them off course. But why hadn't the storm hit the island? One more day passed with no sign of the warship. Mirana said after a very fine dinner of boar steaks broiled with cloudberries, "Something is wrong. I feel it."

Rorik said as he took his small daughter Aglida from her, "We will give them two more days. If they don't return within two days, then we will go to York and find out what has happened."

Everyone was profoundly thankful for his decision since Kiri had stopped eating that morning, had stopped playing and arguing with the other children. She looked like a pathetic little creature. It smote Chessa.

"It was always so when her father left Malverne," Laren said. "Oh, he would be gone a week hunting or trading, but never longer. When he became Duke Rollo's emissary, he would tell her nearly to the day when he would return. Several times he missed the day he'd promised her and when he got home to Malverne, she was a little skeleton, all pale and weak and listless. All of us were frantic. There was nothing any of us could do, and believe me, we tried everything.

"I remember once Cleve added extra days onto the time he planned to be away, but she somehow knew. He told her this time that he would be home by the eighth day. She has counted the days. If you look closely in the far corner of the longhouse, you will see a row of sticks. When she laid the eighth stick down and he didn't come, she lost her faith. No matter what I tell her, she's convinced he won't come back. I stole one of her sticks, but she knew and put it back.

"Perhaps you have wondered why he brought a small child with him. Surely it will be dangerous, the journey to Scotland, his return to his home. The other children were left behind. None of us would allow our children in such danger. But this is different. She would have died if he'd left her. Just look at her. Kiri and her father are very close. None of us knows what to do.''

''What else did Sarla do, Laren, besides try to murder Cleve?''

''She was forced to remain at Malverne until she birthed Kiri. Then Merrik agreed to send her back to her family's farm in the Bergen valley. Her father sent a dozen men to escort her home. She stole Kiri. When Cleve caught up to her, she screamed at the men that he was there to kill her, that he hated her and wanted both her and the babe dead, that they had to protect her. Whilst they argued, she ran away with the babe. Kiri nearly died. She would have if Cleve hadn't managed to rip her from Sarla's arms before she fell to her death. It was a horrible time for him. But Sarla was dead and we all hoped he would heal. He did, truly. He loves Kiri beyond reason. If something has gone wrong in York, then he must be frantic, knowing that she won't continue for very long without him.''

Chessa looked over at the little girl, who was sitting with her thin back against the longhouse wall. At least she was sitting next to Erna, who worked the loom. Erna with her withered left arm, who spoke to the little girl, laughed and jested with her, pretending not to notice that Kiri said nothing back to her, that she didn't react in any way. Gunleik, Erna's husband, tried mightily to interest the child. He whittled a knife for her of the finest oak. She just looked at it and gave him a smileless look. The women cajoled and pleaded. The men held her on their knees and told her stories. Kerzog tugged on the hem of her gown, trying to pull her toward the fire pit and food. Nothing worked.

Another day passed with no sign of Merrik's warship. All planned to leave the next day. Late that night, a storm hit. There was no question of leaving.

Kiri heard the storm and just stared down at the dirt floor. She picked up one of the sticks and began breaking it into small pieces.

The next night Chessa had had enough. She went into the children's bedchamber where ten of them were all packed together like the women's lines of dried fish. She plucked Kiri from among the sleeping children, watching with a grin as their small bodies quickly closed the gap. She carried the sleeping child to the outer longhouse and curled her against her, wrapping a blanket around the both of them.

Before morning, Chessa was aware of a very big, very warm body curved around her back. She froze, then felt a wet tongue swipe over her cheek. She sighed. It was Kerzog.

"Why are you here, Chessa?"

She opened her eyes. It was barely dawn, dim shadowy light breaking the night gloom in the longhouse. No one was yet stirring, but soon there would be enough activity so that no one would be able to continue asleep.

"I decided you're skinny enough. You've driven everyone frantic with worry over you. I won't allow it to continue anymore. I've decided you will now consider me your second father. Whenever your papa can't be with you, then I will be. When Utta has made the porridge, you will eat. Then you and I will go exploring. We will play and run and laugh, and I will teach you a song that's sung by all the farmers in Ireland. It's about a pig who saved his master's life and thus sleeps with the master and mistress of the farmstead. Then we will have lunch, a very big lunch, over on the eastern cliffs."

"You're not my papa. You're a girl."

"It doesn't matter. You may call me Papa if you wish."

The little girl tried to pull away from her, but Chessa held her firmly. She was so thin, even her beautiful golden hair was lank and dull. It scared Chessa to death. She couldn't begin to imagine what Cleve was thinking. She prayed he was still alive so he could think about his child.

"You're not my papa and I won't have you as one."

"Aye, you will. I will tell you something else, Kiri. If your papa doesn't arrive after the storm ends, then you and I are both going with the men to York. Since I'm your second papa, I will speak to Uncle Rorik. Since I'm your second papa, he will say yes, but only—''

''Only what?''

''Only if you do as I tell you.''

''Papa never orders me around.''

''Of course he does. You just don't notice it. Perhaps it's time you had a second papa to do all those things your first papa doesn't do.''

''Do I have to?''

''Aye. Now, lie here beside me again. I'll tell you a story about a little girl who had to grow up with a stepmother who was as nasty as she was beautiful. The stepmother's name was Sira and I was the little girl.''

''Papa's not soft like you are. You don't look like a papa, not even a second papa.''

''That's just because you're not yet used to the idea.''

12

WAVES SPLASHED AGAINST the sides of the warship. The night was black as Chessa's hair, Rorik told her, which was good because there was no one to alert the Danes. The air was heavy with rain, the clouds overhead dark and thick.

Hafter said, "There's not even a gull about to announce us. I pray the rain will hold off until we're done with this business."

Gunleik had steered the warship through the huge York harbor, ringed with its massive wooden palisade to keep out the enemy. Such was his skill that the guards hadn't seen Merrik's ship.

Everyone prayed the Malverne men had been taken alive. But as warriors, they knew in their bellies that it was unlikely. A warrior would fight until he was too weak to raise his sword. Then he would use his knife until he was too weak. Then he would curse until his tongue was dead in his mouth. None said it, but few believed their friends were still alive. And Merrik and Cleve? Rorik said nothing, merely went about his tasks, his head down, calm and still.

Gunleik steered the ship slowly out of the harbor, northward. There were at least three dozen trading ships and warships tied to the dock, their masts like ghosts in the night, tall, wrapped closely in their leather sails, many of them white, swaying slightly with the movement of the ships. They pulled the ship ashore a half mile above the harbor onto a narrow beach covered with driftwood and rocks. There were no lights, no small settlements. They would hug the beach as they made their way back to the town.

They covered the warship with thick-leafed branches from the oak and maple trees just inland from the beach. When it was hidden as best they could, Rorik said quietly, "Kiri, you will stay close to your second papa. I want to leave you here, but it's too dangerous. By the gods, everything is dangerous." He smote his forehead, but knew there was nothing he could do about it. Chessa was skilled with a knife and she carried two of them beneath her wool cloak in a leather belt around her waist.

The child allowed Chessa to take her hand.

Rorik fell into step beside Hafter. "We are Vikings and warriors and now we go to York to find our friends and we take a woman and a little girl with us."

Hafter just shrugged. "Sing not that song again, Rorik. It will gain you nothing more than it gained you the day we left Hawkfell, which was nothing. The child would be dead if she weren't with us."

"So Chessa said," Rorik said under his breath, wondering if this were indeed the case. Kiri had eaten enough on the three-day journey to York from Hawkfell Island. She'd also eaten before they'd left. "It is because she knows she will soon see Cleve," Chessa had said, meeting his look squarely. "If she were back on Hawkfell Island, she would soon be dead. At least with us she has a better chance to survive."

Rorik was impressed by a woman who could lie with such ease and efficiency. But still he couldn't be sure. There were twenty-two warriors, Chessa, and Kiri. All the men were armed with swords, knives, and axes. They held their shields at their sides and wore helmets on their heads. They all knew how to terrify when they appeared suddenly out of the blackness of the night or out of the fog, swords raised, screaming, their Viking helmets covering their faces.

But now they practiced stealth. Gunleik knew York. He'd spent ten years of his life guarding King Guntrum, brother to the current king, Olric. He knew where prisoners were kept and prayed things were as they had been so many years before. It was four hours before dawn. Plenty of time to find Merrik and all the Malverne men, plenty of time to escape. Plenty of time to see if they were dead and seek revenge.

They walked single file, some distance between each of them, so that if anyone saw them, they wouldn't be alarmed, at least not until Rorik or one of his men could silence them. They didn't enter the town, widely skirting the close-set streets with their malodorous alleys, dangerous with thieves. The king's palace stood on the high ground behind the harbor and town, the guards' barracks behind the palace as well as the prisoners' hut. Remaining unnoticed there would prove more difficult.

Gunleik told them where the guards would be and prayed that it was still true. They made their way around to the back of the high ground, scuttling from tree to tree for protection. They killed four guards, quietly and cleanly. At last they were running stealthily toward the low wooden barracks where the soldiers lived. At the end of the barracks was another wooden building, this one cruder, filth all around it. They prayed to Thor that their comrades were inside it, all of them alive. But they all wondered if such a prayer had a chance. None spoke of it aloud.

They saw no more than twenty guards, leaning against the gates that led to the palace, leaning against the walls of the barracks, none of them really paying attention, none of them patrolling, just standing there, perhaps even sleeping on their feet.

When they reached the barracks, still unseen, each of the Hawkfell men picked a guard. Within moments, the men were lying dead on the ground.

Gunleik waved for the men to follow him. There were half a dozen men lolling about outside the prisoner's barrack, speaking quietly. They were all awake.

One man had time to call out the alarm before Hafter cut his throat. They all froze to the spot, waiting for soldiers to pour from the barracks, but nothing happened.

Rorik gently shoved on the door. It was bolted. Sculla, whose arms were the size of a thick oak branch, split the old timber within moments with his axe.

"Now we need a light," Rorik said, and nodded to Aslak. Quickly, Aslak crept to the small fire pit and its still-glowing embers, and lit the wick that floated in the small jar of oil that lay nearby. A smoking trail of light went upward. Chessa stepped inside the barrack and wanted to yell with relief. All the men were there and were alive. Then she wanted to yell with fury.

All the men were chained to huge blocks of wood. All were ragged and filthy. The stench was nearly overpowering. All the Malverne men looked as if they'd been starved.

"Papa!"

Chessa slammed her hand over Kiri's mouth, quickly leaning down. "Be quiet, Kiri. This is dangerous. We want to save your first papa and not be caught ourselves. Don't make a single sound."

"But Papa—"

"I know," Chessa said, so furious she was choking on it. She lifted Kiri into her arms and ran toward Cleve. He was staring at her as if she really weren't there, as if she were a Viking ghost, and she thought she saw alarm in his eyes, but it was too dark in the long room to be certain.

All the men were whispering, so relieved to see their friends they seemed filled with renewed energy. Chessa fell to her knees beside Cleve, her knife already drawn, already sawing on the thick rope that bound him to the chain that was drawn through an iron ring in the huge chunk of wood.

"By all the gods," he said. "Kiri, is that you, sweeting?"

"Aye, Papa. I'm here to save you."

He laughed. Where that laugh came from, he didn't know. He wanted to hold Kiri but he was too filthy to touch her. He feared making her ill. He felt lightheaded. Maybe all this was a dream. He'd thought so much about Rorik coming. Aye, it was a dream to bedevil him. But why had Rorik brought Chessa and Kiri on so dangerous a mission? He shook his head and stared at his small daughter. No dream this. He knew, of course, at least about Kiri. If Rorik hadn't brought her, she'd be dead now. Poor Rorik, damned both ways, no matter what he did. "Hurry," he said to Chessa.

Then Gunleik was beside her on his knees, his own knife joining hers. In moments, Cleve was free.

"Can you stand?" Gunleik said.

Cleve eased himself up with his back against the wall. He felt damnably weak and he hated it that Chessa and his daughter were here to see it.

He immediately said in a furious whisper to his small daughter, "Were you starving yourself again?"

She just looked up at him solemnly, saying nothing. He frowned down at her. She didn't look hungry. There was so much he didn't understand.

Chessa handed him a skin of water. He drank deep. He drank until the skin was empty. Then she handed him a strip of dried beef. He didn't want to stuff it into his mouth, but he did. He'd never been so hungry in his life. Well, he had, but that had been years before when he'd been only a small boy and he hadn't brought his master his goblet of wine quickly enough. Stupid memory. He shook his head again and drank down another skin filled with cool water. She handed him more dried beef. It was the best food he'd ever had in his life.

Chessa looked about. The men were gulping down the water and the food. She knew that if they weren't strong enough to walk on their own, all of Rorik's men would carry them. She saw Merrik. Thank the gods he'd survived, else Rorik would tear York to the ground.

By the gods, in another week, they would have all been dead. She wanted to kill Ragnor. And Kerek. Even Captain Torric.

"Why are you growling, Papa? You sound very angry."

"I'm not growling. I'm swallowing this wonderful food."

"No, not you, Papa. My second papa. She's very angry."

Cleve had no idea what Kiri was talking about. Perhaps he was crazed, for the days and nights had flowed into each other, the hunger and thirst growing and growing until none of the men even wanted to speak. They were waiting for death. When Kerek brought them food and water in the dark of night, they thought he was merely torturing them, making their ultimate death drag out. But he'd come again and again. Not enough times, but he had kept them alive. But the men wouldn't trust him. They knew it was a game, Ragnor's twisted game, and they would die. They were convinced of it, all save Merrik. He just said again and again, "Rorik will come in time."

And Rorik had come and now they had a chance. But for the moment, the only important thing in the world was getting that beef chewed and into his belly.

Each warrior was responsible for one man. Slowly, they made their way from the prisoner barrack, bending low, ever watchful, silent as the night air. Cleve breathed in the clean night air. He whispered, "I never thought to be free again. We all gave up except Merrik. He never doubted Rorik would come. Thank you."

Gunleik grinned. "We're not away yet, Cleve. Hold your thanks until we're in the warship and leagues from this cursed Danelaw."

It happened so quickly the men were stunned. Two men came out of the darkness. One grabbed Chessa, the other grabbed Kiri, and held the little girl in front of him, his hands wrapped around her neck. He yelled, "Don't any of you breathe or I will twist her neck off."

By all the gods, Cleve thought, staring helplessly at his daughter. Someone knew they'd escaped. Mayhap someone had planned it. But why Kiri? Why Chessa? Where were the rest of the men, armed and ready to kill all of them?

When the man grabbed her, Chessa, just like the men, froze with surprise, but for only an instant. She grabbed one of the knives in her belt. She saw the other man had Kiri and knew she had to do something. She left the knife in its scabbard. She went limp.

"She fainted dead away," the man said, grunting as he brought her up against him.

"Wait, Erek, look at her closely. Kerek said she was smart. I don't think—"

Whatever he would have said was cut off by Erek's yell. Chessa shoved her fist into his throat. He dropped her, his hands going around his neck even as he fell to his knees. She had a knife out in a flash. She grabbed Erek by his dirty hair, yanked back, and set the blade of her knife across his throat. She said quietly, "Tell him to set the child down carefully or you're dead." She nicked his throat, just a bit, just enough so he could feel the wet of his blood.

"Drop the babe, Olaf. I have no wish to die."

"Aye, let her go," Cleve said, stepping forward. "Give me the child."

"Forgive me, Cleve, but I must keep her, at least for the moment." Kerek stepped out of the darkness.

The men looked ready to leap on him, but they were powerless. Merrik's men had been chained like slaves for over a week. And now they were helpless again. All were warriors and yet they could do nothing save stand there and watch. Slowly, stealthily, they began slowly moving into a circle.

"You," Rorik said. "Kerek, what is this?"

"By all the gods," Merrik said. "You brought us food and water. You kept us alive. Why, damn you? What is the meaning of this? You play one of Ragnor's perverted games?"

Kerek held up his hand. He turned to Chessa. "If you agree to come with me, Princess, Olaf will give Kiri back to her father. It's a simple trade."

"Papa."

"It's all right, sweeting. Don't move."

"I don't know how to make him let me down, Papa. He's strong."

"I know. Promise me you won't move." Cleve looked at Chessa. Her face was pale in the eerie predawn light but her hand was firm on that knife. The man Erek hadn't moved, had barely breathed. He'd heard Kerek speak with near reverent awe of Chessa, of her strength, her will, the future she would give to the Danelaw.

Cleve said to Kerek, "You wanted this to happen, that much is obvious. But you couldn't have known that Chessa would have brought Kiri. Explain yourself, Kerek."

"On our voyage back to York, Torric and I managed to plan what we would do. When you released him to fetch King Olric, he told the king of our plan to drug you and it worked. I kept you alive because, despite all that's happened, I consider you my friends. Ragnor forgets that you saved our lives, Rorik. I have never forgotten. However, I must have the Princess and now it will happen.

"The day you woke up from the drug, the king sent men to Hawkfell Island with a simple offer. All of you would be returned in exchange for the Princess."

"There was no messenger," Rorik said.

Kerek merely shrugged. "Both the captain and I gave them the best directions we could. It appears they didn't find the island."

"The storm," Rorik said slowly. "There was a terrible storm that lasted nearly four days. We couldn't leave until it was over. They were probably killed."

"Aye, I have thought as much, that or they were blown off course. I knew Rorik would come to rescue you, despite Ragnor, who would have killed all of you if his father hadn't stopped him. Well, not really the king, but never mind that now. Aye, Lord Rorik, I knew you'd come. I've had guards hidden waiting for you. You came. One of my men fetched me immediately. I couldn't believe my good fortune when I saw the Princess and the little girl. It was then I knew the gods blessed my endeavor. Aye, the gods approve what I'm doing for the Danelaw. They sent me the princess and the little girl.''

"You're mad, Kerek," Cleve said. "Chessa is just Chessa. She's a woman, nothing more. Forget this vision you have of her.''

Kerek smiled at him, even as he shook his head. "If you love her, Cleve, I'm sorry. She is destined for other things. Now, Princess, come to me now and Kiri goes to her father.''

Merrik laughed. "Chessa, don't move. Kerek won't kill Kiri. By the gods, this is an irony that cramps my belly. You won't win in this, Kerek.''

"I have won," Kerek said quietly. He saw Hafter take a step forward. He saw the circle tightening. "No, stop, all of you. Don't move, any of you. Not unless you want the little girl dead. I will kill her. I don't want to, but I will. It is the Princess's choice. Will you come to me, Princess? If you do, Olaf will let her go to her father.''

"If she dies then you are dead in the next moment, Kerek.''

"Aye, I know, Cleve. It doesn't matter. I just want the princess. I must have her.''

"Very well," Chessa said. Her knife was still firmly against Erek's throat. "I agree to the exchange.''

Cleve said, "Chessa, I cannot trade you for Kiri. I cannot.''

"I know," she said. "It's my decision.''

Kerek smiled at her, then said to Olaf, "Let the girl go to her father.''

"But she still holds the knife at Erek's neck.''

"She will drop the knife when the little girl is safe. Do as I tell you.''

Olaf looked baffled, but he released Kiri. She stood there a moment, staring from Cleve back to Chessa.

"Go, Kiri, go to your papa. I will be all right. Go.''

"But you told me just one papa wasn't enough. You said—''

"I know, sweeting, but things have changed. Your papa

will take good care of you. Go now.''

Cleve looked at Chessa even as Kiri bounded into his arms. He held her close, but his eyes never left Chessa's pale, set face. He watched her slowly lower the knife and step back from Erek. Then she handed the knife, handle forward, to Kerek.

"Thank you, Princess," Kerek said. He turned back to the group of men. "Merrik, Cleve, I am sorry that Ragnor got past me and came to torment you. But now you will escape and return to your farmsteads. All will be the same again. Your lives will be as they were once more. Cleve, you will simply inform Duke Rollo of the princess's marriage to the heir of the Danelaw. Merrik, you'll find the *Silver Raven* at the far dock. My men moved it from its hiding place when I knew Rorik had come. It is your warship despite what Ragnor claims. You will find food and clean clothes aplenty in the covered cargo space. However, there is no treasure. The king isn't that generous. I bid you good-bye.''

Kerek turned, motioned to his two men, and walked into the woods, Chessa at his side.

Cleve ignored the men's furious words. He took two steps toward the woods. "No, Cleve, not yet," Merrik said. "Not just yet."

"There must be a way to save her, there must."

"We will find it," Hafter said. "But Merrik is right. Not now. You must get back your strength, we must make plans for this. We will get her, Cleve."

Gunleik placed his big veined hand on Cleve's shoulder. "She did what she had to do. She is much like Mirana. She will take care of herself."

But Cleve wondered how. She tended to speak before she thought. She despised Ragnor and she wouldn't hesitate to tell him so. If the king didn't stop him, Ragnor would try to strangle her. He could just picture Chessa goading Ragnor into a black rage. He was very afraid. He felt immense guilt.

He also felt loss. He didn't like it. It was empty and cold, what he felt. Kerek had apologized to Cleve if he'd loved Chessa. That was ridiculous. He'd been a weak fool to believe Sarla, and look what it had gotten him. Well, he'd gotten Kiri, but still, no other woman would make him disbelieve what he knew to be true. He had a scarred ugly face and no possessions worth speaking of. What Chessa wanted of him, he had no idea. But she couldn't love him. He knew that as surely as he remembered Sarla's hatred spewing on him.

Cleve went down on his knees and looked at his daughter. "You didn't starve yourself this time."

"You didn't come home the day I laid down the eighth stick."

"As you know now, I couldn't. You mustn't consider me dead when I don't come back to you on the exact day."

She nodded. "That's what Papa said."

"I know, I just said it. We will speak about this further, but now we must get away from this place. Hafter, please carry her. I'm too filthy."

Cleve said whilst they walked along the beach, the water occasionally flowing over their feet, "I can't let Chessa remain here. She gave herself for Kiri. I must think of some way to get her back."

"Aye," Rorik said over his shoulder. "Cease picking at yourself, Cleve. We'll get her back."

"I'll kill that mangy little bastard," Merrik said, rubbing his hands together. "But I do want a bath first and enough food to fill up all the cracks in my belly."

Gunleik said, "I told you she is like Mirana. Strong. Aye, and she has guile, just as Mirana does."

"You used to curse that Mirana gave you your gray hair, Gunleik," Rorik said.

"Aye, she did. She'll give you gray hair as well."

Cleve listened to the men. The emptiness in him grew. He hated it.

That evening the men camped along a rock inlet some miles north along the coast. They were clean, well garbed again, and hadn't stopped eating.

To Cleve's astonishment, Kiri refused food. He himself cut up a piece of roasted pheasant. She just shook her head.

"What is this? I'm with you again. I'm safe. I'm here. Eat."

"Papa isn't here."

"What are you talking about, Kiri?"

Rorik moved to sit next to Kiri. He pulled her onto his lap. The fire was warm, the smell of the pheasant sweeter than a virgin's mouth, Hafter had said, smacking his lips.

"I don't understand this," Cleve said. "Kiri looks as well fed as a little stoat. Why did she begin to eat again when she started starving herself the eighth day?"

"The truth of the matter, Cleve," Rorik said, "is that Kiri now has two papas."

"What?"

"We couldn't get her to eat. She was becoming skinny as a pole, wouldn't talk, wouldn't do anything. You know her way. We tried everything."

"Aye," Gunleik said. "I even whittled a knife for her, but she wouldn't touch it."

"Finally Chessa said she'd had enough. She told Kiri that she would be her second papa when you weren't about. I don't know everything she told her, but the next morning, Kiri ate an entire bowl of Utta's porridge. Then the two of them went off together. Chessa carried a huge cloth filled with food. When they returned to the long-house that afternoon, Kiri was smiling. All the food was gone."

Rorik sighed then. "By the gods, I let Chessa convince me that Kiri would fade away into a ghost, thus I let the two of them come with us. Aye, she said over and over that Kiri would stop eating again if she didn't see her first papa very soon, that if they didn't come, Kiri would believe Chessa had lied to her, and starve herself again. I had no choice, Cleve. By Thor's axe, I'm sorry."

Cleve looked into the fire, looked at the hissing and spitting pheasant, two of them still on thin long sticks. One of the sticks was beginning to burn. He didn't want that pheasant to fall into the flames. He said nothing, merely leaned forward and pulled it off.

"Papa, what are you going to do?"

"Maybe Chessa will decide she wants to marry Ragnor."

His daughter gave him a disgusted look.

"I agree," he said, and pulled off a wing only to burn his fingers. He yowled.

Merrik took the pheasant and laid it reverently on a rock to cool. "I would have broken your jaw if you'd dropped it in the dirt," he said matter-of-factly.

Cleve said finally, "If I get her back, Kiri, will you promise me you'll eat right now? Some of that pheasant that your uncle is watching like a vulture?"

The little girl studied his face. She touched his golden beard. Finally, she stretched out two fingers and pulled off some meat. "Papa's meat tastes good too," she said when she'd swallowed.

"But I don't cook—"

"She's talking about her second papa."

Cleve looked over his daughter's head. Nothing was right. Nothing had been right the minute he'd met Chessa when she'd forced him to come into that garden at her father's palace. He turned back and said to Rorik, "Now she plans to starve herself if both Chessa and I aren't with her."

Kiri chewed on another piece of meat given to her by her uncle Rorik. "Two papas are good," she said, and licked her fingers.

"Aye, it means you'll get more attention and become as irritating as Ragnor," Cleve said, thinking that he probably should cuff her, but he kissed her instead. He said to Rorik, "Kerek will expect us to do something. We must have a plan that even he won't guess."

"Aye," Hafter said, sitting cross-legged beside Cleve. "He's clever. That's frightening in an enemy."

Cleve suddenly smiled, and it made him look dangerous and terrifying, that scar with the smile made him look like the Christian devil himself. "Kerek won't expect this," he said, and rubbed his hands together.

13

CHESSA SAT AT a long banquet table across from Ragnor. The chamber was long and narrow, benches around all the walls. Many people could dine in here. There were no windows. Dishes of oil with burning wicks floating in them sat at intervals on the oak planked table. Rush lights were fastened to the walls. Guards stood at the two entrances. The ceiling was low, the wooden beams black from years of smoke. There must have been a cooking fire in here at one time. The king's magnificent chair was still empty. Kerek sat next to her, Ragnor opposite her, smiling lazily like a lizard sunning himself.

"I didn't think Kerek could get you for me." Ragnor bit off a large chunk of bread and began chewing, his mouth still open. "Truth is, Chessa, I would rather have Utta."

"Utta is married, you fool," she said, and picked up her own piece of bread. She opened her mouth wide, stuffed it in, and began chewing just as Ragnor was.

"You will stop that," Ragnor said, throwing his bread down. "You revolt me. It makes you look ugly."

"What, don't you believe that when you do it, it makes you look just as ugly and revolting?"

"Princess," Kerek said. "Please, don't push him. He doesn't understand your humor."

"Shut your mouth, Kerek. You don't understand anything. Listen, Chessa, I'll beat you.'' He leaned over the table toward her. "I'll get a whip from the stables and I'll strip you to your white skin and I'll beat you. Then you won't make sport of me. Then you'll hold your shrew's tongue.''

"You stuck your sleeve in the stewed peas, Ragnor. It's dripping. You look ridiculous.''

"Princess. My lord. If you both please,'' Kerek said. "Here comes your father. I beg you to moderate your speech, both of you.''

As King Olric walked to the table, with two very young and very beautiful female servants who were mirror images of each other behind him whose function at the dining table Chessa couldn't guess, Kerek said, "I trust your chamber is sufficient, Princess?''

"No,'' she said. "It is too small, the box bed is too narrow, the pillow is too firm, the—''

"And your servant, Ingurd? She's stupid and insults you? I selected her myself,'' said Kerek.

He'd gotten her. "Your men brought cold bathwater. I am used to much more luxury, Kerek.'' She looked around, her eyes meeting the king's. "This palace isn't at all what I expected. It's dark and smells of old food. It hasn't the grace and wealth of my father's palace in Dublin.''

"You didn't expect anything,'' Ragnor shouted at her. "Damn you, Chessa, stop playing the spoiled bitch. It won't work, no one will believe you, at least they won't once they realize what a stubborn witch you are.''

"I am King Olric.''

She smiled at the old man, who was short, fat bellied, and hadn't a single tooth in his mouth. He looked petulant and vain. He looked as if his wits had begun wandering some years before.

"These are two of my concubines.'' They were each so fair that their hair looked nearly white. Their eyes were down. "They're twins, so alike even I can't tell who is who. I bought them from their father. They suit me well enough. And you are Princess Chessa, King Sitric's daughter. You are here now, just as Kerek promised. Well done, Kerek.''

"I wish you'd asked me, Father. I would have gotten her sooner than Kerek did.''

"Is that true, Ragnor? Perhaps later you can tell me how you planned to bring the princess here.''

She realized in that instant that he was dangerous, that he would lash out and grant no mercy, not just threaten, despite wandering wits. She said, "Your concubines are beautiful, sire.''

A male slave assisted the king into his chair. One of the concubines unfolded a beautiful linen cloth and spread it over the king's chest, to protect the gold chains about his neck, each of them inlaid with diamonds and rubies.

King Olric said to Kerek, "She is passable. Her hair is black, but with the ribbons threaded through the braids, it lessens the coarse effect. Her skin is a strange shade—a pale gold—unusual, but not ugly. She looks foreign. It is her eyes that are interesting. Stand up, Princess. I wish to see if you'll be a good breeder.''

She heard Kerek suck in his breath. She realized he was frightened of what she would do. She looked at Ragnor and watched him sit forward. Very slowly, a gentle submissive smile on her face, Chessa rose from her chair. She walked slowly to where the king sat, watching her. She lightly touched his sleeve. "Do you think I'll breed well, sire?''

He splayed his hands across her belly, stretching them to touch her pelvic bones. She didn't move. Her smile never lessened. Then she felt his hands go around to cup her buttocks. She didn't move even as he pulled her against him and his mouth was moving against her breasts. "Aye,'' the king said at last, snapping his fingers, "she'll be good sport in bed.''

"I thought you wanted to see if she'd breed well,'' Ragnor said, sprawled now in his chair, frowning at his father who was drinking from a goblet held to his mouth by one of his concubines. Chessa sat again. She felt revulsion, but she dared not show it. The father wasn't like the son.

She watched one of the concubines cut off a thick piece of roasted beef. She watched her chew it very thoroughly. She watched in utter surprise when the concubine then removed it from her mouth and gently laid it between the king's lips. Chessa wanted to gag, but she didn't. She just lowered her head and took another bite of bread, a rye bread that was delicious.

Kerek said very quietly, "You're wise, Princess. I didn't have time to tell you that the king's temper isn't as predictable and pleasant as his son's. But you guessed, didn't you?"

"What did you say to her, Kerek?"

"Nothing, my lord. I just asked her if I could have some of the sweet cabbage. I believe there are cloudberries in it. I like it much."

"You're a stupid man, Kerek. If it weren't for you we would never have been caught by that damned Rorik. If it weren't for you we wouldn't have been wrecked on his damned island. Both you and Captain Torric, that stupid slug, both of you are to blame."

The king raised a hand, each finger covered with silver and gold rings. To Chessa's surprise, Ragnor fell silent instantly. "The messengers returned today, Kerek. They didn't find this Hawkfell Island. They said there was a storm and it sent them into waters they didn't know. They said they were lucky to return to York. I would have killed them for their failure except that we do have the princess so it doesn't really matter. One of the men is very skilled, so his death would be a waste."

"I'd kill Captain Torric, Father. He was the one who gave the men the course to travel. Besides, he's lame now. What good is he?"

"Captain Torric and Kerek were the ones who planned how we would get the Vikings and then the princess. I have rewarded him."

"That's ridiculous. It was I who told Kerek that we should drug them, I who told Kerek that you should play a generous role and give them treasures as a reward. I didn't want them to fight and die. I wanted to torture them. I wanted to kill Cleve slowly, that or sell him for a slave. He was a slave once, did you know? Aye, it was my plan and Kerek and Torric have stolen it from me.''

The king said merely after a concubine had gently wiped his mouth with a piece of white linen, ''Don't lie, Ragnor. Remember that slave girl, Mora? The one you raped when you were thirteen years old? You brayed and bragged about your prowess, how you even pleasured her.'' The king paused a moment, then gave his son a gentle smile. It made Chessa shiver. ''I found out of course that it was the captain of your guard who'd taken the girl and you'd watched, then threatened the girl that you'd kill her if she ever told the truth.''

In that moment, Chessa knew exactly what Ragnor was thinking. He couldn't wait for his father to die. If he could get away with it, he'd kill Olric himself. He said, ''The girl lied to you.''

''It wasn't the girl who told me the truth. It was your mother. She is completely in my power, my prisoner, a submissive creature. I allow her to see everything, as you well know, and she tells me.''

Ragnor knifed a huge piece of sea bass into his mouth, the juices running down his chin. ''It was a long time ago. Mother probably forgot. However, Kerek let the Viking prisoners escape. He could have captured all of them, including Rorik and his Hawkfell Island men. He didn't. He failed. I would like to have this Hawkfell Island. Then I could have Utta.''

The king was swallowing from another gem-encrusted goblet held for him by his other concubine, evidently a different drink, for there were now three goblets set in front of him.

''She wanted me. Utta wanted me. She desired me. She gave me her precious mead to drink. Aye, Father, she would have come with me if it weren't for the men.''

Chessa said in a clear loud voice, ''Utta thought you were a fool and a dolt. She kept you drinking her mead so you would be too drunk to cause trouble. She failed, but she did try.''

There was complete silence at the table. The slaves and the concubines froze. A chewed bite of beef was held two inches from the king's mouth. He stared at Chessa.

Ragnor leapt to his feet, his face mottled with rage. He shook his fist at her, yelling, ''Damn you, Chessa. You're nothing now. You're in my power and you'll do as I tell you. I'll beat you if I wish. You will show me respect and obeisance.''

''I never did before. Why should I begin now? You deserve respect and obeisance as much as I deserve to be wedded to a pathetic worm like you.''

She heard Kerek draw in his breath. She knew she was playing a dangerous game, but her life was in the balance.

Ragnor jumped onto the table, hurling himself at her. It was so unexpected, the concubine screamed and her chewed bite of beef fell to the floor. Kerek hurled himself out of his chair, jerked Chessa back, and held himself in line for Ragnor's attack.

Ragnor thudded against him, his hands gouging into Kerek's throat. Kerek grabbed Ragnor's upper arms, but it wouldn't be enough. Ragnor had more leverage. Chessa grabbed her eating knife, a beautiful silver piece, and stabbed it into the back of Ragnor's hand. He screamed, fell away, and slid to the floor, his clothing smeared with cabbage, peas, and apples baked in honey. A platter of boar steaks tilted on the edge of the table and fell, splattering Ragnor's chin and chest with gravy and fat.

Ragnor was on his hands and knees, his hand fiery with pain, so humiliated he could scarcely think. He knew in that moment he would kill her. As soon as he rose, he would kill her.

Then, to his shock, he heard a hoarse sound. He looked up to see his father leaning back in his chair. His head was thrown back. He was laughing. He hadn't heard his father laugh for as long as he'd been old enough to know what a laugh was. Then his father was howling with laughter. His toothless mouth was gaping open, his hands were holding his fat belly. The concubines were fluttering about him, not knowing what to do. The guards came forward, but they just stared, their swords at their sides. Chessa didn't move, nor did Kerek, who just stared in astonishment at the king.

"What is this, Olric? You look ridiculous. Why are you laughing?"

"It's the queen," Kerek said, and quickly bowed to the lady who stood not three feet away from them, looking from her son to her husband. She was dressed in a gown more beautiful than any Sira owned, all embroidered with gold thread in intricate designs of birds and flowers against the soft white wool material. Her hair was braided atop her head, thick braids that were still blond, threaded with strands of white. Her face was thin and beautiful. Ragnor had the look of her. She didn't look at all submissive. She didn't look at all as if she were this fat old man's prisoner.

"Madam," Kerek said. "This is the princess of Ireland, here to marry Prince Ragnor."

Chessa straightened to her full height. She was just as tall as the queen, and she was grateful for that.

"At least you're no whimpering little fool," Turella said. "I am from the House of Tur, in the Bulgar. A mighty kingdom, one that makes the Danelaw look like the remains of a feast. You may kiss my hand."

Chessa lifted a beautiful white hand and kissed it.

The queen said, "Get up, Ragnor. Your father has stopped laughing and now you will stop mewling. Try to be a man. Get up and sit down."

"But she attacked me, Mother. Look at my hand, she stuck me with a knife. I will punish her. I will have my men hold her and I will whip her."

"You are a man. If you wish to whip her then you will do it by yourself." She said to Chessa, "He looks like me, thus I cannot claim that my own child was taken away from me at birth and he put in its place. Give me some wine, Kerek."

The queen then sat herself at the far end of the table.

The king hadn't said a word. His laughter had dried up slowly, like raisins in the sun.

"I heard that you were here now and wanted to have a look at you. Also, I am always about for meals, though I avoid one in this chamber. What did you do to make the king laugh? He's had no laughter in him for twenty years. I had hoped you would be through eating, but you aren't. I see that most of the food is on the floor." She snapped her fingers and Chessa noticed three men who were standing around her chair. She spoke to them and they nodded.

Her own guard? Chessa wondered. She said aloud, "Why didn't you dine with us, madam?"

The queen laughed, a soft musical laugh that was really quite nice. "I haven't eaten at the same table with the king since he lost all his teeth. You see, I refused to chew his food for him."

"Oh," Chessa said. "I think I would have refused also."

"I have been told that your father was once an old man like Olric here. All the skalds sing of his transformation brought about by a sorcerer named Hormuze. What do you know of this? You are the Hormuze's child, are you not?"

"Yes, madam. You see I'm not really a princess at all. The king in his gratitude took me in and treated me like a daughter. My own father Hormuze disappeared, fading like shadows into his own wizardry, into a realm that none of us would understand."

"This is nonsense," the queen said. "Olric, you know she's not a real princess. Why is she here?"

"I wish I had allowed both Ragnor and Kerek to hear me tell all the people at Hawkfell Island that I'm no princess. I have no royal blood. Hear me, Ragnor? Kerek? I am nothing but a simple woman. Release me now."

"She is a princess in the eyes of the world, madam," Kerek said. "Didn't you know that Duke Rollo wants her for his son, William Longsword?"

"He wouldn't want me now, Kerek."

"You're wrong, Princess. You are still the king of Ireland's daughter, regardless of your true kinship to him."

"That is something to think about," the queen said, and drank deeply from a goblet of wine one of the three men placed in front of her. "You didn't poison this wine, did you?" she said to the king, who was contentedly eating a bowl filled with smashed honeyed pears.

"No, it isn't poisoned, not unless someone else did it. I didn't expect you, so the wine is safe. She'll be a good breeder," the king said, looking over at Chessa.

"He felt her, Mother, he rubbed his hands on her belly and on her hips. He pressed his mouth against her breasts. She's to marry me, not him. She let him do it. If I'd demanded to do it she would have killed me."

"Aye, Ragnor, hold your tongue now."

The king pointed to a boar steak that teetered just over the edge of the platter on the floor. "I want it," he said to a concubine, who immediately picked it off the platter, cut it, and popped it into her mouth. Chessa looked away before she could lay the chewed up mess on the king's tongue. So did the queen.

The queen said as she rose, "Have your hand bandaged, Ragnor. There is blood on the turnips. It is fortunate that I don't like turnips. Princess, I will see you in the morning. You won't try to leave the palace."

She swept from the chamber, the three guards at her heels. The king grunted, then smacked his lips. "Another bite of the roasted boar," he said to the concubine.

Kerek said, "Princess, I will see you to your chamber."

The king called after them, "You will come to me before you see the queen. Forget not that I am the king. I rule. Ragnor, see to your hand."

Chessa drew a deep breath once they'd left the dining chamber. "This is all very strange, Kerek."

"Aye," he said. "You see now how badly you're needed. The Saxon kings will overrun the Danelaw if Ragnor comes to the throne."

"I hope the Saxons may serve Ragnor's head up on a platter, just like those boar steaks."

Kerek looked pained, but he said nothing more. He bid

her good night at the door of her chamber, then spoke quietly to the two guards who were outside.

Chessa settled in the box bed, pulled a soft fox fur to her chin, and prepared to think. "Ingurd? Are you still here? You may leave me now."

The young girl was standing there twisting her hands together. "But Kerek said I wasn't to leave you. He said I was to be reverent but I was to stay as close as a shadow. He even said that I—"

"Very well, where will you sleep? No, not on the floor. Have a guard bring you a pallet."

Ingurd's mouth gaped. A pallet, something soft between her and the floor. She couldn't begin to imagine such a thing. But her new mistress was a princess, after all. She supposed that anyone so blessed by the gods could give orders as they pleased. When she eased down on the pallet, the first soft bed she'd known in her short life, she decided the princess wasn't a bitch as she'd heard Prince Ragnor screaming at Kerek.

Chessa moved just a bit, feeling the other knife she'd wrapped into a bathing cloth and tucked beneath her pillow. On the morrow, she would somehow fasten it to her leg.

She pictured Cleve in her mind, his clothes ragged and filthy, his golden hair matted to his head, a scraggly golden beard covering his lean cheeks. He'd smelled very bad. She'd believed him more beautiful than the last time she'd seen him on Hawkfell Island.

She'd decided on the voyage to York that if she found him alive, she would do whatever she must to make him her husband. She decided he shouldn't have to live his life without her. He simply didn't realize yet just how lucky he was.

Now she was the one held captive. She had to stop thinking about Cleve and how she would make him happier than he probably deserved. She had to come up with a plan.

She fell asleep with Cleve's face in her mind. At least Kiri would be all right now. She was with her first papa.

14

THERE WERE THREE guards standing in front of the queen's chamber. Chessa nodded to them, then waited for one of them to open the door. Once she was well inside, the door was again closed.

The queen had sent for her. Chessa had wanted to come, for the queen's behavior the previous night had fascinated her, but now that she was here, as commanded, there wasn't anyone in the large bright chamber. She'd never before seen a chamber so clean, the walls whitewashed so utterly white. There were no smudges, no hints of any dirt at all. There was a small box bed, one chair, a brazier, and a huge trunk sitting at the end of the bed. Nothing else. There were three windows and a narrow door at the back of the chamber. Chessa walked to the door and opened it. It gave onto a small garden closed in by high walls. It was immaculately kept. There were flowers in bloom everywhere. She recognized daffodils and daisies, foxglove, and hyacinth. The water lilies by the small pond in the center of the garden were the most exquisite Chessa had ever seen, white as snowfall in the wilderness, the leaves and pads so green they looked painted. The high stone walls were weathered a soft gray and covered with ivy, pear vines and wild strawberries.

It was a beautiful place. A serene place. A retreat, a

sanctuary. Chessa breathed in a deep breath of the warm morning air.

"You slept well?"

She turned to see the queen, now rising, holding a brilliant red rose.

"Nay, how could I? I don't want to be here. I want to go home."

"You wish to return to Dublin?"

She shook her head. "My home is with a man named Cleve. Wherever he is, that's where I want to be."

The queen narrowed her eyes against the sun, then motioned Chessa to follow her. In the corner of the garden was a stone bench. Above it was an old pear tree, big limbed and thick.

The queen held a rose toward her. "Smell the rose. Isn't it magnificent?"

She drew in the scent deeply. "It smells like sweet velvet. I have never seen such a color. More red than mere red. No, it's not a simple red at all."

The queen smiled. "I produced it myself. Ah, you don't understand. That's all right, none really do, including myself. I try and try and sometimes I succeed. I partially split the seeds of one rose and force it together with the seeds of another color rose or even another variety entirely. This was the result of one of my endeavors."

"That's remarkable. I've never heard of such a thing."

"As I said, few have. Now you're looking at me as if I have two heads."

"I was wondering where the woman was I met last night. You certainly aren't she."

"Ah, but I am, Princess. I am many women. I have to be to survive."

"Please just call me Chessa. I'm no princess. I wish your husband would realize that and let me go."

"Chessa, then. He won't let you go. The woman you met last night, did you believe her to be what you saw?"

Chessa nodded slowly.

"That's good. Sometimes I forget and the king looks at

me suspiciously. I see you don't understand any of this. Kerek told you nothing?''

''Nothing. Last night you acted like the king was half-witted, that Ragnor was a fool, which he is, and that you deigned not to deal with them. I thought you were half-witted as well. You acted as oddly as the king and Ragnor.''

The queen patted her hand. ''Actually, Kerek convinced me that you are the salvation of the Danelaw. I wondered how that was possible. You are just a young girl, after all. Then I saw you last night. At first I thought you stupid in your silly bravery. You took chances that I would never dream of taking, all to see what would happen, all to test the people who were holding you. And you saved Kerek, a man you should want to kill. He has done you in twice, yet you stuck your knife in Ragnor's hand to get him off Kerek. I heard that you let the king touch you. You didn't flinch or shudder and he is a repellent old toad. You again wanted to judge the way he thought, the way he would behave. You were wise. You saw that the king is the one who is dangerous, or he can be, just less and less now that he grows older. He forgets his grievances more and more now. It is a relief. Ragnor is just a sulky little boy. It's strange, but even Ragnor sometimes shows flashes of brilliance, of charm and intelligence.''

''You saw what you wanted to see in me, my lady. I am just that young girl, after all, no more, no less. I love another man. I don't want to be here. I won't marry Ragnor. I've seen these flashes in him but they never last very long.''

The queen merely smiled at her.

''My lady,'' Chessa said slowly, ''who is the true ruler of the Danelaw?''

''You met him last night. A toothless, foul-breathed, utterly ruthless old man.''

''Why are there guards at your chamber door? Why are these walls so high? I have been looking for a gate but I haven't seen one.''

"I'm a prisoner."

Chessa could only stare at her.

"It's true that I'm from the House of Tur in the Bulgar. When my father sold me to King Guntrum, who wanted me for his brother, Olric, I fought him with all my will, all my strength, but it did no good. When Olric saw that I hated him, that I would never be submissive, he was infuriated. He raped me repeatedly. After I gave birth to Ragnor, he imprisoned me and thus it has remained. My babe was taken from me and for twenty-one years now I've been a prisoner in this chamber and this garden. It was a latrine then and smelled foul. I changed it. I had all the time it required. Over time, I was allowed more and more freedom, but still the guards follow me everywhere."

"But you swept into the dining chamber like the queen you are. You insulted the king, your son, and you took charge. I don't understand. Actually, you acted quite mad."

Turella laughed softly. "I told you, Chessa, that Olric is easily led by anyone stronger than he. I am stronger. It is one of the concessions I have gained. At mealtimes I am free to go where I wish, my guards trailing me always, as I said. I ceased eating my evening meal with him when he lost all his teeth and demanded that I chew his food for him. That was all the truth.

"Inside my high stone walls, I function in this court as best I can. Kerek is my eyes and ears. He is in everyone's confidence. The king himself depends on him utterly. Kerek told me that you and I were alike, that you would control Ragnor with ease. After all, I am a prisoner, my chamber is locked, and there are always guards there."

Chessa looked about the garden. The sun was bright and the air was sweet, becoming sweeter by the minute as the sun soaked into the blooms. There were two bees dipping into a purple hydrangea. She saw the truth clearly and marveled at the fluency of the woman seated next to her. She looked at Turella and said, "You're lying to me. Those guards are there to give you warning if someone comes. Those guards are there to hold off people you don't wish

to see. Those guards are there to protect you from the king.
Those guards would die for you. You rule here, not that
profane old man.''

"By all the gods,'' Turella said. She laughed, a soft deep
laugh, then louder, dropping the beautiful rose on the moss-
covered ground. "Kerek was indeed right.''

"No, no, I take it all back. I was wrong. You're indeed
a prisoner and you have no thoughts about anything except
your wretched flowers.''

The queen laughed louder. "By Freya's power, you're
good, but not good enough, my girl. You can't correct your
mistake so easily. You're quite right, I do rule the Danelaw,
but I rule by stealth and guile. It is difficult and many things
slip by me. When the king is dead, you will have an easier
time of it. Ragnor needs flattery and more flattery but then
he is content. You will do it well. I will help you. Kerek
will help you. You must sleep with him to beget a child,
but then you can provide him with concubines as I've done
the king. Weren't the two young girls last night quite
lovely? They're mute, born that way, thank the gods, and
they seem quite happy to do anything the old man wants.
They both desire beautiful gowns. I make certain their
clothing is envied by all the ladies of the court. Aye, even
their loyalty is to me.

"Ah, here is Kerek. She knows now, my friend.''

"Princess,'' Kerek said. "I couldn't tell you before,
surely you realize that. I would never place her in such
danger.''

"It makes no difference. I won't wed Ragnor. You, my
lady, once the king dies, you will rule through your son.
Pick him a wife who will flatter him and let him breed a
boy child off her. I won't do it.''

"I cannot live forever. I must train someone to take my
place. The Danelaw mustn't fall to the Saxons and it surely
will if nothing is done.''

"As far as I'm concerned, my lady, the Danelaw can rot.
If you cannot control your own land, then you deserve to
lose the rule.''

"If I have to force you," Turella said calmly, smelling that incredible red rose, "I will."

Chessa just smiled. "And what will you do with my first child?"

"I will rejoice, as will all the people."

"Ah, but the first child won't be Ragnor's."

Kerek gave a start and then began shaking his head back and forth. "You've done this before, Princess. It won't work twice."

"I am pregnant with Cleve's child. Do you doubt that, Kerek?"

"I don't believe you. He kept you at a distance. He kept yelling at you to begin your monthly flow so you could wed William of Normandy."

"But you knew I didn't want to marry Ragnor or William. You knew, Kerek, that I wanted only Cleve, thus my lie about carrying Ragnor's child. All believed it. I was safe, at least for a while, but Cleve held firm, you're right about that. I became desperate. I came to him at night and he came awake only enough to feel a man's passion. When he reached his climax he awoke fully and saw it was me. He cursed, then took me again and many times after that because the damage was already done. You said to him yourself that you were sorry since he loved me."

Kerek looked as if he'd cry at any moment. He smote his forehead with the heel of his hand. "I am cursed," he said low, and began rocking back and forth on the stone bench. "From the moment I first saw you fishing in the Liffey, I've been cursed. You spin tales and then you make them come true. By all the gods, I don't deserve this. You revile me, then you protect me. It is too much for a mortal man to bear. Tell me you're lying, Princess. Tell me this most recent pregnancy story of yours isn't true."

"Aye, it's quite true. Send me back to Cleve. Leave us in peace. My lady, as I said, you can rule openly when the king dies. Kill him. Or would you like me to poison him for you?"

"He has tasters," the queen said absently. "It wouldn't

work. I tried it once a while ago. The taster died. The king doubled his tasters. Also the concubines taste everything before it goes into his toothless mouth." She paused, staring at Chessa. "If Kerek believes you then I must. Very well, I will rid you of the babe. Kerek, take her inside and I will do it now."

Chessa said very quietly, "If you touch me, lady, I will kill you. Doubt me not."

"Mayhap the child will be a girl, my lady," Kerek said, looking as dejected as a dog who'd just released his bowels in front of his master's guests. "Then no one will care."

The queen sighed. She leaned over to pick another rose, this one a soft pink. She inhaled deeply. "My flowers always agree with me. They give me difficulties, but I can measure their moods and do the right things. But with this girl? I don't know, Kerek. Perhaps we should send her to the Saxon court and let her wed one of Alfred's grandsons. Let her create havoc there. Let her poison all of them."

But she'd done nothing, Chessa thought. She'd only realized the truth about the queen, then she'd been stupid and told her what she realized. Then she'd lied. She'd not done well so far this morning. At least the queen was thinking about her differently now. Just perhaps they'd send her back.

"Actually, my lady, I came to tell you that the king has remembered the princess."

"Someone must have reminded him," Turella said. "That, or the old fool remembers touching her and wants to do it again. Aye, my girl, let's see how you deal with it now when you're alone with him and there's no one to pull him back."

"I'll stay with her. He won't do those things again."

The queen looked at her. "Don't kill him openly, else I couldn't save you."

"I won't. But Ragnor is another matter."

"He has always been another matter," Turella said, and rose from the stone bench. "His father took him away from me when he was born, I told you that, and it quite ruined him. Now, Kerek, take her to the king and stay even if the king orders you to leave. I can't trust her to tell me the truth.''

Kerek said to her as they walked down the narrow passage to the king's chamber, ''Please, Princess, you must begin your monthly flow.''

She just laughed. ''Oh no, Kerek, I very much want Cleve's babe. It will be a boy, I know it. My stepmother has four sons. She always said that boy babes made her puke up her guts. I've not been feeling very well.''

Kerek stopped in the hallway and stared down at her. ''Perhaps Turella is right. Perhaps we should send you to the Saxon court.''

She just laughed. ''All you have to do is send me back to Hawkfell Island.''

Kerek just sighed. ''There is so much to think about. I cannot allow you to ruin my plans. They're good plans. They encompass the future. They cover all possibilities save your character, Princess. It's your character that brings chaos to my plans.''

''Good,'' Chessa said.

Hawkfell Island

Cleve kissed his daughter's nose, gave her another bite of roasted sea bass, one of Entti's specialties, and said, ''Just keep eating. I'm leaving tomorrow for the Danelaw, and no, you're not coming with me. If you stop eating this time, you just might starve to death and both your first papa and your second papa will be forced to stretch out on each side of your skinny little dead body and die themselves. Do you want that?''

''No, Papa.''

''Good. Then eat and keep eating. Keep talking to your aunts and uncles so they won't worry. Keep playing. Keep learning how to weave from Erna. She's very good and kind. If Gunleik whittles you another knife, take it and thank him sincerely. I'll return when I can. I don't know the number of days. Can you just believe that I'll return with Chessa?''

"It's hard, Papa. You won't leave her in the Danelaw, will you? Even if she makes you very angry?''

"Nay, I promise to bring her home, then I'll spew curses at her head.''

Kiri chewed the sea bass, licked the oil from the tartar leaves, and smiled. She nodded.

"Now, here's your aunt Mirana and aunt Laren. Promise me again in front of them.''

"I promise,'' Kiri said, giving each of her aunts a small smile, "to eat and not to be dead when papa returns with my second papa. But I still would like some sticks to count, Papa.''

He tossed her into the air as he groaned. "No sticks. Eat, sweeting.''

York, capital of the Danelaw
the king's palace
One week later

Chessa chewed on an apple. It was more sour than not, and crisp, just as she liked it. Ragnor was sitting in a chair, trying desperately to play the small harp with emotion. He was singing a romantic poem the court skald, Baric, had taught him. It rhymed but Ragnor couldn't seem to make the rhyme fit the music.

Chessa picked up another apple and took a bite. She'd eaten nothing today since she'd been forced to be in the king's presence at both meals. He both frightened and repelled her, a combination that took away her appetite. He'd told her that he'd bed her if Ragnor didn't please her and make her scream with pleasure. Then, he said, if she pleased him sufficiently, he would allow her to chew his food for him.

She shuddered now thinking about it. Finally, Ragnor

looked up at her, his expression both pained and defiant. "Did you like it?"

"Oh, yes. I love music. Your display of ardor moved me, Ragnor. I've asked Baric to teach me lullabies to sing to Cleve's babe when he's born."

Ragnor raised the harp at her, cursed, then threw it to the floor and stomped on it. Each stomp made her smile. "Damn you," he yelled, "you will be quiet. You will not have his babe, Chessa, I forbid it. That damned Cleve. I should have killed him. I should have known that he would seduce you, the damned bastard, just to thwart me. He lied about marrying you to William of Normandy. He just wanted to have you for himself."

"He was relieved that I wasn't pregnant with your babe," she said, and took another bite of her apple. "He was pleased that I was a virgin. He lost his head when he discovered that he was the first. Then he just couldn't stop. The act was quite nice, at least with him."

"My father isn't pleased. You shouldn't have just spat it out at him the way you did and all because he said he'd like to bed you and make you scream. He would have forgotten. He even forgets he's angry at me now. But you had to anger him, didn't you? He was so furious he forgot to have the concubine that stands on his left hand taste every bite he wanted. He could have died from poison."

"Perhaps," Chessa said, "I could bribe the concubine who stands at his left hand."

"Stop that, you evil witch. You try to anger me now. You do it apurpose. My mother warned me that it was your way. She told me not to let you arouse my ire, that you never meant what you said, it was all a ploy. My mother is very smart, but you make it difficult to do as she directs."

"I agree," Chessa said. "She is very smart."

"Ah, here's Baric, here to ask you how you liked my singing and playing. You will tell him that you felt it in your soul, if you have one, or I'll beat you."

Baric was very short and thin. He had a lush dark brown beard that grew nearly to his waist. But he was completely

bald. But he was kind and had merry, intelligent eyes.
Chessa liked him and guessed he enjoyed watching Ragnor
gnash his teeth. At his side was a woman, a very tall
woman, whose head was bowed. She was carrying Baric's
prized harp. She wore white mittens on her hands and her
hair was covered with the hood of her tunic.

Ragnor eyed her as he did every female. "Who is this,
Baric? She's twice your size. Do you like to climb her as
a man would a mountain?"

"Aye, my lord. Her size gives me great pleasure as well
as protection. She's a hardy wench and strong. Her name
is Isla and she comes from Iceland. I sang to her in the
market and she swooned. Now she is mine and gives me
all her loyalty. Such, my lord, is the power of music."

Ragnor cursed.

"Have you given the princess pleasure, my lord, with
your sweet verses?"

"I always gain pleasure in Ragnor's company," Chessa
said, and chewed on her thumbnail. "Who could not?"

"I did mean with his music, Princess."

"Ah, that is another matter. He sought such perfection,
Baric, that when he didn't achieve it, he stomped the harp
into the ground."

Baric looked at the destroyed harp and blinked back
tears. But he did manage to keep his mouth shut. He mum-
bled something and picked at his huge beard.

The woman raised her face. She was beautiful. She was
also painted like a harlot. Her brows were black with kohl,
her one eye lined so heavily with it that it was difficult to
gauge her expression. Ah, and the other eye was covered
with a patch of white linen. The uncovered one was blue.
Her lips were vermilion and looked wet. Her cheeks were
dead white, painted thickly from ground cornstarch and
panza root, mixed into a paste. Chessa blinked at her. Her
face must weigh as much as the armlets Ragnor was wearing, heavy silver, coiled in the shape of snakes.

Ragnor blinked as well, only his blink was assessing and
excited. "Isla," he said, leering at her. Chessa had seen

him once practicing that look when he saw his reflection in a metal shield one of the soldiers was holding.

The woman breathed his name, "My lord Ragnor. I've waited long to see you. Baric tells me you play brilliantly. I wish to hear you sing. Ah, but your poor harp. Did the bitch break it? And you're so noble, you protect her?"

The bitch. Chessa eyed the woman more closely. This was interesting.

"Isla," Baric said, shaking her arm. "This is a princess, not a bitch."

"She is what she is," Isla said. "It was another miserable princess who wounded my poor right eye and thus I have to wear this patch. It makes me look interesting and mysterious, but still I would like the use of both my eyes. This princess is a bitch. I know it."

The bitch. Ragnor nearly burst with pleasure. This Isla was smart and big and he liked big women, at least he did now that he'd seen her and heard her insult Chessa. He also liked that patch over her right eye. He wondered what the eye looked like without the patch.

"What were you doing in the market when Baric came upon you?" Chessa said.

The woman shrugged, not looking at Chessa, her one good eye still trained on Ragnor. "I make the finest mead in all of York. I was selling it in the market when Baric came to have a cup to rest his throat. He drank it and swooned. He begged me to stay with him. I like a man with a lot of hair, particularly a thick beard and handfuls of it on his back. That his head is naked bothers me not at all."

"Thus," Baric said, running his long slender fingers through his beard, "I sing to her and she makes me mead and threads her fingers through the hair on my back."

"Mead," Ragnor said, his eyes lighting with hope. "Does she really make it well?"

"She is an angel," Baric said. "Now, my lord, I have come to teach you another love poem."

Ragnor said, "I haven't any hair on my back. Will that make her dislike me?"

"Nay, my lord. Once you sing for her, she will love you for yourself."

Chessa thought she'd gag. She said in a loud voice, "The babe is making me ill. I think I shall go vomit."

Ragnor was looking at Isla with the hunger of a starving man. He said to Baric, "Aye, teach me a love poem and I will recite it to Isla. For practice."

"Your sweet voice will tire, my lord," Isla said. "Allow me to bring you some of my special mead to soothe you whilst you sing to me. For practice."

Chessa walked quickly from the chamber, ran up against a guard who awaited her just outside. He grabbed her arms to keep her upright.

Suddenly, she heard Ragnor yell from the inside of the chamber, "Begin your monthly flow, Chessa, damn you."

She heard Isla laugh. "Her monthly flow, my lord? What is this?"

15

THE CHAMBER WAS dark. Chessa was alone. She was more worried than frightened. She knew she wouldn't marry Ragnor and there was no way the queen would force her to. But she didn't want to wait until the last minute to see what the queen would try. She knew she had to think of something. She sparred daily with Turella, insulted Ragnor until his eyes were crossed, and tried to avoid the king. Olric no longer terrified her, but he was unpredictable and he could lash out before Turella could control him. Kerek was an immovable rock, always there standing in her path, but she didn't fear him at all. What was she to do now?

Just two hours before, at the evening meal, at least two dozen of the king's nobles dined with them. Baric played his harp and sang, his woman Isla beside him. Slaves served heaped platters of roasted boar, broiled pheasant, and at least four different kinds of fish. There was more sweet wine and ale than Chessa had ever seen, and most of it was being steadily poured down all the gullets present. Men and women alike ate like stoats and drank until they were laughing at nothing at all, giving insults without anger, cheering Baric even when he wasn't singing. The woman Isla was given leers and drunken suggestions from most of the men until surely even she must be horrified. But she hadn't looked it. She just sat there, a besotted look on her face, as she stared at Baric.

After the slaves had cleared away the food, the king looked at all of their drink-flushed faces and said, "You have met Princess Chessa of Ireland. She will wed with Ragnor in three days. She is already carrying his babe, so an heir is assured."

Chessa had nearly fainted.

Ragnor had nearly fainted as well. She heard him say to Kerek, "Damn you, it's all your fault. I didn't want her, I wanted Utta. But now I want Isla. Her mead is as tasty as Utta's—she let me drink out of her own goatskin—and she wants me. Did you see how she smiled at me? How she spoke to me? Baric even commented on it. She doesn't care that I don't have hair on my back, that I haven't a lush long beard. I hate it that all the men here want her as well. Many of them are as hairy as Baric. Chessa won't make me mead. She won't even drink mead with me. She won't even try to make me happy."

The king didn't care that she was pregnant with another man's child. Surely Turella hadn't lied and told the king that it was Ragnor's child she was carrying. Surely she couldn't have done that. On the other hand the king had sounded so certain, so pleased when he'd announced that she was carrying Ragnor's babe. It made her dizzy to try to figure out and keep straight in her own mind everyone and his own set notions. She had to think of something. And she did. She could think of nothing else. She rose slowly, aware that Kerek was nearly choking with fear, pulling at her gown, saying over and over, "No, Princess, keep your mouth shut this time. Please, it isn't wise to go against the king in front of his nobles. Listen to me, sit down, and smile. Drink mead with Ragnor, it will please him."

She sat down, lowering her head as the nobles began cheering, then yelling lewd advice to Ragnor, who looked quite pleased with himself, despite what he'd just said about not wanting her.

"This isn't the end of it, Kerek," she said quietly. "I won't wed that ass."

"As you will, Princess," and she knew he didn't begin to believe her. He was just humoring her. He had ultimate faith in Turella. Truth be told, so did she.

"Did you and Turella lie to the king about the babe or doesn't he care that I carry another man's child?"

Kerek, curse him, just shrugged.

What was she going to do? Whatever it was, she must move quickly. Three days. She found herself wondering if any prince or any king would care if she'd been impregnated by a goat.

She pushed herself more deeply into the woolen blankets. Suddenly she heard a sound. Was it Ingurd to see if she wished anything more? She didn't move when she heard the door quietly open. Was it one of the guards? Surely the queen hadn't dismissed them. Was the queen ready to force her hand? It was too soon for Turella to act, surely.

There was a sliver of light, then it quickly disappeared as the door closed again. She pulled the knife from its wrapping beneath her pillow. She rather hoped it was Ragnor, here to rape her. Just let the little worm try.

She held the knife easily. Her fingers were steady and dry. She was ready.

"Did you begin your monthly flow?"

The words were softly spoken, mocking, and she knew it was the woman Isla.

"No, and I don't intend to either, not that it makes any difference to anybody. I'll just wager that even William of Normandy wouldn't care either. I thought men wanted purity in their brides. It makes no sense."

"Men are strange creatures," Isla agreed and sat beside her on the edge of the box bed. "I wish I could see you, but I won't light the lamp, it's too dangerous. The guards outside are dozing, but not fully asleep yet."

"What do you want?"

"First I want to know if it's true. Are you pregnant with another man's child?"

"Is that what Ragnor bleated to you and Baric after I left you?"

"Aye. He is furious. He said you tried this trick before and thus he didn't want to believe you this time. He said though that Kerek was certain and thus it had to be true. Who is the man this time?"

Chessa sighed. Certainly this was strange to be speaking in her dark chamber to a woman she'd met only today, a woman who called her a bitch, a woman who was obviously teasing Ragnor, for what reason she couldn't imagine. "His name is Cleve. He is a beautiful man, a brave warrior, the only man I want to have for the rest of my life. He's sometimes very difficult, but there is a richness deep inside him. He doesn't yet realize he needs me, but he will. He believed he loved before and the woman betrayed him. I would never betray him and he will come to believe me. He believes himself ugly, hideous even, but he's blind to himself. I will make him laugh until I die. I don't know where he is now, but I pray he's safe."

"He bedded you?"

"No, but I told everyone it was he."

"Your reasoning is pathetic. Listen, you little fool, who do you think I am?"

"You're a painted harlot Baric found in the market. I hope you will seduce Ragnor so he'll keep away from me, although I can't imagine why you'd want to. He's even begun trying to woo me now, doubtless on orders from his mother. Perhaps even orders from his father as well. I never know what Olric will do. When you and Baric came in today, he'd just sung me a romantic song and was demanding praise. He is such a worm."

"Why wouldn't you want to be the future queen of the Danelaw? You're a princess, after all, despite the fact you're really not, but it doesn't matter. I paint my face and make mead, but you, Princess, you can do anything you please, have any man, any prince you wish. Why are you so stubborn about this Cleve?"

"I love him. Perhaps someday he will come to believe

it. But that can't be important to you, Isla. What I please is to leave this place. The king is a strange man, his moods dance about, the queen has been a prisoner for twenty-one years but she isn't a prisoner at all, she rules here, and poor Ragnor is a pawn between the two of them. Now the king thinks I can be forced to marry Ragnor. Actually, he knows that the queen will see to it. All he has to do is belch and drink and fondle his concubines, who are thankfully mute, else they'd be screaming when he touched them. I don't suppose you would lend me your paint pot so I can look like a harlot and leave here?''

Isla laughed. "Perhaps if you paid me enough silver I would try to help you, but you haven't even a valuable armlet, do you? No, I didn't think so. Tell me about Kerek. What is his position here?''

"He worships the queen. He would do anything she asked of him. The king trusts him as well. That's why I'm here. Kerek got this idea that I, a simple woman, was the one to save the Danelaw from the Saxons. He's set on this course. It's utterly ridiculous."

"I agree. As you said, you're just a simple woman. Mayhap you're even more of a simple woman than anyone even realizes."

"Aye, I said that, but I didn't think you'd agree with me so eagerly. I'm not all that simple. I'm not less than simple. Perhaps Kerek is right. Perhaps I am some sort of warrior goddess. I could ride in a chariot as that British queen probably did and men should shout how wonderful I was and they would follow me and—"

"Be quiet. I'm going to puke. You're just a girl, nothing more. I doubt you could save a hair comb. Men follow you? It's beyond ridiculous."

She punched Isla in the arm.

Isla grunted. "What do you plan to do? Nay, don't hit me again. It's an innocent question."

Chessa sighed. She was lying here in the dark speaking to this painted harlot, and yet, she had no one else to speak to. She said slowly, "I suppose I will remain pregnant for a while, until I can escape. My problem is I don't know where to escape to. Hawkfell Island is a long way away from York. Even if I had silver to pay you, where would you take me? The queen thought I should be sent to the Saxon court and cause chaos there.''

Isla laughed. ''I should go console the queen. She's quite right. Wherever you go you bring confusion and trouble. Men grind their teeth at your mischief. They want to strangle you because you dance around them, making up one tale after another, leaving them confused and crazed. You refuse to consider anyone else save yourself. You don't honor your father's wishes. You take it into your silly head that you want only one certain man. You say he has a richness deep inside him. You don't even know what that means. You don't even know this man, not really. You're just like Kerzog who won't let go of a stick. You just dig in your heels and hang on.

''Another thing. This man Cleve is ugly. He's not blind to himself. And what does that mean? That sounds like that deep richness nonsense. The scar on his face makes him look like a devil. It's true, it's you who are the blind one. You refuse to see him clearly because you're so damned obstinate. He has nothing. He doesn't want a wife because he should have had one once before, but by all the gods, that was a disaster. He doesn't need more disasters in his life. He doesn't need a woman who's very nature creates havoc.''

''How dare you, Isla.'' She came up on her elbows, ready to battle. ''Now listen here, I don't create havoc. I may try to change things, but at least I don't wear enough paint on my face so my head is bowed to my knees. Wait a minute, how do you know all this? How do you know of Kerzog? How do you know about Cleve? Oh, goodness, who are you really?''

''Why, who do you think, Princess? I'm the man who seduced you and impregnated you.''

''Cleve?''

''Aye.''

"Oh, I prayed you'd come," she said, and threw herself against him. "You're here, at last. I've missed you, Cleve." She hugged him tighter. He sucked in his breath in pain.

"What's wrong? Oh, I'm sorry."

"You stuck your knife into me. I'm here to save you and you stab me. Keep away from me."

"I didn't mean to." She was frantically trying to find where she'd stuck him, but he slapped her hands away.

"No, don't touch me, you might smear the paint on my face. Put that damned knife down and lie back."

She slipped the knife beneath her pillow again. Her heart was pounding. She'd never been so happy, so utterly relieved. Everything would be all right now, she knew it. Cleve was here. Surely what she'd said had to touch him. At least he should think about her words, shouldn't he? She said, "You don't mind that I'm to bear your child, do you?"

"Not at all. If my seed can be of use to you, why then, drain me of as much as you like."

"I had to do something. Tonight the king announced that I'm to wed Ragnor."

"I know. I was there. I was relieved when you showed the good sense to keep your mouth shut when he did make his announcement."

"I nearly didn't, but Kerek told me to."

"And if Kerek hadn't stopped you, what would you have announced?"

"That the king had lied, perhaps. That it wasn't Ragnor's child I carried. I probably would have gone on about their lack of pride to wed me to Ragnor when it wasn't even his child I was carrying. Perhaps insults about their collective manhoods, that they were shriveled and rotted. Something like that."

"You see, you bring chaos and confusion. Have you any idea what would have happened had you done that?"

"Perhaps the king would have relented since it was all out in the open? That everyone would know what the truth was? Ragnor would choke on the ale you gave him and die?''

He gave her a look of disgust she couldn't see. ''Don't be a fool. The gods know what would have happened. It curdles my blood to even think about it. Now, shall I tell you why you're to wed Ragnor in three days? Well before this pregnant belly of yours begins to swell?''

''You've been here less than a day. How do you know so much? I've been here forever and listened and cajoled and I would have bribed everyone if I'd had any silver. I don't know anything.''

He smiled in the darkness, pleased that she couldn't see his face. He felt the paste cracking around his mouth. ''The queen decided that the babe you bear will be a better future ruler if he's not from Ragnor's seed. I understand she questioned Kerek about what sort of man I am. She didn't care in the least that you, not a real princess at all, and I, a former slave who has no future as of yet, would give the Danelaw its future ruler.''

''That's brilliant. She's a ruthless woman.''

''Aye, and a very clever one. I've heard your threats about how you will yell the roof down if they try to make you wed Ragnor. The queen isn't stupid. She wants this marriage. She plans something. I just don't know what it is yet.''

''I'll find out. I'll use guile with her and she'll confess what she plans to me.''

He laughed, he couldn't help himself.

''By all the gods, Cleve, you're here. That means Kiri is starving herself. Did you bring her? Is she on the *Silver Raven?* Is she safe?''

''She is at Hawkfell Island. She is eating because I swore to her that I would bring you back. She's not even counting sticks, at least she'd better not be.''

She very slowly eased herself against his chest, only to feel what seemed to be very big breasts. He just laughed and pushed her away. ''Don't ruin my paint. This face is desired by Ragnor. Don't hug me again. My breasts aren't all that stable at the moment.''

"After you rescue me, Cleve, will you make me pregnant? I mean *really* pregnant? I'm very close to getting all the fathers of this babe confused.''

"I suppose I must, otherwise only the gods know what poor fellow you will choose as your next victim.'' He paused a moment, and she wished she could see his face. She felt his fingers lightly touching her mouth, her jaw, her nose. She wanted to kiss him, but she didn't want to smear his face. She felt his warm breath against her ear as he said, "I'm pleased that Ragnor didn't force you. A woman who is forced by a man isn't usually eager to have another man bed her, even if she thinks she wants him.''

"How do you know that?''

"I've seen it. Forget not that I was a slave for fifteen years. I saw everything.''

"Ah, but everything is different now. You have me.''

"It appears so,'' he said, and laughed. He patted her cheek and rose from the box bed. "Sleep and don't try to come up with your own plans. I don't want to have to follow after you and put out fires. I will decide what it is we will do. Obey me in this, Chessa, or it will not go well for you.''

Everyone treated her with great deference, including the guard that trailed after her everywhere she went. In two days she was to marry Ragnor. She'd seen Isla flirting with Ragnor, giving him mead, but he'd made no move to see her.

Cleve had told her to leave everything to him. Why? She wasn't stupid or helpless. An entire day had passed and nothing had happened. She had to do something. If she managed to save herself, why then, she could save Cleve too. She was whistling when she was shown to the queen's garden.

It was just beyond dusk, at that shadowy moment before darkness came. The beautiful garden, with its brilliant flowers, didn't look as wildly glorious as it did in full sun. There were shadows in the corners. Everything seemed dull and lackluster, as if every flower, every shrub, every tree, would crumble into dust the moment darkness fell.

Was she being fanciful because she was pregnant? She laughed as she remembered Sira would defend her tantrums by claiming the babes were making her fanciful.

The queen said, ''Ah, you're here at last, Chessa. Do come and sit down and let's enjoy the quiet of the evening. Then you will dine with the king and Ragnor, as I think I'll do this evening as well. One of my people told me that the king is displeased with the concubine who stands at his left hand. It appears he forgot to have her taste something for him and thus could have been poisoned. It is her fault, of course. Aye, I'll go dine with the king and the court and see what's happening. I don't want him to hurt her. Now, sit down, my child.''

''I'm not a child and I'm not yours.''

''You soon will be mine, but enough. You will learn that life doesn't always give you what you want it to. Just look at me.''

''I'm looking, lady, and I see a woman who has everything she could possibly want. I see a lady who rules and meddles to her heart's content. I see a lady who dislikes her only son so much she wants to wed him to a woman who loathes him, a woman who would never let him touch her, a woman pregnant with another man's child. I think I prefer my stepmother, who is truly rotten. At least she's honest in her rottenness.''

Turella felt a stab of anger. No, she thought, the girl was just trying to enrage her. And she was succeeding because what she said was true. She sighed. ''Here is some lemon ale that is very good. Would you like some?'' As she spoke, Turella calmly poured herself a goblet of the ale and drank it down.

''Aye,'' Chessa said after Turella had swallowed all of it.

They sat together on the stone bench as the shadows deepened, Turella telling her about the Bulgar and the immense stretches of barren land that lay between settlements, the trade routes that were jealously guarded and fought over, the Swedes who controlled Kiev and were even now extending their rule to the south and to the east.

Chessa listened to her words. They were becoming more distant and were so very soft. Merrik had brought Laren, her little brother, Taby, and Cleve out of Kiev. She would like to visit such a strange city. It sounded magical. She listened to the gentle buzzing of insects that flew near but never touched her. She began to smell the hyacinths and Turella's magic roses though she wasn't close to them. The flowers didn't die when it was night. That relieved her. When the darkness fell, she felt the softness of the night, the sweetness of the air around her. She was smiling when she slowly fell off the bench onto the ground.

Turella rose and looked down at her. "When I was your age, Princess, I would have fallen into the same trap. You will think yourself stupid to have been duped, but you aren't. I wouldn't ever wait to the last minute to take action. If I had, you would have never touched that lemon ale even after watching me drink it."

The queen called to her guards. One of them wrapped Chessa in a warm blanket and hefted her over his shoulder.

"Follow me," the queen said.

The following afternoon, Baric, Isla at his side, gave Ragnor another lesson on a new harp and taught him another love poem.

"I don't want to learn another love poem," Ragnor said. "I'm to marry the princess tomorrow. Thus I don't have to lie to her, quoting any more of your silly poems. Besides, I won't see her again until the moment she's to agree to be my wife. My mother has her hidden away so she won't try to do something stupid. I hope my mother forgets where she hid the princess, but I know she won't. She never forgets anything."

Isla said easily, looking at Ragnor as if he were a succulent roasted boar, "Ah, my lord, it's a pity that you must marry such a bitch. She has no stature, no gratitude for what you offer her. She has no appreciation for your finer qualities. I still don't understand why she must be forced. It makes no sense.''

Baric strummed on the harp, humming, looking down at his shoes.

Ragnor shrugged. ''I don't understand it either. She claims she loves another man, but how could that be possible? She's seen me, surely that is enough. Once she liked me, but then she changed, for no reason I can think of other than that I tried to seduce her and she didn't want to succumb. She's stubborn.'' He sighed deeply. ''I think she's just like my mother.''

''The queen appears properly cowed by the king. You will deal with the princess in just the same way.''

''Ha,'' Ragnor said. ''You don't know my mother, Isla. You don't understand.''

''Would you like some of my mead, my lord? I thought of you whilst I brewed it. It tastes rich and dark, just like a woman should taste. Just like I taste. That bitch probably tastes like goat weed.''

Ragnor felt saliva pool in his mouth. He watched Isla draw another goatskin from beneath her gown. He stared at her big breasts. He didn't like all the cosmetics she wore on her face, but she'd probably had a disease when she'd been a child and thus her face was badly pocked. As for the patch over her eye, he didn't care about that either. It wasn't important. Her mead was important. Her worship of him was important as were those big breasts of hers.

He drank deeply, knowing she was smiling at him. He wiped his mouth and said, ''Your mead is better than Utta's. Will you bed with me after I am married to Chessa? Will you continue to make me mead?''

''I will think about it. You know, Ragnor, mayhap you need a woman who isn't at all like your mother to tell this silly princess how very lucky she is. Mayhap I should visit her. I would make her see reason. I would make her appreciate how blessed she is, how honored she is that you will take her to wife. Mayhap she isn't really pregnant with this other man's child. Mayhap it is just another ploy, and this Kerek is quite wrong. I could get her to tell me the truth.''

"If my mother couldn't succeed with her, then no one could, even you. Even my mother was forced to drug her. I doubt she's even awake.''

Isla shrugged and poured Ragnor more mead. ''I could see. There would be no harm done.''

"I will think about it. Baric, I want to drink my mead. I don't want to learn any more of those silly poems. I wish to gaze upon Isla whilst I drink. Mayhap she will rub my forehead. You may play for us.''

"Aye, my lord," Baric said, his eyes still on his shoes, thankful his beard covered his face.

"Do you taste rich and dark, Isla?''

"No woman could taste richer and darker than I do, my lord. I'm filled with richness, deep within me.''

"I don't understand that.''

"I don't either, my lord, but I like the sound of it.''

Baric sang louder, his smooth voice filling the chamber.

"More mead, my lord?''

"I feel very tired, Isla. Very tired indeed.''

"Then rest. That's right, just lay your royal head on my lap and rest. Good.''

Ragnor began snoring. Isla looked over at the guards who stood at the doorways. They looked bored.

"Your song is exquisite, Baric. I believe you've put the prince to sleep.''

"I know. But I've a need to relieve myself. Would you like me to carry Ragnor out of here?''

"It suppose it wouldn't look good for me to do it.''

"You carry my harp, nothing more. I would fear your breasts just might fall to the floor.''

16

CLEVE ROSE AS Kerek came into Baric's small chamber, given to Baric by Olric some five years before.

"What is this about you wanting to speak to the princess, Baric? Why is this woman here?"

"Hello, Kerek."

Kerek stared at that face with all its paint, at that black patch over the right eye, at those huge breasts.

"Come, Kerek. Bid me hello."

"Oh no," Kerek said, taking a step back. "You're not a whore at all, are you? Is it you, Cleve?"

"Aye."

"Many of the men want to bed you, including Ragnor. By the gods, you've disguised yourself well. But it's over. You must leave. The queen has Chessa hidden. Even I don't know where she is. You must escape the palace before someone discovers who you really are. I've no wish to harm you, but if Ragnor sees you—sees you as you really are—he'll do his best to see you flayed alive."

"I don't think so, Kerek. That's why you're here. Baric, shut the door. Aye, that's good. Stand against it. Now, another trade, Kerek. I have Ragnor. You have Chessa. He dies if you don't give me Chessa. You have until the tide is in. That's about three hours from now."

Kerek just shook his head back and forth and began to

moan aloud. "Nothing has gone right, nothing. A simple kidnapping began it, and from that moment, everything turned sour. I had believed only the princess could bring me low, but now here you are dressed like a woman, painted like a harlot, and you've teased Ragnor until he's ready to howl. No one realized you were a man, even I."

"Don't tell me you wanted to bed me too, Kerek."

"No, but my mind has been filled with so many details of late."

"I'm relieved. Ragnor's mind is filled only with the desire for my mead. He said it's better than Utta's."

Kerek cursed softly. "You brought Utta's mead, didn't you? I should have guessed something was amiss."

"Of course," Cleve said. "My only concern is that the queen will refuse to give up Chessa because she believes her more valuable than Ragnor."

"She'll give her up. The Danes wouldn't accept a woman ruling openly. But why didn't you just leave her? You can have another woman. Why must it be Chessa?"

"Didn't you tell me you were sorry when you made the trade for Kiri, sorry because I loved her?"

"Aye, but what does love have to do with anything? I've seen little enough of it around. Just look at you—Kiri's mother tried to murder you. Forget love, Cleve, and leave. Chessa will be happy here, you'll see."

"Is that why Turella drugged her and has her hidden? Because she's so concerned about how happy she'll be? Give it up, Kerek. For the last time, give it up."

"I must speak to the queen."

"Why don't both of us speak to her."

They found Turella in her garden, on her hands and knees, sorting seeds. She was humming.

"Lady," Kerek said and lightly touched his hand to her shoulder. She grew very still, then slowly, she looked up at him and Cleve saw that the look on her face was too tender for a queen toward her subject. He wondered how he could turn it to his advantage.

"Ah, Kerek. What have you done? You brought Baric's woman. Why?"

Cleve said, "I'm really not a woman, my lady. My name is Cleve. I'm the father of Chessa's babe. I'm here to fetch her and take her home."

The queen slowly cleaned off her hands and rose. She looked at Cleve for a very long time, then said, her voice irritated, "I want to see what you look like as a man. I want to know what my grandson will look like."

"Perhaps the babe will be the picture of Chessa," Cleve said.

"You can't have her, Cleve. It is done. You will leave willingly or I will give you to my son. He treated you badly before. Just imagine what he would do now."

"Ragnor won't do anything, lady. Your son is right now snoring blissfully, drugged to his brows, just as you drugged the princess."

The queen staggered back. Kerek grabbed her arm to steady her. "Is he telling the truth, Kerek?"

"Aye, he is. I don't know where he's got Ragnor hidden. He wants to trade Ragnor for the princess."

"I want it done now," Cleve said. "Take me to Chessa."

Slowly, the queen shook her head. "I cannot. She must wed Ragnor. She must someday rule the Danelaw."

Cleve only smiled. He slipped a small very sharp knife from his tunic, grabbed Kerek, and stuck the knife point into his neck.

"Then first I will slit Kerek's throat and then I will kill Ragnor. You can keep Chessa, but I don't know what you'll do with her. She'll make you regret it too, if I know her. Ah, I see that you do. Give over, lady." He pressed the knife tip into Kerek's throat. A drop of blood trickled over the smooth blade.

Turella stepped forward. "No, don't hurt him. By all the gods, what am I to do, Kerek?"

"Let him kill me, Turella, it doesn't matter. But he will kill Ragnor as well and then where will we be? Cleve is right. It's over. We must think of something else."

The queen frowned down at her hands, at the black rich dirt beneath her nails. "We can find a silly little girl for Ragnor, I suppose. But it means that I must remain as I am, Kerek. I cannot die."

"You won't die," Kerek said.

"This is all touching," Cleve said. "Let's end it. Will we trade?"

The queen nodded. "Release Kerek."

Cleve did, then wiped the tip of the knife on his sleeve. "Take me to the princess."

The queen started to protest but Kerek gently laid his hand on her arm. "You can believe him. He will release Ragnor. He will keep his word. He is that kind of man."

Chessa lay on her back atop several soft furs in a small storage chamber. Two guards sat near her, rising quickly when the queen came into the room.

"Leave us," she said.

Cleve dropped to his knees beside Chessa. He shook her gently. "She's still unconscious. You drugged her yesterday."

"She will be all right. I planned to lessen the drug tomorrow morning until she was just conscious enough to do as she was told during the marriage ceremony."

Chessa moaned, but she didn't awaken.

"Kerek, wrap her up in the furs. You will come with me. When I have her safe on board the warship, then I will tell you where Ragnor is."

It was quickly done. Cleve's last view of the queen made him smile. She was tapping her fingers against her temple. She was thinking and planning and plotting. He imagined that some poor girl would soon be in Ragnor's bed.

They were out of York harbor within an hour.

"I have a gray hair," Cleve said to Chessa, who was lying still unconscious across his thighs, "and I have known you only a short time. What will I look like when I reach Rorik's advanced years?"

Rorik laughed as he rowed. "It's true," he said over his

shoulder, "I'm aged. I am thirty at the beginning of summer. How can you see this gray hair? Your hair is golden."

Hafter said, "He feels the gray hair, Rorik, and I understand that. Many times Entti will make me so angry I want to strangle her, I can actually feel my own gray hairs pushing to come up through my scalp. Is the princess awake yet, Cleve?"

"No, and it begins to worry me. She's very pale. Her flesh feels too dry. I was stupid. I should have found out what drug the queen gave her."

Gunleik said, "Wet a cloth in the water and wipe her face with it. Mayhap it will shock her awake."

He lightly touched the wet cloth over her dry skin. He smoothed her eyebrows, touched his fingertips to the tip of her nose, and rubbed the cloth over her throat. Her lashes were thick and long. He hadn't noticed that before. Her mouth should be soft and moist, he'd noticed that, but now her lips were dry and cracked. How could this happen in just one day?

He began to worry when darkness fell that night. He ate the dried herring Hafter handed to him and chewed on flatbread Aslak had bought at the marketplace. She didn't move. Cleve shook her, slapped her face several times. She still didn't awaken. Gunleik told him to continue wiping her with the wet cloth.

He carried her to the covered cargo space, laid her gently on several blankets, then stretched out beside her. He picked up her hand. It was small and dry and limp.

He stripped off her clothes and began wiping her with a wet cloth. Still, she didn't wake up.

It was Gunleik who said just after dawn, "She must not have borne the queen's potion well. We've got to make her wake up. I fear she'll just fade away from us if she remains unconscious."

Cleve had felt helpless in his life, many, many times, helpless and impotent, but now it was not just his need to do something to help her, it was necessary for him, she couldn't die. She was Kiri's second papa. By all the gods, she was also important to him. He felt fear in his guts. "What are we going to do?"

Gunleik rose. "I'll get Rorik's packet of medicines Mirana always sends with him. Perhaps there is something that will help."

Gunleik was back with a large skin lined with soft linen and holding vials of creams and liquids. Rorik came in behind him. "There is nothing here that can help else I would have said something before."

"She must wake up," Cleve said. "She must wake up and see that I'm a man again. She's been unconscious for nearly two days. She'll starve to death if she doesn't awaken."

"Then we will pull close to shore and you can go overboard with her. Hold her in the cold water. Mayhap that's what's needed to shock her awake. Mirana did that once with our little boy, Ivar, and it worked."

Cleve thought it a crazed idea, but he was desperate.

When they were within feet of the shore, Cleve lifted Chessa, held her tight against him, and jumped into the water with her. They both went under. The water was so cold it shocked the breath from him. He shoved upward, found he could stand on his feet, and kept Chessa close, the water to her neck. He held her there until suddenly she heaved and shuddered, and shoved hard at him, moaning, hitting at his chest.

"You're killing me," she yelled, her voice harsh and raw. "I'm dying of cold. Please, Cleve, don't kill me. I won't be pregnant anymore with your babe, I swear it."

He was so relieved, so very happy, he lifted her in his arms and kissed her mouth. "I should have known the moment you woke up you'd talk about my babe. Come, let's get you dry."

She looked at the boat, at the men all leaning over the side, all cheering now. "This is strange. You're no longer Isla. What's happening? Oh, dear, where is the queen?"

Cleve just laughed and handed her up to Hafter, who

hauled her into the warship. "I tried to throw her to the fish, but she wouldn't let go of me."

"What happened? Where are we?"

Cleve climbed over the side of the warship, shook himself like Kerzog, and said, grinning at her, "We rescued you. The queen gave you a potion. I gave Ragnor a potion. Then we made a trade. The queen didn't want to, but she realized that you couldn't rule the Danelaw without Ragnor as the nominal king. Unfortunately, the sweet prince never awoke before we gave him back to Kerek and the queen, else I would have enjoyed telling him that he'd fallen in love with Isla, who was really his worst nightmare, namely I, and it was Utta's wine he was drinking. You're safe now, Chessa. Now, let's go get us both dry."

"I'm very hungry, Cleve. I haven't eaten since last night."

"You," Rorik said, cuffing her shoulder as he would a boy, "you haven't eaten for at least two days."

"Perhaps you don't have to feed her. Just look at her, she still yells and talks," Rorik said. "Any minute now she'll want you to impregnate her again. How do you feel, Chessa?"

"Very cold. I shall collapse very soon since you haven't fed me."

"Come along," Cleve said. "Would you like to try on my breasts? I brought them back with me. Poor Baric didn't want to keep them. I think it would have saddened him to have them near him without me being attached to them. Ah, we did share some interesting moments together."

"You should have let me stack up my sticks, Papa. I wouldn't have run out this time."

Cleve kissed Kiri, then said, "No more sticks. Now, I kept my promise to you. Here's Chessa."

"Papa!" Kiri jumped into Chessa's arms and hugged her thin arms around her neck.

Chessa was laughing and kissing the little girl's face. "Your papa—your first papa—was a great hero. Everyone

in York believed he was Thor, come down with his lightning bolts to terrify the king and queen until they gave me
back to him. As for you, you were wonderful, Kiri. I'm
very glad you didn't starve yourself again.''

"Aunt Laren said that since I now have two papas, I'm
more important than ever. She said my papas couldn't bear
it if something happened to me. So I ate and ate.''

Chessa rubbed her palm over the little girl's stomach.
"Cleve,'' she called out, laughing. "I fear we will have a
very fat little creature on our hands if we leave her often.
Instead of starving herself, she will cram food down her
gullet until she waddles.''

Kiri laughed and pulled out of Chessa's arms. She
grinned at Cleve and Chessa then ran to Aglida to play.

"Behold our true importance,'' Cleve said. He turned to
Mirana. "Chessa and I will wed. I can't hold out against
her any longer. I don't want any more gray hairs. I will
send a messenger to both Duke Rollo and to King Sitric.''

"Tomorrow,'' Old Alna said, and cackled. "You'll wed
tomorrow. Finally, you'll plant a real babe in her belly.
Lord Rorik, I wish you'd brought back Captain Torric. Aye,
what a fine lad he was.''

That evening, both during and after a dinner of roasted
pheasant, fried halibut, and Entti's delicious rye bread,
Cleve told of his adventures in York. His disguise was
brought out and admired and laughed over. Everyone
begged him to dress just once for them as Isla. He refused,
saying his daughter would swoon from disgust and shock.

Laren asked many questions about the people at the palace in York. Cleve provided her with all the details, as did
Chessa. They knew that soon Laren would weave a skald's
tale. Cleve asked her at the end of the evening, "I beg you,
Laren, let me remain a man. I dread thinking of how I will
be greeted in future years if you tell about how Cleve of
Malverne disguised himself as a whore with big breasts and
more paint on her face than a whitewashed wall in order
to rescue the damsel.''

Laren punched his arm and laughed. "I will think about

it. Actually, I will ask Chessa after you've been married for several days. If you've pleased her, Cleve, why then, I will let you remain the mighty Thor.''

Cleve grinned down at her, sweet Laren, as beloved as a sister. "I'll try my best, Laren, I'll try my best."

Just before the ceremony the following afternoon, Kiri said to Cleve, "You're certain you wish to wed Chessa, Papa? I think she's a very good second papa, but a wife is different. You've never wanted another wife since my mama."

"I think those things that make her an excellent second papa will also make her a good wife. I have to marry her, Kiri."

Kiri said slowly, frowning up at him, "But why?"

"If I don't she'll begin to count sticks and soon she'll be so skinny she'll blow off the eastern cliffs here on Hawkfell Island. She doesn't want to be parted from us, Kiri, thus I must wed her."

"I'll talk to her, Papa," Kiri said and ran to where Chessa stood with her aunt Mirana and her aunt Laren.

"Ah, my little beauty," Chessa said and picked Kiri up in her arms. She groaned. "You're a big girl now. I can't lift you much longer."

"But you're my second papa. Papas are strong."

"That's true," Chessa said. "I will have to grow more muscle." She set Kiri down. "Now, sweeting, what do you think of my gown?"

Kiri walked around her, just looking, saying nothing. Chessa cocked an eyebrow at her. "Well?"

"I don't know what to call you now."

Mirana said, "Perhaps you can call her mama sometimes."

"You just think about it, Kiri," Chessa said. "I would like that, but it's up to you. Now, do you like the saffron gown?"

Kiri nodded slowly. "Papa said he had to marry you

because you'd count sticks and starve yourself if he didn't.''

"That's right.''

Kiri just nodded then and skipped away.

"Children,'' Entti said, shaking her head.

"And men,'' Laren said.

When the men came to stand in the circle for the ceremony, it was to hear the women giggling.

17

THE AFTERNOON SKY over Hawkfell Island was brilliant with light, sweet with the scent of the gorse and heather, and tangy with the salty spray from the sea. There were plump white clouds to soften the force of the sun. There was no wind. The crashing of the waves against the rocks was rhythmic and heavy.

As was the Malverne custom, the men stood behind Cleve, the women behind Chessa. The children stood off to one side, the oldest children responsible for relative silence among the younger ones. The pets stayed with the children, all except Kerzog, who nestled his nose between Chessa's feet.

"Since Sira is your stepmother," Old Alna said to Chessa, "you'll not have to worry about her coming to steal Cleve, like she tried to steal Rorik. To think of Sira as a queen, it makes my brain spin. Aye, she tried to seduce Rorik from Mirana, you know, nearly killed my little sweeting. Ah, but I saved her."

Mirana began to whistle.

Rorik, Lord of Hawkfell Island, yelled out for silence. "We're graced with fine weather, a sure sign that this marriage is blessed by the gods. Cleve of Malverne is here to wed with Chessa, daughter of King Sitric of Ireland. Listen all of you to their pledges of faith."

Cleve stepped forward, clasped Chessa's hands in his, and gently tugged her to the center. "Kerzog," he said, pushing the mongrel away, "leave her be. You can sniff her toes and sleep on her feet after I'm done with her."

There was laughter.

Cleve felt the coldness of her hands. "Don't be afraid," he said low. "A papa shouldn't ever be afraid."

"I'm not afraid. I'm terrified. I've never been married before, Cleve."

He just smiled down at her and said in a loud voice that carried to the waves crashing against the black rocks at the base of the eastern cliffs, "I offer this woman all that I have and all that I will ever have." He raised her hand in his. "Our future is shrouded in the unknown. She stands with me in this. When it is clear to me who and what I am, she will still be at my side. I hold her in honor. I will pray to Freya daily that we are blessed with many babes and that all of them will be mine this time."

There was a spurt of laughter, then silence again as Chessa clasped Cleve's wrist and raised it high. "You will be my mate, the man who will be with me forever. I give you all my loyalty, my fidelity. I will protect you with my life. We will conquer Scotland together. I love your daughter as my own. I love you, her father, with all that is within me and I have since the first moment I saw you in the queen's garden. You are my husband now and forever."

Love wasn't usually spoken of in a Viking wedding. Honor and fidelity were the important vows. Loyalty to one's people, to one's king. There was a moment of sharp silence. Cleve stared down at her, his head cocked to one side. "You loved me that soon?" he said, his voice low, but since no one was saying a word, everyone heard him.

"Aye," she said. "I'd never seen a man as beautiful as you. You were golden and strong. You shone beneath the sun in the garden that day."

He leaned over and kissed her mouth. The silence broke with cheers from men and women alike. Cleve took her in his arms and pressed her face against his shoulder.

"Papa!"

"Which one?" Chessa said, turning to look at her new daughter.

"My manly papa," Kiri said.

Laughter took the place of cheers.

Cleve picked up his daughter, hugged her, and said, "Now you've a new mama who is also your second papa."

Kiri frowned at Chessa. Slowly, she reached out her hand and lightly touched her fingers to Chessa's cheek. "I just don't know," Kiri said.

"I don't either," Chessa said. "We'll all find out together."

It was very late, but the wedding banquet hadn't slowed at all. It just got louder and more raucous. Laughter filled the air. There were several good-natured fights between Malverne men and Hawkfell men, but as Cleve told Chessa, it was their responsibility to remain sober and watchful so that no one got his head broken. No one did.

"It's magic," Chessa said to her new husband.

"Will you truly give me your loyalty, Chessa? Will you stay with me until I can no longer breathe?"

"Aye," she said, stood on her tiptoes and kissed his mouth. There were cheers and shouts of advice. She felt his tongue on her lower lip and started with surprise. He raised his head and grinned down at her.

Old Alna said, "She'll be more giving, Cleve, if you pour some of Utta's mead down her gullet."

Cleve lightly stroked his fingers over her throat. "Is there a gullet in there that wants mead?"

Her stomach growled and he laughed. "Come, wife, let's stuff you with some boar steaks. Ah, smell that. They're sizzling, just the way I like them."

Food was piled on every surface. Ale and mead filled casks whose ladles were never still. Laren told three stories until she was giggling so hard from the mead she'd drunk, she fell from the corner of a table, thankfully into Merrik's arms. Both of them went down amid a tangle of arms and legs. Kerzog was too full to do more than lift his head every once in a while to see if anyone was bringing him more food.

The children were all inside the longhouse, hopefully asleep, for it was very late.

Chessa hadn't drunk even a sip of ale, hadn't even sniffed Utta's infamous mead. She was too excited. And Cleve knew it. He would look at her and smile, a small and mysterious smile, one that promised things she didn't yet know, and he did. He was teasing her and doing it very well.

Rorik, whose stomach turned on him if he drank more than a goblet of mead, was as sober as Chessa. He said to her as the evening stretched toward midnight, "You have brought more change to Cleve's life than I can imagine. I had worried about him, as had my brother, Merrik. He has known a lifetime of hardship, a lifetime that gave him nothing but pain and humiliation. That he survived it is amazing. That he still smiles, that he's able to enjoy the beauty of the sunset, appreciate the beauty of a woman's white breasts, ah, it bespeaks strength that only a Viking can know."

"I will protect him, Rorik, I swear it," Chessa said. "I will give him all that I can."

He smiled down at her. "That is what you said in the ceremony. The women were moved, the men disbelieving, save those who have dealt with my wife."

"Men always disbelieve. It makes no difference. I will always be there for him. He knows I can wield a knife as well as he can."

"Not quite," Cleve said, coming up behind her. He lifted the hair from her neck and kissed her damp skin. She shivered. He laughed, dropped her hair, and just stood there beside her, stroking his long fingers through her hair, saying to Rorik, "Black as a Christian's sins, just like Mirana's. Forget not that I have spent five years at Malverne. Merrik has become like a brother. He's a vicious fighter, and he taught me everything he knows. He also taught me to trust.

I have been blessed, Rorik, truly. Now, I would like to take my wife to a very private place and teach her how a man goes about planting a babe in a woman's belly. The next time she brays about such things, at least she'll know what she's talking about. Aye, Freya has been nudging me all evening to begin my duties.''

''I do use a knife as well as you do,'' Chessa said, and skipped next to him to keep up.

Rorik laughed and called after them, ''Mirana and I give you our chamber. You can't escape the jests of our people though.''

''We will come in a moment,'' Cleve said. ''First, I want to walk a bit. Unlike my wife here, I drank my share of Utta's mead.''

He took her hand and led her through the palisade gates.

''No, you didn't. I've been watching you. You've smiled and nodded and even laughed at all the advice everyone's given you, but you didn't drink. You broke up that fight between Aslak and Hafter.''

''Be careful, the path can be treacherous,'' he said, drawing her closer to his side. ''You're right. I drank only enough to make my fingers curl when I thought about all I would do to you tonight. I still can't decide where to begin. Perhaps with your breasts, but I must give it more thought. Or perhaps I'll just stroke my hand over your belly and let my fingers go where they will. Have I made you turn red, Chessa? Turn around and let me see.''

He gently pulled her around to face him. He lifted her chin with his fingertips. Slowly, he stroked his fingers over her shoulders, then downward until he cupped her left breast. ''Ah, this is nice. Your heart is beginning to pound. Aye, this is a good place to begin.''

He didn't move his hand, just held her breast. He leaned over and kissed her mouth. His hand lifted and his fingers began to caress her breast. ''Open your mouth, Chessa.''

She did, coming onto her tiptoes, pressing her breast more fully into his hand. She felt his tongue lightly glide over her lower lip.

"Oh, Cleve, that is rather strange. I want to come closer and I want to yell."

"Do it." His tongue slid into her mouth and she gasped with surprise.

"Please don't bite my tongue off," he said, and kissed her ear, licking the soft flesh, then nibbling on her earlobe.

"I'm sorry but you surprised me. That's surprising too. I don't like this. You've got all the surprises and I'm just standing here like an ignorant fool."

He drew back from her and folded his arms over his chest. "A full moon. It's magnificent, don't you think?"

Her heart was pounding; she ached in her belly. She wanted to kiss him and to touch him as he touched her. She wanted to bite his earlobe.

"Aye," she said. "The moon is so brilliant I can see the two plovers in their nest over beneath that gorse bush."

He stepped to her again, pulled her against him and without hesitation or warning, he ran his hand over her belly, downward, to cup her. His hand was very hot through her clothes.

She could only stare up at him. "No one's ever touched me there before."

He moved his fingers slightly and she jumped. "I trust not, though you've been pregnant with so many babes surely someone must have touched you somewhere. You look worried, Chessa. What's wrong? Don't you like me pressing my hand against you?"

She looked up at him, all her feelings for him clear on her face. "I don't know if I like that. It isn't what I'm used to. But I will tell you, Cleve, that I love you. No, if you don't love me yet, it doesn't matter. I just wanted you to know."

He groaned, jerked her against him, and let her feel the heat of his body, the hardness of his sex against her belly. He was breathing deep and thick, he wanted to have her now, at this very instant, over in the gorse and heather where the two plovers were nesting. "Chessa," he said into her mouth. "It's too much, sweeting. Now, I want you now. I don't know what's the matter with me, but I can't wait. I'd thought to go slowly with you, but somehow I can't. I'd thought to tease you and caress you until you were whimpering and moaning, but I can't.''

She nearly knocked him onto his back so quickly did she throw herself against him. He staggered, laughed, then began kissing her again. Slowly, he eased her onto the path, only to realize that they were on an incline, the ground was hard, and it was her first time. He cursed, lifting himself above her. ''We can't stay here. It's too rough. Come, Chessa. Hurry, by all the gods, hurry.''

He was holding her hand so tightly he knew her fingers must be white, but he didn't care. He was dragging her, not letting her run to catch up with him. He looked neither to the right nor to the left. All their friends were still laughing and drinking, but they stopped when Cleve pulled Chessa through their midst and into the longhouse. There were shouts of laughter, Old Alna yelling, ''Give her your tongue, Cleve. A woman loves a man's tongue.''

''Ha,'' Hafter said. ''You can't even remember a man's tongue, Alna.''

''Alna, pay Hafter no mind. Here's some mead,'' Utta said, giggling as Haakon patted her buttocks.

Kerzog barked and ran after them, then abruptly stopped just inside the longhouse. He cocked his big head, then turned and bounded back into the laughing and shouting people.

''At last,'' Cleve said, panting, his chest heaving. He quickly pulled the bearskin over the opening to Rorik's and Mirana's chamber. Bless them, they'd left a lit wick in a bowl of oil. The light was gentle and shadowy, the air warm and soft, and this was his wife. She was his.

He lifted her and laid her on her back, then immediately pulled her up again. ''Your clothes,'' he said, and nearly tore off the brooches at her shoulders.

Suddenly, she was laughing. He stopped then.

''Let me remove my own clothes, Cleve, else I'll have

to beg a gown off one of the women on the morrow.''

He stepped back and yanked off his own clothes. He was naked and staring at her when she looked up at him, still in her long linen shift. He was breathing hard. He didn't understand this urgency, but he accepted it. He wanted her and he would have her as soon as he could get her onto her back.

''Oh,'' Chessa said. She swallowed. ''Oh,'' she said again. She looked at him, every inch of him, from the whorls of golden hair on his chest to his flat belly, lower, to the golden bush at his groin. She swallowed again. ''Oh.''

''Chessa, hurry. Don't be frightened. I'll fit, you'll see. I promise I'll fit and you'll like it. I swear it to you. Hurry. By all the gods, I don't believe this. Hurry.''

When she was standing in front of him, the linen shift at her feet, he looked at her and groaned.

''I wanted to go slowly with you. I teased you all evening, but I suppose I was just teasing myself and look what's come of it. Now, Chessa, now.''

He lifted her, her breasts against his face, and when he suckled her nipple, she arched her back, her body taut as a sapling. Then she was on her back and he was between her legs and he was breathing hard, his hands all over her. It was as if he didn't know where to begin, what to do first. He cursed, lifted her, and brought her to his mouth, his breath deep and hot on her flesh.

She froze, then twisted, so surprised she didn't know what to do. Cleve straightened over her. His mouth was glistening with her. He looked to be in pain. He pushed her knees against her, stared at her woman's flesh, and groaned again. ''I can't wait,'' he said and he was in pain, she thought, his teeth clenched, his eyes closed, his head thrown back.

She didn't know what to think, what to do. In the next instant, he was pushing himself into her and she wondered what was happening to him, what she was supposed to do now, if she was to move and if so, how was she to move?

What was she supposed to feel? There was no longer an ache deep in her belly. There was no deep ache anywhere.

But she loved him, she wouldn't forget that no matter what he did, and she was curious, but she was also aware that he was very large and she wasn't.

She felt pain and shoved her palms against his chest. "Cleve, please stop a moment. Just a moment, please."

"I can't, Chessa, I can't. Try to ease yourself for me. By all the gods, you're small, too small, but I must come deeper into you, I can't wait, please try to ease yourself, Chessa. If any woman can do it, you can."

"All right." She felt his hands holding her thighs apart, felt him pushing slowly into her. The pain grew. She didn't like it. This act gave a woman a child, she accepted that, but it was also supposed to give her pleasure? Suddenly, he thrust again and again, and she felt tearing pain, felt as if a part of her had ripped apart deep inside her. She screamed, her fists against his chest shoving at him, striking him, anything to get him off her. Then he heaved over her, groaning and trembling, sweat making his golden body glisten. She didn't know what was happening to him but whatever it was, he appeared to want it, thus she did too. Ah, but it hurt. He was his full length inside her body. That was strange that he was deep inside her, that he was part of her. He was hot and tense, ramming into her, sealing himself against her, groaning deep in his chest, then pulling out just to shove forward again. She didn't move. She hurt badly, but she didn't move.

She loved him. If this was what he wanted, then he would have it. She stuffed her fist into her mouth. It was over soon enough. He arched over her, his throat working madly, and he cried out again and again, and she felt the wetness from him fill her. She lay very still. The pain lessened and so did he.

He was lying over her now, balanced on his elbows, breathing hard and fast. He was sweating. He smelled wonderful. She leaned up and kissed his shoulder—sweat and his unique scent. She kissed his shoulder again.

He drew a deep heaving breath. "By all the gods, that was not well done of me. I hurt you, didn't I, Chessa? I hurt you and I'm sorry for it but I couldn't have done it differently. Do you understand? Do you forgive me? I was as clumsy as a raw boy and I am sorry for it. I didn't want to take you this way, at least not the first time. Did you hate it? Do you hate me now for hurting you?"

She was adrift in the feeling of him still inside her and he was over her, kissing her and talking and she said, "You want to know many things, Cleve. Not now, all right?"

He lowered himself so he was flat and heavy on her and she didn't want him to move at all. He was pressed against her belly, his sex still inside her. "Do you know how you feel to me? No, of course you don't. You're a woman and you were a virgin and I hurt you." He withdrew from her and rolled off her.

"Could you come back, please, Cleve?"

He came up on his elbow and looked down at her. "I'm here. I feel like a sorry husband. Forgive me, Chessa."

"Is it always like that?"

"Like what?"

She raised her hair and lightly stroked her fingers over his jaw, his lips, his nose. "Will you always touch me like you just did? Like every part of me is yours to handle freely? You'll use me and do exactly as you please to me and hurt me?"

He bit the end of her finger. "Aye. But it works both ways, Chessa. You can do exactly what you wish to me. No, I won't ever hurt you again."

She doubted that, but kept silent. Then she wailed, "But I don't know anything." She grabbed his ears in both her hands and pulled him down to kiss him. He was laughing, then quickly moaning. She put her tongue in his mouth, not realizing really what she was doing, how it would make him feel, not at all how it would make her feel.

"Oh," she said into his mouth, felt his tongue touch hers, and felt a jolt of pleasure so intense she whimpered. "That's very nice."

"Good," he said and kissed her until she was struggling to get closer to him, her hands on his back, his chest, all over him, save his belly and groin. He said as he licked her ear, "Touch me, Chessa. Touch me."

She knew where he wanted her hand, aye, she knew, but still she wasn't certain. When she touched him, felt the heat of him, the wetness of him and knew it was from both of them, this wetness, she jerked back her fingers. He moaned.

She closed her fingers around him again as she kissed him. It was incredible. He was warm and tasted of sweet ale and of her and of himself. He was hard and strong against her fingers. He fascinated her. She was beginning to feel those feelings again, deep in her belly, and in her breasts, that was very nice when he'd kissed her breasts, but he'd stopped only a moment after he'd begun. She wanted him to do it again.

"Cleve?"

He kissed the side of her mouth. His hand flattened on her hip bone. He was slipping from her hand.

"Cleve?"

He moaned softly, falling away from her onto his back.

She lurched over him and stared down at his face. He was asleep. She wanted to hit him. Instead, she lightly kissed his mouth. She snuffed out the wick.

"Well," Chessa said to the dark chamber, "I suppose it's a beginning. Not much of one, but a start."

Dawn light shadowed the chamber. Chessa suddenly cried out in pain and jerked awake. She remembered she was married, she remembered everything. She felt sore between her legs and sticky. Again she felt a sharp jabbing pain in her ribs.

She shook her head, realized that Kiri was between her and Cleve and Kiri's elbow had poked her twice.

She and Cleve were on the two edges of the bed. Kiri was lying flat on her back between them, her legs and arms sprawled away from her body. She was dreaming, tossing a bit now, and that elbow flailed again.

"Nay," Chessa said, grabbed the child's hand and brought it down. "Cleve, do wake up. We have a guest."

Cleve awoke immediately, a habit he'd quickly learned when he was very young from his first master, an old merchant who sold furs and young boys. Thankfully, he'd believed Cleve too young to be used, and thus kept him in his shop, counting and sorting furs. Cleve looked at Chessa's shadowed face, then down at his daughter. He groaned.

"Papa," Kiri said, and yawned. "You were holding her really tight. It took me a long time to get between you."

Cleve groaned again and fell off the side of the bed. When he opened his eyes, his daughter and his new wife were on their hands and knees, staring down at him.

"Papa," Kiri said. "You don't have any clothes on."

Chessa threw him a woolen blanket, drawing Kiri back to the middle of the bed. "Now, sweeting, what are you doing here? Couldn't you sleep?"

Kiri smiled and slipped away from Chessa. She called out, "Kerzog! You were right. Come here, Kerzog. No, stay, I'll come with you now."

"What was that damned dog right about?" Cleve said as he eased back between the woolen blankets.

"I'm afraid to know," Chessa said, and snuggled against her new husband.

"No," he said firmly, "don't touch any part of me, Chessa. You're sore and I won't ravage you again until you've healed."

She cursed and he laughed.

18

CLEVE STARED DOWN at Utta's porridge. For the first time since he'd tasted his first blissful spoonful, he didn't even like the looks of it. He set his bowl aside. He heard a laugh and looked up to see Chessa grinning and shaking her head at something Laren had said.

How could she laugh after what he'd done to her? She was strong, this wife of his. She wasn't one to complain or cry. But still, did she have to act so very contented? So happy? Didn't she realize what he'd *not* done to her? And she'd smiled at him and wanted to have him hurt her again after Kiri had left at dawn. At least he'd been civilized enough to be firm about it. He didn't begin to understand her.

He rose from the bench only to be pounded on his back, in turn, by Hafter, Rorik, and Gunleik.

"She looks pleased," Hafter said. "Not as pleased as Entti after our first married night together, but still, she's smiling and laughing."

"Aye, it appears you didn't exhaust her with your lust," Gunleik said. "It's always uncertain what will happen with an innocent girl like Chessa."

"I'm just pleased she can still walk," Merrik said, walking up to them. "You'd been a long time without a woman,

Cleve. Truth be told I was a bit worried you'd be too enthusiastic.''

Rorik said. ''Mirana told me Kiri ended up between the two of you.''

Cleve nodded. ''She kicked me off the edge of the bed, then called Kerzog, thinking it all a great jest.''

Gunleik said, frowning at Cleve, ''You don't look like a man who's enjoyed himself all through a long dark night with a new wife who worships you.''

''Gunleik's right,'' Hafter said, adding his frowning to Gunleik's. ''You look like you've got a cramp in your bowels, that, hmmm, or you've done something incredibly stupid with your new bride.''

It was too much, damn their interfering eyes. He shouted, ''Damn all of you. My bowels are just fine. You want the truth, you damned meddlesome sods? Very well, I failed her. I fell asleep like a stuporous goat.''

Rorik groaned and struck his fist against Cleve's arm. ''You didn't. Truly, you fell asleep? Quickly? Aye, I see by the guilt in your eyes you did. By all the gods, Cleve, you give us all a bad name.''

''I'm going to the bathing hut,'' Cleve said and left them to stare after him. He rubbed his arm as he walked out of the longhouse. He didn't look at his new wife, the wife who'd hounded him since he'd met her, the wife who'd stood firmly against a marriage to either the future king of the Danelaw or to the future Duke of Normandy. It made no sense that she'd always wanted him. Now she had to regret her choice, surely now she didn't want to see him again. Then why was she laughing with Laren? Why did she look so happy?

Chessa was very aware of every movement he'd made since he'd picked up a bowl of Utta's porridge, then quickly set it down again as if it were a bowl of snakes to bite him. She saw the men jest with him, doubtless questioning him about what he'd done the previous night. She smiled. She couldn't wait to kiss him, to touch him again. Then he turned from them and walked out of the longhouse, never looking back, not even at her. What was wrong with him?

Rorik came up, kissed his wife, then turned to Chessa, a big grin on his handsome face. "So Cleve finally confessed that he'd failed you. The men have berated him unmercifully. Tell me, Chessa, did he truly fall asleep?"

Ah, so that's what it was all about. Chessa looked shyly down at her shoes. In a voice so soft Rorik had to lean down to hear her, she said, "He did finally, just before dawn. I have to admit I was relieved. It was more than I expected. No one told me about how it would be." She gave Laren and Mirana a reproachful look.

"Relieved he fell asleep?" Rorik said, looking at her closely. "That makes no sense at all. Why the devil would you be relieved?"

"I was so very tired, Rorik," she said, eyes still on her shoes, her voice very faint now, a thin thread of a sound. "Ah, it's not that I didn't enjoy it, for Cleve is a man who demands passion and knows how to call it forth from a woman." She shuddered delicately in memory. "But truly, isn't mating five times sufficient for a man? Must he continually want more? Does he never tire?"

Rorik just stared at her. "Five times?"

She nodded, shy as the shyest maiden, eyes still down, mute as the babe in Entti's arms.

Rorik frowned. "Chessa, are you certain you counted correctly? That is, to be five times, it's not just that he comes into, well, never mind that. It's *separate* times with time in between so that, well, it means—" Mirana poked his arm. Rorik shook his head. "By all the gods, you'll be pregnant by the end of the day if he continues as he's begun. Five times? You're sure it was five *separate* times?"

She never looked up, just nodded. Her voice was tiny now in embarrassment. "Very separate. The fifth time was difficult for I was very tired, but Cleve just laughed and kissed me and wouldn't stop. The pleasure he forced upon me, well, it nearly sent me into oblivion. But even then I fell asleep before he did. I have to admit it. I was glad he was kind enough to let me sleep. He said he fell asleep then? I wondered for he never slowed, never stopped touching me and giving me pleasure.''

Rorik strode off, shaking his head. Mirana looked at Chessa, saw the wicked gleam in her eyes, and began to laugh. ''Ah, that was very well done of you. You rival Laren as a skald. My poor husband will now believe he's failed me, Chessa. Actually, I can't wait until tonight. He'll believe he must prove himself. By the gods, all the men will feel as if their manhood has been called into question. Ah, the women will love this. Well done, well done.''

''I thought it was,'' Chessa said, grinning like one of Mirana's sons when he'd managed to fool his father. ''I believe I'll go to the bathing hut.'' She turned. ''Is five times more than a man can accomplish in one night?''

''I honestly don't know. I hope to find out tonight. Rorik will do his best now that he knows the new standard. A standard that every man on Hawkfell Island will know before the day is out. *Separate* times. Ah, that was well done.''

When Chessa entered the outer room in the bathing hut Cleve was already dressed. She walked up to him, took his face between her hands and brought his head down to kiss him. ''Hello, husband,'' she said, and kissed him again. His hair was wet, the thick golden strands brushing his shoulders. He looked so barbaric, so wonderfully alive she never wanted to let him out of her sight.

''I'm going hunting with Merrik and Oleg and the Malverne men,'' he said, clasping her wrists and pulling her arms down. ''You will help the women dry meat and fish. We will need a lot of food when we leave for Scotland. I wish to leave in four days. I've already spoken to Kiri.''

''All right. I don't know anything about drying meat or fish, but Mirana will show me. Do you have time for another bath, Cleve?''

He felt the hunger in her, felt her absolute acceptance of him, and he felt like garbage tossed in a refuse mound. He'd failed her, left her wanting and not understanding what it was she'd missed because he'd been such a frantic pig. He had to gather himself together. Even now, after she'd just kissed him, he wanted to fling her down to the pounded earth floor, rip up her gown and come into her. He wouldn't. He couldn't begin to imagine what Merrik would think of him if he knew how he'd treated his virgin bride the previous night. She wanted him to bathe with her? He shuddered at the thought, seeing her naked and wet, his hands slick with soap, stroking over her, seeing himself lifting her and coming up into her. By the gods, it was too much. He'd kill himself before he shamed her again.

"Nay, I can't now, Chessa. I will see you later." He kissed her quickly and strode to the outer door. He turned and said, "I'm sorry about last night. I don't know what happened to me, but I just had to have you and that's never happened to me before, but—" He looked furious with himself and embarrassed and desperate.

She said, looking at him straightly, "I want to touch you again, Cleve, wrap my fingers around you, listen to you moan, feel you shudder. The feel of you makes me very happy. Don't you like it when I touch you there?"

He looked as if she'd just shot him with an arrow. He was gone in an instant.

Chessa looked down at her toes and smiled. Men were strange. They were also fascinating. She couldn't wait to get him alone tonight.

What to do about Kiri? She grinned, remembering how the little girl had called in Kerzog and told the damned mongrel that he'd been right. She'd thought it all a game, the two of them in the same box bed, both of them naked, laughing, tugging at Kerzog, racing out of the small sleeping chamber. She'd lifted Kiri that morning after she'd finished her porridge, tossed her into the air and told her she was going to tie her to Kerzog's tail so she couldn't come in and attack her poor papa before he was even awake.

"Which Papa?" Kiri had said, laughed at her own cleverness, and wriggled out of Chessa's arms.

She hadn't known what to expect that morning, but she'd

been hopeful. Her hope hadn't lasted long. He'd acted ashamed, embarrassed. He'd quickly left the chamber, saying little to her. Now she understood. She wondered what the men had said, what he'd said to the men.

Cleve was red-faced, the cords in his neck pulsing madly. "You told Rorik I took you five times? *Five* times? Five *separate* times? And you asked him if it was enough? You asked him if men never tired?"

She looked down at her shoes. She gave him a furtive look, all shy and flustered. "Aye," she said in a small little voice, scuffing the toe of her slipper into the dirt.

"Damn you, Chessa, stop it. I don't believe your act for an instant. Look me in the eyes and stop the smiling you're doing inside."

"All right." She grinned up at him shamelessly. "I thought Lord Rorik would drop his jaw on the ground. He wanted to question me to make sure I knew what five times really meant. He kept saying, Were they *separate* times, with time in between? It was very important to him that I understood."

Cleve could still see Rorik's face in his mind's eyes, staring at him, marveling at him, wondering if he could have that extraordinary stamina. He sighed, saying, "What a day it's been. It's all the men can talk about. Surely you didn't think Rorik would keep such a bit of wickedness to himself, did you? No, of course you didn't." Cleve sighed, plowed his fingers through his golden hair, loosening several strands to frame his face, and said, "I mauled you and then I fell asleep. That's the truth of things and—"

"And what, Cleve? I'm pleased that you desired me so very much that you couldn't slow yourself. I can't believe you told the men you'd failed me. That's ridiculous. You didn't hurt me overly. I look forward to this evening."

He wanted to shake some sense into her. Instead, he growled at her just like Kerzog when someone was trying to pull a stick out of his mouth, turned on his heel and strode away.

Laren came over to her and held out an apple. "Here, chew whilst I tell you about men."

Chessa took a big bite.

"Men," Laren said, staring after Cleve, who was nearly running out of the palisade gates, "can't bear it if women take away something they consider to belong to them."

"Men consider mating to be theirs?"

"Oh, yes. It involves their prowess, you see. Even more than that, it is how they see themselves, it is the very core of what they are. They must see themselves as the masters in this. It is they who decide how the act is to be done properly, and this is based on certain rules they've developed from father to son over the years. Women are never to talk openly about such things."

"What rules?"

"A man such as Cleve is thoughtful, slow to temper, a man of thorough habits. Since I overheard what you said, why then, he feels as though he failed not just you, but himself, and all men. He's ashamed. However, what you said to Rorik was excellent. All the men now consider Cleve near to a god's throne. I've heard '*five times*' more than I ever wish to hear two words again in my life. Actually '*five separate times*.' And that embarrasses him even more because, Chessa, you made it up to hide what he views as his failure. You, a mere woman, are trying to protect him, to save him from humiliation. He can't bear that."

"By all the gods," Chessa said, tossing the apple core onto a refuse pile, "that's ridiculous. There are two of us, not just Cleve doing things according to some sequence. I'm half of this business, aren't I?"

Laren hugged her. "Aye. The women are all delighted at what you've done. You've made them laugh at how easily you drew the men's manly noses into your drama. Perhaps Kerek was right."

"Right about what?"

Laren just shrugged. "Perhaps I can picture you in an open wagon, hundreds of men following your orders. Perhaps I can see you as the woman warrior Boadicea, the queen of the Iceni. You think, Chessa, and you act. Whether or not you see things clearly—well, it doesn't matter. You can't be right all of the time. The point is, you don't dither. You act. I like that. Cleve does too, just not now when his man's feelings are raw. Will you handle him tonight?''

"Oh, yes," Chessa said. "Mirana wants me to search out some plover eggs. I'm taking Kiri. She and I must decide how we're going to divide up her first papa at night. She's very smart, you know, Laren. It's difficult to keep a step ahead of her. I must ask her about Kerzog too.''

"I agree. Too, since Kiri isn't a man, you will come to agreement very quickly, I doubt it not. What's this about Kerzog?''

"I don't know. As you said, Kiri's a female. Already, she loves mysteries.''

That night after all had eaten roasted herring, rye bread dripping with hot fat from the baked pheasant, and stewed onions and cabbage, and drunk Utta's mead, Laren stood and cleared her throat. In an instant of time, all were turned to her, leaning toward her, waiting expectantly. Even Kerzog looked alert, which was something, Chessa thought, since he'd eaten more than three starving men.

"I have a story to tell you," Laren said.

There were cheers and all sat forward even more, the longhouse completely silent. All anticipation.

"This is a story about a man beyond any man, a man who didn't want it known that he had powers no other man could claim. He was calm and thoughtful, never loud or boisterous. He was looked upon as a kind man, a man who was a good friend, but surely, not a man who could claim such powers, such endurance.

"It came to pass that this man married a woman of extraordinary lineage. He hadn't wanted to, but she was strong and sure of what she was and what she wanted, and thus it was done. That first night of their union he took her to his bed and mated with her five times before the dawn sent the shadows into mists of the sunlight.''

''Stop this, Laren,'' Hafter yelled, tossing down his mead. ''I don't believe it. I have never taken Entti more than three times in a night.''

''It couldn't be five *separate* times,'' Rorik said. ''That isn't possible. Chessa just doesn't know how to count things like that properly. She's mistaken, that's all. By all the gods' beards, she was a virgin. How could she know how to figure out anything at all?''

''Yes, I do know,'' Chessa called out. ''Cleve explained it all to me before we began. He said he would give me more pleasure than any woman had ever had before. He wanted me to be able to compare my pleasure last night with my pleasure in the future. He said he knew I was innocent and thus I might be sore if he was too enthusiastic, thus he said he would go very gently with me until I became more used to him.''

''Cleve lied to her!'' Merrik shouted. ''He's very nearly my brother, yet he can lie as well as I can. He learned to lie from me. Don't believe any of it.''

''I understand now,'' Hafter said. ''Chessa didn't drain Cleve the way Entti drains me. She caresses and kisses me and fondles me and then forces me to do that to her. It takes a lot of time, for she is a stern taskmaster. Thus, I've never been given the chance to reach my full potential. Whereas Chessa, an innocent despite the number of times she's been pregnant, knows nothing about the act, and thus Cleve simply kissed her and took her. Mayhap he didn't even kiss her. There was nothing to it, no soft words, no caressing, nothing that took any time at all. He did it quickly, then rested himself only to do it quickly again. Any man here could do that.''

Laren raised her hands. ''Enough now, this is just a tale, a simple tale for your enjoyment.''

Merrik said, ''Are you certain you wish to proceed, wife? You're treading where the gods wouldn't be seen.''

She nodded, grinning down at her hands. ''Five times he

loved her and each time was wondrous because this man was a fine lover, giving her all his skill and his caring and speaking soft words to her, telling her how beautiful she was, how she moved him, how her flesh felt to his fingers, to his mouth. He made her pleasure exquisite because he knew that a man's responsibility was first to his wife. He was a husband that every woman dreams of having. Ah, and he was so gentle with her since she was unused to a man. Each of those five *different* and *separate* times left both of them lying in a brief stupor, sated, happy, yet eager for more after but a short time had passed.

"The following day left all the men slack-jawed when they found out how he'd treated his new wife. He, naturally, didn't say anything, because he wasn't the kind of man who bragged and carried on about his own greatness. Indeed, he probably believed it just a normal way of things. But his innocent wife spoke of it and why not? She thought that was simply the way things were done as well. The men couldn't believe it. They couldn't accept it because none of them had ever managed to achieve such a superior number and done in such a perfect way.

"They didn't know what to do. Before, they'd all admired him, liked him, called him friend, but now? They looked at him now and saw a man who was more than they. A man who had reached heights other men only dreamed of. And surely men are always dreaming of heights. It is their nature to do so. What should they do? My lord Merrik—my mate, a brave warrior, a man whose choler comes swiftly to the fore then recedes after he's made the earth shake with his wrath, a man who gives me—"

"Be quiet, Laren," Merrik said very slowly, very precisely, his eyes burning with a desire to strangle her. "Be quiet or it won't go well for you."

"Very well, my lord. I got carried away, actually only the skald part got away, but both of us are back again. Forgive me. I'd always believed you the most perfect of men, the very . . . well, forget about that. Things are differ-

ent now, what with Cleve's skills and . . . nay, forget that
as well. My lord, please tell us what do you think the men
should do.''

Merrik roared to his feet. "Enough of this, Laren. You're
causing mischief and we won't have it.'' He turned to the
men, who were all speaking amongst themselves, tempers
rising, and he bellowed, "I don't want to hear more of this,
do any of you? It's nonsense, she's baiting us and—''

Rorik rose, laid down his mug of ale on the bench,
paused a moment, and said, "Well, I would like to know
what you think the men should do, Merrik. I really would.
That is, you may go first, then the rest of us will tell Laren
what is to be done with this man who is so damnably perfect he should be dead, a knife sticking out of his gullet.''

Merrik could only shake his head. "Don't let her goad
you. She's my wife, I know her. She oils her tongue around
her words. She's dangerous. Listen to me. Cleve is one of
us. He is as much my brother as you are, Rorik. If he
happens to be able to repeat the act more times than the
rest of us, what does it matter?''

"I say hang the bastard,'' Haakon said. "Now my Utta
will look at me, her mouth all sad, but she won't tell me
that I've failed her, maybe not for at least another five
years, but then, if she's too used to me, she will throw up
Cleve in my face. I say kill him, cut out his guts. I want
to boil his guts and feed them to Kerzog.''

Entti, who held her sleeping son in her arms, rose and
said, "Haakon, Utta would never make you feel less a man,
even after five years and her being too used to you. None
of us would. We are kind. We understand that certain men
simply aren't—well, no matter.'' She paused a moment,
and looked at Chessa. "I suggest that we end this with a
very simple solution. All the women will speak to Chessa
and she will tell us what it's like to have a man with such
endurance, such skill, such pride in his work. We will enjoy
it through her. We won't shame any of you. We love you.
We are understanding.''

Hafter had turned red. "I'll kill the damned bastard

LORD OF FALCON RIDGE   217

now.'' He rushed at Cleve, his hands raised to go around his throat. Merrik blocked him, and the fighting began.

Cleve jumped onto the table and yelled at the top of his lungs, "Stop it, all of you! Can't you see the women are just having sport with you? Are you so lackbrained that you don't understand what Laren's done to you? And Entti? And all the others, including Utta, who makes the best mead in all the world? It's all a jest, nothing more. They are laughing at us. I will tell you the truth. Listen to me— I fell asleep. Aye, that's the absolute truth. I fell asleep with Chessa wide awake beside me. I failed her. I gave her no pleasure. I rutted her like a stoat and gave her nothing but pain and she was a virgin. Don't break Haakon's arm, Gunleik. I'm a failure as a man. I'm nothing but offal on the refuse pile. Believe me, for it's the truth.'' He gave his wife a malignant look, shook his fist at her, and strode from the longhouse. Actually, he stomped from the longhouse, Chessa thought, watching him. She looked up to see Laren wink at her. Why, she thought, Laren was as wicked as she was. It was heartening.

There was utter silence where only the moment before it had been pandemonium.

19

Gunleik released Haakon's arm. Hafter stood silently, staring after Cleve. Merrik looked at his wife without a glimmer of affection. Hafter said to Entti, "If you weren't holding my sleeping son, I would strangle you. You're dangerous, mayhap more dangerous than those damned Danes and Saxons."

Rorik cleared his throat. "Chessa, did you lie? Did Cleve truly fall asleep and you were still awake, left wanting? Cold and alone? No love words, nothing at all save his obnoxious snoring?"

She sagged against Rorik's chair. She covered her face with her hands and sobbed, low racking sobs that brought Kerzog to sit at her feet, his paws scratching against her leg. No one said a word. Mirana would have gone to her, but Rorik held her back. He waited until those pained sobs finally stopped and Kerzog had been patted by Hafter. He said more gently, "Chessa, it's all right, no one blames you or Cleve, at least not now. Just tell us the truth. Nothing more, just the plain simple truth."

But she wouldn't look up at any of them. Her voice was thin and liquid from her crying. "I'm so sorry, Rorik. I didn't know anything was wrong until this morning when Cleve didn't kiss me upon awakening. He was ashamed. I didn't understand why he was ashamed, but he was. He believed he'd failed me. That's why he acted so strangely. I couldn't bear that, so I lied since he was ashamed and I wanted to spare him that.''

Rorik said carefully, mindful of each of those dozens of giant boulders in his path, ''That's the truth, Chessa?''

She looked up then, her face flushed with embarrassment, her lower lip quivering. ''But he didn't fail me, Rorik, it's just that he believed he did. All right, so he only took me three times. I lied about the five times. But he believed he'd failed since he came to me only three times and then he fell asleep and didn't awaken to love me again, which was what he wanted to do. I'm sorry I lied.''

''Is this the absolute truth, Chessa?'' Merrik asked.

She was silent for the longest time. Everyone was silent as well, staring at her, waiting. Anticipation made the air thick. No sound, even from the pets, except Kerzog. He whined, pawing at her foot.

She said in a choking voice, ''All right, it isn't the absolute truth, Merrik. It's just that—''. She stopped, swallowed and continued, ''Ah, this is so difficult. It's embarrassing for me. The fact is that Cleve is very big. When he first bared himself to me I knew it wouldn't work. I knew he would kill me, his member is so massive. I was afraid. I cried I was so afraid, but he was gentle, despite this huge part of him, and I let him advance. He was kind to me, but his size—'' She shuddered, then continued quietly, ''I thought I would die, but I didn't, of course. He took care of me after he'd finished the act. He soothed me and kissed me and told me he would allow me time to heal, but the bleeding was awful. This is why he feels guilty. He hurt me and he despises himself for it. Aye, he fell asleep finally, after seeing to me and assuring himself that I was no longer hurting so badly. He told all of you that he'd fallen asleep. He did this because he didn't want to embarrass me. I failed him, not the other way around. I failed him because I couldn't accommodate him. Because I wasn't as other women. Something's wrong with me, for I was too small for him. I've failed as a wife. He isn't to blame. I'm the only one to blame here. I only sought to protect him because he is so good and so noble.''

Laren cleared her throat. ''Now, my Lord Merrik, do you believe you know all the facts? Are you now satisfied with what Chessa has told you? Very well, what do you think the men should do?''

''Chessa,'' Merrik said slowly, aware that everyone of the men were sitting forward, waiting for his words, ''just how big is Cleve?''

''What do you mean, my lord?''

''I mean is it length or breadth or what exactly? Or is it that you are simply very small? Are you deformed?''

''I don't know.'' She looked about until she saw a very thick bolt of wood what was a joint in the chain of the pot hanging over the fire pit. She pointed to it. ''I suppose the breadth is like that.'' She then said very quietly, ''And the length? Perhaps it is like that chair post. I couldn't caress him even with both my hands. To stroke the full length of him took a long time. I failed him.''

''What is the truth, Chessa?'' Rorik said. ''Did he take you once or three times or five times?''

''Just once because he was so large and hurt me. He was kind though he wanted me again. He was stiff and hard beside me all through the night. I couldn't sleep because I knew he was in pain and in need, but whenever I told him to do what he wished to do, he refused, saying I had to heal.''

''I think,'' Merrik said at last, ''that the men should be grateful that Chessa lied. Cleve took her only once. We will all assume that she is smaller than most women. We will assume that she cannot judge either breadth or length. She is a woman, she knows naught of such things. Aye, let's forget it and remember that Cleve is one of us.''

''I say we should be grateful that Cleve felt such guilt about hurting Chessa that he fell asleep,'' Rorik said, and he laughed.

There was arguing, cursing, and some laughter. Entti laughed and Hafter looked at her with lust and murder in his beautiful blue eyes. As for Chessa, she merely smiled down at her toes and said nothing more. She knew the men were turning in circles. She really didn't care now, she just wanted her husband.

Cleve stood on the ramparts of the palisade. He felt relief when he heard sporadic laughter coming from the longhouse. By all the gods, what had Laren told them now? That he had the skill of a wild dog? The stamina of a girl? He was a laughingstock. All because of his damned wife.

"Cleve?"

He turned to see her staring up at him. The night was bright with a near full moon and a sky full of stars. He saw tear streaks on her cheeks. He forgot his anger at her. "Did they hurt you, Chessa? By the gods, what did they say to you to make you cry?"

That was surely a good sign, she thought. She managed a pitiful smile. She even managed a credibly thin little voice. "I'm all right. I was worried about you. Please come with me, Cleve. I'd like to sleep on the warship. There are blankets on board. We'll be alone and comfortable."

"Nay. There's Kiri."

"Kiri is sleeping with the other children. I spent time with her today searching for plover eggs. We came to an agreement. She won't sleep with us unless we ask her to. She did say that she might begin to count sticks though if we didn't ask her enough times. She's a very independent little girl, Cleve."

In his embarrassment, Cleve laughed. "Why the warship?"

"The men are still of an uncertain mood. I think it's best that they not see you again tonight. They spoke of stripping you naked to see how you're made."

"Why would they want to do that?"

"Well, I told them I'd lied. I admitted that it wasn't really five times or three times because you were so massive you hurt me badly, but you were gentle and kind to me and didn't take me again as you wanted to. As I was walking out of the longhouse, I heard Rorik say it wouldn't matter if they stripped you naked because that meant nothing. He said different men gained different size when they wanted a woman. What they began with wasn't all that important.''

"Chessa,'' he said slowly as he walked down the wooden rungs of the ladder, ''you told them that I had a huge member?''

"It's surely the truth. I looked at you and nearly fainted. And that's what I told them, Cleve. Can we go to the warship now? All that talk of separate times and length and breadth. It's left me wondering what all this mating is supposed to be about.''

He plowed his hands through his hair, a habit, she was learning, whenever he was unnerved. ''I failed you, but tonight, Chessa, tonight I won't. All right, I want no more fighting. We'll go to the damned warship. I might as well show you that I'm no hero, that I'm just a man and have the endurance of any other man, no more. Please, Chessa, tell me you didn't compare my sex to that huge oak trunk over there.''

"There were no oak trees in the longhouse.'' She looked disappointed.

"Thank the gods for that. I don't want to know what you compared me to. Doubtless I'll hear it from the men tomorrow. Come along now and learn you're married to a man, a simple man who doesn't have an oak tree attached to him.''

"That's splendid,'' she said, and tucked her hand through his arm. ''It's a beautiful night, isn't it? I love the smell of the salt water, the sound of the waves hitting against the rocks. The rocking of the warship will be very nice.''

He looked at her as if she were mad. He grabbed her hand and together they ran through the palisade gates. Old Olgar looked after them, shaking his head, grinning in the bright moonlight, his two remaining teeth glittering.

"Just look at him hauling her out of here,'' Hafter said to Gunleik. ''He's taking her away because he doesn't trust that we won't be listening, that we won't be looking through the bearskin covering to see what he's doing, to see how big he is. He's a sneak, this damned man I thought was a good friend. What should we do?''

Rorik said, ''Leave them be, Hafter. If Chessa is barely able to walk on the morrow, then we'll flatten him.''

''Aye,'' Gunleik said. ''I felt the same about Rorik when I realized he was husband to my sweet Mirana. I would have killed him if he'd hurt her.''

''Sweet?'' Rorik said, choking. ''Mirana? Sweet?''

''Be quiet, boy,'' Gunleik said. ''You're the luckiest bastard alive.''

Hafter, who wasn't paying any attention, said, ''Very well, we'll wait until tomorrow to see if Chessa can walk or not. Aye, that will suit. Now, where's Entti? I will show her just how it's done and it will be she on the morrow to give fodder to Laren's tale.''

''Amaze her with your breadth, Hafter,'' Rorik said, clapped his friend on the back, bade Gunleik good night, and went in search of his own wife. He wondered how much she'd had to do with this. He smiled remembering some of her more outrageous mischief, each time making him more furious than the last, each time making him laugh harder than the last, like the trousers she'd made for him with too much wool in the front. The trousers looked ridiculous with the bagging groin until he was fully aroused. He hadn't realized what she'd done until it dawned on him that the women were looking at his crotch every time they saw him, and giggling.

They'd been lucky over the years they'd been wedded. There'd been two raids by landless Danes and they'd lost only two men and one boy in the fighting and gained two warships. There'd been enough game to hunt, the rain had kept the crops plentiful. They had two fine boys and a little girl. He wondered, as he walked back to the longhouse, whistling, if perhaps she wouldn't become pregnant with another babe by morning. He would try his damnedest. Five

times. Five *separate* times. It was a goal now, despite
everything.

"By all the gods, I don't believe this." Cleve sat back
on his heels and just stared down at his wife. "This is the
god's punishment for my finally agreeing to marry you.
How many times did everyone ask you if you'd begun your
monthly flow? More times than I can remember. It's too
much."

"My stomach hurts, Cleve."

He just shook his head, plowed his fingers through his
thick hair, freeing it from the leather tie at the back of his
neck. Then he really looked down at her, saw her pallor in
the faint light coming into the small cargo space from the
moon, the tensing of her mouth.

He cursed softly, then eased down beside her. "Shall I
go ask Mirana if she has something for the cramping?"

"She'll be with Rorik having a splendid time. I just pray
there won't be any attacks tonight, for all the men are so
busy with their wives they'd never hear a thing."

"I'll hear it," Cleve said and sighed deeply. "I'll hear
every damned thing. You want me to rub your belly?"

"No, just hold me."

The following morning, Chessa felt tired, for she'd not
slept well. There were faint purple smudges beneath her
eyes. As for Cleve, he'd not slept all that well either, because he saw her pain, hated it, and tried to distract her
from it. When they left the warship after dawn, he said,
"Do you always have such cramping?"

She ducked her head down, watching the narrow winding
path upward to the summit of the island. A plover raced
across the path.

"Don't be embarrassed," he said, more irritated with her
than he could say. "By the gods, you were carrying on to
everyone about my man's size and the number of times I
took you on our wedding night."

"This is different," she said. "Nay, it isn't always bad.

Perhaps it was because of our wedding night. You might have pulled something loose, do you think?''

''Don't be ridiculous. How many times do I have to tell you? I'm just a man, a simple man. Now, I want you to rest.''

''But Mirana is giving me instruction on drying meat and fish.''

''That can wait. Rest, all right?''

He cupped her face between his palms and raised her to him. He kissed her lightly, gently rubbed his fingertips over her eyebrows to smooth them, kissed the tip of her nose, and lightly stroked his hand over her belly. ''Rest,'' he said again, and left her.

''I'm sorry, Cleve.''

''I know,'' he said over his shoulder even as he grinned and shook his head. ''We'll both survive.'' Odd, he thought, how marriage had focused his mind, nay, all of him, particularly his man's parts, on sex. He couldn't remember being so completely a slave to his body before. If he'd felt the urge, he'd slept with a woman, enjoyed himself, and hopefully given her pleasure as well, and then it was morning and time to go about his business again. But with marriage it was different. Sex seemed to be all he could think about. Or it was Chessa. No, that couldn't be true. He liked her, admired her, was terrified of her ability to think and act and do it well. Her results weren't always what one could wish but she never sat about and cried, unless it was a part of her latest strategy. No, this desire of his, always there, prodding at him, making him lose his concentration and look for her, it was just because they were married. She now belonged to him and that changed everything. She was his and only his. The only problem was that he couldn't have what he was supposed to have, at least not for a number of days yet. He moaned, wanting to cry.

''Didn't you sleep at all?''

It was Haakon frowning ferociously at him. Cleve thought Haakon would really prefer to be looking down at

Cleve's slain body. "You look like you've worked harder than a thrall for the entire night. I worked hard last night too, yet my eyes are at least open and my shoulders squared."

"I did sleep, Haakon. Not a spit of work for me." He said nothing more. Damnation, it wasn't anybody's business what he and Chessa did at night.

As for Chessa, the women were grouped around her, commiserating. Most of them were looking quite delighted, and Chessa knew the reason, but not how it felt to be delighted like that. Freya was punishing her for all her lies. "This will take away any cramping you may have now," Mirana said. "Just mix this in a bit of water and drink it."

"Poor Chessa," Entti said after her.

"Poor Cleve," Old Alna said. "He's a randy lad and will be more randy by the moment as the hours pass. Mayhap I should stroke his fevered brow, mayhap sing to him."

"Please, Alna, don't," Mirana said.

To Cleve's immense relief, no word was spoken about either his size, his prowess, his endurance, or his death at the men's hands. He noticed that the men did look at Chessa, saw that she was very tired, and wondered at it, but this time, they didn't ask. Had they learned that the women were making sport of them? He didn't know. He wasn't about to ask.

Over the late afternoon meal, Merrik said, "We leave in two days for Scotland. I've looked through the stores and all is ready to be stowed on the warships."

"I want to stop in York and kill Ragnor," Hafter said. "That bastard, making you go to such lengths, Cleve, that you had to wear breasts and paint on your face."

Cleve just laughed.

Chessa said, "He was beautiful, all the men admired him. When he came to my room he wouldn't let me hug him because he was afraid his breasts would slip and all the paint on his face would crack."

"But his eyes," Mirana said. "Didn't you recognize him immediately, Chessa?"

"He wore a black patch over his right eye. I just saw

this whore with big breasts who finally came to my bed-chamber and kissed me.''

"And you stabbed me," Cleve said. "Aye, she thought I was one of the guards bent on mischief and she stabbed me. Then she hugged me so hard that my breasts were in danger of falling to the floor."

There was much laughter, jests that made even Chessa's ears burn. Most importantly there were no more threats of killing Cleve for his superiority.

Kiri was invited to sleep with her two papas, Cleve told Chessa, and looked as if he would cry. They wrapped up in blankets near the fire pit, Kiri between them.

"We're going to a place called Scotland," Cleve told her, kissing her forehead. "Actually, we're going to a place called Inverness that's a trading town inland on the Moray Firth. There are many Vikings there, but also other peoples as well."

"Aye, Kiri," Chessa said. "There are people called Picts, an old race of people about whom I know nothing at all, Britons, Saxons, the Dalriada Scots—"

"I heard Gunleik tell Erna that none of them are clean like we are. He told her that the wool she spins is far too good for the likes of those dirty pigs. I think he kissed her then."

"That's possible," Chessa said.

"Her arm is all strange looking but it doesn't make any difference to her weaving," Kiri said.

"Nay, her arm is withered, but it doesn't make a whit of difference," Cleve said. "Never forget that, Kiri."

"Everyone loves her," Chessa said. "Your second papa also believes you should never forget that. What a woman is has nothing to do with how she looks."

"A man as well," Cleve said.

"Ah," Chessa said into his ear, "then you will finally know how much I love you. Not only your beautiful face and body, but your spirit, that deep richness in you?"

"You're mad," he said, and kissed her, then sighed deeply.

Kiri snuggled about to face her father, poking Chessa in the ribs with her knee. "You mean these strange people don't have bathing huts?"

"No," Cleve said. "I've heard that many of them never bathe for as long as they live. We won't live near them, I promise you, sweeting."

Chessa took Cleve's hand, freed from Kiri's for the moment. "They also have different beliefs, Kiri. The Vikings, like us, believe in Odin-All-Father, the chief of all our gods, the creator, the warrior, the keeper of heaven and earth. But there is Thor as well. In Dublin where I come from, we're called the tribe of Thor. He's our sky god, the god of thunder and storms whom our seafarers pray to for good weather. He's closer to us than Odin-All-Father, more personal to us, I suppose."

"Are you going to remember all this, Kiri?"

"Aye, Papa. Freya will see to it."

He moaned. "Did I ever tell you that you were too smart? Nay, don't answer that. Now, did you know that Vikings have also become Christians? That means they have priors and monks and priests and bishops, all sorts of men who tell them what they're supposed to believe and what they're to do and none of them agree with the other. All they agree on is that there is only one god and He is God. They have a Valhalla just like ours, but they count on this one God of theirs to see to their fertility, their battles, their crops, everything. It's a big chore for just one deity."

"Duke Rollo of Normandy and the Vikings who rule and live in the Danelaw are Christians, at least they profess to be."

"So you see, sweeting, we're going to sleep now because I want very much to kiss your second papa and I can't because it would send me very great pain. Good night, Kiri."

"Good night, Papa. Good night, Papa."

"Soon, Kiri," Chessa said, kissing Cleve's fingers, nibbling the pad of his thumb, "we're sailing to Scotland for a very great adventure."

"Why can't you kiss Chessa, Papa?"

"Go to sleep, Kiri."

Cleve didn't go to sleep for a good while. They were going on an adventure, that was certain. He was scared. He had no idea what they would find. How could anyone even remember him? Surely all had changed in the twenty years he'd been gone. Who was Cleve to them? A little boy maybe, that had been thought dead so many years before. What if what he remembered, all those landmarks, weren't there anymore? What if nothing were the same? What if they went, found nothing, then what? He had a wife and a child. What would he do?

Damn her, it was as if she'd read his thoughts. She said low, so much love in her voice that he wanted to run, "It's all right. We're together. It will be all right."

"If you're so smart then why did you begin your monthly flow now?"

Chessa laughed, took his hand, and kissed each of his fingers again. "I love the taste of you," she said softly so not to awaken Kiri.

"Why are you putting my first Papa's fingers in your mouth, Chessa?"

"I'm kissing them just like I'm going to kiss yours now."

The child laughed, turning back to Chessa, when she grabbed Kiri's fingers and kissed each one.

The next day was warm, the inside of the smoking hut so hot the women had tied their hair up with kerchiefs. "Now," Mirana said to Chessa, "you see that we have enough racks here for hundreds of fish. The gods know we need them with Kerzog's appetite. The ones here are clean and split open. We hold them open with wooden skewers hung on thin wooden rods passed through the heads. Now this fire that's making us all miserable isn't as hot as it could be. I've banked it down with sawdust and woodchips so it just keeps on smoking and smoldering. This dries the fish out very slowly."

"Aye," Old Alna said. "I like my oak sawdust the best. It gives the herring a nice sharp taste."

Mirana laughed. "And I prefer pine and fir. You will experiment to see what you and Cleve like best. Now, all the cod, the hake, and the salmon turn yellow. See? Tomorrow, we'll pack them in barrels with lots of salt between each layer. They'll last probably longer than we'll live."

"With all that salt," Chessa said slowly, "I imagine the smoked fish would last longer than any of our children or our grandchildren."

"It does, probably forever. You see that we smoke the meat in just the same way. I'm glad you'll be living next to both a lake and the sea. You'll never have to worry about food. There'll be abundant fish, trout, I've heard, and now you know how to make it last forever."

"Och," Old Alna said, "I remember when you ruined it all, Mirana. The stench drove us from the longhouse."

Mirana buffeted the old woman very gently on her bony shoulder. "Old Alna's right. You must smoke the fish long enough or else it will rot and nothing smells worse than rotted fish." She then walked Chessa through each step in the process, Old Alna cackling advice and disagreements with Mirana often enough to keep the women amused.

"What's that?" Mirana said suddenly, turning toward the door of the hut. Then she smiled, pulled the kerchief from her hair and shook it out. Hair as rich and black as Chessa's swept down her back and over her shoulders. She wiped the perspiration from her face. "It's Kerzog barking his head off. I'll just wager the men have killed a boar, perhaps even a deer. Let's go see. Ah, it's a feast we'll have tonight."

20

Moray Firth, Northern Scotland

THE DAY WAS cool, the sun trying to burn through the light mist that stretched out over the water and veiled the land. Only the very tallest peaks poked through that heavy mist.

Merrik said, "Kiri, my little pet, this is a fine summer day in Scotland from all I've heard."

"But there's no bright sun like at home."

"As I said, a bright summer day for Scotland."

Kiri was sitting on his knee. "Then we're nearly there, Uncle Merrik?"

"Aye, Kiri. We'll sail down the Moray Firth to the trading town of Inverness, which is nestled right there where many bodies of water come together. Then just southward is the river Ness. It's a narrow canal that feeds finally into Loch Ness. Your papa remembers a huge circular promontory or a long arm of land and rock jutting out high into the loch on the western side. On that promontory is a large wooden house, something like Malverne farmstead."

"Will they know me? Will Papa have a mama who will be my grandmother?"

"I don't know, sweeting. So much time has passed and

life doesn't just go on and on because he would like it to. But there will be perhaps cousins and aunts. It's been twenty years, Kiri, since your first papa left here. None of us know what we'll find.''

"My second papa calls it a grand adventure.''

"It hasn't been so far," Merrik said, then laughed at himself. He didn't really want to come stern to stern with a marauding Viking warship, not with all their supplies, Chessa, Laren, and Kiri aboard. Ah, but it had been a long time since his warship the *Silver Raven* had rowed directly at an attacking raider. His men who were the best archers would shoot at the enemy. His men in their narrow helmets and long war coats would be on both the platforms at the stem, ready when they were close enough to leap aboard the raider's warship and then the fighting would begin. Merrik's hand itched for his sword, once his father's sword and his brother Erik's sword, called the Slasher, three feet long, its blade of iron, its hilt of bronze inlaid with silver and rubies he himself had added just three summers ago south of Kiev in a tiny trading town called Radovia.

"No, not yet," he said, bringing his attention back to the little girl. He looked over at Eller. "Does your nose smell anything? We're quite close to land now. I can't see much of anything through the morning mist. The *summer* morning mist that will probably last all day. By all the gods, this is a land that confuses the senses, aye, but it's a rich land and there's magic here, even I can sense it. Chessa is right. This will soon become an adventure.''

Eller tapped the side of his nose, shook his head, and kept his hand firmly on the rudder. He'd done well this trip, Merrik thought, had learned nearly everything Old Firren knew. Old Firren had died the previous winter.

"I hope Eller doesn't get sick in his nose, Uncle Merrik," Kiri said.

"It happened once," Merrik said. "We were in the Baltic Sea, just coming from Birka. His nose was all clogged up and he couldn't smell a thing. We had a close call because of it.'' Ah, that had been fun.

"Inverness!"

At last they'd arrived. It had taken only eight days from Hawkfell Island, thank the gods for the warm weather and the constant summer westerly winds. There had been but one brief rain squall that had passed quickly. Everyone was excited. They'd finally reached Inverness.

There were thirty men, most of them from Malverne. All were warriors, all were ready for anything, all skilled with axes, swords, and guile. All of them had brought goods to trade at Inverness. Merrik hoped for a fine profit from this trip as well as helping Cleve regain what was rightfully his.

The trading town of Inverness looked much like the town of York some years before. Inverness was smaller, cruder, and its fortifications weren't as impressive as those at either York or Hedeby or Kaupang. It was more like Birka, Merrik thought, but then he changed his mind. Its paths weren't covered with planks of wood and thus the ground, when it rained, would be muddy and dangerous. That had to be often. It probably sweated rain here, he thought. It reminded him of Ireland, so very much green from all the rain, but the mist was different here, like fine spiders' webs, open here, yet opaque over a tree or a rock. The mist was lifting as the morning lengthened toward noon, but not entirely, hardly ever entirely.

They tied the *Silver Raven* and the Malverne fellow trading ship to the far dock beside a trading ship from Dublin. Next to it was a vessel from the northern islands called the Orkneys and another from the Shetland Islands.

Half the men remained on board. Cleve, carrying Kiri in his arms, walked beside Chessa to the center of the small town. There was row upon row of wooden buildings, all of them shops close together selling furs, jewelry, shoes, swords and axes, bows and arrows, some for trading or selling slaves, so much more. There were open-air fish markets, farmers' goods were arranged beneath leather covers to keep the sun off them, when there was sun.

There was noise and activity everywhere, men and women bargaining, shouting, cursing customers who outwitted them, rubbing their hands together when they'd gotten the better of the bargain—once the customer had left their shop, naturally.

"Where are we going, Papa?" Kiri said, her first words since they'd left the dock. She'd seen Kaupang, but this was new and exciting. This was Scotland.

"We're going to find a bathing hut. You're as dirty as that louse I just picked off Eller's head this morning. So is Chessa and so am I. I want you smelling like honey again, sweeting, so I can kiss your ear without wrinkling my nose."

She laughed and was still laughing when Cleve left her and Chessa with an old crone at a bathing hut. It was a wooden hut with a thickly thatched roof, as were most all the other buildings. Inside it was steaming hot, a huge wooden tub in the middle with woven mats beside it. It looked like Valhalla to Chessa.

When Cleve, himself now clean, came to fetch them two hours later, a good dozen of the Malverne men with him, he brought new gowns, and for Chessa, two beautiful silver brooches, made only in the Shetland Islands, he told her. They were called silver thistle brooches because of the thistles carved into the sides and top of the brooches. And from Orkney, he gave her a gold finger ring, made of five rods twisted and plaited together. Chessa just gazed at that ring. She'd had fine jewels given to her by her father in Dublin, armlets, finger rings, brooches, many so dazzling with the purity of the gold and silver, the sheer delicateness of their fashioning, that they made Sira jealous, which was always an interesting thing to watch, but this ring was surely the most exquisite she'd ever seen. Despite all the men standing about and the old crone and Kiri, Chessa threw herself into Cleve's arms, nearly toppling him over so unexpected was her pleasure. "Oh, they're beautiful, the most superb jewelry I've ever seen. You're wonderful, Cleve, the most perfect man, the best of—'' She looked demurely at the men standing behind him, now beginning to frown, and just smiled down at her feet, saying low, but not low enough that they couldn't hear her, "and you're such a splendid lover and husband, more than any wife could wish for."

It was difficult, but he didn't strangle her. "Be quiet, damn you, or I'll thrash you right here. By all the gods, do you want them to kill me?"

"All right," she said, smiling at him, "I'll hold my peace, thought it is all probably true," and kissed him on his closed mouth. "Aren't you an excellent lover, Cleve?"

"I'll strangle you."

"What did you get for me, Papa?"

It took Cleve a moment to focus on his daughter. He smiled, handing her a small arm ring of shining silver. He let her touch it and stare at it, then slipped it onto her upper arm, tightening it because her arm was very small.

"Your second papa is the daughter of the King of Ireland. I suppose that must make you some sort of adopted princess too. That's very fine, Kiri."

The men looked jealous and wistful. Chessa knew they missed their wives and children. She wondered if they wanted to kill Cleve again. She imagined all of them had traded their goods for jewelry. But it could be a long time until they returned to Malverne.

"Och, yer white gentiles!"

All the men whirled around to face a graybeard who looked as if he should have died twenty summers before. He had a long scraggly beard that hung nearly to his waist, and no hair at all on his head. He wore a black robe that was tied at his sagging middle with a thick rope. He was giving them a big toothless smile.

"We get many black gentiles trading here," he said when he reached them, and Chessa thought, *Ah, here's a perfect mate for Old Alna.* "They don't stay long. They go back down to the Danelaw. They're not fit for our climes."

"What's that, Chessa?" Kiri asked, unable to take her eyes off the old man.

"I don't know. Cleve?"

"We're from Norway, thus we're white gentiles. Black gentiles are Danes. We're taller and have lighter hair, that's all, that's the only difference, that and we have more honor than the damned Danes."

Merrik smiled down at the old ancient. "I am Merrik, Lord of Malverne, in Norway. We're bringing our friend home. He's been gone since he was a small boy. His family rules Kinloch. Perhaps you know of them?"

It seemed the old man shriveled before their eyes. The scoring wrinkles on his face seemed to deepen. He stared at Cleve and began backing away. "Och," he said, crossing his fingers in front of him to ward Cleve off. "Yer one of them, one of them fiends what call out the monster."

"What fiends?" Chessa said.

"What monster?" Merrik asked.

The old man was trembling, his gnarly hands opening and fisting. "The Kinloch, he calls himself the Lord of the Night. He rules as harshly as the earls of Orkney. He orders his men to kill and take what they want. He's a fiend, a man of evil, lower than the Christian's devil, who draws nearer to us everyday. We don't know if the Christian God is more powerful than the Christian devil. Who wants to take the chance? But we're already got our devil here, and it's yer kin—the Lord of the Night—the Lord of Evil. Get away, get away from here if yer a part of him and his. Aye, ye are, a monster, just like he is. I see it clearly now. Jest look at ye."

"This is interesting," Cleve said, frowning after the old man, who was surprisingly agile in his escape for one of his advanced years. "I come from the family of fiends? The Lord of the Night? Of Evil? As bad as the Christian's devil? He must not like my hideous face. This sounds like one of Laren's tales. Where is Laren?"

"She will be here shortly. She and Eller were trading soapstone bowls. Ours are the finest in the market. Sarla made them before she became, well, maddened."

No one said anything to that.

*   *   *

They left Inverness several hours later, well before it was dark. They sailed down the narrow river Ness, seeing small settlements on both sides of the shore, looking for a deserted cove to stay for the night. At the mouth of Loch Ness, they pulled the warship and the trading vessel into a small inlet that seemed deserted and pulled both boats well up onto the shore.

The mist became thicker during the evening, the summer air chill. Laren cooked a red deer stew that made everyone groan with pleasure.

"I remember now," Cleve said as his knife tip speared another piece of the tender deer meat. "I remember that red deer abound, as well as rabbits and grouse. With all the salmon and herring in the loch, no one ever starves, even in winter, for it is never as cold here as it is in Norway."

"A land of plenty," Merrik said to Cleve. "But this fog or mist—it's summer, and just look. We're shivering off our bearskins. Tomorrow," he continued, smiling now at Cleve, "we'll find out what kind of a friend you really are."

Chessa was holding Kiri between her crossed legs as she sat close to the fire. She said, "Cleve, tell us about this man who married your mother after your father died."

Cleve flinched; he couldn't help it. "His name is Varrick. You know, what I remember most clearly is the coldness. Even curled next to the fire pit, I was always cold. Everyone in that longhouse was cold. And he was the coldest one of all. He made the cold. I think he's a white gentile, just like you are, Merrik, despite the darkness of his hair. My mother was a Dalriada Scot. I can see him as if I were a small boy again, standing in front of him, staring up at him—he was a giant to me for I was small—and I knew he must hate me since my older brother and I were the heirs to Kinloch, that he must want us dead, that he would kill us, it was just a matter of time. I was terrified of him. He never hit me, never touched me. He would just look down at me as if I were something of mild interest to him, nothing more. He was big, as are most Vikings, but he was thin I remember, for once I saw him naked in the bathing hut and I could see his ribs. He was very young, no older than I am now. As I said, his hair was dark and he usually wore it loose around his face. His face, by the gods, his face was so cold, just as he was, and he treated everyone with that same coldness, even my mother and my sisters, particularly my elder brother. Everyone was terrified of him, why, I don't know. He liked to lift me up so my face was right in front of his and he'd shake me—never hard enough to hurt me—and I'd shrivel into nothing. But then he'd smile at me and that made me all the more terrified of him. Many times he hugged me against him and I was so frightened I often forgot to breathe. I remember he told me I was his, only his, and I would be what he wanted me to be. And I wasn't to forget it, ever.

"I remember one night he came into the longhouse after standing on the edge of the promontory that overlooks Loch Ness. A storm was raging outside. He was wearing black, I think he always wore black, and there were strange blue markings on his face. No one said a word. But I remember again the coldness of him and of how he made me feel.

"I remember he hated filth. He wouldn't allow any blood to be seen on anyone. When the men came in from a kill, they couldn't show themselves until their bodies and clothes were clean. He abhorred animal flesh, I remember that clearly. I can see him looking at my mother when she once forgot and offered him a platter of roasted deer. He took the platter from her and then put it on the ground at his feet for his dogs. He looked at her and said she would regret that.

"It's strange, but before that, I remember laughter and fighting and quarreling, everyone, the men, the women, the children, and everyone shared and worked together." Cleve sighed. "Then again, I must have been very young. Maybe I dreamed that once everything was different, mayhap it wasn't. But I do remember my mother coming to my pallet at night and holding me and telling me that one day my brother would become Lord of Kinloch and my brother would see that I served him well and honored me. She had to know that he would rid himself of my brother and of me. She had to."

Laren leaned forward, her vibrant red hair glistening in the light of the leaping fire, thick and damp with the mist that hung low over them. "I remember you told us your mother died. Do you remember this, Cleve? Did this Varrick kill her?"

"I don't know. She died just before I was taken. I remember thinking when I was well enough to think, Why me? Why not my brother? He was, after all, the heir to Kinloch. But I was the one struck, I was the one left for dead, I was the one found and nursed back to health, then sold as a slave." He paused, "Look over Loch Ness. Look at how very murky it is. That's because of all the peat moss in it. Even when there's no mist, even with a bright sun overhead, you can't see very far beneath the surface. It's also said that the loch is bottomless, that any who fall into it will never come up. It's said that there are caves honeycombing the sides and that bodies wash into those caves and are held there for the monster."

"You remember all that?" Merrik asked, knifing down one final bite of the deer stew. "Ah, Laren, that was delicious."

Cleve grinned. "Nay, I listened to several men at the market today. A fisherman had just disappeared in the loch. They told me all about it. They made little attempt to find him since they know he's dead and there's no hope of regaining his body for burial. Never does anyone venture onto the loch after sunset."

"This man you describe," Laren said, "He does rather sound like this Lord of the Night, this Lord of Evil. He wore black and pranced about in raging storms, he painted his face blue. What sort of markings were they, do you remember, Cleve?"

"I only remember squares and circles. I was only five or six years old, Laren. Perhaps not even that."

"This was all twenty years ago," Chessa said. "That's

a very long time, but it seems your stepfather is still very much alive. I am anxious to see him. I like the notion of him wearing black and prancing about. It makes my mind spin.''

''Oh, no,'' Cleve said, and slapped his hand against his forehead. ''Not more chaos from you, Chessa. Be quiet, and think only calm thoughts.''

''We'll discover the truth tomorrow,'' Merrik said. He turned to his wife, who was leaning against his shoulder, staring with her skald's dreamy eyes into the fire. ''Have you already begun to weave your tale, sweeting?''

''Aye, my lord. It is the ending that eludes me. I want to know more about this monster.''

''There is one,'' Cleve said, and every man leaned forward, silent and alert. He felt a ripple of fear, of the unknown, grip them. It gripped him as well. ''It's said that the monster lives in Loch Ness and has for thousands of years. Whether it is good or evil, no one knows. The men who were speaking of the monster said he's seen not just on clear nights beneath the moonlight, but during the day as well, at any time. It's said the monster comes out during storms only when it's called. Perhaps that is why my stepfather is a fiend. They believe he calls the monster out.''

''This has all the makings of a fine tale,'' Laren said, and yawned. ''My lord.'' She offered her hand to her husband and he pulled her up and into his arms.

There was no choice that night. Kiri would sleep with her two papas. Cleve wanted Chessa so much he nearly moaned aloud with his need for her. As for his wife, she just looked at him wistfully, kissed him when Kiri turned away, then sighed when the child whipped about and frowned up at her, jealousy clearly writ on her small face. Chessa said, ''I'm a princess, Kiri. I can kiss anyone I want to. Even you.'' She grabbed up the little girl, tossed her into the air, then caught her and kissed her loudly on her little mouth.

Laren said to Cleve, "She does well with Kiri. I knew that one day you would wed, but I also knew that Kiri wouldn't like it at all. You made an excellent choice, Cleve."

"Ha," he said. "I made no choice at all. It was she who picked me with my hideous scarred face and my eyes that don't match."

"I wish you would stop that," Laren said, shaking his woolen sleeve. "You're a dangerous-looking devil, aye, that's true enough, and it makes all the women shiver with the thought of what you'd do to them. As for those eyes of yours, well, if it weren't for Merrik standing not an inch behind me, I'd leap on you, just like Chessa always seems to want to do."

"Aye, and after you'd leapt at me, Laren, Merrik would kill me," Cleve said. "You think me dangerous, Laren?"

"Oh, aye," she said. She said over her shoulder as Merrik just laughed and tugged at her hand, "Your eyes will very likely seal your claim to your birthright. No one could be certain you were the same child who returned as Cleve, but your gold eye and your blue eye, all would remember that."

"She's right," Merrik said. "I fear only that this Lord Varrick will simply stick a knife between your ribs or poison you. Now, wife, I'm weary to my bones. But not weary in other places." He led his wife to their small tent, set apart from the other men's, her merry laughter sounding in their ears.

Chessa grabbed Cleve by his ears. "You mustn't listen to other women, husband, even Laren. Saying she would leap on you if Merrik weren't close. Bah! They will make your head grow fat and filled with thoughts of your own beauty. You must only listen to me. I will never lie to you."

"And what will you tell me, Chessa?"

"That when you look at me I want to make you part of me forever."

He just stared down at her. "I asked, didn't I?"

"And I would leap on you even if Merrik is close. As for Kiri—"

"Papa, I'm tired."

"Aye, sweeting, we'll sleep now." He sighed again, very deeply. Chessa sighed as well.

21

Lოch Ness glistened beneath a morning sun. There was no soft mist to bathe the surrounding green hills and sloping forests of pine and oak beneath a mysterious white veil. The land looked lonely and magical, savage and unforgiving. Chessa could easily see the undergrowth of holly and hazel from the warship. Heather was everywhere, colorful blooms rioting over rocks, very close to the shore. The land had a wild and forlorn look. A golden eagle flew overhead, an osprey close behind it. She heard buzzards squawking. It was warm, the water was calm, and the men rowed smooth and cleanly through it. It was a large loch, fresh water, and very wide. But still the water wasn't a clear rich blue like the fjords at home, no, just below that clear surface it was dark. Chessa didn't want to fall in that water.

"Is it really bottomless, Cleve?" Chessa said, gazing down into the murky water.

"That's what the men said."

"Perhaps we'll see the monster. Did the men say what it looked like?"

"There are many descriptions, beginning with Saint Columba over three hundred years ago. A sea serpent, most say, with a long skinny neck and a small head. The men talked of humps, but none could agree on the number."

"There it is," Eller called out, "Kinloch." He pointed

to the outcropping on the western side of the loch. It was high and stark and there was a huge wooden fortress atop it, no simple farmstead. It would be impenetrable, save from the land, which was a narrow strip that had been shorn of all foliage. Just a barren wide path that led to the long-house. Only it wasn't a longhouse, it was nothing like Malverne. It was a fortress. There were no outbuildings beside it, just the stark huge wooden building that sprawled over the entire top of the promontory.

The outbuildings, at least twenty of them, were clustered around the loch at the land end of the promontory, low squat wooden buildings with sod roofs. There were pens for cattle and sheep and goats. There was a large smokehouse, a bathing hut, a privy, two slave huts. It was a huge farmstead with fields of barley and rye and oats growing thick and tall behind the outbuildings, climbing upward to the fir-covered hills beyond, the barley turning the fields gold. Surrounding the entire land was a high wooden palisade, thick pine trunks lashed together with leather cord, reaching at least eight feet high. The end of each pine was sharpened into a fearsome point.

"It is a safe place," Merrik said. "I would never worry that my property would be overrun by the Scots or the Picts or the Britons. As you did, Cleve, I listened well in Inverness yesterday. There are always raids, just forays really. There are no longer the ferocious fights between the Vikings and the Scots and the Picts since McAlpin became king in the last century." He turned to Chessa. "He united the Scots and the Picts and moved their center far to the west, in Scone. Their king now is Constantine."

Cleve said slowly, staring up at that immense wooden fortress. "I remember that just to the left inside the huge doors extends a thick wooden joint in the shape of a long sea serpent head. There are deep grooves in it and the cooking pots hang from it by chains. When the meal is done, one of the women simply moves the head from over the fire pit. I remember looking up at it, terrified because it looked so very real. My mother laughed and told me the monster served her and thus it wouldn't ever hurt me.''

"Cleve, you said your mother died shortly before you were nearly killed. Do you remember any more about her?''

He shook his head. "No, I just remember that her hair was nearly as red as Laren's, her eyes as green as yours, Chessa. She was small.''

"Now," Merrik said, stroking his brown hand over his chin. "What do we do? I can't imagine that your stepfather particularly wants to see your face again. I imagine he believes himself long safe from you after he sent you away. He must believe you long dead. We cannot storm that fortress, Cleve. It is impossible. There's something else, and I know you've thought of it. Your brother, he must be dead, perhaps struck down when you were.''

"I know," Cleve said. "I know. Now, I will go alone to the palisade and ask to see Lord Varrick. I will tell him that I am here to discuss matters of grave importance to him.''

"Ha," Chessa said. "I don't like your diplomat's voice, Cleve. This man doesn't sound reasonable like my father or like Duke Rollo. There is no chance I will let you go in alone. I've thought about this as have you.''

"I'll count sticks, Papa, if you leave me," Kiri said.

"Aye, you may accuse me of coercing your daughter," Chessa said. "But we won't let you go in there alone. Laren and Merrik will come as well. With the women and Kiri, no one could believe us to be enemies. Also, my lord Cleve, I am a princess. Never forget that. And Laren's uncle is Duke Rollo. Surely your stepfather isn't stupid.''

That was beyond foolish, but Cleve let it pass as did Merrik's men, though they stared at their lord as if he'd just relieved himself on his own leg. None knew what could happen. But they also knew they couldn't just stand here and wait. Chessa was a princess, the gods knew they'd all suffered enough for that fact.

Cleve didn't want Chessa or Kiri anywhere near him, but when he tried again to argue with Chessa, she just looked at him and said, "Nay, don't even think it. You are my husband. I will not let you go into that place alone. I will count sticks with Kiri.''

Cleve cursed. Their small group left all the men aboard the ships on the loch and walked to the wide palisade gates.

An old man called down to them from atop the rampart that ran along the inside of the wooden palisade. Cleve, as Chessa listened with a grin on her face, said, ''I have news for Lord Varrick. As you see, we have a warship and a trading vessel and both are in the loch. All our men await us there. We mean no harm nor do we mean to attack. We are but two men and two women and a child. Take us to Lord Varrick.''

The old man spat, nodded, and opened the gate. Four men immediately appeared, ferocious-looking men in red deerskins, none of them either white or black gentiles, but men shorter than Cleve and Merrik, dark haired and dark eyed. Their faces were etched with dark blue paint in circular and rectangular patterns. They looked vicious and deadly.

Kiri tried to climb up Cleve's leg. ''Papa, they're monsters.'' She buried her face against his knee. ''They'll cut off our fingers and roast them over a fire.''

One of the men laughed, actually laughed, and it was a terrifying sound. ''Nay, little one, we're not monsters save to our enemies. Come and we will take you to Lord Varrick. Whether he will see you is another matter.''

Two of the men marched in front of them, the other two behind. Cleve's knife was secured at his waist as was his sword and axe, Merrik's as well. None of the men tried to take their weapons. A weapon was just part of a man's clothing. Chessa had her own knife strapped to her thigh, as did Laren. Neither husband knew, and the women had decided that ignorance would suit them best.

''Men,'' Laren had said as she handed Chessa a piece of stout leather to secure the knife to her leg, ''men just don't understand that women need to know they can protect them. They would scoff at such a notion. But Merrik is mine. I won't allow anyone to hurt him. He was stabbed once in Rouen and didn't tell me. I wanted to kill him.''

Chessa was entirely in agreement with Laren.

It was about one hundred steps, the land slightly rising with every step, to the huge fortress atop the promontory. Cleve was right, Chessa thought, as she gazed at it. She was getting colder by the moment even though the sun shone starkly down on her head. Oddly enough, the cold was on the inside. It made no sense at all.

The man who'd spoken first to them turned at the great door and said, ''You will stay here. Hold the child. There are dogs and they might run over her and hurt her.''

Cleve lifted Kiri into his arms. She was frightened, but she didn't say a word. He was proud of her.

They stood there before that huge oak door, weathered to dark brown, the iron bars on the door looking older than time itself. Surely this fortress hadn't been built all that long ago. Had his father built it? His grandfather? Cleve stared up at the fortress, trying to bring memories of it from his boyhood. It didn't seem smaller. Surely that couldn't be right. It seemed the same yet very different. He had a flash of an ancient memory—streams of people, all carrying things, chatting, yelling at each other, dogs barking, children screaming and playing. Then it was gone, replaced by this impossibly cold fortress that looked older than the hills themselves. The air itself was laden with pervasive silence. They'd seen slaves working in the fields, but there'd been no talk amongst them. There were men, some Vikings, others like these four who were short and dark and painted with the blue markings on their faces. A score of women were washing clothes, others were stringing salmon to dry for the upcoming winter. Everyone was busy but everyone was silent. It was eerie. Cleve felt Kiri shiver in his arms.

''It's all right, sweeting,'' he said against her ear.

The man opened the door and said, ''Lord Varrick will see you.''

They walked through the door into a huge house of darkness. The immense hall wasn't empty. Women stood over the cooking pot at the fire pit, stirring with a huge wooden spoon. Two other women sat at their looms set against the wooden walls. There were at least a dozen men working their weapons, all of them silent. At the end of the immense hall, light flooded into the darkness through two huge open wooden shutters. The stream of light was harsh and heavy. In that stark light, standing on a wooden platform, stood a man dressed in black. He didn't move, just stood looking at them, silhouetted in the beam of bright sunlight. He remained motionless, as if he weren't really there, as if he were some sort of ghost appearing suddenly to drive them mad. Kiri whimpered softly and pressed her face into her father's neck.

There was still no movement, no talk. No one seemed to breathe.

"Come here," the man said, his voice deep and resonant, filling every corner of the huge hall.

Cleve gave Kiri to Chessa. "Stay with your second papa. Don't be frightened. He is entertaining us just as would Laren, only he does it with light and shadow, black and white. More black than white, but that's all right."

Cleve said aloud as he walked toward the giant of a man standing with legs spread atop that high wooden platform, "You are lucky there is no mist overhanging the land and loch today. Otherwise you wouldn't look like a demon from the Christian's hell."

"Ah," the man said, still not moving, just staring down at Cleve, whose face was alight with the sun and couldn't see the man's face clearly because he was in the shadows. "What you say is true, but there are other ways to make men shudder with fright, to bring them to their knees, to make them obey me. You understand this. Who are you?"

"I am Ronin of Kinloch, but I have been known as Cleve for so many years that I think of myself as Cleve of Kinloch."

At last there was noise, people staring at him, speaking now behind their hands, none knowing what to do, how to react. Not one of the men moved from their posts. Cleve thought Varrick had them very well trained. He had no fear of this man, just hatred, and yet he didn't know how he was going to wrest what was rightfully his away from this man who looked like a demon standing there, his face in the shadows even as the light cascaded around him. Cleve was a man of thought. He was a diplomat. He would trust his wits.

The man merely stared down at him, not moving, not speaking. There was a sudden shift of breeze from behind him, sweeping into the immense hall, and his black tunic billowed, making him look all the more terrifying.

"Where are my sisters?"

"They are here. You say you are Ronin? We have long believed you dead. You disappeared twenty years ago, surely too long a time for a child to survive into manhood. Are you truly who you say you are?"

"I remember my mother telling me I was the very image of my father. Look closely at me, Lord Varrick. Do you see resemblance between me and the man you replaced so very long ago?"

The man said in that same cold voice, "No, there is no resemblance to you and your mother's first husband. How came you by the scar on your face?"

"A woman, my lord. She struck me with a whip when I refused to bed with her."

The man laughed. It was a cold rusty sound, and quickly stopped. Chessa saw several of the men stare openly up at their master.

"Why?" he asked. "One woman is much as another. Why did you refuse her?"

"She was with three other young male slaves, all of them naked surrounding her. She wanted me to pleasure her, then to mount her and show them how it was done. She said she'd seen me with another girl and had decided then that she would have me as well. I wouldn't do it. She was enraged. She took her whip and sliced open my face. I bled on her."

"I would have killed her for maiming me."

"I had not that chance," Cleve said. "I was a slave. But you know that, don't you, Lord Varrick?" He stepped forward. "Let us continue, Lord Varrick. Do not think you can crush me like you did the small boy twenty years ago. Do not think I am a nightmare come only for the space of a single hour to torment you. I am here to stay. This is my home and I belong here. Where is my brother? No, I see that he isn't here. You killed him as you tried to kill me, didn't you?"

"You will crush me beneath your heel, Cleve?"

"I will come to an agreement with you, my lord. But I will not fade away. This is my wife, Chessa, she is the daughter of King Sitric of Ireland. This is Lord Merrik of Malverne. His wife is the niece of Duke Rollo of Normandy. If something happens again to me, you will be crushed, your magnificent platform that sets you above all others torn asunder, this fortress leveled. You will have nothing left, no huge windows at your back to give you presence and terrify people with your magic. I tell you this so that you will not act precipitously."

Chessa felt the intensity of his eyes on her. Like Cleve, she couldn't see him clearly for the sunlight blinded her.

"You are Hormuze's daughter," he said to her. "Are you truly of his blood?"

"Aye. I was very young when he gave King Sitric back his youth. I loved him dearly, but he left me, disappeared into the mists of time, giving me into the guardianship of the newly reborn king."

"He is the greatest magician I have ever met," Lord Varrick said. "Were any of you present when he worked this feat of magic on King Sitric?"

Merrik said, "My brother, Lord Rorik of Hawkfell Island, was there. It occurred just as Hormuze had promised. King Sitric wedded the virgin Hormuze selected for him. The following morning, he greeted his soldiers and the people at Clontarf as a young man, vital, handsome, the greediness of the old man melded back into the nobility of the young man."

"And you are his daughter."

"Aye, he taught me as well." Chessa raised her chin just a bit. "He taught me potions and spells. But I was a child and learned only a little."

Cleve said, "I want no battle with you, Lord Varrick. I want only what is mine and should have been mine. I spent fifteen years as a slave. I didn't remember who I was until the dreams came to me over the past three years. Now I know who I am. I want what is mine. I will kill you if I must to regain it."

At those words, the men very quietly stood, their weapons at ready. The man with his black tunic billowing out from the breeze coming through those open windows said, "You needn't threaten me. I know you are your father's son. I recognize you as your father's son. Now look upon me, Ronin of Kinloch."

"I am Cleve of Kinloch."

Varrick merely nodded as he stepped down from that high wooden platform, and for the first time Cleve saw him clearly.

"By all the gods," Merrik said. "I don't believe this."

"You are his stepfather," Laren said. "His mother married you after his father died. This isn't possible."

Cleve stared into the man's eyes—one golden eye and one blue eye. He stared into his own face.

"You are my son. I believed you lost to me for twenty years. You are home again." Lord Varrick stretched out his hands and clasped Cleve's upper arms. "You are my son," he said again. "You are mine."

"Papa," Kiri said loudly. "I don't like this. I want to count my sticks."

A soft voice came from behind them, "She is the image of you, Cayman, the twin of you when you were small. She is beautiful. My brother, welcome home."

Cleve had turned at the woman's voice. He knew his sister, indeed he recognized her. She looked like their father, like a Viking woman, tall and blond and fair skinned. "You are Argana? Truly?"

"Aye, Cleve."

Still, he didn't touch her. She was only his half sister, he thought, still reeling, feeling the nearness of his father, the man he'd believed all these years to have sold him as a slave, to have taken what he'd wanted, not caring, only taking. This man in his black robes, standing on the platform, calling forth monsters during storms. It was difficult to think. He could feel Chessa beside him, questions flowing through her, no fear now, just all these questions and surely there had to be sense in all this. "Argana," he said again. "It was our grandmother's name, I remember mother telling me, for it is an odd name. I am only your half brother."

"Our mother is still the same. What difference?"

"It is all too new to me as yet. I don't know."

"These are my sons, Cleve," Argana said, turning to show him three boys standing behind her, protecting her, knives in their hands, the eldest nearly a man, the youngest about twelve years old. Cleve nodded to each of them. He froze at the sight of the youngest boy. He had one gold eye and one blue eye. His father was this boy's father as well? He'd mated with Cleve's sister?

Chessa said clearly, "I am Chessa and this is my step-daughter, Kiri. You say she looks like Cayman. Who is Cayman?"

"She is my younger sister. Come here, Cayman."

She was the most beautiful woman Chessa had ever seen in her life, all blond and white, with eyes so blue they pierced the gloom of the great hall. Her coloring was identical to Merrik's, to most Vikings', yet there was great fascination in her face, a face that surely looked younger than it really was. Would Kiri truly become this beautiful when she reached a woman's years?

"Cayman," Cleve said. "I remember you were skinny and your hair was always in tangles around your face. You were ten years old when I left."

But surely that was impossible, Laren was thinking. She

looked impossibly young and pure and so very innocent and at the same time alluring.

"Aye," Cayman said. "And now I am nearly thirty years old, little brother. I am glad you're not dead. None have spoken of you in many many years." Suddenly, Lord Varrick said, "I have no small daughters. Kiri, you are my first grandchild. Will you come to me?"

He held out his arms to her. Kiri, as was her wont, studied him closely, his flowing black linen tunic with its billowing sleeves, his face that was like her papa's, yet thinner and older. "You're my grandfather?"

"Aye, I'm your grandfather. I am an old graybeard."

"Will you let me stand in the light like you did? Will you let me look like a demon as you do?"

"Aye," he said, and there was that same coldness in his voice, in the very presence of him, that made Chessa draw back. "I will let you stand in the sun if you like."

Kiri slowly held out her arms to him.

Still, there was utter silence in that huge fortress. There were many men, women, and children standing about now, but they were saying nothing at all. Argana's three boys were perfectly still and silent. Chessa watched Lord Varrick carry Kiri to the huge open shutters. He turned then and held her, facing them, the harsh sunlight streaming over both of them, sending their faces into shadows. Kiri's head became a halo of spun gold.

22

CLEVE DISCOVERED WHEN darkness came that his wife was dangerous. She didn't give him a chance, just jerked him into the small chamber Lord Varrick had offered to them, and pulled him down onto the box bed atop her. He'd never realized how a woman could tangle herself so completely with a man, but she did it. He was breathing hard, and she was biting his chin, kissing his ear, his jaw, all the while pulling madly at his clothes.

"Please, Cleve, now, hurry. I want you."

"This is too much," he said, eyes glittering in the soft dim light. "By the gods, I want you naked." His hands were frantic on her clothes and she had to slap them away for she didn't have that many gowns and he would surely rip this one.

But then, just as quickly, she didn't care. He wanted her and what he wanted she would give him. She would take care of him. "Hurry," she said, and didn't know where that had come from, but it was deep inside her and she couldn't wait for him to remove those brooches, to pull off her overtunic and her gown and untie her stockings. She just couldn't wait. Her hands were on his trousers and now he was above her, looking down at her, seeing her clearly enough in the shadowy light, for even in this small chamber, there were shutters that were open to the moonlight streaming into the room.

"Chessa," he said, and kissed her and kept kissing her, molding her to him, fitting his hands over her breasts, caressing them. He wanted to feel her naked flesh with his fingers. Her hands were wrapped around his back, kneading his flesh, pulling him close, drawing him toward her as if she wanted to consume him.

She lurched up, yanking hard at his trousers. "Hurry," she said again. "Please, Cleve. Hurry."

He knew she'd never known pleasure. How could she? He'd been a pig on their marriage night and she must have hated it, but she'd protected him, making the other men want to kill him because he was such a fine lover. Now it was she who was the frantic one, as urgent as he'd been. He didn't know what to do. Then his own need swamped him and it didn't matter. He jerked up her clothes, feeling her naked flesh beneath his hands, and his fingers were pushing apart her thighs and he felt her then, her dampness, her softness, her readiness for him and he couldn't believe it. He groaned and mounted her. "Part your legs wider," he said into her mouth, and she did, her hands on his buttocks.

"Hurry," she said again, and he laughed even as he lifted her hips in his hand, stared down at her beautiful woman's flesh and thrust forward, his head thrown back, his back arching, coming deep into her, filling her and letting the warmth of her fill him until he wanted to weep with the joy of it.

Ah, but that joy was mixed with a lust that drove him to the brink. He tried to pull back, but she pushed upward, drawing him deeper. He hadn't hurt her this time, yet he'd felt the pull of her flesh when he'd come into her. She hadn't been as ready for him as he'd believed, damn her, but now she was twisting and turning beneath him, arching upward, saying over and over, "Hurry, hurry."

He didn't want to hurry, but seeing her there beneath

him, her eyes closed, her black hair strewn about her head, her mouth open, and the soft moans touched his soul.

"I want your pleasure," he managed to say even as he knew it was nearly over for him. She was tight and small and she was moving beneath him, drawing him deeper into her even when he tried to pull out of her, just for a moment, just to get a hold on himself, so he wouldn't—

He felt himself explode. It was that simple and that complete, his surrender to his need, his surrender to her. When he drove to his hilt into her, feeling his seed touch her womb, he moaned deep in his throat like a wild animal, like a man whose pleasure was so great he cared naught who heard him.

Surely he would die now. No man could exist beyond that pleasure, no mortal man, aye, it was over for him. He was flat on top of her, their sweating chests pressed together and he was breathing hard against her cheek, kissing her between breaths, still shoving into her, his legs heavy on hers.

"I won't go to sleep," he said, and managed to draw himself up on his elbows. "Chessa, speak to me."

She smiled up at him. "You're very deep inside me, Cleve. I love the feel of you, the strength of you. You're smooth and hard and it pleases me."

"Foolish words," he said. "You don't know what you're saying, you're just talking. Don't you dare even hint to the men that I'm smooth and hard or anything else or I'll strangle you. I see what you've done now. I should have known. You got no pleasure and you didn't care. Damn you, Chessa, you just wanted to wring me out again, to take me and give me joy and not receive any for yourself. Well, that's not the way of it. I won't let you control me, not like you have every other damned man who's been unfortunate enough to swim into your waters. I won't ever again listen to your siren's song. Damn you, I will make you scream."

"But Cleve, it's your pleasure that is important, your pleasure that gives me joy, your—" She sucked in her breath when she felt his mouth hot on her belly, his hands working over her flesh, touching her, smoothing her, the heels of his hands massaging her pelvic bones, squeezing her hips, drawing her ever upward. He was on his knees between her legs and he looked up at her then. He was frowning ferociously. "You damned woman, you will scream for me."

He lowered his head and his mouth touched her. Her back arched and she gasped with the surprise of it. This was too much, she thought, her mind sharp with the pleasure of his tongue, the soft bite of his teeth. This was too much for a woman to bear. Surely he shouldn't be doing this to her, surely he should be resting now, for there was much to be done. "I don't know, Cleve," she said, striving to find somewhere in her body that wasn't pounding with urgency. She felt his tongue, his fingers sliding inside her, felt the dampness of herself and his seed and this felling pleasure that gave no mercy, no respite. She cried out, unable to help herself.

"Scream, damn you," he said, lifting his head just a moment to look up at her face. The scar was livid in the dim light and he looked like a demon, hard and cold and she knew he would gain what he wanted. He was more beautiful than the carvings she'd seen of the Christian saints or the Viking gods. "Aye," he said, seeing the change in her expression, and lowered his head again. His hands lifted her and she knew there was no hope for her now. He'd told her about a woman's lust but she hadn't really believed in it, not in feelings that seemed to make men animal-mad, that drove all their wits from them and left them panting and growling and helpless in their own cravings.

No, it couldn't be the same, it couldn't. She wouldn't believe, no, it was his pleasure that was important, not hers, not that a woman's pleasure existed anyway, but still—

She screamed. From one instant to the next, she was with herself, within her body, with him, then the next instant, she was wild and uncontrolled and crying out like an animal. She was mad and she was thrown into a frenzy she couldn't begin to imagine. She didn't care. She just wanted more. Her hands were frantic in his hair, on his shoulders, and she was keening, the feelings only making her wilder and wilder until suddenly she felt as if a soft rainfall had begun to fall on her and it was calming her, bringing her back into herself, not that she wanted the rainfall or being back into herself. No, she wanted more of that demented pleasure that was surely too great for a human to have to suffer.

"Cleve," she said. "I will surely die from that."

"Every night then," he said, and he was grinning down at her, triumphant, satisfied, everything male and strong in him, everything dominant, sublimely content. "You scream well, Chessa. I like it. You respond to me well. I like that too. I suppose I knew it would be this way between us. But you will not lie to me again, Chessa. I will have your pleasure as well as my own. Do you understand me?"

She said in a small thin voice that made him smile, "Since it is so very nice then I suppose I must do as you wish."

He gathered her into his arms and pulled her against his side. "In a few minutes we'll do that again. You've been a wife far too long to have suffered from a husband's neglect."

"I can't do that again, can I?"

He smiled at the utter bewilderment in her voice, at the sudden shyness, but he'd held her, caressed her with his mouth, moved his fingers inside her. He kissed her nose. "You thought you were so smart. You believed you could control me." He kissed her ear. "I'll make you do that as often as I wish to. You will have no say in the matter. I will say to you, 'Chessa, I'm putting my mouth on you and you will scream.' And then you will." He kissed her jaw.

She was silent for the longest time, then whispered against his shoulder, "Do you promise, my lord?"

His hand, stroking over her buttocks, stilled. He eased his fingers between her thighs. She was wet with him, with herself, with their passion. She quivered as his fingers lightly stroked her. "Aye," he said, "I promise."

It was Chessa who fell asleep but moments later, leaving Cleve to smile up at the shaft of bright moonlight that came through the open shutters. The fresh night air was strange. In Norway it was simply too cold during most of the year to allow such a thing. The thick wooden planks of the long-house had to overlap tightly to keep in heat. A window would be unthinkable. He looked up and saw the moon.

It moved him. He didn't remember seeing the moon as a child when he'd slept in this fortress. He closed his eyes and there was his father, looking at him with his one golden eye and his one blue eye. His father, not his stepfather, not the man he'd feared so completely as a small boy, not the man he'd believed had ordered him murdered. There was so much here at Kinloch, too much, and Cleve still had no idea how to sort it all out. He prayed no fights would break out between the Malverne men and Lord Varrick's men. But that was foolish. There'd been silence, just more deep, calm silence. Deadly frightening silence. Even the Malverne men, even Eller with his sensitive nose, hadn't said more than three words all during the long evening.

His sister, Argana, was his father's wife, and a mother of three boys. He remembered her as a girl, laughing and always in motion, always moving, picking him up in her arms and giving him great smacking kisses. But last evening, her silence had been absolute. And Cayman, thirty yet unwed, so beautiful she made a man ache just to look at her. Why hadn't she married? Like Argana, she'd said very little even when Laren had tried with all her skald's skills to learn more about her. He had very little memory of her as a child. Perhaps she'd always been silent, but he doubted it.

Kinloch was filled with an unearthly silence, and an eerie darkness that seemed to hiss through every corner of the huge hall, that shadowed around that profound light that his father brought into the fortress, keeping that light unto himself, keeping it from everything and everyone else. He pictured again Varrick holding Kiri in his arms, the bright light framing them together, making them one, that strange breeze that had lifted their hair, making them look other-worldly.

Chessa murmured in her sleep, her hand slipping down onto Cleve's belly. He felt her hand move over his groin and grunted when she tangled her fingers in his hair. He kissed the top of her head, squeezed her closer to him be-cause he couldn't seem to help himself. She'd come so very close to him. He'd fought her, the gods knew he'd fought her, but it had done him no good, no good at all. And she'd become Kiri's second papa. Chessa was smart. He was go-ing to have to be careful of her. There was too much of her papa, King Sitric, in her.

Ragnor of York had been lucky to escape. He smiled at that. He wondered if Turella had removed the king finally, setting Ragnor nominally in his place, with her ruling, nat-urally.

Chessa's hand tightened on him and he moaned deep within himself. He said as calmly as he was able, "Listen to me, Chessa. You're my wife, but I won't allow you to control me. I am myself. You will not dominate me, so you may forget your machinations." He thought he heard her yawn. Aye, a close eye on this wife of his who was too smart and had as much ingenuity as he did, which was bothering, but he'd accepted her, as had his daughter. Kiri was sleeping with Laren and Merrik, a good punishment for them, he'd told Merrik, who'd wondered aloud to him how Cleve was ever going to know his bride again. And Laren, beautiful red-haired Laren, closer to him than these two sisters of his, took Kiri and asked her if she'd consider a skald for her third papa. Merrik had stared at the vaulted ceiling high above them and sighed.

There was so much Cleve had to learn. And there was his wife, whose hand was holding him, and he knew she was awake, for her breathing had quickened. He grinned and rolled over atop her.

"I did promise," he said, and began kissing her. She was warm and willing. He expected that, but he knew it

would take her time to accustom herself to the pleasure he
would bring her every time they came together. When she
finally cried out softly in his mouth, his fingers slick on her
warm flesh, he felt in that instant free and whole and complete. It was frightening and it pleased him enormously. He
said again, softly against her parted lips, "You won't ever
try to control me, Chessa. Don't forget what I've said. You
may try, it will give me amusement, but don't forget I'm
like no man you've met before in your life."

She hugged him. The witch hugged him. He would have
to be careful of her. And that seemed an interesting thing
to do.

She would have killed Ragnor of York.

As for William of Normandy, Cleve was grateful William had never laid eyes on her. William wasn't stupid like
Ragnor.

Argana looked at Cleve closely. "Strange," she said,
"that when you were a small boy I never realized that your
eyes were exactly like Varrick's—one gold, one blue. Perhaps they weren't then and changed over time."

"I don't know," Cleve said. "I don't remember ever
looking at myself."

"I believed our mother when she said you were the son
of my father. But then he died a violent death, as most men
do. Varrick killed him. I've never doubted that. And Varrick married our mother."

"I know," Cleve said. "I'm merely surprised that my
father would then wed his wife's daughter. It isn't usually
done. If you were Christians, I believe it would be forbid-
den."

Argana, nearly as tall as Cleve, straight limbed, eyes as
blue as the summer sky, dimples in her cheeks, didn't
smile. "Mother died. I was almost thirteen, nearly ready
for a husband. Varrick didn't touch me until I was fourteen,
then he told me that he would bed me, to test my innocence,
to see if I would respond to a man's touch. He told me if
I proved to be what he wished, he would wed me. I asked

one of the women how I should behave. She told me exactly what to do. Varrick was pleased. Understand, Cleve, there was no one else. We are isolated, except for trading at Inverness and to the northward islands. The men naturally trade southward at York and enjoy themselves raiding Pict and Briton holdings. I had believed my eldest son, Athol, would be the Lord of Kinloch upon Varrick's death. But you're back, Cleve, and Varrick is more pleased than I've ever seen him. I mourned you for a very long time. I'm glad you're alive even though my son is no longer the heir to Kinloch.''

He looked at her closely, heard the disappointment in her low musical voice, felt the pain she felt for her son. "I spent fifteen years in the Christian's hell, Argana. Surely I didn't deserve that. I was a boy of five and I was cast forth only to become a slave. Surely I deserve to have what now is rightfully mine. Athol is a fine boy, nay, he's nearly a man. He is also my half brother. I pray he will feel no hatred for me, that he will recognize what is mine. But heed me, Argana, what is mine is mine. Surely you must agree with that. You're my half sister.''

"Aye, it is a logical thing you say, but there is still Athol, nearly a man grown as you said, and now he has nothing. You don't remember my father but I do. His passions ran deep and strong. He believed in his family, in his sons. Then he died, fighting outlaws, so it was said, but as I told you, I believe Varrick killed him.''

"Athol will make his own way, as most sons do. I would have had nothing if our brother had lived. Varrick told me last night that Ethar disappeared soon after I had gone, that all believed him to have fallen into the loch and the monsters drew him down into its depths and devoured him.''

"It is more likely that he was sucked into one of the caves that honeycomb the loch. I know not, but our mother died, then you were gone, and finally Ethar. There was Varrick, always Varrick. I soon realized that our mother lusted after him. She came to fear him. He was sometimes harsh with her. Of course, all of us fear him. It is what he wants. It is what pleases him. He is a strange man, his origins murky, cast in dark tales, but my mother took him and that was that.''

"Do you still fear him?''

She smiled then, her white teeth strong and straight. She was still a lovely woman, not of the same beauty as Cayman, but she seemed more real than Cayman, as if there were more substance to her, more sheer force and will. The lines on her face were from living, from suffering, aye, it made her more human, and thus more to be feared, perhaps, or to be studied, before Cleve came to a decision about her. He was nothing to her, merely a small boy who'd disappeared so many years before. He remembered adoring her when he'd been just a babe. Ah, how she'd made him laugh.

"Fear Varrick? Certainly I fear him. Everyone fears him. It pleases him to have the stench of fear around him, created by him. He expects all to worship at the veil of darkness that he sweeps over himself.''

"You speak eloquently, Argana,'' Varrick said.

She started, but she didn't pale or move back from him. She said, "I have been wedded to you for a very long time, Varrick. You have taught me as much eloquence as a woman can learn. Have I done it well enough to suit you?''

Cleve watched Varrick reach out one hand, the long pale fingers so slender, so finely carved as if by a Rune master, no callouses, no sign of any labor, nothing but the purity of white flesh. "Nearly eighteen years,'' he said. "It's a long time, Argana, a very long time. Athol is sixteen, as you said, nearly a man grown. He will revere his brother, Cleve, who has come back to us magically, as if transported by the netherworld gods. Cleve will follow me now, not Athol. You understand that, do you not, Argana?''

"Actually,'' Cleve said to Varrick, "my escape and rescue was far more practical. The netherworld gods would have spat upon the dullness of it.'' Aye, this man was his father, looking at him was like looking at his own image, and it surprised him deep inside, and was also frightening.

"By the winter solstice," Varrick said, "your escape from Kiev with Lord Merrik and his lady, Laren, will reach even the limits of a skald's talents. Tell me, Cleve, why did you not try to return here the moment you were free?"

"I'd forgotten everything until the dreams came to me. Finally I remembered almost everything. I remember now that I was riding my pony when a man stopped me. I was speaking to him when someone struck me hard on the head and left me for dead on the eastern side of Loch Ness. A trader found me, nursed me back to health, named me Cleve, and sold me. I remembered nothing of this life until the dreams began three years ago."

"Fetch me porridge, Argana," Varrick said. "Mayhap I sent the dreams to you, Cleve. I have that power and it comes to me when I am not even aware of it."

"If it pleases you to believe so, then why not?"

Argana gave Cleve a look that clearly told him to be careful, but she said nothing, merely nodded and walked to the huge fire pit whose flames burned sluggishly in the summer morning. The iron pot was huge, much larger than those on Hawkfell Island or at Malverne.

"How many people live at Kinloch?"

"There are nearly one hundred. My men produced many children after I married your mother. Aye, I can see it in your eyes. You are my son, yet you remember the man you believed was your father, an animal of a man, a man of little reason, really, something of a warrior, but without the brains to keep himself safe. I forced your mother, Cleve, forced her because I wanted her and she was bathing in the loch and I took her and you were the result. Since your father didn't know of me, he saw your different colored eyes as a gift from the Dalriada god. Ah, my porridge. Come and sit with me, Cleve. We have much to discuss. I wish to hear all about the dreams.

Cleve looked toward Chessa, who was playing with Kiri, tossing her a small leather ball. Laren was speaking with Cayman, Merrik with Varrick's soldiers who were working on their axes and swords.

Suddenly, with no warning, there was the sound of a great wind. The huge wooden fortress actually shuddered with the force of the wind. There was utter silence amongst the forty-odd men, women, and children in the great hall. No one screamed, no one moved. All stood still as stones, as silent as the immense iron pot suspended from its chains.

Then there was the sound of churning water, so much water twisting and roiling, crashing against rocks and spuming surely hundreds of feet into the air, all that water bulging upward to surge over the fortress, which was surely wrong since the fortress sat high on a promontory.

Varrick rose from his beautifully carved oak chair, its arm posts serpents, but not the sea serpents of the stems of Viking warships. These serpents were like none Cleve had ever seen before. They were magical serpents, knowing serpents who seemed to stare back at the men who beheld them. Varrick stepped up to the raised wooden dais and walked to the huge shuttered windows. He flung them open. Cleve saw that he held some sort of odd-looking wooden stick in his hands, that now he was thrusting it upward, toward the open window. What was that stick? How long had Varrick been holding it?

It was early morning, the sun had been bright one moment, the light mist burned off, yet now, it was black. The light inside the fortress seemed to be sucked out through those shutters into that deep, forbidding blackness. The wind was so powerful that Varrick had to hold onto the clawed post carved into the base of the shutters. Cleve would swear that he saw huge sprays of water rise up before the darkness outside, then heave downward, splashing loudly, spuming outward.

Varrick turned his back to the open shutters and that eerie blackness. He raised his arms. The full sleeves of his black tunic billowed outward. He said, "I have called to Caldon. I must see what has happened. All will be well. Have no fear. Remain within. No one is to venture outside."

He stepped off the dais, strode to the great front doors, and flung them open. He looked like a man of Cleve's years, Chessa thought, watching him, certainly not a man twice Cleve's age, certainly not the man who had fathered Cleve. He looked young and strong and agile as a goat.

Kiri pressed her face against Chessa's neck, and whispered against her ear, "Varrick is very strange, Papa. What's a Caldon?"

"Aye," Chessa said slowly, "very strange. He likes it, Kiri, else he wouldn't do it. I think Caldon is the name he's given to the monster that lives in the loch."

"But it's morning, Papa. Why is it dark?"

"That," Chessa said, "is something I can't explain. Now, sweeting, let's give your first papa some porridge. Surely all this will cease soon enough. Don't be frightened."

"You're not afraid. Why?"

Chessa was thoughtful. "I'm not sure, but you're right, sweeting, I'm not. I think it's all a fine performance, like the ones your aunt Laren gives when she tells us tales of monsters and heroes who become real to us when she weaves her magic. And then her tales are over and the magic with them. It is the same with Varrick."

"All right," Kiri said. "I'm hungry again, Papa."

23

"**H**OW DID YOU do it?"

Varrick merely smiled, or at least his lips curled slightly, giving a brief illusion of pleasure. "You should ask your wife. Her father is the most powerful magician I have ever seen or heard of. She knows some of his magic. I can tell this by looking at her, at her eyes—an odd green, her eyes, holding secrets and power. You are lucky, Cleve, for she will protect you from your enemies."

"If ever she protected me, it would be because she is smart and cunning, not because she cast some curse. Ragnor of York wanted her. William of Normandy wanted her. Now she's my wife and I just pray that neither man will come to skin my hide, including her father, King Sitric. Now, Lord Varrick, how did you manage that terrifying wind, the utter blackness, and all that thrashing water?"

Varrick picked up that odd-looking stick. Cleve saw up close that it looked more like a carved wooden spear. It wasn't really a spear, for it was much too short, not more than a foot long. It wasn't a knife either, for it wasn't sharpened at its tip. It was wood, but a heavy wood that really didn't look like wood. There were strange designs on it: circles and squares, in bright reds and blues. "This comes from a Pict chieftain who ruled not farther than a long day's ride from here, to the east of the loch. I knew it had power, this *burra,* for that is what it is called. It comes from the Druids, used for hundreds of years in their ceremonies. It is older than Caldon, older than Thor and Odin-All-Father perhaps. I have studied it for years, learned all its secrets. I let it take my magic and focus it.''

"How did you get it from the chieftain?''

"I killed him and took it. Here, hold it.''

Cleve took the *burra*. It was heavy on his palm, so heavy that it dragged his arm down with its weight. He couldn't believe such a small slender piece of wood could be so heavy, yet Varrick had held it easily. He felt something in it, something that made him want to shiver.

"I call it Pagan," Varrick said. "What do you feel?''

"Nothing, merely that it is heavy, that the man who fashioned it added something to the wood." He willingly handed the *burra* back to his father. He never wanted to see or touch the thing again.

Varrick called out, "Chessa, please come here. I have something for you to see.''

Chessa, who was speaking with Laren, looked up, saw that Cleve was seated perfectly still, and walked quickly to Varrick. "Aye, my lord?''

"Here," he said simply, and handed her the *burra*.

Chessa cocked her head to one side as she accepted the strange looking spear that wasn't at all a spear. It looked to be naught more than a simple stick of wood with strange markings on it. Suddenly she gasped and tossed the wooden piece into the air, then caught it again with three fingers. It was very light. Strange, because it looked heavy, but it wasn't. "It's very hot," she said, and tossed it back and forth from her right to her left hand, as if it were naught but a feather. "Very hot indeed and it weighs nothing. Why is that? It looks heavy, as if I wouldn't be able to lift it, but it isn't.''

"Look at the markings on it, Chessa.''

Suddenly the wood was different. She dropped it to the earthen floor. "I'm sorry, but it became so very cold, pain-fully so. I couldn't hold it." She frowned at Varrick, then leaned down and touched the *burra*. It felt warm to the touch, not hot or frigidly cold. She picked it up again and studied the circles and squares on it. "It's very old," she said. "I feel that it's older than this promontory upon which this fortress rests." She frowned in confusion at her husband. "Cleve, this is very strange. I touch these circles and these squares and my fingers seem to sink down into the wood, yet they don't, not really. But I can feel how very deeply they're carved, and you know, it's not like they're really carved at all, for they're smooth and deep and there doesn't seemed to be an end to them." Then she was silent, looking down at her fingers as they traced each pattern very slowly. Suddenly she turned white, her eyes wide and deep with fright. Cleve jumped to his feet and grabbed that damned heathen stick from her hands. He tossed it to Varrick. It was difficult, for it was so very heavy. Then he took Chessa in his arms. "It's all right, Chessa. What happened? Can you tell me?"

Her face was against his shoulder. She said, "I saw my mother, Naphta. I saw her as clearly as if she were here, standing before me. She was so real, Cleve, and then she smiled at me, and I knew I was very small, no more than a babe. She was so very real, Cleve, so very real."

Cleve felt his flesh grow cold, felt the hair rise on the back of his neck. He didn't like this—not the damned darkness, black and impenetrable in the morning, the raging wind that had shaken the fortress, or the roiling waters that had seemed nearly alive, wanting to engulf the fortress and swallow all within. He didn't like this *burra* that had touched something strange in Chessa. He suddenly very much wanted to leave.

But he couldn't. This was where he belonged. Kinloch was his birthright. But he didn't like this, any of it. To soothe Chessa he said, "You are your father's daughter. He is a wizard. It's natural that you would have some affinity for things old and sacred. It's not important, Chessa. Now, I would like for us to fetch Kiri and see the land. I have memories and I would like to see if they are anything now as they were for the small boy.''

Varrick said nothing. He gently placed the *burra* in a lined scabbard, then tied it to his waist with a strap of leather that was also painted with red and blue circles and squares. It looked as old as the *burra*. It was leather and it was still strong, no hint of fraying or decay to be seen. It made no sense. Cleve hated things that made no sense. Men were helpless enough as it was, but with this, all this unexplained magic, this confusion of senses, the fact that the damned *burra* weighed no more than a feather to both Varrick and Chessa. "I will have your brother Athol show you the land, Cleve. The boy knows every glen and hillock. He will take care. There have been few attacks by the Picts or the Britons. The Scots are the ferocious ones but they usually don't bother us. We must always be on guard against the outlaws and the thieves, homeless men who roam the land and steal and murder. The Scot king, Constantine, encourages them, at least against us. We fight back, naturally. My men are ferocious warriors. They show no mercy. You must have at least a dozen men with you if you ride south. I am pleased that you want to learn all about what will be yours one day when I am dead.''

Varrick gave them horses to ride. Cleve had ridden a pony before he'd been taken from Kinloch and then learned to ride again only after he'd come to Malverne. He was comfortable enough astride the raw-boned bay stallion, but he would have preferred to walk, something he couldn't do, for Kinloch lands stretched far to the west and to the south. Chessa was at her ease on a mare with white stockings who kept tossing her head, making Kiri laugh. Laren rode well and she looked thoughtful. As for Merrik and the other Malverne men, they looked uncomfortable. They looked wary, as if they expected demons to rise from the dark waters of Loch Ness and attack them.

Several of Varrick's men, all of them with their faces painted with blue lines and circles, garbed in bearskins, rode at their rear, eyes alert. Varrick had told him they were Pict warriors and owed their loyalty to him. Their leader,

Igmal, as evil looking as the Christian's devil, had very white teeth, a blue-painted face, and a ready smile. Kiri ordered him about and he would smile that evil-looking smile and throw her into the air. Such a contrast, Cleve thought. Silence within the fortress and at least a bit of an occasional smile without, smiles that Kiri brought, no one else. He wondered if Kiri would lose her smiles soon enough living here. He wouldn't allow that.

Chessa pulled her mare close to Cleve's, saying, "Look at the mist coming toward us, like a tide, and you know it won't stop until there is naught but chill and gray and no sunlight. This place is savage and as pure as the sweetest music, but it is summer and this mist will take getting used to. Ah, but the green, such a deep pure green, just like in Ireland, where it rained all the time as well."

"It isn't Norway," Cleve said. "Do you find it beautiful, Chessa? Truly? Can you make your home here?"

"Aye, I find it splendidly untamed, yet the sheep and the cows graze so peacefully, and the birds, Cleve, there are so many birds. Mirana would be blissful were she here, so many birds. I can't begin to identify them all and I'm trying so I can tell her all about them. Aye, Scotland is a perfect place. And why shouldn't it be? It is our home now." She paused a moment, then added, "Cayman won't say anything to me. Neither will Argana or her three sons. They don't treat me badly, but I know they don't want me here. None of the women will speak of anything but cooking and weaving and dyeing. Nothing at all. All fear Varrick."

"You don't."

"Nay, but then again, there is my father, the greatest magician the world has ever known. It would be cowardly of me to fear him."

"Tell me the truth, Chessa. Is your father really a magician? Did he really renew King Sitric? Did he really then just disappear leaving you to be raised by the king?"

"I would have told you," she said, turning to smile at him. "I just didn't think of it. So much has happened since we've come together. Too, I've been silent for so very long. Merrik and Rorik know, of course, and all the people of Hawkfell Island and Malverne. King Sitric is my father. He is also the magician, Hormuze. He killed the old king and then became the king himself. My father's only magic is his brain. He understands people, understands what makes them do what they do. There's nothing more to it save that he wanted to wed Mirana. She looked very much like my mother, you see. But since she was already wedded to Rorik, my father had to settle for Sira. Unfortunately, she pleases him greatly. Four sons, yet she hated me for no reason save, naturally, that I hated her."

"I remember thinking that you and Mirana looked alike, not really your features, but when you and she both smiled and nodded, you know, with your head to the side? I've been a fool."

"Oh, no. It's just that no one ever speaks of it. It will remain a miracle wrought by the powerful magician Hormuze. That Varrick believes him great makes me want to giggle. Your father amuses me, but he is dangerous, never forget that." She touched her hand to his sleeve, saying again, "Never forget he is dangerous."

"No, I shan't, but you mean more than just danger, don't you?"

"Aye, but I can't really explain it."

"Think of that *burra,* Chessa. When I held it I felt only that it was heavier than it should be. I could barely pick it up it was so heavy. When you held it, it was as light as a mote of dust. And the heat and cold. Surely that's magic of a sort. My father was pleased that you reacted to it the way you did. It was light for him as well. There is something there, as much as I hate to admit it."

She was frowning, looking out over the loch, at the smooth water, darker now beneath the blanketing soft mist, so very gray and fine that there were patches of blue sky that shone through it. But it would keep coming until there was naught but the soft blurry gray and it would become colder, this summer mist that lived in this land. There were several small boats with men aboard fishing. They were very close to shore as if the men feared going out beyond the shallows. She shivered, pulling her woolen cloak more closely. "How did it work? Was I just thinking of my mother and my brain brought her forth? Since my father isn't a wizard, then why would the *burra* be light to me? Why would I see my mother?"

"Like Ragnor of York, I have great respect for your brain, Chessa, but to bring forth your mother? I don't think so. I think it was something Varrick did—cast some sort of spell. Perhaps he has the ability to look just a bit into your mind and he saw your mother there."

She shivered and it had nothing to do with the mist that was now swirling lightly around them. It was as if the mist caressed them. It wasn't wet now or chill, it was there, as light as a lover's fingers touching them. They were nearing the far south end of Loch Ness. Low hills spread out around them, sheep grazing on them. Buzzards and falcons flew overhead. Gulls dove into the loch. There were barley fields being tended by slaves. There were thick stands of trees. Huge boulders lay in piles as if tossed there by a mighty hand. "Varrick's lands go on forever," Cleve said. "He told me that this is called Falcon Ridge, a name he gave it when he called the birds to him and three falcons landed on his outstretched hand to welcome him."

"They will never be your lands, brother." It was Athol and he jerked on his stallion's reins, making the horse rear up on his hind legs. "These are my lands. Go back to Norway. You have become a Viking like those men who come to trade in Inverness. We are different here. We are Vikings, yet we are more, more than you can imagine. You are too ignorant to know anything. You aren't welcome, despite the words my father now mouths to you. He doesn't know you even though it was his seed that filled your mother's womb. Go away, Cleve of Malverne. There's nothing for you here."

Cleve studied Athol's face. Nearly a man, he thought, with passions boiling too close to the surface, too much passion and not enough control. He said, "I wonder whether when you reach your man years you will gain control and perhaps a bit of wisdom. Many men never do. I know you feel displaced. I can't blame you for that. I am new to you. Like everyone else you believed me dead. But I'm here now and you will have to make the best of it."

"No," Athol said. "Never." He wheeled his stallion about, to ride back at the fore of their group.

"I want you to keep your knife close," Cleve said to Chessa. "Damn, I wish Kiri weren't with us."

"But why?"

"I have this feeling, nay, it is more than that. Keep close watch, Chessa. By all the gods, we shouldn't have come with this half brother of mine."

The attack came so quickly there was no chance for her to answer. Cleve took a wild look at Kiri, now tucked securely against Merrik's side, even as he drew his sword.

There were at least three dozen of them, not at all like Viking warriors, but wild men garbed in bearskins and wolfskins, their trousers filthy and ripped, their feet bound in coarse leather sandals, all of them wielding small swords over their heads. They carried wooden shields and wore wooden helmets. They looked strong and ready to kill. They were yelling their heads off and their faces were painted with the blue and red circles and squares. Picts, Cleve thought, and his eyes glittered. He didn't doubt for a moment that Athol had summoned them after he'd spoken to Cleve but minutes before. No doubt at all, the little bastard.

Cleve calmly rode forward, even as the Malverne men and Varrick's men were shouting and positioning their horses, preparing for the attack. The loch was at their back, the outlaws hemming them in. There was no escape, not that a Viking would ever avoid a fight or want an escape.

He watched Athol even as he brandished his sword above his head. Ah, aye, he was right, it was some sort of signal to the outlaws. Cleve was on him in the next moment, his arm about Athol's throat, his knife poised directly above his heart. He pulled the boy off his horse and over onto his. He said in his ear, "Call off your men, Athol."

The boy struggled, nearly shrieking, "They aren't my men, Cleve, they're outlaws, thieves. They want our swords and our jewelry. They want the women."

"You call off your men now or I will stick my knife clean through your heart. Do you understand me?"

"I would rather die than let you have—"

The knife slipped through Athol's tunic, touched its cold tip to his flesh and then gently eased in. The boy screamed.

"You see, death is never preferable. I learned that during the fifteen years I was a slave. A man can bear anything if he believes he can survive. Call them off or you will never draw another breath."

Athol shouted, "Sarva! Stop! Nay, come no nearer. You and your men withdraw. Now, or I will die."

The man in the lead paused a moment, and Cleve could see the frown on his painted face. These were no Scots. They were indeed outlaws, men loyal to Athol. But how had Athol gotten to these men so quickly? He shook his head, but Athol, feeling Cleve's knife pressing deeper, screamed at him, "Go back! Don't attack."

Sarva slowly raised his hand. The men behind him stopped, then circled around him, speaking amongst themselves.

Merrik said, "Why don't we go kill them?" As soon as he spoke, he realized he was holding Kiri against his side, her face pressed against him. "Nay, I didn't mean that. Everything's all right, Kiri. See, your papa's solved the problem."

"Papa always solves problems," Kiri said, and brought her face out of Merrik's armpit. "Papa, who are those men?"

"Soon they will be gone, sweeting, and then we will find out," Cleve said. He whispered in Athol's ear, "They were here so fast, all ready to kill us. You'd better hope that Sarva listens to you, Athol. Do you like the feel of this?"

The knife went in just a bit further. Athol groaned, not moving.

Then the men melted away behind three low hills, behind the piles of massive boulders, simply disappearing into the mist. It seemed to swallow them, pulling them through a gray veil.

Cleve withdrew the knife. Calmly, he sheathed it at his belt. Then he lifted Athol by his tunic and threw him to the ground. He jumped off his horse's back and stood over the boy. "Stand up, you puling coward."

"So," Chessa said, riding her mare to within a foot of Athol. "This was your idea. You wanted to kill all of us. *You wanted to kill Cleve, to kill Kiri.*" Her voice rose to a near shriek. She slid off her mare's back, pulled her knife and dove toward Athol. Cleve managed to catch her. "No, Chessa, no. I don't want his miserable blood on your hands. Kiri is all right. We're all fine now. Think of him as another Ragnor of York, the poor fool. You really didn't want to kill him, you just wanted him to be gone."

"He put you and Kiri into mortal danger," Chessa said, panting hard, still held in her fury. Cleve shook her. "Come, Chessa. Come back to me." He leaned down and kissed her hard, then squeezed her against him.

Kiri said to Igmal, whose horse was next to Merrik's, "My second papa won't let anyone hurt me or my first papa. Her eyes turn red when she's really mad. I've seen her dive at a man who wanted to hurt someone she loved. She's wonderful, my second papa. But I wasn't sure I wanted her to marry my first papa. We did well before she came." Kiri sighed, much put upon. "But she has brought excitement to our lives and I think my first papa thinks she's splendid. She's not my real mama, you know."

Igmal nodded. "She's a Viking woman. She's strong and proud and she very much loves your first papa, if I'm not mistaken, and I'm not. You could do worse for a step-mother, Kiri. You call her your second papa. You must explain this to me."

Cleve leaned down and pulled Athol to his feet.

"I'm bleeding, you cut me."

Cleve just smiled at the boy's outrage. "He reminds me so much of Ragnor, both whining little worms." Cleve sent his fist into Athol's jaw. He wished he'd heard a crack but he hadn't. He would have liked to have broken the little bastard's jaw.

"Too bad," Merrik said. "A broken jaw would have done him good. Every word he tried to say would have killed him. He just might have starved to death. But you tried, Cleve." He grinned. "Five years with you and I didn't manage to instill enough killing instinct in you, but you did hurt him, and I trust you enjoyed it."

"Aye, I enjoyed it." Cleve then sent his fist into Athol's belly, doubling him over, and then he kicked him, sending him sprawling to the rocky ground. Cleve turned to Varrick's man, Igmal, and said, "We will take him back to the fortress. Varrick will decide what to do with him. I don't want his blood on your hands any more than I want it on my wife's hands. Do you agree, Igmal?"

Igmal looked down at Athol, who was lying on his side, knees drawn up, hugging his belly. He looked both sad and yet not surprised. "I saw him come from his mother's womb, whole limbed, squalling, ready for life. I watched him grow tall, but he didn't grow straight. A darkness grew in him, a cramped black place I didn't understand. I've watched him since you came, Cleve, watched the fear in him, knowing he would lose everything, then I saw the calculation, the hatred, the determination. And now he would have killed you, his flesh and blood, the women, and the little girl who makes me laugh. This is a shame that drowns all of us." Without saying another word, Igmal pulled a short slender knife from its scabbard, leapt from his horse, and bent down. Cleve grabbed his arm even as it was descending to Athol's heart. "No, Igmal, no. This must be up to Varrick. He must decide. You speak of shame. It isn't your shame, but my family's. We must return him to Varrick."

"As you will, Cleve," Igmal said, and straightened, slipping that knife back into its scabbard. "You will be master and lord here someday." He turned to spit down at Athol. "He saved you," he said, staring down at Athol as if still uncomprehending that the boy had done such a thing. "You would have killed him, yet he saved you. He saved you from his wife and from me." Igmal spat on Athol, then turned his back and motioned his men back onto their horses.

"Igmal," Kiri called out.

The ugly man looked at the child and gave her a ferocious smile that showed those blazing white teeth of his. "Aye, little one?"

"I will ride with you back to the fortress."

Merrik just shook his head and handed Kiri over to Igmal, who tucked her neatly in the crook of his huge arm. "I begin to believe all of us are here just for her pleasure."

Cleve nodded, then said, "Let's get him on his horse. I don't know what Varrick will do."

Athol, now alive and knowing Cleve wouldn't kill him, looked about for the outlaws, then said, "My father loves me. He will take my side. He will forgive me."

"Actually, he won't," Chessa said. "Or if he does, then he has no more wisdom than you do."

"You're a damned witch. My mother said you were a witch after she saw you holding the *burra,* and I knew then it would be best if you died, your evil with you. You're just a woman, yet you would have stuck that knife in me."

"Mayhap you're right that I'm a witch," she said, just smiling at him. "You're a fool, Athol, if you think you can ever overcome me. Don't forget that. Your father knows me for what I am. You're stupid if you forget it." She knew he was watching her with fear and hatred as she walked to her mare. She stood there, waiting for Cleve to hand her up.

One of the men gave a shout. "It's the monster. It's Caldon! By all the gods, it's Caldon."

Chessa whirled about to look out over the loch. There

was naught but the heavy gray mist, veiling everything in sight.

"Over on the eastern side, just yon!"

Then she saw it, a shadow, a long neck, it seemed, with perhaps a head atop that long curving neck, a small head that looked upward, then slewed about and looked toward them. But then she couldn't be certain, for the mist divided that long neck into three parts, showing dark mottled flesh and then thick sheets of mist, mingled together until nothing was clear, nothing was certain.

The men murmured amongst themselves. They believed they saw Caldon. They believed they saw the monster of Loch Ness.

Chessa didn't know what she saw. She looked toward Cleve, who had managed to get Athol atop his horse. He just shook his head, saying nothing.

Kiri was staring in silence toward the loch, just staring, her head cocked to one side. Igmal said to her, "The monster is a good creature, Kiri. There's nothing to fear from it. It has a family, babies, just like you." He paused, and Chessa knew he'd lied, and he'd done it well, cleanly and without hesitation. She wanted to kiss him, for Kiri just nodded and leaned back against his chest. Suddenly she straightened and said, "Igmal, the bearskin smells bad. I'll wash it for you."

The ugly man just stared down at the little girl on his lap. "You'll wash it for me?"

"Aye, unless you have a wife. You don't have a wife or the skin wouldn't smell, would it?"

"You're right about that," Igmal said. He looked over at Chessa. "Cleve is blessed in his women."

Athol screamed, "He's a damned bastard! He's nothing. You'll see, Igmal, my father will kill you for trying to harm me. He'll kill Cleve and he'll kill that damned witch."

"I wonder if he'll leave anyone alive," Igmal said. "Be quiet, Athol, else Cleve just might break your jaw, and I think all the men would like that."

Chessa wondered if Athol's mother, Argana, knew what

her son had planned. She prayed it wasn't so, but there was
the woman's silence, the woman's utter devotion to her son.
Argana was Cleve's half sister, but still, blood was blood.
She didn't want to return to Kinloch. She didn't want to
see Varrick.

24

WHERE THE HELL was Kiri? Cleve had looked in the sheep byre, in the privy, in the bathing hut. Where was she? He turned to look back toward the fortress, but he didn't see her amongst all the people standing there. He strode toward the barley fields. He'd shake her good for disappearing like this.

Inside the huge fortress, Varrick, as was his wont, stood on the raised dais, regarding the fifty-some people in the great hall. He said in a calm voice that seemed to ring from the blackened wooden beams above, "Argana, you will come here to me now."

Chessa frowned. Where was Cleve? Why was Varrick calling Argana to him? She looked to see Athol, standing next to Igmal and his men, but he didn't look frightened. Indeed, there was a stark look of pleasure on his thin face. He looked triumphant. She frowned, puzzled. What in the name of the gods was going on here?

Argana walked tall and proud to the dais, to her husband. She stood below, flinging back her head to look up at him. "Yes, Lord Varrick? What is your pleasure?"

"You will learn of it shortly. Answer me now. Would you agree, Argana, that our son, Athol, is only a boy?"

"Aye, he is but sixteen. But he is nearly a man. You yourself have been seeking about for a suitable wife for him. You have said you wish him wedded soon. You wouldn't want a boy to be a husband.''

"But he is still not of full reason. He is still easily swayed by those he admires, those he loves, those he trusts. Like you, Argana.''

"I trust that will be true when he has reached even your years, Lord Varrick.''

Varrick was silent, just staring at her, but Chessa wasn't fooled, the insult had made him furious. Suddenly, a wind came from the wide-open shutters behind him. He was holding the *burra*, fingering its surface with his long white fingers. There was conversation all around her, low and frightened. Where was Cleve? She looked over at where Merrik and Laren stood, Laren holding Kiri. The little girl looked bored, but she stayed quiet in Laren's arms.

Slowly, the winds died. Varrick said nothing until there was utter silence both inside and outside the fortress. He sheathed the *burra* once again at his belt. It was a quick gesture, a furtive gesture. She wondered if anyone else had noticed that he'd had the *burra* out when the winds had so suddenly arisen. "A mother has great influence over her children, particularly her sons.''

"Aye,'' Argana said quietly, "that is usually true. But here at Kinloch, with you, Lord Varrick, it isn't. Athol takes his direction from you and from no other. All here take their direction from you and none other.''

"Didn't you call Chessa a witch?''

"Aye, she is a witch. What of it? Did you not tell us that her father was Hormuze, the greatest magician you'd ever known?''

"Didn't you tell your Athol that she was a witch and she would be better dead?''

"Nay, I didn't say that.''

"But it is what you believe, is it not?''

Slowly, Argana turned and looked at Chessa. She was frowning slightly, as if she didn't understand something that she should understand. There wasn't particular dislike in her look, but confusion. "Perhaps,'' she said, and it was clear to all that she was uncertain, that she didn't know where Varrick was leading with all this talk. Chessa felt the flesh on her arms rise. She was frightened. Where was Cleve?

"Athol has told me that you ordered him to kill Cleve and all the visitors with him, including the child and Chessa. He has told me it wasn't his fault. He was only following your wishes, your orders."

"Nay, I did not. Cleve is your son. Why would I want to have one son kill another?"

"Ah, Argana, then you call your beloved son a liar and you want to see my knife slide between his ribs for his supposed treachery?"

Argana smiled. "That was well done, husband. My only question is why?"

Varrick didn't answer. "Athol will learn honor. He will come to regret his actions of this day. He will no longer have a mother who incites him to violence, to betrayal." He drew a long slender knife from his belt and slowly walked to Argana, who just stood there, staring at him, accepting.

Chessa couldn't believe this. Argana, just standing there, watching him walk toward her, his knife raising, ready to come into her heart. All his talk, it had been to convince everyone that the mother had incited the son to violence. Chessa screamed, "Don't you dare kill her, Varrick! By all the gods, what are you doing?"

She ran like a madwoman to Argana, shoved her aside, and stood blocking Varrick, whose right arm was raised, the dagger ready to plunge downward.

"I don't believe you would do this. Listen to me, Varrick. You won't kill her, damn you. I won't let you. You will have to kill me first to get to her."

Athol shouted, "Kill her, Father. Kill them both. Save me from the witch and from a disloyal mother."

Chessa said to Varrick, her voice low and calm as his, "You see what you fathered? He deserves to die. By all the gods, I wish Cleve hadn't stopped me. I would have plunged my knife into his black heart. His years don't matter. He will but become more of a bully, a tyrant, a dishonest fool, as he gains years. And he is of your seed, yet you protect him. You blame the mother. Rather blame yourself, you miserable bastard.''

"Move aside, Chessa."

"Ah, your soft, persuasive magician's voice, Varrick. I won't move. You won't kill Argana. She has done nothing save call me a witch and what is wrong with that? You believe me a witch, indeed, you pray I am a witch. Place your blame where it deserves to be.''

"Move, Chessa."

It was Argana, and she was trying to shove Chessa aside, but Chessa was strong, stronger than the woman who was taller and built more powerfully than she. Chessa didn't move at all. "Nay," she said, still looking directly at Varrick who was staring down at her, his one golden eye as bright as the most brilliant sun, the one blue eye dark and turbulent as the stormy sea, his body utterly quiet, the knife still held in his hand. "Be quiet, Argana, I won't let him kill you and that's that. Just be quiet. You will not die for your son. It isn't right. I wondered where Cleve was, Varrick. I realize now that you sent him away. You feared if he were here, he would protect his sister. It's true. He returned Athol to you for punishment, but you seek only to kill Athol's mother. Why, Varrick?''

"Move aside, Chessa. Argana, wife or no, must pay for her betrayal. Death is her punishment.''

"Why, damn you, Varrick?'' This from Merrik, who strode forward to stand beside Chessa. "You touch Argana and I will kill you here and now. Then I will kill that little beast that sprang from your seed.''

"You have nothing to say about anything, Merrik of Malverne. Move aside and take Chessa with you.''

"Tell us why, Varrick?'' Chessa said, now grabbing Argana's wrist to hold her in place.

"Think, Chessa, and you as well, Merrik. It's because he no longer wants my sister as his wife.''

Chessa whirled again, still keeping her body between Varrick and Argana. "Cleve. You're here, thank the gods." She wanted to run to him, but she didn't dare. She knew in her deepest soul that Varrick would strike the moment she moved.

"Aye, he told me that Kiri had run away from Igmal and I've been searching for her. I see that she's been here all the while, with Laren and Merrik. It's true, isn't it, Lord Varrick? We've been here but two days and you decided you wanted Argana dead so you could have Chessa, my wife, the daughter of Hormuze the magician. But then what was your plan? Athol could have easily killed Chessa as well as the rest of us. He had a good two score bandits to do the job for him."

"It is Argana who wanted her dead, not I," Varrick said. "Doesn't that convince you, Cleve?"

"Nay," Cleve said, slowly shaking his head. "I believe Athol went beyond what you wanted. Athol wants us all dead. You would have lost, Father, had Athol won. Who then would you have killed?"

"You're wrong, Cleve, quite wrong."

Cleve said, "Let us say that Chessa survived, that I survived. Then what was your plan after you killed Argana? To murder me, your son? Somehow force Chessa to wed you? By all the gods, Father, you don't know Chessa. She would have you slavering to be free of her within three days if you did that, if, that is, she'd allowed you to live that long."

Slowly Varrick lowered the knife. He slipped it back into his belt. He said nothing for a very long time. Then he said in that calm deep voice, "Chessa is a woman, a woman just like any other woman. I don't want her. Why would I want her? She's your wife. Aye, she's naught but a simple woman. She does as she's told. Watch, Cleve." He said to his wife, "Argana, fetch me a cup of mead. I'm thirsty."

Argana said nothing, merely turned and walked toward the huge barrel that held Kinloch's mead. The men, women, and children parted for her, as would two parts of cloth rent apart.

He waited for her to return.

Cleve said, "You will answer me. What would you have done? Murdered me, your son?"

Varrick merely waved his hand, waiting until Argana handed him a silver cup of mead. Cleve wondered from whom he'd stolen it. He watched his father drink deep, then toss the silver cup to one of his men, who caught it deftly, then wiped his mouth with the back of his flawless white hand.

"Answer me," Cleve said.

Varrick said very quietly, "What you say, Cleve, is painful to me. I am your father. I don't wish to kill Athol because he is also my son. I believe the mother to be the one to have incited him to this treacherous deed. I sought only to punish the guilty one. What you have said wounds me deeply. You must believe me that I don't want your wife. I don't know where you got such an idea."

Cleve waved his words aside. "You would have killed her if not for Chessa."

Varrick then turned his eyes to her. "Why, Princess? Why did you save her? I believe her guilty. Surely you have your doubts, do you not?"

Chessa just shook her head at him in disgust. "You weren't there, Varrick. You didn't see what Athol did. You didn't hear what he said. He is like a mangy dog, blaming us for his fleas. He is unworthy of you as a father or of Cleve as a half brother. You won't harm Argana."

"She's right, Lord Varrick," Igmal said, stepping forward. "It is just as I told you. Athol doesn't deserve any leniency from you."

Chessa said, "Do as you will with Athol, but you won't harm Argana, ever." She looked at Cleve, saw him nod, and took his hand. He drew her against his side.

Varrick smiled, then laughed, a rusty sound, deep and frightening, for he hadn't laughed in so very long. All his people stared at him, but they held themselves quiet, saying nothing, not moving. Chessa believed she could smell their fear. That was it, the stillness in this great hall. It was the air, dark and heavy, weighing down on them. It was filled with year upon year of fear.

"You think, you foolish woman, to prevent me from doing whatever I wish to do?"

Chessa dropped Cleve's hand, and calmly strode up onto the dais to stand in front of him. She looked up at him as if she were looking at an insect that faintly interested her. "If you harm Argana, I will kill you and none will know how I did it. Argana is right. I'm a witch. I am the daughter of Hormuze, the greatest sorcerer who's ever lived. You said that yourself. You said yourself that as his daughter I carried his magic. Believe it, Varrick. Believe also that Cleve is the only man who will ever have my loyalty. He and Kiri are deep within me, deep within my woman's soul, my witch's soul. No one will harm either of them, or he will die." She didn't turn from Varrick, merely said louder, "You hear what I said, Athol? I pray so, for if you try anything, I will see you dead before the dropping of the sun into the western sea. Don't doubt me. Men have before and they've paid for it."

She didn't wait for Varrick to speak, merely turned on her heel, and walked away from him, stepping down from the dais and walking directly to her husband. When she was close to Cleve, she looked up at him, smiled, and winked.

Cleve just stared down at her for the longest time. He knew no one else had seen that wink, just him. He said finally, his voice low and deep, "Now I understand exactly what Kerek meant. But heed me, Chessa, you play with things you don't understand. It frightens me and angers me. You will take care and you will act only when it is necessary, only when I am not present—"

He broke off, shaking his head, for she'd been in the right of it. He'd been gone. She'd been alone and she'd acted. She'd done exactly what he would have done. "Damnation, what is a man to do with a woman who could have led soldiers into battle against the Romans?''

"That is Kerek's nonsense and you well know it.''

"Do I?'' he said. "I wonder.'' He added very quietly, "I suppose I shall just have to keep you close to me. I suppose I shall just have to love you. Will you accept that?''

She stared up at him. She'd wanted these words from him for so very long. She said only, "Aye, I'll accept that, husband, just as I accept you, forever.''

Three days passed without incident. Athol gave all of them a wide berth. As for Argana, she said nothing at all to Chessa, but since she'd never said anything in any case, nothing had changed. As for Cayman, she seemed more beautiful as each day passed, her flesh glowing, her eyes brighter than the gleam of the noonday sun. It was odd, but it was so, and she too remained silent.

Ah, but Varrick. He held himself apart from all except Cleve. It was as if he knew if he didn't make Cleve trust him, he would lose everything.

On the fourth day, Merrik said to Cleve and Chessa as they walked along the narrow path beside the loch, "Laren and I begin to believe we should return to Malverne. The men are restless. No, I will be honest with you. They are afraid of this place, of this monster Lord Varrick calls Caldon. They don't want to leave you here, Cleve, but they are afraid.''

Cleve looked at Laren, who was looking over the loch, searching for the monster, he knew. She spent all her time studying the loch at different times of day, searching, always searching.

Merrik said, "She wants to see the monster again. She remembers it vividly from that day of the attack, but she says it isn't enough. She wants it to come to her so she may speak to it. She will weave a skald's tale that will last until more generations than we can imagine believe in this monster and search for it as she does. She tries to seduce the beast from the depths of the loch.''

"I saw the monster just yesterday," Kiri said, and everyone stopped and stared down at her. She was holding a piece of bright purple heather, sniffing it, and nodding up at them. "Caldon isn't a monster. Igmal is right. Caldon is a mother and she has many children, just like my two papas will have. She came to me and smiled. She has a very long neck, but she can bend it low enough so I can see her face. I told her that Lord Varrick isn't like my papas. I don't think she wants to come when he calls to her. She looked sad. She made me feel that there is something even beyond her that beckons her to him. Then she just sank beneath the water and I didn't see her again."

Cleve stared down at his daughter, wondering if this story was real, knowing that it couldn't be, yet pleased that Kiri could tell such a splendid tale. Perhaps she had skald's blood in her as did Laren.

Laren said, "Kiri, you will tell me everything before you go to sleep tonight, all right?"

"Yes, Aunt," Kiri said, and skipped away to break off more heather, as purple as the bruise on Chessa's upper thigh from Cleve's loving the previous night.

Cleve said, "This is my home. Chessa insists that where I am she will be also. She swears to me that she loves this savage land, that the mist now caresses her face like a lover's fingers."

"Did I truly say that, Cleve?"

"Perhaps not so eloquently," Cleve said. "We will stay. It is my home, my birthright. There is nothing for me at Malverne, Merrik. You are lord there and Laren is lady. Aye, Chessa, Kiri, and I will remain here. We must. And I have an idea that I hope my father will approve."

"You could return to Duke Rollo's court in Rouen," Laren said. "My uncle believes you to be the greatest of all diplomats, Cleve."

"Chessa dislikes me as a diplomat."

"Aye, he's like a snake his tongue is so smooth. If he weren't so beautiful I would never have paid attention to him at my father's court."

Merrik laughed, shaking his head, but it ended quickly. He looked out over the loch. "The mist is rolling in from the sea again. It never ends. In Norway, there is frigid weather and more snow than a man can sometimes bear, but in the summer months, then the sun scarce ever leaves the sky, it is more beautiful than Laren's eyes."

"We will become accustomed," Chessa said. "Now, you wonder what to do. You fear to leave us here alone. If Varrick wanted us dead, then he would see that all of us were killed. Your men would make no difference. Leave, Merrik. Return to Malverne and your children. This is now our home."

Merrik just shook his head, took his wife's hand, and said, "We will leave in two days, if nothing more happens."

"I want to speak to Kiri," Laren said, and hurried off after the child, who was trying to pat a sheep that was grazing on a hillside near a clump of heather.

"She wants to see that damned monster again," Merrik said. "I pray she will, else my life will be a misery." He smiled and walked swiftly after Laren.

25

THE FOLLOWING MORNING Chessa took a final bite of porridge, and slowly licked the wooden spoon, for Argana's honey was as sweet as Cleve's kisses. She offered to assist Argana but the woman only shook her head. "Once you live here and aren't here as a guest, then you will have duties you select but not before then. Is it true that Merrik and Laren and all the Malverne men will leave soon?"

"Aye," Chessa said. "There is no reason for them to remain. This is my husband's home, not Malverne."

Argana gave her a look she couldn't begin to understand.

"What will you do, Argana?"

"What do you mean, Chessa? Do about what? About Varrick, my husband of eighteen years, the man who would have killed me with little regret? I will do nothing. What can a woman do about anything, save serve and hold her tongue when she's angry, mayhap even bite her tongue until it bleeds?"

"You could tell him he's a swine."

Argana stared at her, then threw back her head and laughed. She couldn't seem to stop laughing. Chessa began to laugh with her. All looked at them, mouths agape, eyes furtively searching out the Lord of Kinloch. Chessa said, "Why is there no joy here? No laughter? You laughed and it is very nice, Argana, yet look at your people. They are shocked that we laughed and perhaps even frightened.''

"Cayman laughs sometimes," Argana said. "But she goes off by herself to do it. I've seen her in the hills, walking about, picking flowers just as your Kiri does, and she'll sniff the flowers and then smile, then perhaps she will laugh. It is a sweet sound. Cayman was always a sweet child and a sweet girl, but she has lived here all her life, and that, Chessa, is too long. You saved my life. I've said nothing about it to you because I—'' She paused, staring down at the cut on her thumb. It was red and swelled. "I wonder how I did this. I have no memory of it."

"It's ugly and must be tended. I have some cream that Mirana of Hawkfell Island gave me. You will rub it into the cut. It will heal."

She left her then to go to the small chamber. In the sea chest at the foot of the box bed, she found the medicinal herbs Mirana had given her. She fetched the cream back to Argana and handed it to her. "Rub it in well, at least three times a day, and keep it clean. Mirana said healing comes more quickly if left to the open air."

As Argana touched the white cream to the cut, there came a shadow that covered both of them. Chessa shivered, looking over her shoulder to see Varrick watching his wife as she smoothed the cream into the cut. "What are you doing, Argana?"

"I seem to have cut my finger, though I don't know how I did it. Chessa gave me some healing cream for it."

Varrick looked for a brief instant as if he would grab the cream from her and hurl it into the fire pit, but then he only shrugged and said, "Chessa, I would speak to you. Cleve is with Kiri and Igmal, both of them teaching her to ride the pony I had Athol bring back to her from Inverness."

Argana didn't even look up. If her finger that was smoothing in the cream paused a moment, that was the only sign that she'd even heard what her husband had said.

"All right," Chessa said, smiling at Argana. "Don't forget, rub in the cream at least three times a day. The cut will heal very soon. Now, Lord Varrick, what is it you wish to say to me? Something that will make me laugh? You need some laughter here at Kinloch.''

"I wish to speak to you of Caldon. I called to him early this morning, but he didn't come to me."

"Perhaps Caldon is female," Chessa said, her voice as cold as the spring to the south of the loch, surrounded with mossed rocks and slippery grass and overhung with full-leafed branches of maple trees. "Perhaps she grows tired of your orders and your domination."

"Perhaps," he said, and his voice was even colder. "Come walk with me, Chessa."

She nodded. There was no reason not to. This man was her father-in-law. She would know him until he died. Unfortunately, at this moment, he looked fitter than the goat that was chasing Kiri into Igmal's arms. For an instant, she wondered about his magic, if there was such a thing, and she looked at the *burra* in its sheath at his belt. She remembered clearly the stark cold and frightening heat of it, and the image of her mother. She said to Argana, "I will walk with my father-in-law, Argana." She felt him stiffen beside her, knew he hated her saying that, and it pleased her. She was determined that soon there would be laughter at Kinloch, that there would be normalcy—bickering, arguing, jesting, wrestling, children yelling at each other, all of it, all of what life was meant to be, not this coldly oppressive atmosphere that Varrick had brought to Kinloch.

"So, you wish to speak of Caldon?"

He said nothing until they were beyond the hearing of any of the Kinloch people. "The sun is bright this morning," he said finally. "It is a fine day."

She laughed. "Not for long, I wager. Every time I've believed that the sun would remain strong and bright, the mist rolled in and reduced it to nothing in but minutes. Should you care to wager about this, Varrick?"

"Why don't you call me lord?"

"You're my father-in-law. Why should I? Don't you know that I respect you since you're my husband's father?"

He looked as if he wanted to strangle her. "I will wager

that the sun remains high and strong today," he said, his white slender hands still fisted at his sides. "If I am right, I want something from you."

"What would that be?"

"I want you to bear my child."

"You what?" She stared up at him, so surprised that no other words formed in her mind. "You *what*?" she said again.

"I can't kill my own son and take you. Thus you will be my concubine and bear my child. Cleve will never know. But the child we produce will have more skill in the magic arts than I have, than your father had, Chessa. You owe it to the force of all that remains hidden from mortals to produce a child who will claim an inheritance no man has ever possessed. Forget the stupid wager, I did not mean to say it. This is more important than you or your husband or anything. Tell me, Chessa, will you be my concubine? Will you bear my child who will be a great sorcerer?"

She stared up at him and said very calmly, "So Cleve was right. You would have killed Argana to have me. But it was a stupid plan, Varrick. Cleve was right again. What would you have done then? Killed your own son?"

"Nay, he wasn't right. I would have killed Argana because it was a matter of honor. I want you, but not as my wife since you are married to Cleve. Answer me now, Chessa. Will you bear my child?"

What was she to say? To do? She forced herself to say calmly, "Perhaps sometimes in the future, Varrick."

"Nay, we mustn't wait. Men die in the flicker of an eyelid. It must be now."

"I can't, Varrick," she said, still calm, now smiling at him. "I am pregnant with Cleve's child."

"You *what*?" Cleve stared down at her, too many memories running riot in his mind, unable to take in what she'd said. He'd been kissing her, caressing her breasts when she'd told him, just blurted it out without adornment. He just shook his head at her. He cupped her chin in his hand, which was difficult to manage since he was on top of her. "Again, Chessa? Yet again you carry my child? I had believed we were well beyond your games by now. At least it isn't Ragnor's child this time."

"Listen to me, Cleve, and you'll understand how clever I've been. Your father decided he wanted me to bed with him and bear his child."

"He *what*?" Cleve smote his forehead with his palm, nearly falling on her. "You wait until you're making my eyes cross with pleasure and then you tell me that my father wants a babe by you? He's an old man, curse him. I'll slit his damned throat for this. He's as perfidious as Ragnor, just smarter, but this wasn't very smart. He wants to bed you? I'll kill him, Chessa, and you'll not gainsay me."

"Nay, I won't gainsay you, Cleve. But listen to me. Varrick doesn't really want *me,* he just believes with all his soul that a child we would produce would be the greatest magician ever to live. He is old enough to be my father. When he wanted to speak to me, I looked at him and then at Argana and agreed that I'd go walking with my father-in-law. I thought he would choke me, but he didn't. He had this on his mind, you see. No, when he told me that the child he and I would produce would be the sorcerer of the millennium, that was when I told him I couldn't do it since it was your babe I carried in my womb. I don't know if you should kill him just yet."

Cleve lifted himself off her. His desire was like the cool ashes in the fire pit, banked for the night. He sat on the edge of the bed, naked, his hands clasped between his knees. "My father wants my wife. Aye, I knew that, but after you stopped him from killing Argana, I believed it over. He knew that all of us realized his motive, thus I believed you safe from him. But this. By all the gods, what am I to do? I should kill him. That would end it once and for all. Ah, but that would leave Argana and her sons alone as well as all his people."

She came up on her knees and hugged her arms around his chest. She kissed the back of his neck, breathed in the scent of his flesh, the scent of his golden hair. She kissed the scar that ran down the side of his face. This time, to her joy, he didn't flinch away from her. She kissed his shoulder. "I'm sorry I told you when I did. You now have no more interest in matters of the flesh, do you?" She was looking over his shoulder.

He grunted but didn't turn to her.

"I told you, Cleve, because you must make me pregnant. We can no longer just think of lust, as we did last night and the night before and the night before that. We must now think very hard of a babe."

He did turn back to her then, shoving her onto her back and coming over her. He balanced himself above her on his elbows. "My life has taken many strange turns. You're the strangest, Chessa. Nay, don't argue with me, you know it's true, you know that you've twisted me about and made me question everything that I was, everything that I ever wanted to be. You've been pregnant more times without producing a child than any woman alive. Now you've done it again. I have to think lustful thoughts. Every time I look at you I think of loving you, caressing you with my mouth, coming into you. A child follows when these thoughts become actions. There is naught more either of us can do. I don't suppose you told him how many months you were pregnant with my child?"

"He didn't ask," she said, kissing Cleve's chin. "I think he was so surprised, that what I'd said was so unexpected, that it didn't occur to him. He's probably been thinking about it all through the afternoon and evening," she continued, trying to pull him back down to her, but he wouldn't move, just stared down at her, now balancing himself on his hands. She stroked her hands down his back to his buttocks. He frowned at her, but she just squeezed and smiled up at him. "You feel so very nice," she said, and arched up, but it didn't encourage him. Her fingers were between his thighs now, lightly touching him, searching, enjoying him.

"Don't," he said, shaking his head at her. "I love you,

aye, that's true enough, though I never wanted to, but now that I do, I will just have to accept it, but even with this love I have for you I still have no interest in this, at least right now. Pay attention, Chessa. You must know that my father is at this very moment deciding what he will do. It worries me, Chessa, for he is ruthless. He wants you. By all the gods, must every man on this wretched earth want you? Must I constantly look at every man to see if there is lust in his eyes and that his eyes are fastened on you?''

"Ragnor didn't really want to marry me. He wanted to marry Utta or you."

"I wish you'd say that another way. Now, be quiet and stop doing that with your hands. I mean it, Chessa, I must think, I must decide what is best to do. You're right, I can't kill him yet. Tomorrow you may be certain he'll want to know when the babe will be born. Oh, damnation, part your legs and let me take you. Perhaps my seed will come deep into your womb and you will accept it."

He didn't touch her further, just pushed her legs apart and came into her, sliding deep and hard. He closed his eyes against the feeling of her soft flesh around him. She'd taken him, she'd been ready for him, yet he knew if he didn't slow, she would gain no pleasure. It would be her own fault for being pregnant yet again with his babe, but he shook his head even as he thought it. He wasn't thinking of a babe when he brought his mouth to her, nor did he think of a babe when he watched her arch upward, yelling in her pleasure. He smiled when he came again into her, harder this time, and she brought him deep and stroked her hands over his back as he moved within her. "I love you," he said when he reached his pleasure.

When he was lying in a near stupor, his head beside hers, his body heavy on hers, she said in his ear, "What is this plan you have that you spoke of to Merrik and Laren?"

Cleve said to his father, "I would like to build a farmstead to the south of the loch where there are the hills and the glens and meadows, filled with flowers. I remember the waterfall and the lushness of the trees and bushes. I remember the boulders and the thick moss that covered the earth. The land to the east flattens enough to grow the crops we would need. Perhaps some of your men would like to join me. They would learn loyalty to me, which is something I know you want.''

Varrick said, ''Naturally my men will also owe you their loyalty. Igmal already would die for Kiri. She is your image, save for that scar on your face. You have yet to tell me of her mother, Cleve. Did she die birthing the child?''

Cleve only shook his head.

''This place you describe, you spent much of your time there when you were a small boy.''

''I was small when I was left for dead,'' Cleve said. He paused and looked toward the fire pit. The sweet smell of mead rose strong in the air. Cayman made it. It was as excellent as Utta's. He smelled the breakfast porridge, the honey Argana gathered. ''After I remembered everything, I believed it was you, my stepfather, who'd tried to kill me. Now I know that can't be true.''

Varrick stretched out his black-clad legs and looked at the rich leather of his boots, dyed as black as his trousers. He wore the *burra* at his wide belt. His tunic was the softest wool, the sleeves full-cut. Black, he wore all black. He said finally, ''I know who tried to kill you. There were no doubts because there was no other who would have done it. I'd hoped you wouldn't ask me. I have no wish to cause you further pain.''

''Who was it?''

Varrick looked directly at his son. ''I'm sorry. It was your brother, Ethar. He was fourteen at the time. He looked at your eyes and knew that you weren't his father's son. He knew you sprang from my seed. He knew you were mine. The girls never realized it. But Ethar did. He hated you from that moment as much as he hated me.''

Cleve rocked back with the pain of it. ''Nay,'' he said, shaking his head, his voice hoarse and low. ''Not Ethar. I worshipped him. He never showed dislike toward me, never.''

"That's true. He tried to kill you very soon after he realized the truth. I believe he wanted to kill me even more than he wanted to kill you, but he couldn't do it. He failed with you as well, thank the gods. I'm sorry that you were a slave for fifteen years. I cannot imagine what you did during those long years, what you suffered. I know you must have many scars, Cleve, not just the one that shows on your face, but scars no one else can see. But it's over now. You're home again. You're safe."

Cleve thought of those long fifteen years, of the different masters and mistresses who'd made his life a living hell, of that one kind old man who'd told him stories and fed him regular meals. The old man had died and he'd been sold then to a man who was a pig. So much had happened. So many years. His father was right. It was behind him. He was home again. His father had said he was safe. He thought of Athol's attack. He imagined Varrick would deal with Athol. He looked at his father now. He knew the answer even before he asked him, "I've been told that Ethar drowned in the loch."

Varrick stared off into the pale smoky air in the hall. "Aye," he said finally. "That is what happened."

Of course Varrick had killed him for what he'd done to his small son. All during those fifteen years Cleve hadn't questioned who'd tried to kill him. He'd been sure it was Varrick, his stepfather, thus his hatred had had a focus. But now, Ethar was long dead, killed by Varrick. He supposed he should thank his father for avenging him, but he couldn't find it within him. Ethar, his brother, nay, his half brother. It had been so very long ago. Ethar had been so young. Ah, but he'd been only five years old. Too young for Ethar's revenge. He cleared his mind. It had been a lifetime ago. He couldn't even remember his brother's face.

He looked at his father, so still he sat, his long white hands utterly motionless, fingers splayed on the carved chair posts. Surely then he could trust his father, in everything except where Chessa was concerned. He couldn't trust any man where Chessa was concerned.

"You're to have another child," Varrick said at last.

"Aye," Cleve said without hesitation.

"She isn't ill."

"Not as yet. It's early days. Kiri's mother vomited constantly after all the other women said she'd be fine." He smiled at his father. "Why did Chessa tell you?"

"I'm her father-in-law. Of course she would tell me. I'm pleased that you will give me a grandson."

He was a liar, but he was as smooth as stones washed over by the waterfall. Cleve said, "I would like to begin today to build my farmstead. Eventually, perhaps Athol could live there."

"And you and Chessa and your children would move here after I die?"

"That is the way of things," Cleve said. He looked up and smiled at Chessa, who was walking to him, a cup of mead in her hand. She handed it to him, then placed her hand on his shoulder. He covered her hand with his. He felt the warmth of her, the softness of her flesh. He turned to smile up at her. Let his father see that she was his and only his. He not only wanted her. He not only admired her and found her both humorous and aggravating, he also loved her, and it was nothing like the feelings he'd had for Sarla, Kiri's mother. He'd believed he'd loved her more than a man could love any other being, but it wasn't true. Much of what he'd felt for Sarla, he realized now, was anger and pity at how her husband had treated her. And he'd desired her, wanted desperately to protect her, to be her champion, to prove that he was no longer a slave but a man who could take care of his woman. But he was stupid enough to confuse lust with caring, and that's what he felt for Chessa. Caring. Deep caring. He hadn't even realized that something so intense, something so profoundly altering, could exist, but it did, and he felt it for her in full measure. He loved her. He loved her more this moment than he had the previous moment. He shook with the realization that this love he felt for her would continue into the future until they were both bones and dust. He knew now what it was she felt for him. He didn't understand it, for he was just a man, nothing special, just a man who'd been a worthless slave, but yet she'd not seen the hideous scar on his face. She'd always believed him beautiful, and that was the truth of it. He hadn't understood her, thus he'd believed it a sham. But it wasn't. These feelings were as real as the high mist that hung over the loch. The caring he had for her, this bone-deep pleasure at her closeness, all of it made him feel warm and filled with hope and energy and the blessedness of being human and *knowing* what she was to him and what he was to her. He smiled at her, what he felt making his golden eye brilliant as the sun. "I will take you to see where we will begin our building."

"Aye, I'd like that," Chessa said, leaned down, and kissed his mouth. In front of Varrick. But he knew she'd kissed him because she'd looked into his eyes and seen his soul. She was accepting him into her and her delight was plain for him to see. For his father to see.

26

Merrik, Laren, and all the Malverne men left two days later, on a bright morning that Chessa now believed would stay bright, the mist biding its time, but not closing in about them until the evening. Eller sniffed the air and grunted. "Aye," he said. "'Twill serve."

Chessa and Cleve, Kiri in his arms, waved until the two ships disappeared around a slight bend in the loch. "This is our home now," Chessa said.

Kiri said, "Papa, let me down. I want to go find Caldon. I haven't seen her for two days now. She misses me. I told her I wanted to meet her children."

He merely nodded and set her on the narrow path that led to the wooden dock that stretched out into the loch beside the promontory. "Her imagination rivals Laren's. Unfortunately, Laren never saw the monster again. Merrik says she will droop like a withered flower for a while."

"Let's take Kiri and go back to work," Chessa said. "I would have our own bed soon."

Varrick looked at her belly every single day, asked her how she felt every single day. She merely smiled at him, nothing more.

It was soon after that things began to change at Kinloch. There was some laughter now, some arguments amongst

the men as they ate, as they drank, as they worked. The
children, led by Kiri, battled with their wooden knives and
swords and axes. They threw their leather balls. They ran
about the hall, tumbling over each other, insulting each
other. The women chatted as they wove the wool into
thread. Varrick frowned, but remained quiet. Chessa
laughed more than she'd ever laughed in her life, most
times not because she was amused, but because she wanted
all the Kinloch people to know that laughter was a wonderful thing, that they could do it and not be struck down.
She wanted them to know that Varrick would do naught to
stop it. Cleve must believe he'd become the greatest wit in
all of Scotland, she thought, for she laughed at nearly every
thing he said. She looked over at Cayman, who still only
spoke to either of them when it was necessary, never vol-
unteering a word or a thought or an opinion. She was gone
most of the time, out in the hills, Argana said. As for Argana's sons, they called Cayman a madwoman, singing to
the goats, they said, speaking strange incantations over
rocks, they said, then they'd stare toward their father.

The day Chessa broke Athol's leg began with a dull gray
mist, then cleared into a magical morning that smelled crisp
and clean. A falcon perched on the high ridge of rocks that
formed the eastern perimeter of their new farmstead. All
the men were working on the farmstead, to be named Karelia, named after an isthmus between Lake Ladoga and the
Gulf of Finland, a place Cleve remembered with pleasure.
When Chessa questioned him more closely about this pleasure, he simply kissed the tip of her nose and told her it
would go with him to the grave.

"Karelia," she said. "It sounds pleasant, thus I will allow it, husband, even though I know you knew a woman
there. What was her name?"

"Tyra," he said, and kissed the tip of her nose again.
"If I remember aright. There were so very many."

She fisted her hand and hit him in his belly. He grinned
down at her. "Do you yet carry my babe?"

She frowned. "So many times I've claimed to be pregnant and yet now when I truly want to be, it won't happen. Do you think I'm barren, Cleve?"

"Nay, sweeting, I think your husband isn't trying hard enough. Mayhap you're worrying about it too much and it makes my seed wary."

"It's true you're very tired every night now with all the work."

He clasped her neck in his hands and squeezed lightly. Then he kissed her hard on her closed mouth. He looked at her closely, at those beautiful green eyes of hers, as green as the moss-covered rocks near the waterfall he'd shown her. "Has my father said anything to you? Bothered you in any way?"

"He just stares at my belly every time he sees me."

"Papa, is it true?"

Both looked down to see Kiri frowning up at them, an apple in her hand, three children trailing after her, all bickering over a leather ball.

"Is what true, sweeting?" Chessa said.

"I heard Athol tell his brother that you were having my first papa's babe."

"Aye," Cleve said, his single word as bald as the goat that was chewing on a discarded tunic near the newly built privy.

"He then said it wasn't true, the tale you were telling. He said Chessa was carrying Varrick's babe, not yours. I told him that wasn't right and he laughed at me. I don't like Athol." Kiri looked at the ground for a moment, frowning ferociously. "Athol somehow isn't right in his head."

"No, he's not, you're right about that, Kiri," Chessa said. "You keep away from him. He's a coward and a troublemaker."

But Kiri didn't. Luckily, it was Chessa who came upon the two of them. She heard Kiri shout up at Athol, who was sneering down at her, "You lied to me, Athol. My second papa won't have Varrick's babe. It's my first papa's babe.''

"You're a stupid little girl," Athol said. "You don't know anything. Go away. She isn't your second papa, she's nothing but a silly woman, worth little save for breeding."

"Not until you tell me you lied."

Athol swore at her. Then when she kicked him in his shin, he leaned down and picked her up. He shook her. "You miserable whelp," he shouted in her face, spittle spewing out. "You damned miserable whelp. You're his and you don't deserve to live, much less to live here and take what is mine."

Chessa had no idea what he intended, but the look on his face terrified her. There was a complete lack of control there, his eyes dark with rage. She said very quietly, "Let her down, Athol, now."

"You," he said, and shook Kiri again. She fisted her small hand and shoved it into his nose. He yowled and threw her down.

Chessa was on him in the next instant, shrieking in his face, cursing him with all the words she'd learned in Dublin from her father's soldiers. When he raised his hand to her, she sent her knee into his groin. When he was bowed and yelling with pain, she kicked him in the leg and knocked him to the ground. She kicked him in the ribs, then again in the leg and heard the bone snap. Still, she didn't stop. She was panting hard, her anger making the air around her as red as the Christian's hell, making the loch look black as midnight.

"Chessa!"

She tried to struggle away from him, to keep kicking Athol, who was cringing at her feet, holding himself in a ball, but Cleve pulled her off. She whirled about, panting, "He was shaking Kiri. Then he threw Kiri on the ground, Cleve. *Threw her*!"

"Kiri is all right. I taught her how to roll off her shoulder if she ever fell. Stop it, Chessa. Look, Kiri is just fine."

"Papa, see, I'm not hurt, not like Athol is."

The red mist fell away from her as she heard the satis-
faction in Kiri's voice. She took a deep breath. "I wonder
why I didn't draw my knife and send it into his black
heart," she said, then shook her head. She stared down at
him, raised her foot, then lowered it. "Nay, that's enough
for him."

"My leg," Athol said, holding it and rocking back and
forth, moaning. "You broke my leg."

"Aye," Chessa said. "I heard the bone crack. Hold still
and I'll see to you."

Athol screamed and tried to scramble away from her.

"You bullying coward, hold still."

Cleve said, "She won't kill you now, Athol. Do as she
says, else I'll have to hit your head with a rock so you
won't move while she takes care of you."

"What is this?" Igmal said as he strode to them, wiping
his hands on the leather apron tied around his waist. "Aye,
Athol, you forgot her warning, eh? You're lucky she didn't
kill you."

Athol groaned. "Don't let her touch me, Igmal, I order
you."

"Hold your damned tongue in your throat, Athol. She
won't kill you now."

"My father—"

Cleve leaned down and sent his fist into Athol's jaw. He
fell back, unconscious.

"Papa, can you teach me how to do that?"

"No," Cleve said and picked up his daughter. "Are you
truly all right, sweeting?"

"Aye," Kiri said. "Igmal, can I come with you now and
help you work?"

Igmal grinned, those beautiful white teeth of his glistening in the sun, and took her from Cleve. "Aye, little one,
I think I'll let you play in the tar pot. Your papas will like
that, I think."

In late September, when in Norway the air would have
turned frigid in the early afternoon, it was still warm in

Scotland, the air soft and sweet from the smells of the heather. Karelia was finished. The wood smelled fresh and new and Chessa loved it. It was small, but there was enough room for three of them and the dozen men and the four families that came there to live. There was a bathing hut, just like the one in Malverne, only smaller, a privy, a barn for the grain, several storage huts, a barn for the cows, goats, and two horses, a blacksmith's hut, and a small slave compound. Now the men were erecting a palisade some ten feet high that would surround the farmstead.

"It's ours," Chessa said with relish as she rubbed her hands together. Argana had given her pots and dishes and spoons and knives. She even gave her a beautiful linen cloth for the long narrow eating table. The first time Cleve lit the fire pit, the first time Chessa pulled the thick piece of wood attached to the roof beams with the serpent's head at its end, adjusting its thick chains hooked to the iron cooking pot over the pit, she laughed aloud with pleasure. Varrick was there. He frowned at her. Argana laughed as well. Cayman just stood back, watching, saying nothing, just watching. Athol stood on crutches, watching as well, his expression so sullen Cleve wished he could kick him out.

It was that night, their first night at Karelia, the first night in their own box bed with a soft new bearskin, given to them by Ottar, one of Igmal's men, when Chessa said, "I'm with child."

Cleve, on the point of coming into her, stiffened, looked at her in bewilderment, then came into her, deep and full, and she laughed, pulling him closer, drawing him deeper. "I wondered what you'd do," she whispered into his ear, then nibbled his earlobe, kissed his jaw, then his mouth and tasted the sweet mead on his breath from their feast, and said, "I love you, Cleve. I'm not barren."

He withdrew from her, came between her thighs and brought his mouth to her. When she screamed, bowing upward, he laughed. "My babe will hear his mother shrieking," he said, then came into her again, feeling her tighten about him, feeling her quiver from the tremors of pleasure still holding her.

"You will forget about controlling me," he said, coming up over her, leaning his head down to kiss her as he spoke each word. "You believed I would become so befuddled at your news that I would fall off the bed and you would give me a smug smile. Ah, don't move like that, Chessa, else I'll—"

He said no more. He loved her again, only this time, it was different, for his babe nestled in her womb and he wanted to show her how pleased he was, how much he loved her, how he would cherish her for the rest of his life. When she moaned softly into his mouth, he took that moan deep within himself. When he could speak again, he said, "I love you, Chessa. I never thought you were barren."

She sent her elbow into his ribs, then brought his mouth down to hers. "Do you really love me, Cleve? It's not that I haven't believed you before when you've brought yourself to say it, but you're still a man, and I don't think men like to speak of such things. It makes them feel silly."

"Who told you that? Surely not Mirana or Laren?"

"Nay, it's just what I've observed."

"And you're such an old woman, just like Old Alna, cackling, her gums showing, preaching about all men's failings, even her beloved Rorik's."

"Well, perhaps a bit. But you've only told me a few times, a very few times. Usually you just rant at me and yell at me and lust after me, which is something else that men want to do all the time."

"That," he said, kissing her deeply, "is true. When will our babe be born?"

"In March."

"That's when Kiri was born," he said, and rolled off her, bringing her against his side.

"What happened?"

He told her about Sarla then, how he'd believed he'd loved her, how she'd betrayed him, but he'd forced her to remain at Malverne until Kiri was born. "I remember how she cursed me as she was birthing Kiri.''

''Why?''

''It hurts, Chessa.''

''Are you certain? Sira said it was nothing. She said she grunted a few times and another boy came out of her body.''

Cleve winced at the hopefulness in her voice. What did he, a man, know about birthing babes? He said, kissing her ear, ''Why don't you ask Argana about it?''

''Did it take a long time for Kiri to be born?''

He started to lie then knew it wasn't fair. ''A very long time,'' he said, ''but I know that it is different with every woman.''

''And many women die.''

''You won't and I forbid you to speak of it. I'll be with you and it will be fine.''

''My father never went near to Sira when she was birthing each of the boys.''

''Merrik was with Laren with both boys. Is there some sort of rule in Ireland that a husband must leave?''

''I didn't think that men wanted to be close to their wives whilst they were birthing a babe. My father always left the palace and went hunting.''

''I won't go hunting.''

She kissed his chest. ''I remember that Sira wouldn't let my father near her when her time grew near because she was fat and ugly, I heard her say to one of her women. Of course she'd never say anything to me. The truth is I never thought she was ugly even when her belly was huge.''

He caressed her flanks, then slid his hand between them to her belly. ''I won't leave you,'' he said. ''I won't ever leave you.''

''You swear it?''

''Even if you look like Laren's pet pig, Ravnold, I'll stay close. I'll even try to hold you every night. At least I'll come as close to you as possible.''

She bit his chin, then came down over him.

He said, puzzled, ''I don't understand, Chessa. You're

pregnant. My seed took hold inside you. You mean we must continue to do this?''

She leaned down and bit his chin again. ''This is for me, not for a babe,'' she said as he came high and deep into her.

''It is a messenger from King Sitric,'' Igmal said. ''He claims he knows you, Chessa.''

Chessa wiped her hands on a woolen cloth, straightened her tunic, pulled off the linen kerchief from around her hair and came outside the farmstead. There was Brodan, her half brother, behind him two dozen soldiers, her father's bodyguard, Cullic, at their fore.

She yelled his name and ran into his arms. ''Ah, Brodan,'' she said between kisses, ''you're here! I thought never to see you again, oh my, you're here. How much you've grown. How did you find us? Oh, you're quite a young man now, so very big. Your eyes are dark, just like father's. The girls must adore you, Brodan.'' Since he was only eight years old, this didn't please him, and Chessa quickly called out, ''Cleve, come here and meet your new brother, Brodan.''

He had grown over the past nearly six months, she thought. He would become a handsome man. She thought of Athol and said a prayer to every god she knew that Brodan wouldn't grow crooked as Athol had. She watched him stare up at Cleve, eyeing him as another grown man would, for strengths and weaknesses, something their father had taught him. ''I remember you,'' Brodan said. ''You were the emissary from Duke Rollo. When your messenger from Hawkfell Island came to Dublin and told my father of your marriage to Chessa, he cursed and ranted and kicked furniture and yelled at everyone who came near him for three days. He even yelled at mother. She didn't understand that. It confused her. Then he smiled again. I remember his telling mother that you were a good man and that Chessa thought you nearly perfect, especially your face. He said she never saw the scar and thus she must love you very much. He is content now, not happy, but content."

"I am relieved," Cleve said, gripping the young boy's shoulder. "I didn't want your father to come here and slit my throat."

"My father said Chessa would slit your throat if you ever deserved it."

"She would," Cleve said, nodding.

"Father let you come to Scotland," Chessa said, marveling, for Brodan was only a young boy, after all, and such a journey was always fraught with danger.

"I wanted to see Iona where Saint Columba lived and preached. Did you know that Kenneth moved his remains from Iona many years ago to near Scone?"

"Aye," Igmal said. "My grandfather told me that after Kenneth united the Scots and Picts together, he wanted to prove that the Scots were the better ones and he moved his capital from Argyll to Scone in Perth. He took poor Saint Columba's bones away from Iona and moved the Stone of Destiny from Dunadd to Scone. My grandfather hated the little man for that, said that he'd gotten the Pictish throne through the female line and everyone knew that was madness."

"What's the Stone of Destiny?" Chessa asked.

Brodan's voice dropped to a whisper. "It looks like a simple slab of sandstone, but it was the pillow on which Jacob, the son of Isaac and grandson of Abraham, had his dream about the angels and the stairway to heaven."

"You've become a Christian, Brodan?" she said, not recognizing these names, but hearing the awe in her brother's voice.

"Aye, Chessa. I've told Father that I want to live on Iona and practice the old ways."

"Oh," she said. He was only eight years old and he believed he'd already found what he was meant to do? He'd always been a serious child, older than his years, but he'd loved fishing with her. She remembered the *glailey* fish they'd caught that had been served that one night at the evening meal to Cleve in Dublin. "Father is all right, Brodan?"

"Aye, he is the same. Mother had another boy. I told father that with four other sons, he didn't need me. He said he would consult the stars. He told me later that the signs were good, that I would be safe."

"Ever the sorcerer," Cleve said. He looked up to see Cullic, King Sitric's personal bodyguard, stride forward to stand beside Brodan. He still had the coldest eyes Cleve had ever seen and his skin was even darker after their journey from Dublin. Cullic gently placed his hand on Brodan's shoulder, saying, "We will remain here for three days, then the prince wishes to journey to St. Andrews. We have been told that a new abbey has been founded. The bishop there will become the leading man in the Scottish Church."

"Aye," Brodan said. "Iona is the old and the abbey of St. Andrews is the new. I wish to worship at both." He seemed to struggle with himself for a moment, then blurted out, "I have heard also that the monster in Loch Ness was seen by Saint Columba. Surely it can't be evil, not if that great man saw it. Have you seen it, Chessa?"

"Aye, I did, just once. It has a very long neck and a small head. It appeared, then quickly sank beneath the water again. Kiri has seen the monster many times. She says it isn't a monster, but rather a mother with children."

"Kiri?"

"Cleve's daughter. Ah, here she is. Kiri, sweeting, come and meet my brother, Brodan, from Ireland. He wants to know all about Caldon."

The eight-year-old stared down at the small girl and looked immeasurably depressed. "You're telling me that this little girl has seen the creature?"

"Her name is Caldon," Kiri said.

Brodan sighed. "How can this be possible? How can this be just? Little girls have imaginations that bubble over like stew pots."

"Trust me, Brodan. Not this little girl. Now, brother, come into our new farmstead and bring your men with you.

We will prepare a feast that will even make Cullic belch.''

The Spaniard didn't smile, but he nodded, then turned about to give instructions to his men.

A light drizzle fell, graying the air, a soft sweet sound against the roof of the longhouse, bringing the mist to hover over the hills and sink slowly down to sit upon the dark waters of the loch. Chessa loved the rain for it stopped as suddenly as it began, bringing forth the sun to shine down upon the lush green. She left the front oak door open so that smoke from the fire pit could escape. The small hole in the roof never allowed enough smoke out at any one time. At least here in Scotland, they didn't have to worry about freezing.

Not an hour later the drizzle stopped and the sun shone over the loch. Chessa left the longhouse for the privy. She patted the small curve of her belly. ''Will I make even more trips to the privy for you when it is winter and cold and snow is blowing off the loch? Does that ever happen? I wonder.''

She was humming softly to herself when she left the privy and walked to the barn where Varrick had sent hay to feed the animals for the winter. It was dark inside and smelled of cow and goat, of closely packed grain and men's sweat. When the hand came over her mouth and her arms were pinned to her sides, she froze, her first thought: Varrick.

But it wasn't Varrick. ''Don't move, Chessa. I don't want to hurt you.''

27

"KEREK," SHE SAID through his fingers. "I've missed you." He loosened his grip and slowly turned her to face him.

"Aye," he said, looking down into her face, "I have missed you as well. You're more beautiful than I'd remembered, Chessa, but you look tired. You've had to work too hard. You need more slaves, more families. The farmstead looks sturdy, I doubt outlaws will attack it. I've watched you now for three days, waiting to find you alone. There are always so many people about."

"What do you want, Kerek? Why are you hiding like a thief? This is our new home. Cleve calls it Karelia. We've all worked very hard, aye, that's true enough, but it's worth the work, for it's our home. Why didn't you just come and greet us like a friend?"

He sighed. "I wanted to but I couldn't. I don't want this, Chessa, truly, but Turella believes it the only way. She sent me. Ragnor is now king. Olric died from a piece of meat one of his concubines hadn't chewed well enough. He choked to death with many looking on. It is said that Ragnor tossed a bone in the air once his father had fallen face forward into his plate and said that he wanted his father's concubines and now they would chew his food.

"He plans to attack Hawkfell Island and take Utta. You

might believe this is his boy's bragging, but I know it isn't. He will do it. He won't listen to Turella. He blames his mother for Isla disappearing, and since he doesn't know where she is, he claims his mother killed her. Thus, he says he will settle for Utta after he's taken Hawkfell Island. He was mistreated there, he yells to all, thrown into the water to drown, given no respect as the prince of the Danelaw. Now that he's the king, he will show them. He will kill all of them or make them slaves. He does mean it, Chessa.

"You'll not credit this but he truly mourns Isla. He talks about her breasts, surely, for he is a man, but he liked the way she treated him, so easily, and yet with the respect due him as the prince of the Danelaw. He liked her eye patch more than anything else, I think. He wanted to remove it to see what was underneath."

"If he had he would have seen Cleve's golden eye."

"Neither Turella nor I told him this woman he desired above all others was really Cleve, come to York to rescue you. Thus, Princess, we are back to you. You are the only one he ever heeded. He fears you, aye, don't interrupt me, you know it's true. He would never admit to it, but he does fear you in a strange way that I don't understand. Turella believes you would hold sway over him where she no longer can. You must come back to York with me. You must take him in hand. You must control him."

"No, never. He would kill me, Kerek. I would never have control over him. It's nonsense, all of it. Please, you must stop this now."

"Turella doesn't want to have to kill her own son, but to save the Danelaw, she might be forced into it. He thinks only of revenge against Rorik and taking Utta. I think he also plans to kill her. He won't listen to the advisors about the increasing raids by the Saxons, about the lands they're conquering, what we're losing to them. He drinks and complains that the mead isn't as good as Utta's or Isla's. All despair, not just I, not just Turella. A kingdom despairs,

Princess. It is your duty to come back, to contain Ragnor, to master him.''

"Let her kill him. I care not. The Danelaw will fall eventually to the Saxons. All know it. It's just a matter of time. Leave me be, Kerek.''

"Not if you are there, not if you and Turella join together and rule.''

She clasped his arms and tried to shake him. "Look at me, Kerek. I'm but a woman. I bathed in the bathing hut this morning. I just went to the privy. I'm wearing a cloth around my head. I was just kneading bread dough. See, there is flour on my hands. This is our farmstead, this is my life. I have nothing to do with the Danelaw, nothing to do with Turella. *I'm not a warrior woman.*''

"I will take you to Turella, Chessa. She has commanded me to. I have no choice.''

"I won't go with you. If you try to force me, you will come to regret it, Kerek, I swear it to you.''

The threat, very real, didn't have the effect on him she'd expected it to. He smiled hugely. "Ah, you see? I will have to guard you very carefully else you will kill me. It is that passion in you, Chessa, that promise that you'll do exactly as you say, that utter resolution that is such a deep part of you, that makes you formidable, that will make Ragnor and the Saxons think hard before they attempt to go against you. You're not stupid either, and you're willing to act, regardless of the consequences to yourself. Why do you not accept this? Aye, you will come with me and Turella will be pleased and the Danelaw will survive longer.''

She wanted to hit him over the head to make him think clearly. But he was holding her and he was strong. She said again, "I won't do it.''

Still, he appeared to hold to his patience. "Hear me out. Turella has thought of everything. She believes Cleve will forget you, he will come to believe you dead when he cannot find you. He will mourn you, but how long does a man mourn a woman, any woman? Not that long, Princess. Then he will find another and soon he will be happy again. You won't have to worry that he will suffer long once you've gone. Turella wants you to wed with Ragnor. None will know that it isn't a true wedding, save Turella, you, and I. She says you'll agree to it to save Rorik and Mirana and Hawkfell Island. Remember, Chessa, Ragnor now has many warriors to command. They would follow him even though they wouldn't want to. Loyalty runs deep in Vikings, you know that. He would take Hawkfell Island. He would destroy it. He enjoys destruction, you remember that, don't you?''

"Aye, I remember, but it makes no difference. Come, Kerek, come back to the farmstead and speak to Cleve of this. We will plan something that will help you and Turella as well as Hawkfell Island. Please, come back with me.''

"Nay," he said, and there was strength in that one small word and deep resolve, and she knew he wouldn't change his mind. She drew a deep breath, smiled up at him, and said, "I'm pregnant with Cleve's child.''

He stared down at her, then threw back his head and laughed. A cow mooed and a goat kicked over a wooden pail. The smell of hay was heavy in the air.

"Cleve laughed as well when I told him," she said. "But this time it's true, Kerek. I am pregnant. You can believe me. Cleve and I have been married since midsummer.''

His laughter stopped as suddenly as it began. He splayed his fingers over her belly, felt the slight thickening, and went pale. "No," he said, "oh, no. We never considered this." He ran his fingers through his hair, making it stand on end. He clasped her arm and pulled her close, then stared toward the goat. He was deep in thought. "It doesn't matter," he said at last. "We will get you back to York as quickly as possible. We will simply tell everyone it's Ragnor's child, just like before. Turella will be pleased. She'll be ecstatic. Don't you remember? She wanted you to rule and Cleve's child to rule after you? Aye, all will be well. This is better than either Turella or I expected. Once again you've not disappointed me, Princess.''

"I won't leave Cleve or Kiri," she said. "Even if you

get me to York, I won't do what you wish me to do, namely
wed Ragnor and become Turella's daughter. I won't do it.''

Kerek smiled sadly at her. "You will, Chessa. You now
have your babe to protect."

Cleve tapped the leather ball with his foot, sending it
bouncing to Kiri, who scooped it up and threw it to little
Torik, who let it hit his chest and bounce off.

Kiri immediately scolded him until Inga, Askhold's wife,
bent down and put her face right up to Kiri's. "He's but a
little bit of a boy, sweeting. He doesn't know what to do
with his hands yet. Be patient. It's a female's lot in this
life—patience. You must begin to learn it now."

Cleve laughed. "Aye," he said, nodding, "it's true. Listen to her, Kiri. Then you will tell your second papa, for
sometimes she rushes off without proper patience."

"Aye, little one," Igmal said, coming down on his
haunches in front of Kiri, "you must be patient with boys
just as Inga says. They take a goodly time to ripen, many
take more than a goodly time."

"All right," Kiri said. She held out her hand to Torik.
"I'll take him to the loch and call out to Caldon. She'll
come when I call her."

"Aye," Igmal said, "but you take heed, little one.
You're the big sister here, so pay attention to little Torik.
You come back soon."

Kiri nodded, took Torik's dirty hand, and pulled him
from the longhouse.

Cleve just shook his head. It was like Malverne, like
Hawkfell. Every man and woman attended every child
when they were close, and all worked for the good of the
farmstead. He felt an overwhelming sense of belonging that
had been denied to him most of his life until he'd found
Laren and Merrik and lived as one of them at Malverne.
But this was different. This was his home. His and Chessa's. He felt warm and secure. He wanted to hug Chessa,
he realized, perhaps kiss her mouth, and lick her lower lip,
something she liked very much.

"Inga, where is Chessa?"

She said, "She was kneading dough but an hour ago, then she just shook her head and said she had to go to the privy again. I haven't seen her, Cleve. Let me ask."

"Aye, and I'll look outside."

Chessa loved to visit the waterfall, to sit on the moss-covered rocks and lean back against the gnarled old sessile oak tree and dream, that's what she'd tell him, dream about the babe she carried, if it would be a boy or a girl, and would the babe have his golden hair or her black hair? But if she'd been kneading bread, why would she simply leave the longhouse and go off?

It was at that moment that he felt a chill in the air, a raw current of air that ruffled his hair and made him shiver. Then the cold died and the air warmed, touching his flesh, making him wonder what had happened.

Everyone searched for her but she wasn't to be found. Toward evening, Varrick came, alone, and he said to Cleve, "Chessa's been taken. I don't know by whom, but a man took her. I saw it all clearly."

Cleve stared at his father. "It's true we can't find her, but who would take her? Who could come into the farm-stead and take her?"

"I don't know but he got in here and has been waiting to get her alone and take her."

"How do you know this?"

Varrick pulled the *burra* from its sheath at his belt. "I felt it and then I saw it just a short time ago. I saw a large man, muscled and thick, a man with fierce eyes, and thick red hair threaded with gray, but I also saw pleasure in his eyes at the sight of Chessa. I saw them speak. They argued, but he was pleading with her. Then, finally, he stuck a gag in her mouth, bound her wrists, covered her with a blanket, and pulled her over his shoulder. He's gone now, but I don't know where. The images stopped. But he has her."

"How old is this man?"

"He has my years, but he looks older, more rough-hewn, more lines on his face. Do you know this man, Cleve?"

"Aye," Cleve said quietly, "I know him very well. His name is Kerek and he is Queen Turella's man."

"Turella?" Varrick said, looking off into the distance. "Turella? That's odd, isn't it?"

"Once I tell you the history of all this, you'll believe it more than odd. Turella is the queen of the Danelaw. It's put about that the king has kept her prisoner for many years, but it's a false rumor. She rules. He is a fool, but she allows him to think that he is the important one. Something must have happened in York. Turella was convinced that Chessa should marry her son, Ragnor, that she could control him, that she could lead after Turella and secure the safety of the Danelaw. Ragnor is a selfish little toad with no more sense than Athol."

Varrick said, his voice as stiff as the *burra* that he still held in his right hand, "Athol improves. Once you left Kinloch, he began to regain his balance. His broken leg mends."

Cleve only grunted. "Do you wish to accompany me to get Chessa back?"

"Aye," Varrick said slowly. "We'll find Chessa."

And Cleve thought, he still wants her, he's just biding his time until the babe is born, then it will begin again. He prayed Argana was safe from Varrick, at least until Chessa birthed their babe. By all the gods, he hated it, but now he needed his father's help. He watched Varrick gently slip the *burra* back into its leather sheath and fasten it to his belt. What would his father be without the *burra*?

Cleve, Varrick, and Igmal discussed which route Kerek had taken. By sea or traveling overland through Scotland into the Danelaw?

"By sea," Cleve said. "Kerek would never risk Chessa's life by traveling through Scotland. He doesn't know the land or the dangers. Besides, it would be quicker to go by sea, if the weather holds steady."

"It's nearly winter," Varrick said. "Storms in the North Sea come in the blink of an eye, without warning, and with deadly effect."

Varrick had three warships, Cleve, one. In all, they had sixty men, most of them Pict warriors, so honed in their skills, so ruthless, that they would challenge the Christian's hell itself. But they weren't good sailors, and that worried Cleve. He wanted to go after Kerek and Chessa this very moment, but it was dark now and no man would venture onto the loch when it was dark. It would do him no good even to discuss it with the men. They would leave at first light. There was no choice. He thought and thought all evening, listening to Igmal, to his father, to the other men as well. It was just before Varrick left Karelia to return the short distance to Kinloch that he said, "I have a plan. Will you be willing to obey me, Father, in order to rescue Chessa?"

Varrick stared at his son. He saw strength and intelligence in him. He wasn't surprised. How else would Cleve have survived for fifteen years as a slave? He was his son and he would rule Kinloch after him. But that wasn't what made Varrick nod. It was Chessa. He had to have her back and who better to get her back than her husband? "Aye," he said. "Tell me your plan."

Cleve told him, working out flaws as he thought, then spoke. When he finished, Varrick slowly nodded. He pulled the *burra* from its sheath. It was pulsing with warmth, and it was so light he wondered if he released it, if it would rise to the roof of the longhouse. He gave it to Cleve and said, "What do you feel?"

Cleve looked at the heathen stick, for that's how he thought of it now. He didn't want to touch the damned thing, but he knew he had to. Slowly he took it from his father, nearly dropping it, so heavy it was. It was eerie and it made the hair stick up on the back of his neck. It shouldn't be so heavy. He had to hold it with both hands. By all the gods, the thing was just a stick that was a foot long and with a dull point on the end, nothing more except for those strange markings, truly, there shouldn't be anything more, but he remembered Chessa's face when she had held it, her surprise, her fascination, and finally her fear.

He gave it back to his father. "Take your *burra* and sheath it. I have no interest in it. It is heavy and cold. I accept that it has qualities that are not of this land, mayhap even of this earth. I don't want to know its mysteries or its powers. Take it, Father, and force it not upon me again."

Varrick accepted it from his son, balancing it on one finger even as he smiled at Cleve and knew that Cleve recognized that he had no power over it. Ah, but Chessa did have power. "We will leave then at first light. Are you certain this is what you want to do?"

Cleve nodded. "A large force would have no hope of rescuing her. No, we will do it another way." Then he smiled, an evil smile, one that promised revenge and death.

"I don't need a *burra* to make rain and turn the loch into boiling chaos or to bring that poor monster to me," Cleve said. "I have a man's brain and that is what will succeed."

"Ah," Varrick said as he turned away to slip into the night, "there is much that is uncertain. I agree to your idea. A small force of men, disguised as the guards at the palace in York, aye, I believe that will work well enough, particularly since you know the palace. But if it doesn't work, then you'll see, Cleve, aye, you'll see. Then you'll need me. Never discount the power of magic."

Heavy mist hung over the loch, touching the water, swirling around the single longboat. It was cold and damp on the water and Chessa's teeth chattered despite the warm woolen cloak Kerek had wrapped around her. He had only six men, all rowing the small longboat with all their strength. They knew the monster lived in this loch that was said to be bottomless. They knew if one of them fell into the water, he would disappear forever, either pulled into the monster's maw, or sucked into the oblivion that swirled ever downward in the loch. Each man was grunting hard now, not wanting to stop his frantic rowing, just praying to

Thor that they'd reach Inverness and safety. They needed no encouragement, for fear of the unknown pushed them and gave them strength.

She sat in the bow of the longboat, trying to see through the thick gray mist, but unable to. There were no stars above, just this gray mist that gave off an eerie light. She said quietly, cupping her hand to her mouth, "Caldon, if you are there, come to me as you do to Varrick, as you do to Kiri. I don't have his wizardry or that *burra* of his, nor do I have Kiri's child's belief, but I call you to me. Help me."

"What are you saying, Chessa?"

She smiled at Kerek who was drawing on his oars as hard as the other six men, panting so hard she could barely understand his words. "I'm calling to the monster of the loch," she said, raising her voice so all could hear her. "Cleve's father calls her and she comes. He's a sorcerer. Kiri calls the monster as well. We will see. If she comes, she will save me."

The men turned to her and she saw such fear on their faces that she knew she had to push them. "Aye," she said louder now, "just look at this mist. It isn't natural, just look at the dull light it gives off. Look closely, soon the monster will appear. Caldon is larger than a warship, a sea serpent that's lived in this loch for hundreds of years, mayhap thousands, mayhap since before time began. It's said the Romans never came close to this loch because they feared the monster. Fishermen never come to the middle of the loch and never set their nets in the water after the sun sets. They know they will die and their bodies never again be found. Listen. Is that Caldon coming?"

One of the men yelled. "Kerek, we will die!"

Kerek said low, "Be quiet, Chessa, or I will have to stick that gag in your mouth again."

"If you strike me, Kerek," she said, smiling at him, "I wonder what Caldon will do."

"Stop this, you know—"

With no warning, a huge wave slapped against the longboat. It sent cold water splashing over the men. They dropped their oars.

"Damn you, row," Kerek shouted. "We will go to shore. Row to shore, it isn't far. If there weren't this wretched mist, you'd see how close we were. Do it or you will have no chance to survive."

Another wave slapped against the side of the longboat, sending another curl of frigid water over the men. The water didn't touch Chessa, nor did it wet the man next to her, but it poured over Kerek, as if meant only for him. The men knew it and were terrified. Kerek had stood up and was pointing. "The shore is just there. Row, damn you, row!"

There was a soft whistling sound just off the bow of the boat. Another wave struck, but this one wasn't so big. It rolled against the side of the longboat as if something large were coming and making the water shift and pulse. The whistling sound was closer now and coming even closer. The men froze, knowing that the monster was here and that soon they would die. One of them yelled, "Princess, tell the monster to leave us. Tell the monster we will release you if we can but live. We won't obey Kerek, tell the monster that."

"Caldon," Chessa called out, "You heard the man. If he speaks true, then you can release them from your death grip. If he lies, then kill them."

The whistling sound changed. It was more like the hiss of a snake, a huge snake, nay, the sound a sea serpent would make to warn its prey just before it struck. The hissing was close now, in every man's ear. The warmth of that hissing breath against every man's face. All of them could imagine that huge sea serpent strike its immense tail against a longboat and send it spinning into the depths of the loch, down and down into nothingness. The men could hear the hissing closer now, as if it were right beside each of them, as if it were burrowing inside them. They could feel the damp scales of the monster's flesh, they could smell death in the monster's breath. Small waves crested, shimmering in the strange light of the mist, then slapped against the longboat, one after the other.

"Thor save us," one of the men shouted, and pointed. "Look yon. It's upon us!"

28

KIRI SCREAMED. SHE woke the other six children who all slept pressed against each other in the large box bed. She screamed again, arms thrashing, her body heaving. Torik began to cry. Eidalla, a year older than Kiri, shook her arm. "It's a nightmare, nothing more. Be quiet, Kiri. Hush, wake up now and stop crying."

But Kiri threw herself out of the bed and ran to her father's small chamber where he was already in the doorway, pulling on his trousers.

"Papa!"

Cleve grabbed her up into his arms and rocked her. Men and women surrounded them now, shaking hair from their eyes, concern on their faces. Cleve just shook his head. "Nay, it's all right. She'll be fine. She's afraid for Chessa and dreamed a bad dream. Isn't that right, sweeting?"

But Kiri was shaking her head against Cleve's neck. He felt her tears on his skin, felt the cold of her flesh. He kissed her ear, the top of her head.

He walked back into his sleeping chamber and sat down on the bed, holding her on his lap. He pulled a woolen blanket around her. "Tell me what happened, Kiri."

She shuddered, then whispered, "Papa, Caldon is trying to save Chessa."

"*What?*"

He saw she was confused. She huddled against him, shivering violently. "It's all right, Kiri. It was a dream, just a bad dream."

Kiri shook her head and burrowed deeper against her father's chest. "No, Papa, I did dream, but it wasn't really a dream. There was Caldon and she heard Chessa calling to her. Chessa's in a boat on the loch with Kerek and some other men. What does it mean, Papa?"

He didn't know. By all the gods, was he to be surrounded by wizardry? By things he didn't understand but had to accept? He hugged his small daughter tightly. She said in that matter-of-fact way of hers, "I'm proud of Caldon for trying to save Chessa, but she doesn't always do what I ask her to. I wanted her to bring her children so I could play with them, but she didn't. I hope she saves Chessa, Papa."

He didn't know what to say. Was it all Kiri's imagination? Laren hadn't thought so, neither did Varrick. He found himself asking her to tell him more about Caldon. She did, but her answers were becoming more vague and her eyes soon closed again on sleep. He sat there, holding his now-sleeping daughter, her small head pressed close to his heart. He simply didn't know. He couldn't bring himself to believe this monster business, but what else could he believe? What else made even a whit of sense? One thing he did believe was that Chessa was indeed on the loch in the middle of the night. And that made his belly cramp with fear.

He knew none of the men would go out on the loch at the word of a child after darkness fell. Or at his word either, despite his conviction that she was indeed there and that there were only six men holding her. Their fear was too deep, and he supposed it was a healthy fear, for it kept them alive.

He didn't doubt the existence of the monster, of Caldon, as Varrick and Kiri called it. But that it could feel a human being's thoughts, that it could be beckoned by Varrick's *burra*—he didn't want to believe it, but he was holding proof of it on his lap. His small daughter somehow knew

what was happening. He now accepted what she'd
dreamed, or the vision that had come to her whilst she slept.
He said quietly, shaking her slightly until she was again
awake, "I'm sorry, sweeting, but this is important. I want
you to lie still, Kiri, and think of your second papa. Can
you see her? Is she still in that boat with the other men? Is
Caldon near?"

Kiri drew a deep breath and sank down into her father's
arms. "That's it," he said. "Breathe deeply, sweeting.
Close your eyes and think of Chessa. Do you see her?"

"Now I see Lord Varrick. He's staring at Pagan. He's
fitting his fingers into the holes those circles and squares
make, Papa. He's humming and his eyes are closed."

"What's Pagan?"

"The stick, Papa. It's what Lord Varrick—"

"He's your grandfather—"

"Aye, I know that, but he doesn't like it. He told me to
call him Lord Varrick. He told me he was young, younger
than you even, that years fell away from him, that he would
still be as he was when I was grown and had babes of my
own."

"Then he sees Chessa as well?"

"Aye, I think somehow he sent thoughts to Chessa and
to Caldon. I don't know, Papa."

"What do you—"

Kiri screamed and struggled from the woolen blanket.
"Caldon hit the boat. She butted it with her head! Everyone
is screaming, Papa!"

It was just a soft nudge, but the men nearly fainted from
fear in that first moment, then screamed in the next.
"Row!" Kerek yelled as loud as he could. "Damn you
cowards, the shore is nearly beneath our feet. Row!"

There was another nudge. Oh, no, Chessa thought, Caldon was pushing the longboat to shore, not away from it.
Well, if she forced them to shore, then there would be a
chance of escaping.

It was then that the men yelled with relief, all of them

leaping from the longboat into the shallow water, thrashing to the shore just feet beyond them. Kerek grabbed Chessa's arm and pulled her after him. He lifted her over his shoulder and climbed over the side of the boat. He yelled to the men to pull it ashore.

But they were too late. Once Kerek set Chessa's feet on the pebbly beach, Caldon rose from the water beside the longboat. The mist cleared, forming a frame for that long curving neck, the small head. The mouth opened and Caldon trumpeted loudly. The men dropped the ropes to the boat and froze into statues, staring, too frightened to scream, too frightened to move.

Chessa grinned as Caldon lowered her mighty head and shoved at the side of the boat, butting it away from the shoreline back out into the loch. Kerek yelled and strode into the water, screaming at the monster, who was now lost in the thick mist again, the longboat as well. There was silence and the smell of fear. Finally, Kerek said loudly, breaking through to the men, "The monster is gone and has taken our longboat. All of you come out of your damned fear now. Shake yourselves. Bring your brains back into your heads. It's over. We must stay here until it is morning. Halak, see to building a fire. The rest of you gather wood and branches. We will stay warm, at least, until the sun comes out tomorrow."

"I wonder if it will," Chessa said loudly, turned, and gave Kerek a big smile. "Did you forget, Kerek, that I am the daughter of the greatest wizard who ever lived?"

He stared down at her, fear making him pale, the thick mist leaching the rest of the color from his face. His hair was wet around his head. He was soaked, as were the rest of the men. She was completely dry, save where Kerek had pulled her over his shoulder to carry her ashore. He shivered. She didn't know if it was from cold or from fear. She never stopped smiling up at him. He hated the fear, she knew it, and it pleased her.

The men built a huge fire. By the time they lay down beside the banked embers, they were dry. Chessa was still wrapped in the woolen blanket. The mist was soft on her face, like damp fingers tracing over her flesh.

Kerek left to go into the woods to relieve himself. The moment he was out of hearing, she said to the men, "You saw my magic. You saw the monster. The only reason Caldon didn't kill all of you was because I was in the boat and she was afraid I would be harmed. When it is light, if I allow the sun to shine on the morrow, you must return me to my home. If you obey Kerek, then you will all perish."

"Don't listen to her." It was Kerek and there was deep anger in his voice. "She isn't a witch or a wizard or anything else. The monster lives in this loch, all of us knew that. It simply came to our boat and wanted it. Nothing more. Now, the sun will be bright and hot on the morrow, despite its being fall and the leaves are now golden and red and yellow. I swear it to you. Sleep now and don't listen to her."

Then he said, "You wonder why Queen Turella wants her. I will tell you. It is because of her strength, it is because of what she is that she will wed Ragnor and she will rule, not that fool. The Saxons won't overrun the Danelaw once she is there. You have seen witness of her strength. Think of that whilst you sleep."

Chessa said, "Kerek has said two very different things. Which will you believe? Look at me. Do any of you think I'll allow Ragnor to be my husband?" She shook her head and spit into the fire, causing the embers to hiss and spew. "I will by myself destroy the Danelaw. I will by myself give it over to the Saxons. You don't want me for the king's wife."

"Better the fool dies," one of the men said.

"Aye," another said. "Kill him."

Chessa sighed. There were so many currents here and she didn't know which way to swim. She'd decided upon wizardry and threats to kill Ragnor but it hadn't worked. These men wanted him dead. She looked at Kerek, who was smiling very slightly at her.

"The princess is of great value," he said. "Now, go to sleep, all of you. The sun will be upon us soon."

She slept. She didn't want to, but she did, deeply, with no dreams. She awoke when Kerek shook her arm.

"Look at the bright sun, Princess," he said, thick pleasure in his voice, or was it stark relief? She didn't know. "Aye," he said, "bright sun, just as I promised."

It was so strong, even after the passing of the dawn hour, that it hurt to look directly into it. The loch glistened beneath it, pure and dark. The longboat was nowhere in sight. She smiled. "Now Cleve will find us, Kerek. We have no boat. Did you plan to walk to York? Perhaps fly?"

"Look, Princess."

She followed his finger. They were at the narrow channel. Just beyond that channel was the trading town of Inverness. She wanted to weep with disappointment.

"Come, Chessa, resign yourself. Your life will be pleasant. You will have all the luxury you could desire. If you want a lover, I will provide one for you after you've birthed the heir to the Danelaw. Don't worry about Cleve's babe. He will be safe. And you can have lovers. Turella has lovers, you know."

The men were cheering, pointing wildly, quickly pulling their clothing straight, throwing sand on the dying embers of the fire.

"You have no longboat," she said even as he pulled her to her feet. "Will you steal one to get back to York?"

"I have something better," Kerek said, and dusted her off. He took her blanket and carefully folded it. He whistled as he took her arm and pulled her to the fore of the men. "Keep a sharp eye out for outlaws," he said, and covered the rock-strewn ground with long strides.

Chessa cursed.

They reached Inverness by early afternoon. The weather held mild, the breeze soft and warm against their faces. Kerek bought her a new tunic of saffron and an overtunic of softer yellow, two beautiful brooches from Orkney to fasten the overtunic around her shoulders. He bought a reindeer comb and told the old woman at the bathing hut not only to bathe her but to arrange her hair as well.

"Why?" Chessa said, but Kerek only shook his head. He stayed on guard outside the bathing hut whilst the other men spent their silver coins on what they needed.

It was nearing sunset when Kerek led Chessa and his men out of the trading town, through the palisade gates, down to the dock. "Come, Princess."

He led her onto a warship whose stem was carved in the shape of a black raven. It was a big ship, and there were at least fifty men on board, standing there, watching them come. One of the men shouted, "It is Kerek! He's brought her! By the gods, he managed to do it."

Kerek pulled her up the rough boards that were securely roped together. He gave her a shove and she walked up those boards to the warship. She stepped down and onto the center plank that ran the full length of the ship. There was a covered cargo space at the bow, but it looked larger than any Chessa had seen before, the wadmal cover brightly painted with white and red stripes, just as was the huge rolled sail of the warship.

"You're a wizard," Kerek whispered in her ear. "Tell me what you expect."

She just shook her head. He pushed her gently through the opening into the covered space. There, seated in a beautifully carved chair was Ragnor, holding a pale blue glass in his hand, Turella, standing just behind him, her hand resting lightly on his shoulder.

"Welcome, Chessa," Ragnor said, and he raised his glass, saluted her, and drank deep. He belched even as he grinned at her. "You're here. I doubted Kerek could do it, for he's an old man and my mother surely has too much trust in him, but he managed to get you. You're not very smart, are you, Chessa?"

"You've done well, Kerek," Turella said. "We expected you sooner. I was worried."

"The Princess has many tricks, my lady. She called forth

the monster of Loch Ness and we were forced to shore. We had to walk to Inverness.''

"The monster?" Ragnor said, leaning forward, paling.

"Aye, the monster. It exists."

"I doubt that not," Turella said, "but you beat the monster, Kerek. As for the princess, she looks none the worse for her adventure.''

"I had her bathed and newly garbed," Kerek said. "She is beautiful, sire, is she not?" He would tell Turella all that had happened later, after Chessa and Ragnor were married, when they could finally be alone. He wondered if she would believe it, or just smile at him in that mysterious way of hers.

"Aye, she's well enough, but she's still not Utta," Ragnor said, his first words to her. "This mead is foul." He threw the empty glass from him and it crashed onto a bare plank and shattered.

Turella sucked in her breath. "That belonged to my mother," she said. "I brought it from the Bulgar."

"She was an old crone," Ragnor said. "I remember she hit me when I was a small boy. She only came to York that one time, and she hit me. I will break all of them since I know now where they come from."

Turella said gently, "Chessa will be your wife, Ragnor. You will wed with her this evening. Kerek has agreed to travel to Hawkfell Island and memorize the way this Utta prepares mead. Then you will have a queen who will breed your heirs, and the mead that suits you so well.''

"I still don't have Isla," Ragnor said.

"No, and you never will," his mother said. She tightened her hand on his shoulder and he winced. "Now, my son, tell the princess that she's lovely and that you desire above all things to have her for your wife.''

Ragnor looked at Chessa, a sullen look, but then suddenly that looked changed. He stared at her breasts. There was lust in his eyes. Her breasts were fuller now, from the baby, and she saw that he wanted her.

She said loudly, her voice clear and carrying far, "I can't

marry you, Ragnor, no matter how much I would wish to since you're such a splendid man, since you would give me jewels and splendid clothes, and the gods know that's what I've always wanted in life, but listen, Ragnor, I'm pregnant with Cleve's child.''

Why had she said it? she wondered, watching Ragnor laugh until he was holding his sides. It was unfortunate that lies always seemed to come back to torment.

Turella said to Kerek, ''Will anyone be looking for her?''

''Aye, Cleve will search everywhere for her, but he won't even consider that we came for her. It would be a mad thought. If he thinks about it, he will dismiss it. Eventually he will have to believe she's dead, perhaps fallen into that miserable loch and drowned.''

''She is married to Cleve?'' Turella said.

''So, the bastard's still not dead,'' Ragnor said, and shouted to one of the men, ''Bring me more mead! Pour it into one of the blue glass goblets.''

''Aye,'' Chessa said. ''I'm married to Cleve. He's very much alive and he's returned to his home on Loch Ness. But he'll come after me. He'll search for me, not find me, and then he'll sit down and think. He'll realize you kidnapped me again and he'll come to York and kill all of you. He should have killed Ragnor before but he held his own anger in check because he believed the Danelaw should remain in Viking hands as long as possible. Aye, he'll come for me and all of you will regret it. If you don't believe that, you're all fools, you most of all, Turella. You met Cleve. You know the kind of man he is.''

Ragnor looked at his fingernails and frowned at the hangnail on his thumb. ''I wanted to kill him, but Kerek, you stopped me, then told my mother to stop me.'' He sent his mother a drunken frown. ''How do you know Cleve? Surely he didn't come to you, did he?''

''Nay, son, the princess is mistaken. Don't think of it further.''

''I tried to kill him before, but the damned assassin failed. I would have slit his throat had not Cleve killed him first. Who would have believed a damned diplomat could be skilled as a warrior?''

Chessa stared at him. She said very quietly, ''What do you mean, 'you tried,' Ragnor?''

''Your beautiful bitch of a stepmother. Aye, Sira. Both she and I wanted him dead. He came to negotiate a marriage between you and William of Normandy. She didn't want it. She wanted her son to marry into the French royal family. By then I decided that I would take you. But Cleve killed the assassin and there was no other chance.''

Chessa felt rage strangle her. She opened her mouth, but there were no words. She was on Ragnor in an instant, her fingers closing around his throat, squeezing, screaming at him, ''I saw it all, you damned coward! I myself threw a knife into the assassin's back, but Cleve's knife went into his throat and you're right, he killed him. It was you? It was that wretched stepmother of mine? The two of you plotted his death? Oh, aye, I believe it. I saw her too, hiding in the shadows. I didn't recognize who it was. Damn you, Ragnor, I'll kill you now!''

She would have killed him if Kerek hadn't pulled her off. Even he needed help. She was held against his chest, panting, rage unbanked in her eyes, wanting only to kill him. ''I wouldn't marry you no matter what you threatened. If you force me to somehow, I'll kill you, Ragnor, and unlike the assassin you and Sira hired, I won't fail.''

''Stop it,'' Turella said very calmly. ''Quiet, child. Come now, I didn't know about this. You must be calm. You must think of the child.''

''Child?'' Ragnor said, staring at her breasts again. ''That's just a simple jest, Mother. Chessa has been pregnant many times and it's never true. No one ever believes her. Now she tried to kill me. If I weren't a man who was gentle with weak and fragile women, I wouldn't have let her touch me, but I didn't want to hurt her. You understand, don't you, Mother?''

''Aye,'' Turella said. ''I understand, my son. Chessa,

come with me and we will speak together. Just you and I, two reasonable women.''

But Chessa just smiled at her and shook her head. ''Nay, my lady. I won't speak with you. I won't do anything.''

''You've changed,'' Turella said, frowning at her. ''Ah, Ragnor, here's your mead. Why don't you take it and go speak to Captain Torric. We will leave in the morning at first light. You and Chessa will wed tonight.''

Ragnor, Kerek holding his arm, managed to stagger from the enclosed space. He drank down the mead in another blue glass goblet, looked back at his mother, and threw the goblet over the side of the warship. He giggled.

''He is paltry,'' Turella said. ''I don't know how I could have birthed him. But Olric, you know, my child, he was weak, and stupid, wanting only to wench and to drink.''

''You have already told me that. I'm sorry, my lady, but I won't help you. You're right, I've changed. I'm a wife and I love my husband. We live at a new farmstead on Loch Ness, near his father's. That is where I will spend my life, where I will live with my husband and raise our children, not in York.''

''You are pregnant, truly, this time, you are pregnant. When Kerek nodded to me I understood. I also see, just as he does, just as you do, that you will protect this babe in your womb. You will wed Ragnor to save the babe. No one will ever know that Ragnor isn't your true husband. Even if you bleat it about, why then, can you really believe that anyone would care? There's really nothing more I have to say to you. You're not stupid, Chessa. You know when to retreat.''

29

"By all the gods, I don't believe this," Cleve said, wanting to yell with relief. "Are you certain?"

"Aye," Varrick said. "They're still here in Inverness and Chessa is still their prisoner."

The old woman at the bathing hut had told them about the little sweeting whose hair she'd plaited with lovely yellow ribbons. "Looked like a princess, she did," the old woman had said.

If only she knew, Cleve had thought, giving her a piece of silver.

Igmal slipped around the side of a jeweler's stall to join them. "Ragnor and Chessa are to wed tonight. A mock ceremony, but none will question it. I overheard one of the queen's men telling another whilst they traded here in Inverness. They plan to sail back to York at first light in the morning."

"There are sixty men," Igmal said, "more or less. Queen Turella is with them."

"Even if she weds him, it means nothing," Varrick said. He said to Cleve, "I see from your face that your plan won't work now. It is time for Pagan." He drew the *burra* slowly from its sheath. He held it up in front of him, fitting his fingers into the circles and squares. Cleve didn't want to watch, but he did, and it did seem that his fingers were sinking down into those markings, as they would into soft wax, though he knew that wasn't possible. Varrick said quietly, "I see Chessa. She's seated beside Turella beneath the cargo covering. By the gods, either Turella or that idiot son of hers has brought the king's chair. Has the woman no sense? Chessa is all right. She's thinking, trying to decide what to do. I can feel purpose flowing through her, and anger and determination to return to you—and to me, naturally. Ah, yes, she knows we're here. I can feel the quickening in her. She knows and now she'll look for a way to aid us to get to her." Varrick fell silent, his eyes closed now, but he was still seeing on board that warship through the magic of the *burra*.

Cleve stared at him with the fascination of a man cornered by a snake. This snake with his magic stick was his father.

It was Varrick, Chessa thought, and he was calling to her, but now she realized that it wasn't really Varrick, it was Varrick using the *burra*, calling through that ancient magic. She felt calm flow through her. She'd been thinking and thinking, trying to figure out how to escape and had decided that her best chance would be once she was alone with Ragnor after the wedding. She thought of him touching her and grinned. She'd break his fingers if he tried.

What to do? She knew they'd have to wait until it was dark. She rose, stretched, and walked from the covered cargo space. She said idly to Captain Torric, "Will there be a moon tonight, do you know?"

"A half-moon," Torric said and no more. He was uncomfortable. He hadn't wanted this, not after Rorik, Merrik, and Cleve had saved him and Kerek, even that ass, Ragnor. He looked up at Chessa, thought her beautiful with her hair in soft plaits, the saffron ribbons matching her tunic and falling around her face. "I'm sorry about this, Princess. So is Kerek, it's just that he—"

"Why do you call me that when you know it isn't true, Torric?"

"Habit," he said, and spat over the side into the dark water of Inverness harbor.

"If I jumped into the harbor would you jump after me, Torric?"

"Nay, Princess. My leg didn't heal straight. I'd rather let you swim away than drown."

"Good," she said, and ran toward the side of the warship. She didn't get far. Kerek's hand closed over her upper arm. "You would ruin your beautiful gown, Chessa," he said. "Come now, you must wed with Ragnor."

She stared down at his blunt fingers holding her. She knew then, knew exactly what she would do. Cleve was near. Aye, she knew what she would do. She smiled up at him. "I have no choice, just as you said, Kerek. Let's get it done."

"Why are you smiling?"

She shrugged. "Why not? If this is to be my fate, then so be it. Are you not pleased that I will obey? Don't you want me to marry Ragnor now?"

Kerek frowned after her. She was walking briskly, as if she were looking forward to wedding Ragnor. Only a slug would look forward to wedding Ragnor. He felt something different about her. He felt a shock of fear. It angered him. He went after her and grabbed her arm again and pulled her back. He would have to watch her carefully.

The ceremony took very little time. Chessa stood beside Ragnor, who was already nearly stumbling with drink, but he said in a loud, clear voice, "I take you, Princess Chessa of Ireland, as my queen. You will bear my children and the future heirs of the Danelaw. You will be submissive and obey me. If you please me, you will have a long and pleasing life. I, King Ragnor of York, vow this to you."

She didn't strike him, but it was close. Instead, she smiled up at him and placed her hand on his forearm. "I, Chessa of Ireland, will come to York with you, Ragnor, and be the queen of the Danelaw. Being what you are, life will not continue as it has. All know this. If anyone doesn't know this by now then he will learn it soon enough."

She stopped, nodded to Turella and then to Kerek. "There is nothing else to say," she said. "Nothing at all."

Ragnor called out, "She's now the queen, Mother. You can leave and take the rest of those blue glass goblets with you. Chessa, bring me more mead and then we will retire and I will take you as I should have that first time, only Kerek stopped me. I still haven't punished him sufficiently for that. Now you're not even a virgin. Aye, I'll punish him for that as well."

"Certainly, my husband," Chessa said, her voice sweeter than the mead that she handed to Ragnor. "To be taken by you is something I've scarce ever even imagined. Here is your mead. Drink deeply, husband. I will think of a punishment for Kerek. He shouldn't have abused you so."

"Mayhap you shouldn't drink more," Kerek said. He knew that Ragnor would fall into a stupor very soon now and that was when Chessa planned to try her escape. Was he to watch them throughout the night? He cursed to himself. Ragnor turned on him. "I am the king of the Danelaw and you are naught, Kerek. After we return to York, I will take men to Hawkfell Island and we will destroy that miserable pile of stone and bring back Utta. Come, Chessa, it's time I was your husband, at long last."

"Certainly, my husband," she said again, tucked her hand through his arm and helped direct him toward the enclosed cargo space.

Turella stood beside him, staring after them. "She will try to outsmart me, Kerek, but she won't succeed. Don't worry so. If Ragnor is too sodden with drink to take her tonight, why then, he'll do it when he's sober, tomorrow. Besides, once he's taken her, then we will just keep him drunk. It will make things easier."

Kerek turned to Turella. "I don't like this, you know that. I never did."

"You are too soft," she said. "Come now, there is nothing she can do. The men are everywhere and there are at least a half dozen on watch all through the night."

* * *

Cleve motioned the men to hunker down within the deep shadows of the fortress walls. "Stay back, all of you. I don't want to take the chance that any of their warriors will see us. We don't need to see the warship. Varrick will tell us what we need to know."

"I see eight men, holding these watches," Varrick said. He drew the men's positions in the sand, all their men hunkered down in a circle to look. "Ragnor is in a drunken stupor in the enclosed cargo space. It's here. Chessa is sitting next to him, waiting."

"Waiting?" Igmal said.

"For us," Cleve said. "For me. Then she plans to act. That frightens me. I think Turella would rather kill her than let her go."

"Nay," Varrick said.

Cleve frowned at the certainty in his father's voice, but said instead, "Each of you pick your man. We must kill them quickly and with no noise. Allow none of them to fall into the water. I will get Chessa. We must be fast and silent for this to succeed. Does anyone have any questions?"

But the warship wasn't tied securely to the long wooden dock as Varrick had told them it was. It lay at least fifty yards out, moored to the dock by stout ropes, held in place with an iron anchor. There were three more men pacing forward and back in front of the boarding plank. They looked alert. They were well armed. There was no chance Cleve and his men could swim to the warship without being seen, no chance at all. Besides, four of the men couldn't swim.

Cleve cursed.

Varrick looked puzzled. "This isn't right," he said. "When did they move the warship away from its moorings? Damnation, I saw the warship moored to the dock."

Igmal just shrugged.

Igmal said, "What will we do? Your plan can't work now, Cleve."

Cleve looked toward his father and said, "Can you do it?"

Varrick merely smiled. He withdrew the *burra*. He walked away from the men to higher ground at the far end of the fortress wall that protected Inverness. Cleve didn't know if his father left them because he wanted himself to appear more the sorcerer or because he needed it. He stood on the high ground, closed his hands over the *burra* and raised it high in the air in front of him. He began to chant the strange words he'd learned so many years before. Soon a slash of lightning knifed through the still night, striking the wooden dock, not many feet from where one of the warship guards was pacing, sending smoke gushing into the night air. The man froze, then yelled.

Another streak of lightning came, then two more together, then one more, this one searing away the end of the wooden dock. Thunder boomed right overhead, so loud Cleve's men held their hands over their ears.

The warriors on board the warship were running about, looking at the heavens, looking toward the men on the dock that was falling away beneath their feet.

Captain Torric yelled, "The ropes will break. Row to the dock and save the men. Quickly now, quickly!"

Rain poured down upon them. It had been silent and dry one moment, then the rain flooded over them. "Hurry," Torric yelled. "Hurry!"

The men were rowing frantically, others with wooden pails were filling them from the bottom of the warship and tossing the water over the side, but the rain only came down harder and harder still in the following minutes.

"Aye," Igmal said to Cleve, "see how they come to us. They're like dead chickens that don't yet know they're dead. Soon now, very soon, and we will have Chessa back."

But Cleve wasn't so certain of that. He had seven men. There were nearly sixty men aboard the warship. What chance did they have even amid all this confusion?

Lightning struck the huge mast of the warship, tearing it

in half. Men screamed in pain and fear as it fell on twelve of them, pinning them beneath it. It was then Cleve saw Chessa. She was standing in the entryway of the cargo space, staring toward shore, staring toward Varrick, whom all could see now, if they looked, his black cloak billowing out behind him, standing tall on that higher ground, which seemed even higher now than it had before, the *burra* held in front of him, his head flung back, his throat working. Cleve knew he was speaking, but the words were low, nearly a whisper, and blown away by the wind that was now whipping the warship closer and closer to the dock. It would crash into it. The warriors on board were praying to Odin, to Thor, to Freya. They were terrified. Both Kerek and Torric yelled at them to row back out to sea, but the wind was shoving them harder and harder toward the dock and the shore.

Chessa stood there, smiling.

Turella ran to her, the wind so strong she could barely remain upright.

"You're doing this," she screamed at Chessa. "I can see it in your witch's eyes. You're doing this. Stop it, damn you, stop it before we're all dead."

"Aye, I am doing it. I won't die. When the warship strikes the dock, the men will flee in terror. Then, Turella, I will leave you, and I hope never to see you again. If I do, I will destroy you. You think this storm is strong? I haven't stretched my powers yet. This is only the beginning."

Suddenly, the warship struck the dock. The sound of rending wood sounded through the night, so powerful the crash that it was heard even over the wind. Men screamed and leapt from the warship, jumping onto the remains of the dock and running as fast as they could toward shore and safety.

"Cowards!" Turella screamed after them, but her voice was smothered in the wind, her mouth filled with the thick rain that poured down over them.

"Stop it, Chessa."

"Nay, Kerek. You'd best save your queen. As for Ragnor, I believe he is still unconscious from all the mead he drank. I'm leaving now. I wanted to call you friend but you wouldn't allow it. I don't wish you well, Kerek. Goodbye."

He grabbed her arm. "I won't let you go."

It was then Cleve said, "Release her, Kerek. She's right. It's over now."

Chessa said quickly, "He knows I brought the devastation, he just doesn't want to accept it. I will bring more if you don't release me, Kerek, that or Cleve will kill you."

Kerek dropped her arm.

"Save your pathetic king," Chessa called back to him even as Cleve lifted her into his arms and lightly tossed her to Igmal, who stood on the dock.

But Kerek shook his head and ran toward Turella. He grabbed her and pulled her over his shoulder. "We will survive this," he said, and jumped to the dock. He slipped on broken planks and dropped her. Both of them went down, knocking the breath from each.

Then, as suddenly as the terrifying storm had begun, it stopped. The air was quiet. The blackness no longer weighed so heavily. There was no more rain. A single bolt of lightning slashed through the black sky, but it was nothing, really, just an afterthought of the storm the demons unleashed during those endless minutes.

Turella sat up. She shook her head. "She could have killed us," she said to Kerek.

He was staring after Cleve, who had reached the dock and now carried his wife in his arms. The rest of Turella's men, those who hadn't run for shelter into Inverness, stood on the shreds of the dock, just stood there, panting, not understanding what had happened, thankful they were still alive.

"The princess did this," Torric said. "I don't want her in York. She will kill all of us next time."

"Aye," the men said.

"She's a witch."

"The night was darker than an old man's teeth. Now the moon is bright overhead."

"We must leave."

Kerek listened to the men, knew it was lost, and stood. He held out his hand and pulled Turella, sodden, her hair plastered to her head, to her feet.

"You are all right, my lady?"

She nodded. Then she froze still as a rune stone. Kerek stared at her. He didn't think she was breathing, just staring beyond him. Slowly, he turned to see a tall man dressed all in black striding toward them. The moon seemed suddenly brighter overhead, indeed, it seemed to shine more brightly over the man who was coming ever closer to them. He carried no huge sword, his white hands were empty. The wind came again, but it wasn't a raging wind, just enough so that the man's black cloak billowed out behind him.

He didn't look of this earth.

Turella's warriors, one by one, became aware of the man coming toward them. They stared. They prayed and huddled together. One man drew his sword. As if he'd seen that sword drawn, the tall man paused a moment, then turned to look directly at the warrior. The warrior fell back a step, lowering his sword until its tip was buried into the wooden dock at his feet.

Turella said very softly, "Varrick? Is it really you? After all these years?"

"Aye, Turella, it is I. You dared to take what belongs to me. Should I kill you, I wonder, or acknowledge your ignorance this one time, and let you live?"

"Who is this man?" Kerek said, aware that his voice wasn't steady, and hating himself for it. Surely this was just a man, nothing more than a single man, and he wasn't even armed. He could walk to him and strangle him. He could kill him, but he didn't move. "You know this man, my lady?" Kerek said, seeing the pallor of her face. She looked suddenly like an old woman, bent and frail, not the proud queen he'd loved for so many years.

Turella said, "He is Varrick. He is my brother." It was

then she seemed to remember she was a queen, not some sort of frightened old woman. She drew herself up. "You still wear black, I see, Varrick. Do you still streak blue and red paint on your face and dance around fires, chanting an ignorant babble of ancient rituals? Do you still seek out those things mortals shouldn't know about? Do you still terrify people with your tricks?"

"Did you like the storm, Turella? Did you feel terror? Your men did."

"Nay, Chessa brought the storm."

"Do you really believe so, sister?"

She didn't believe it, and Kerek saw she didn't. She swallowed, afraid, and Kerek knew she was afraid, and so did this Varrick, this sorcerer all garbed in black, standing so tall and stark white beneath the half-moon that shone so brightly down upon him.

She was staring at him again, studying his face. She said suddenly, "By all the gods, I should have known. His eyes, they're your eyes—one gold, one blue. I saw Cleve once in York and I remarked his strange eyes. And again tonight, just for a moment. He is your son, Varrick?"

"Aye, he is my son."

"Chessa is his wife," she said, her voice absent. "Their child will be formidable."

"It is possible," he said. "That is none of your concern, Turella. Listen to me. Your warship isn't destroyed. Gather your men, awaken your sodden son, or give him to me and I'll kill him. Leave my land. Never return here, Turella, else I'll make you regret it even into eternity."

"Aye," she said slowly, "we will leave. I know there is nothing here for me now. The Danelaw is lost. Chessa wasn't for me, Varrick, I wanted her for the Danelaw, to lead when the time came, to control Ragnor."

Varrick stood quiet, staring out over the dark sea. There was no wind, yet his black cloak billowed out behind him. He said finally, "I have a stepdaughter. Her name is Cayman. She is the most beautiful woman I have ever seen. There is no man for her here and she will grow old alone, without children, without purpose. If you request it, Turella, I will ask her if she wishes to join you. She is very smart. After all, she's lived with me since she was a child. She would listen to you, Turella, she would deal well with this wretched son of yours. She would replace Chessa.''

"She is truly beautiful?''

He nodded. ''She is the most beautiful woman I have ever seen. I don't lie.''

"Can she make mead?'' Kerek said.

Varrick's brow went upward. ''Mead? Aye, her mead is excellent. If she decides to go with you, she will have to tell her sister how to prepare it, else all of us will be greatly saddened.''

Kerek rubbed his hands together. ''If this is true,'' he said to Turella, ''then Utta of Hawkfell Island is safe, Ragnor will remain sodden, and you and this Cayman will rule.''

Turella stared at her brother, with his billowing cloak in the still air. ''I will take her.''

Varrick merely nodded. ''Remain here for two days. If she decides to come to you, I will bring her. I wish you farewell, sister. Treat my stepdaughter well. If you do not, you will answer to me.'' He nodded to her once again, turned on his heel, and began to walk quickly down the wooden dock. Kerek saw him take a stick from his belt and raise it over his head. He saw a wind begin to rise, but it was only around Varrick. It spun around him, making the cloak flap up and down, making the loose sleeves of Varrick's black tunic billow out. A mist came up suddenly, but it seemed to be only directly in front of Varrick, and he walked toward that mist, into it, and then, suddenly, the mist began to fade, holes appearing in it, the holes spreading, like a fire spreading over cloth. In moments the mist was gone and the night clear again.

Varrick was gone as well.

To Kerek's astonishment, Turella laughed. ''He did that when he was naught but a small boy,'' she said. ''The wizards in Bulgar taught him that.'' And she laughed and laughed.

"But he vanished, my lady,'' Kerek said, so frightened he thought he'd choke with it.

"Aye,'' she said. "He vanished. When I came here to wed the king of the Danelaw, he came with me. He'd learned all the wizards could teach him in the Bulgar. He'd heard of the West, of the Druids and their ancient magic. He wanted to visit the land called Scotland and learn the Picts' ways. I see he stayed. I still can't believe it, Kerek. Cleve is his son. Those eyes—I am a fool. I should have realized the moment I saw him in York that he was Varrick's son.''

"Nay,'' Kerek said, and drew her against him. "Ah, you're wet and you're tired. This night has been something I don't wish to repeat, ever. Whilst we wait for Cayman, we must gather up our men again and soothe their terrors. We must see to repairs on the warship.''

"She makes excellent mead,'' Turella said, and giggled against Kerek's shoulder.

She'd giggled? Kerek had never heard a more wonderful sound in his life.

Captain Torric limped to them, stared at them a moment, then cleared his throat. He said matter-of-factly, "Ragnor slept through the storm, all the lightning, the thunder. He slept through the warship's crash against the dock. He's awake now and calling for mead.''

30

CHESSA SAT ON Cleve's lap in the longboat. All the men were huddled around them waiting for Varrick. She saw him first, tall and slim, his head thrown back, that damned cloak of his billowing out and yet there was no wind, not even a small breeze, and she knew that he'd saved her, just as she knew that she must act and she must act now, else they would never have peace. Varrick would always be there, waiting for her. It had to stop.

When he was nearly on them, she turned on Cleve's lap and burst into tears. She cried and sobbed and shivered violently, huddling against him, burrowing against him, as if she wanted to crawl inside him to protect herself.

Cleve, completely taken by surprise, nonetheless gathered her against him, kissed her hair and rocked her, whispering meaningless words to soothe her, but they didn't seem to. She cried harder and harder.

Varrick stared at her. He said, "What is wrong? Has something happened to her? Is she in pain?"

Chessa whispered through her sobs, "I'm so afraid. I thought I would have to go to York. I believed I would have to be his wife. You saved me. All of you saved me."

"Chessa," Cleve began, "it's all right, sweeting. I'll protect you always. No, love, don't cry more, you'll make yourself ill."

As he spoke he looked up. Varrick was staring at her as if he'd never seen her before. His expression was cold. He looked more dangerous than his son in that moment. "What she said is nonsense. What is wrong with her?"

Igmal shrugged and said, "She's a woman, lord Varrick. She was frightened. The storm you called up terrified her."

Varrick continued to frown down at her, a wealth of distaste on his face, but he said nothing more.

The mist lifted and the air was cold and clear. The waters of the loch were smooth and dark. Chessa looked up to see Varrick coming, a good dozen men trailing behind him. His cloak billowed behind him. She was used to that now. She wondered idly how Argana managed to make the wool so very lightweight.

They hadn't seen Varrick in seven days. Argana had come to tell them that Varrick had taken Cayman to Turella in Inverness to return with her to York. "She sang and she smiled," Argana had said. "She will enjoy herself and she will enjoy this fool, Ragnor, you've told me so much about, Chessa. There are depths to Cayman, aye, and she will suit herself."

After his return Varrick still hadn't come to Karelia. Chessa knew that he would come. She wondered how he would look at her now.

But here he was, on the seventh day. Chessa welcomed Varrick, Argana, Athol, who looked as sullen as a goat deprived of a tough boot, and Igmal, who waved to Kiri, and when the child shrieked his name and ran to him, he threw her into the air and brought her tight against his chest. The other men flowed into the crowd of Karelia people, conversation lively, laughter free, the four Karelia dogs barking in a frenzy, jumping and leaping about all the people.

Varrick stood off to one side, staring at the people. He wasn't frowning, nor was he smiling. He heard Kiri say to Igmal, "I just sniffed you and you smell clean. Did you bathe like I told you to, Igmal?"

"Aye, little one, I bathed not three days ago."

"Your bearskin isn't too bad either," Kiri said, and smelled it again.

"Nay, I kept it on and bathed it with me."

Kiri laughed and laughed. "I will ask my papas if I can do that as well."

It was nearing the winter solstice and yet there was no snow yet, no frigid nights to make everyone's teeth chatter. Chessa gently patted her swelling belly. It seemed that more and more often the people from Kinloch were here at their farmstead, and why not? she wondered. There was laughter here and fights. There was no magic here, nothing to frighten anyone. There were no billowing gowns or cloaks when there was no wind.

Chessa smiled toward Varrick, squeezing Cleve's hand. What would he do? Had he finally given over? Was he finally ready to leave her alone?

"Welcome, Father," Cleve said. "Chessa believed you would come. The women are preparing a feast. If you would like to send one of your men back to Kinloch to fetch the others, you should do it soon."

Varrick gave his son a superior smile. "There is no need for that." He pulled the *burra* from its sheath at his belt. "I will call them with this." He lovingly stroked the *burra* and stood back. Then he looked at Chessa, his eyes on her belly, and there was uncertainty in his eyes, and determination as well. She sighed to herself. Her bout of hysteria after her rescue had done no good. She crossed her hands over her chest and yawned. Varrick still stared at her, and now there was anger in those strange eyes of his. She'd wondered several times when she'd angered Cleve if his golden eye grew more enraged than his blue one. When she'd told him that, both of them forgot their argument in their laughter.

Varrick walked to the edge of Falcon Ridge, the only high strip of land at Karelia. He performed nicely, bringing thunder and cold white streaks of lightning. He didn't bring rain, for which all the people were profoundly grateful.

When he finished, he turned. He froze. No one was even looking at him. Igmal was showing Kiri how to toss the knife he'd carved for her. Other children were looking on, begging him to teach them as well. Three of his men—*his* men—were drinking and poking each other. Several other of his men were speaking to Karelia men, formerly his men, none of them even looking toward him. His two younger sons were throwing stones into the loch, seeing who could throw the farthest. Argana, silent, obedient Argana, was speaking to Chessa and several other women. They began to laugh at something Argana said. Argana saying something funny?

None were looking at him except for one dog, who sat on his haunches, his head to one side, staring up at Varrick.

Varrick strode to Chessa. "Come with me."

She smiled up at him. "Did you call the rest of the Kinloch people?"

"Aye, I called them," he said, and she heard the child's temper in his voice.

"Good," she said. "That stick is a handy tool to have about. I'll tell the women to prepare more boar steaks. Also, Cleve and his men brought in more than a dozen pheasants this morning. We'll have a fine feast."

"It's called a *burra*. I told you to come with me."

She never let her smile slip. "I forgot. You wish to speak to me now? I'm so busy, but, ah, very well, Varrick."

She walked beside him into the farmstead. Unlike Kinloch, there was no raised dais here, just a long room filled with the smell of roasting pheasant, baking bread and the soft smell of rising smoke, a narrow blue line streaking upward. Varrick strode to the table and climbed up upon it.

"Be careful, Father," Cleve said. "The table doesn't always hold itself straight."

"Aye," Igmal said, grinning. "Cleve didn't cut all the legs evenly."

Cleve poked him.

"Be quiet," Varrick said. "Come here," he said to Chessa.

"I hope you don't want me to climb up on that table," she said, and rubbed her stomach.

He frowned at her, and she would have sworn he growled.

He climbed down. He withdrew the *burra* from its sheath and handed it to her. "Take it. Take it and tell me what you feel, what you see."

Slowly, she reached out her hand and took the *burra* from him. She cried out and brought her other hand up to help her hold it. "It's so heavy," she said, and quickly lowered it to the table. She still held it between her hands, but let its weight rest on the tabletop.

Varrick didn't move.

"It's hot, isn't it?"

She shook her head. "Nay, it's just very heavy, so heavy that I know I can't hold it.

"It's cold now, isn't it?"

"Cold? It isn't cold at all. It just feels like wood, very heavy wood that's got something else inside it to make it so weighty."

"What do you see?"

She looked down at the *burra.* "Circles and strange squares. The paint looks faded as if it will flake off very soon now. It looks old and strange. It's very heavy, Varrick. Won't you take it back? I don't like it."

He looked baffled, then angry. "Damn you, I asked you what you saw, not what the *burra* looked like."

"Saw? I saw nothing, save the table and I'm worried that it won't hold all the food we're preparing."

He grabbed the *burra* from her and shoved it back into its sheath. "It's the babe," he said. "Aye, it's the babe. It's stolen your powers."

"What powers?" she said. "You have the powers, Varrick, not I."

He sighed deeply and called out, "Argana, bring me a goblet of mead."

There were still the remnants of laughter in her voice when Argana called out, "I can't, Varrick. My hand is filled with cabbage."

He turned slowly to see his wife of eighteen years cutting huge chunks of cabbage and laying them onto a large wooden platter. "Athol," she called out. "Take your father a goblet of mead."

"I'm a man, Mother, not a slave."

"I'm a woman, Son, not a slave. That has nothing to do with anything. I'm busy, as are your brothers, if you'd bother to notice. You are doing nothing at all. Your father deserves obedience from all of us. Do as I tell you or you won't have dinner with us."

To Chessa's utter delight, Athol poured a goblet of mead and gave it to his father. He didn't do it with pleasure, but he did it.

This, Chessa thought, holding perfectly still, not about to draw more attention to herself, was surely the beginning of the end for Varrick's reign of terror and silence.

The feast went very well. There was plentiful food, more laughter than Chessa had heard since leaving Hawkfell Island. Chessa remembered the tale and riddle Laren had spun about Egypt for them all and that weasel Ragnor had answered. She told all the people the story, put the riddle to them, and it was Athol who answered it. No one could believe he'd answered it correctly and they hadn't been able to. Perhaps, she thought, there was a bond between Athol and Ragnor. She decided she would have Varrick send Athol to York. He could befriend Ragnor.

Late that night when everyone slept, many of the Kinloch people wrapped in woolen blankets and packed next to each other, close to the fire pit, Cleve brought his wife close and said, "Tell me, Chessa, what did you see?"

She said very quietly, "Ah," she said, "It was wonderful, Cleve. I saw our child. He hasn't your beautiful eyes, but rather mine, all green and yet deeper than mine, all filled with secrets and joy and mysteries and adventures.

He has your golden hair, thick and pure.''

"What is his name?''

She grinned against his throat. "I didn't have time to ask him.''

Author's Note

BACK IN ROMAN times, Scotland was called Caledonia. By the middle of the ninth century, it had become Scotland. Loch Ness was also called Loch Ness by Viking times. However, I couldn't very well call the Loch Ness monster Nessie. I decided to call her Caldon.

Loch Ness is twenty-four miles long, on average a mile wide. It has never been known to freeze. It's fed by eight rivers and countless streams, the course of all these waterways having changed dramatically over the centuries and millennia. The loch's only outlet now is by the river Ness into the Moray Firth.

It's true that Saint Columba was the first person to record sighting of the Loch Ness monster way back in the sixth century. From that time onward, there have been countless sightings, reports, descriptions, most of them surprisingly alike. The number of reported sightings took a huge leap upward during the 1930s when the thick trees were cleared around Loch Ness's western shores for the construction of the new A82 Highway. It was during the 1930s that Nessie became well publicized and looking for Nessie became the thing to do.

Do I believe in Nessie? Back in 1990, when my husband and I were traveling through the Highlands, we decided to get out of the rented car and do some exploring on foot.

We left the car at Urquhart Castle near Drumnadrochit, one of the favorite Nessie-watching sites. It was a damp warm day. There was a heavy mist—a perfectly normal day in the Highlands in midsummer. We fetched a picnic lunch and hiked to the ruined fortress that stood on a promontory that hung out over the loch. Because of the thick mist, there were few tourists, and those who were there eyed our lunch and were nice enough to leave. We spread out our table-cloth and feasted. The mist dampened the baked chicken, the bread, even the wineglasses. We didn't care. My hus-band fell asleep. I read a novel. The afternoon was lazy. The mist got thicker. I looked up at the sound of a soft hissing right in front of me. Hissing sound? A snake? In the water?

The hair on my neck stirred. My heart went south. There it was again, that soft hissing sound, but it was closer now. Then, suddenly, there was an abrupt clearing in the mist, as if someone had taken a knife and cut out a square in a swatch of filmy material. Framed in that rough square was a small head. Slowly, with no sound at all, the head rose higher and higher out of the water. I realized then that I was staring at Nessie, just sitting there crouched forward over that promontory, staring, not really believing that I could be seeing Nessie, but then there was this long neck, incredibly long, rising, rising out of the water. I remember reaching out my hand. I remember whispering something. Just as suddenly, the mist filled in again. And there was nothing. I sat there for a very long time, not moving, won-dering if I'd lost it, wondering if the chicken had gone bad before it had been baked, wondering if that sweet red wine had held more than eleven percent alcohol. And I decided, finally, that the picnic had nothing to do with anything.

Nessie is there and so are her children. I have no idea how many of her generations have passed since Saint Co-lumba saw her in the sixth century. Five? Ten?

It doesn't matter. She's there.